LIN FINITY
AND THE
ISLANDS OF TIME

Other Books By Edward Allen Karr

* * * * *

SERIES: Fringes Of Infinity

Lin Finity And Her Mayhem Rising – Book One

Lin Finity In Holding On
(A Fringes Of Infinity Novella)

Lin Finity And The Words Unspoken – Book Two

Lin Finity And The Flights To Forever – Book Four

* * * * *

SERIES: Thrills N Kills In The Hills

Dayzee Dazzle And The Kildare Killers – Book One

Dayzee Dazzle And Her Manic Mansion – Book Two

* * * * *

LIN FINITY
AND THE
ISLANDS OF TIME

Fringes Of Infinity
Book Three

Edward Allen Karr

LAKESIDE LETTERS, LLC

Lakeside Letters, LLC
30628 Detroit Road, #247
Westlake, OH 44145

Lin Finity And The Islands Of Time
Fringes Of Infinity Book Three
©2020 Edward Sechkar.   All rights reserved.

First Edition, 2020
www.lakesideletters.com

Cover design by JD Smith Design
Front Cover Model: Kim Hendrickson as Lin Finity
Back Cover Model: Gloria Ervin as Queen Gloriana
Editing by Preferred Proofreading, LLC

ISBN-13: 978-1-950886-08-1

"But I didn't just see it—I felt what you felt. How is any of that possible? That all happened so long ago."

"I tell you again: time is not what you believe it to be. If you can move between the Islands, you can find any Islands that your intent seeks to hold. Any Islands that are past. They persist even as the living continue across their centuries."

"What islands?"

Lin looked down from the tower at the unbroken expanse of water.

"I don't see any islands. You're not making any sense."

"Islands of Time, Lin Finity. And no, I do not make sense. For you to be here, you must know that sense is weak. It is an empty promise. It survives only until it is challenged."

From Chapter 3 – Here I Remain

Dedication

This work is dedicated to:

All who travel from moment to moment
and have sensed the magic of time passing.

May you always remember that you are forever on the
Fringes Of Infinity.

Table of Contents

Chapter 1 – No More Magic

"No more magic!"

Lin Finity shoved the blanket covering her to the floor and powered her reclined seat higher. She took a long look through the windshield at Jack, who was slumped over a picnic table and motionless despite the first few raindrops finding him. She snapped her head to the right and stared through her car's passenger side window. Her heart began to race.

"Lin, you probably need to rest. You're—"

"No, Gabby."

She turned quickly and shook back her long blond hair. Her chest heaved from her rapid breaths, and her unblinking green eyes focused on Gabriel.

"I remember everything that happened. That was the most terrifying thing I could ever imagine. Worse than I could imagine."

"It was frightening for us too. You were—"

"I remember it all. That queen, the one who created the Scroll with the Words of God . . . she's still out there! How could that be? She pulled me in there, or out there, or back there, or—"

"Lin, try to slow down. That blanket will help you. It will take you some time to recover."

She turned to stare out her window through the lines traced by the cool rainwater.

"I brought that on myself," she said between urgent breaths. "I shouldn't be playing around with the magic. Why did you let me? Why did you encourage me? I should have stopped the first time I spoke any of those damn Words. I felt things moving around inside, and I knew it wasn't right. Saying the Words changed me. That prepared me. Set me up somehow. And when the time was right, that damn queen—"

"Gloriana?"

"Yeah, her. From way back when. She didn't just show me what happened and how she felt—I lived it. I've never felt such frustration and anger as that. And determination. She'll never quit. If I stop and don't use the magic anymore, maybe that will be the end of it?"

Gabriel tugged on Lin's sleeve until she turned from the window she'd fogged.

"I'm glad you're getting some energy back, Lin. That's a good sign. Maybe it's too soon for you. How about if we think of today right now, and we can talk about Gloriana later?"

"I don't feel safe."

Her head began to lean forward, and her voice grew soft.

"I'm not strong enough for this. I can't. I just . . . I . . ."

Lin's head tipped and rested against the glass, and Gabriel reached over and pulled the blanket back up over her cold body.

* * *

Five silent minutes later, Lin opened her eyes, but she let more time pass before she moved. She snugged the blanket up tight under her chin and turned to look at Gabriel with her eyebrows raised.

"I thought you were joking, Gabby. You really do drive?"

Gabriel laughed and patted Lin's arm through the heavy blanket.

"Yes, Lin. And I got all the hood lights to turn on too."

"That must have been fun—you really have to accelerate for that."

"I enjoyed it, but it wasn't for fun."

"Where are we again?"

"Hickory Run State Park. We're only a short drive from your home."

Lin peeked over her blanket from the passenger side of her Temt8tion and watched Gabriel for several seconds. She glanced back through the windshield to see Jack still lying over his folded arms on the weathered boards. The rain was still light, but it had become steady.

He'll notice it soon, she thought and turned back to face Gabriel.

"This car's fast. How did Jack keep up? There's no way his pickup could do it."

"He didn't keep up with us. But at that moment, Jack had to do his best on his own. I'm here only for you."

"Why? What happened?"

"It's more important right now to make sure you're okay. We can talk about the rest soon. I imagine even that short nap helped you?"

"Yeah, some. I guess I'm not surprised you'd be worried about me. I'm starting to feel more like myself. Still a little strange, though. I can't believe I was asleep for three days."

"And you shouldn't believe it. Because you weren't."

Lin continued to look only into Gabriel's eyes, and she didn't speak for several seconds.

"But . . . how could—"

"We can talk more about that later."

"Sure. It seems more like a dream now, but I remember everything before I was taken. I was sitting on the couch with you at the cabin. We'd just finished that crazy battle with Wolfe and his ungodly army. I remember how tired I felt, and then . . . something strange and powerful happened. It was a nightmare without end, or maybe it just felt that way. And I woke up here."

Gabriel's head shook slowly, and big brown eyes stared into Lin's.

"Okay, so I didn't just wake up. Something else is going on."

"We can talk soon, but for now, we should keep moving. It won't be safe here for long."

Gabriel pointed out Lin's window and said, "And look. Jack is going to find your daughter and your dog."

Lin watched as Jack hiked into the thick pines bordering the trail and out of sight.

"I told you he was okay."

* * *

"Taylor, it's starting to rain here too. Why don't we get Nomad back? He's probably had enough exercise for now."

Jack Madison had felt the rain pelting him until he'd made it under the trees. The forest above them rattled and swayed as the wind worked to sift raindrops through to the dry trail below.

"I have no choice, Jack," she said and brushed back her shoulder-length blond hair. "He's losing his mind out here. Just a few minutes ago, he started whining and pulling me back down the trail. He's really strong!"

"Let me give you a hand, then."

Together, they held Nomad's leash, and their combined strength still couldn't hold the big dog at a walking pace. His bushy tail swished, and his agitated panting increased as he pulled them both down the path.

"I'll try to hold him still, and you see if you can unhook him, alright? Let him run the rest of the way."

"It's either that or he'll drag us."

Jack reached his brawny arms around a thin tree and held the leash with both hands.

"Hurry! He's ripping my arms out of their sockets!"

Taylor fumbled with the clasp but finally got Nomad free of his leash. His huge paws clawed into the soft trail dirt and pine needles, throwing it all up and back as he dug in and rushed between the close pines.

* * *

"What do you mean, 'it won't be safe?'"

"Lin, I'm just saying—"

A loud crash shook the car sideways, and Lin turned to look out her window and saw a massive snout smudging against the glass from the center of a bushy red mane. Two big happy eyes stared into hers, and she was sure she saw a smile on that familiar face.

"Nomad, my sweet fluffy boy!"

With the heavy dog's bulk pressed against the door, she pushed with all of her slowly returning strength to get it to move. And when it did open, all two-hundred pounds of Tibetan Mastiff climbed in on her lap, where he proceeded to lick her face and nuzzle her neck.

"Ugh . . . Nomad! I might have to start watching your diet again!"

Lin tried to hug him, but she could barely get her arms around his thick mane.

"Lin, we really should get going. As soon as Jack and Taylor get back."

*   *   *

"Jack, look! It's Mom!"

"Oh my God . . ."

They both raced to the car, Taylor in tears and Jack fighting his.

"Mom, you're okay! Gabriel said you would be, but I was scared— I didn't think I'd ever see you awake again!"

"Oh, Taylor, my sweet girl. I'm so happy to be back and to see you again. Have you been okay?"

"Me?" Taylor wiped at her eyes. "What about you? You were . . . you were—"

"She's fine now, Taylor," said Gabriel. "Jack, you must be relieved. I did tell you."

Jack ran both hands up through his wavy brown hair and held them there.

"God, I don't know how much of this I can take. Lin, this is the happiest moment of my life. Don't ever do that again, alright? Promise?"

"I don't ever want to do that again, whatever it was. You can believe that, Jack."

And she looked into his big brown eyes as they pleaded with her through a film of tears that she loved and hoped she'd never cause again. When he leaned in and wedged himself between her and a grumbling and protesting Nomad, she hugged them both. But she made sure most of her kisses landed on Jack.

"I feel like driving some more. How about you, Jack? And you, Nomad, are you ready for the ride home?"

No one could argue with Gabriel since the rain had picked up, and the parking lot's puddles had merged, leaving only small mounds of mud and gravel. Taylor leaned in to hug and kiss Lin, then she and Jack and Nomad sloshed back to Jack's truck.

"Gabby, why did you say it wasn't safe at the cabin? I watched you scatter that Wolfe thing and all his evil buddies. Did Anna and Tayo come back?"

"There's nothing to go back to, Lin. Your cabin is gone."

"But . . ."

Lin could only stare out the windshield at the persistent rain bouncing off the empty picnic table. The tall pines leaned and tangled into each other, and even in the luxurious confines of her car, the rising winds couldn't be ignored.

"Someone else shot another rocket? And I wasn't awake to stop it?"

"No, nothing like that. It was the weather. It seemed angry."

She turned to stare at Gabriel as the big motor fired up, and soon, the two vehicles bounced and splashed toward the service road leading to the state route.

* * *

"Jack, this has been a crazy couple of days. Ever since Lee healed me in Philadelphia, I just can't believe all the weird stuff going on."

Taylor still fought her tears and took deliberate breaths.

"I should be more used to it, but I'm not. All I know, Taylor, is that I love your mom. And if Gabriel were here, I'd be reminded to love

Nomad too. So, yeah, I love Nomad too. But this is all a lot to accept. I'm trying, though. You seem to be holding up alright."

"Yeah, I think I'll be okay. I saw all the stuff my mom did, and I can't hardly believe it. It's real, though, isn't it, Jack?"

"Yeah, there's no doubt about that. It's a really big deal that Lee healed you too. Do you still feel alright?"

Taylor stretched her slender legs out as far as she could and then kicked them a couple of times.

"I feel so good, Jack, like I never did before. And you might not believe it, but I never met Nomad until that day at the hospital. My mom mentioned him on the phone, and I knew he was big—but not that big!"

"Well, don't feel bad. I never even heard of you until a couple of days ago."

"Really? My mom never even mentioned me?"

"I think she's been pretty sad about how things have been between you."

"Yeah, I've been sad too. And you know what else, Jack? I'm mad too, but not at my mom—just about how long I haven't felt good. It's not just that I felt lousy. It was feeling like I was about to die any day, and I never even knew what from. I still don't, Jack."

"That had to be rough. You must be very strong, though. You seem to have made it through all that."

"Yeah. And while I was lying around in stupid hospital beds, I thought maybe I should become an author someday if I ever had the strength. Well, now I do. I feel strong enough for anything. Words kind of fascinate me, Jack."

"All words or just some?"

Jack looked over quickly with a grin.

"Some more than others. As long as my mom doesn't—"

"She won't. She won't."

Jack shook his head and smiled and tried to keep a close eye on the road. The rain continued a steady downpour, and without the

Temt8tion's taillights, he knew he would have easily driven off of the road.

"Like back at the cabin when Mom was . . . you know. I don't know why, Jack, but I started thinking about the word 'pigeon.' It's a weird word, you know? Why is it pronounced that way? And why is it . . . oh Jack, I know why I was thinking about that word.

"I can't count how many days I lay in that damn hospital bed and watched pigeons outside my window. They weren't sick, and they weren't alone. They were outside in the fresh air and sunshine, and they could all fly away wherever the hell they wanted. I wished I could fly away too.

"Even on rainy days. Especially on rainy days. They looked so content to just sit there out of the rain. When it started to rain back at the cabin, it reminded me of the pigeons and the word 'pigeon.' It's a funny word, Jack, if you think about it. If you really, really think about it."

Jack hurried a look at Taylor and saw that she stared out through the windshield with an odd grin. He looked back at the road and rain that seemed determined to become a waterfall.

"Well, that could be the first word in the first book you write. How does that sound?"

"Maybe it's too funny of a word for that, Jack." She continued to gaze out through the windshield.

"Just how long have you been sick?"

"I never really felt right, but it didn't get serious until about four years ago. I'd just turned nineteen, and I got my own apartment. It sure went downhill from there. I've been in hospitals ever since."

"Not anymore, though, right?"

"No, not anymore. I've never felt like this. I don't know how Lee did it, but it seems like a miracle."

"Yeah, a miracle. Your mom works miracles too. God, *she* is a miracle . . ."

Jack gripped the wheel tightly with both hands, and he didn't risk another look at Taylor.

"At this speed, we still have about an hour to go. That seat reclines some if you want. Why don't you take a nap? It's been quite a day."

"Good idea. I think I will."

With her seat tilted back, Taylor was soon asleep, and Jack was left with the challenge of keeping his truck on the road and thoughts of his impossible life with Lin. Even Nomad had sprawled across the back seat and snored, with his big dirty paws twitching in time with the wipers.

*　*　*

"Gabby, what about the weather? Was there a tornado or something?"

"Rain mostly. Then wind too. Too much of both. I don't think there's much left of the place. We had to leave, Lin."

"I have insurance, and we're all safe—that's the main thing. But that cabin was sturdy. No ordinary storm should have affected it at all."

"Maybe it wasn't a normal storm."

"What does that mean?"

"Just that it was a very powerful one. And the storm was only . . .'"
Gabriel paused.

"Only what?"

"And you're right. We're safe, and that's what's important."

"At least the rain here is tapering off. It was getting a lot worse there for a while. But look at that—I think the sun might be coming out again."

"It's always wise to be thankful for the sunshine. Perhaps it will last a while."

"I bet you're hungry, aren't you?"

"Always. I pray you have food at your house."

"You're praying for food?"

Lin turned to Gabriel without a smile. Gabriel smiled but didn't look over.

"Yes. It's a perfectly good use of prayer."

Chapter 2 – An Ancient Knowledge

Under cloudy skies free of storms, Gabriel led them all back to Lin's home on Kingsbury Court. Gabriel pulled her Temt8tion into the garage, and Jack pulled onto the driveway and shut down his pickup. Before he'd cracked his door open, Nomad had climbed onto his lap and began to bark and bump his nose into the window. And as soon as he could break loose, he galloped straight to Lin and offered a big furry hug.

"Oh, Nomad, you do want to keep my legs strong, don't you, boy?" she said as he pressed down on her shoulders, and his back paws alternated, trying to climb up her legs.

"No, Nomad, I can't carry you!"

Taylor woke up from the sounds of barking and slamming doors and jumped down from Jack's truck.

"Thanks for the ride, Jack. Are you coming in?"

"Yeah, of course. After the scare your mom put us through, I want to make sure she's alright."

"Good. I like having you around. I think Nomad does too."

At that, Nomad ran to Jack and jumped up against him with his broad paws reaching for his shoulders, shoving Jack back against his closed door. Jack accepted a few sloppy kisses then turned and took off.

"Come on, boy, try to catch me!"

Down the sidewalk he jogged, with the barking dog close behind. Lin's first smile since she'd returned to life made an appearance.

* * *

"Taylor, how was the ride back? Jack's pretty good company, isn't he?"

"He's a good guy, Mom. And Nomad—oh my God, I love Nomad!"

"He's a big baby. A real good boy. Were you serious about staying here? There's plenty of room, and I'd love to have you around again."

Lin held the gaze of her daughter's bright green eyes, and the years of strife and misunderstanding continued to fade into a past that neither wanted to remember.

"Yeah, I do want to stay. Do you still have a guest room?"

"Oh, Hon, I still have *your* room. I haven't touched it. Well, except to clean it."

"Aw, Mom, that's sweet. I'm going to take another nap right now. In my room. I like the sound of that. I haven't slept much the last three days."

"Sorry about that, Hon. Rest up. I'm glad you're home."

Taylor had little to bring inside. Her years of traveling between hospitals and clinics had left her with few possessions. She grabbed her small bag and walked inside.

"Gabby, tell me you're sticking around."

"Yes, I'm not leaving. And I'd like to know more about what you experienced after you left us."

"I can tell you what I remember, but I can't say I understand any of it. Come on in."

Jack and Nomad had finished their romp and filed in through the garage. Nomad headed straight for his empty bowl.

"Lin, where's the forklift? It's time to feed your dog," Jack said with a big grin.

Lin smiled again.

"Okay, Jack, he eats a lot. We all know that."

* * *

With Taylor back in her room for the first time in years, Lin felt a satisfaction that had escaped her long ago. She thought of all the wonders she'd found in the magic, and her powers still fascinated her. But something so simple—the company of her own daughter—could never be taken for granted.

She and Jack took the couch, and Gabriel slouched into the recliner.

"First of all, Gabby, how could I have been out for three days? And you said I wasn't asleep?"

"No, you weren't."

"What was that, then?"

"You were dead."

She looked at Jack, who only nodded, then she stared at Gabriel with her mouth open. But no words came out. Only the loud crunching from the kitchen broke the silence in the room, which was lightening as the clouds cleared.

"Dead? What the heck does that mean?"

"As in . . . no pulse?" said Jack.

"You can't be serious. How could I have been dead for three days?"

"It's because of where you went, Lin. I've briefly visited that place, but long ago, I chose to focus my life elsewhere. There's nothing worth pursuing there, and certainly nothing we'd ever want to meet."

"And while I was there, I was dead? Here, I was dead?"

"Completely dead. Do you remember when you first looked out and saw Jack at the picnic table? He was very distraught. I told him you'd be back, but he had no reason to believe me. You were dead."

"I didn't believe Gabriel. You really didn't have a heartbeat, and you were getting cold."

"But what about Taylor? And Nomad?"

"They were upset too. Nomad approached you very slowly and whined. It was a sad sight. All three of them stayed by your side, and they rarely slept. When Nomad rammed into your car at the park, it was because he'd sensed that you'd come back."

Lin took turns staring at each of them.

"Jack thought at first that we should call an ambulance or take you to a hospital. Do you remember that, Jack? Aren't you glad we didn't? It's good that I was able to talk him out of it. That could have been a disaster."

"So, I was dead. And I sat on the couch for three days?"

"No, we put you in your bed. You looked quite comfortable, but a lot like a corpse too."

Lin felt a twinge inside, and she remembered the entire previous week and how many times she'd felt things shifting around inside. It had started the moment she'd returned from the magic, her first trip there with Gabriel, when she'd seen the color that exists only there and not in the world. A foundation that she never knew existed had begun to weaken, and so many other events had continued to pick away at it.

But she understood that it was all necessary. To keep learning, she needed to escape the confines of her mind and find the strength to survive. Gabriel pushed her for a reason. Gabriel didn't just save her from a bottomless darkness when her mayhem had first erupted back when she was only fifteen. Gabriel was also leading her and guiding her, helping her sort out the limitless magic that supported everything in the world.

"Was I a good-looking corpse?" Lin said with a smile.

"Yes, of course you were. Even dying couldn't change that," said Gabriel.

They shared a gentle laugh as they gazed at each other, with Lin's green eyes moistening.

"Jack, I'm so sorry for putting you through that. It wasn't by choice, that's for sure."

"Just don't do that again, alright?"

Lin saw in his eyes how horrible that had been for him. Never again, she told herself.

"I won't, Jack. It was terrifying. There was no way to control what was going on. Even in the magic, Gabby,"—she looked away from Jack—"I feel like I'm learning to be okay there. But this other thing? No way. It was overpowering."

"And do you remember any of what happened there?"

"All of it. It was Gloriana. Somehow she pulled me into there . . . somewhere. And I remember what she was trying to tell me. Or show me. Why she asked God for an answer. Why she saved that answer with the Messenger Scroll. And I remember that she wasn't at all happy with God's answer, like she said in the Telling, that note that Anna gave us. How could any of that have happened? It felt like I went back in time."

"Perhaps there's no such thing as 'back,' Lin. It might all be there, every moment of it, if you can survive the journey. It looks like you did."

"My intent. I found my intent, and I held onto it so tight, and there was nothing else. It was like that for an eternity."

"Well, three days anyway," Gabriel said.

"Yeah, that's right—only three days. Not a big deal at all to come back from being dead for three days."

"It's happened before."

Again, Lin could only stare, and she noticed her heart rate jump up.

"Oh no, you don't mean—"

"Yes, the last person to read the Scroll two-thousand years ago. Maybe he visited with Gloriana too?"

*　*　*

Jack's fatigue was obvious, and he admitted that what he wanted most right then was to crawl off somewhere and sleep. Lin walked with him into the kitchen, where she gave much-appreciated attention to him and Nomad before the two lay across the guest room bed, their backs pressed together. She stood a moment to watch them sagging into the blankets with their eyes closed.

It feels so good to be alive again and back at home, she thought. How could I have been dead for three days?

"I just ordered a giant pizza, Gabby. It should be here in about fifteen minutes. Think you can wait that long?"

"I'll try. Don't forget—I've only been real for about two weeks, after being with you for over three decades. I'm enjoying this like you can't imagine."

"I know, and I still can't thank you enough. You saved me. I never would have made it. After I destroyed my uncle Ray, I felt like I couldn't go on another minute. Then, you showed up, and you kept me safe. I have no idea how, but you stayed with me through everything.

"And I've been wondering . . . if I *did* hurt Ben instead of healing him, would you have stayed in the background, and I still wouldn't remember who you really are?"

"Maybe. Or worse."

"I'm afraid to ask. What do you mean?"

"You were already very powerful by the time you confronted Ben in Allentown. You had an unbreakable hold on your intent, and your mayhem was right beneath your surface, ready to rise up in an instant. It still is. It always will be. If you'd hurt Ben instead of helping him, I don't know, Lin . . ."

"What? Tell me."

Gabriel laughed.

"You don't want to know."

"You mean—"

"Yes."

"You couldn't."

"I wouldn't have wanted to."

Lin shook her head and stared at her best friend, the being she could barely believe was real.

"So, I need to be careful all the time . . ." Lin frowned and looked at her hands in her lap.

"You must have noticed, Lin. Don't I always ask if you've hurt anyone?"

"You always encourage me to choose good, that's for sure."

"I really want you to always choose good. Yes, that's very important. For both of us. But don't worry about being perfect. Mistakes are allowed. Constantly choosing good and nothing else is nearly impossible."

"Not for you, Gabby."

* * *

Gabriel grinned at the rapping on the door, and Lin rose to answer it. She traded cash for pizza, and before long, the open box sat on the table in front of them. After each had devoured a slice and felt they could slow enough to talk, the conversation resumed.

"You must be wondering about your cabin at St. Mary's."

"Yeah, of course. The weather, you said. But how could the weather have gotten that bad?"

"I don't believe it was just the weather. Not by itself anyway."

"Oh, here we go again. What's going on this time?"

"I wouldn't have thought of this—it's something no one has dealt with for many centuries. But your little vacation,"—Gabriel stopped to smile at her—"to visit with Gloriana brought it to mind. I almost forgot about it."

"What on Earth are you talking about?"

"It's an ancient knowledge, forgotten long ago. Or so I thought. Somehow, it might be back."

"What knowledge?"

"It's a very old practice involving language. The use of words is intertwined with everything in how we relate to the world. Words are more essential to our world than most people suspect. We all use them to describe things to each other and ourselves. And also to shape things. They help form how we perceive the world. We control which words we use and what they mean, but it's easy to forget that words control us as well."

"What? How?"

"It's probably easiest if I demonstrate the concept of it."

Gabriel asked Lin for a pen, and she brought one back from the kitchen.

"I'm going to write something on the box. All I ask is that you look at it."

Gabriel pulled the pizza box over, closed it, and wrote the word "sex."

Lin laughed out loud when she read it, and then she quit smiling and frowned. She looked up at Gabriel with eyes open wide.

"Gabby, I'm a little shocked. What are you getting at? When you were with me all those years, you never watched, did you? Or wait, do you mean . . . you can't be thinking—"

"Lin, slow down. I meant absolutely nothing by it. It just happens to be a good word to explain my point."

"And what exactly is your point?"

"That there are many different levels of perception when it comes to words. Other things too, but for now, we're talking about words."

"What on Earth are you talking about?"

"That's just a word written on a pizza box, but it affected you at a very high level. That's where most people stay. That's the effect many words have."

"I still don't know what you mean."

"If I'm judging your reaction correctly, you immediately thought I was talking about something to do with sex and you and me. Whether I'd witnessed it, or . . . well, let's not consider any other possibilities."

Lin laughed, and Gabriel joined her.

"You saw it from a high level. As an idea. And even higher than that—you immediately tried to determine my *purpose* in communicating an idea. Now, think of the lowest possible level when your eyes observed what I wrote."

"I'd see just a word, is that what you're saying?"

"Yes, that's lower."

"I don't—"

"You'd see a word and not wonder at all why I wrote it, but the word's meaning would cause you to imagine something—I won't ask what. But you wouldn't wonder why I wrote it. That's one step lower.

"Next, you'd see it and understand its meaning, but you would only read it and be aware of the word's definition—you wouldn't imagine anything."

"That's kind of impossible to get that low."

"Oh, let's go lower. Even if you tried as hard as you could, would you ever be able to look at it and not see a word? Could you see only individual letters and remain unable to see a word?"

Lin stared in silence until she could speak again.

"No, how could I?"

"That's my point. Your mind keeps you at a higher level. But let's go a step lower. Could you look at it and not even understand that those are letters? Could you make yourself see just lines and swirls and circles that don't add up to anything?"

"No, how could—"

"Could you see those lines and swirls and circles and not understand that someone wrote them there?"

"Gabby—"

"Or could you look at it and not even comprehend that the box is white and the ink is black?"

"No, that's—"

"Lin, could you look at it and not have a single thought about it? Not understand anything about it and just witness it?"

"No one could live like that."

"No, because our world is built on the higher levels. It's where we live."

Lin stared in silence.

"And that's just with your eyes."

"What other—"

"Could you hear your language being spoken and not understand any of the words? If you wanted to, could you put aside that skill that you learned—that you weren't born with—to the point where you only hear sounds that mean nothing? Can you turn that off if you wish?"

"No. No one can do that."

"That's the connection of words to your mind."

"So, what is this all about?"

"We started at a high level, where we all live, and we talked about lower levels. But there are even higher levels, higher than where our minds keep us."

"I don't understand. What's higher than thinking about your reason for writing a word?"

"It's an ancient knowledge, Lin. There are techniques that I know of, different ways to observe a word, even one on a pizza box. Very dangerous and unpredictable for beginners."

"What does any of this have to do with my cabin being wrecked?"

"I believe that ancient knowledge raised the storm that destroyed your cabin."

She stared but said nothing.

"Your cabin sat in the middle of a large clearing. The storm didn't touch any of the surrounding forest. It only covered the clearing and your cabin."

"Gabby, I feel it again. Things moving inside. You talking about the weather and now, some crazy ideas about words. I feel like, I don't know . . . like—"

A pinpoint of blackness appeared before her, and her eyes were drawn to it. She could look nowhere else as two thin streams of tears trickled down her cheeks.

"Lin, remember your intent . . ."

Gabriel's voice faded, but Lin heard the reminder.

It was all she could hear from Gabriel as the darkness grew and raced toward her, swallowing her whole. When the night had chased away her world, her lungs locked, and no more air moved in or out. Her thoughts and feelings left her, and she knew only the beating of her heart.

And then, it stopped.

Lin had again become only a captive of that endless emptiness. Frozen in silence.

Chapter 3 – Here I Remain

A tiny dot of light was all Lin could see as if a hole had been poked in the blackness that surrounded her, and it raced toward her and chased away the darkness. A radiant world that appeared ancient dragged behind until it covered her completely.

Her heart began its familiar steady rhythm, and she found she could think and feel once more. She drew in a deep breath of air that evoked childhood memories of the sea, and she knew that an ocean was near before she opened her eyes.

She looked down and saw that she stood on the edge of a stone floor next to a low stone wall. All of the irregular blocks were fitted together in joints that seemed too perfect for even the most skilled workers. She leaned out over the wall enough to see waves crashing against the flooded remains of a palace far below. No land could be seen anywhere, and when she looked to her left, she saw half of a sun beginning to burn its path into the sky.

She looked to her right and caught her breath.

An elegant, athletic woman stood close enough to touch and stared out over the ocean. Without a word, she turned and looked at Lin with unblinking eyes that glowed a rich caramel. Her wild dark hair spilled down far past her uncovered shoulders, where a light breeze bounced it across her dark skin. She wore a gown the color of cinnamon that couldn't hide the body of a warrior.

"I am Gloriana, Queen of these islands that I intend. Here I wait for you."

"Me? How do you even know about me?"

"As the Messenger knows you, so do I."

"How can this be happening? How could you bring me here?"

"The Scroll connects us. It serves as I intend."

"You created the Scroll?"

"We cannot create. We only give new form to magic that exists."

"How is this even possible? What am I doing here?"

"I invest in you, Lin Finity. My power grows weak as your centuries pass. I spend much of it to bring you to me."

"And where exactly are we?"

"We are nowhere. This is but a memory of the last moments of my islands. It is all that I intend for you. This is enough that we may talk."

"About what? What do you want from me?"

"To join you. To live on the Islands of Time once more. There is no path for me without your help."

"Islands of what? What are you talking about?"

"Time is not a thing that you know. Not yet. I seek a life on the Islands again."

"I don't understand anything you're saying. I don't know who you are, or where I am, or how—"

"In time, you come to understand. Agree to help me, and we discuss time."

"You're talking in circles. I don't think I can help you anyway. How could I?"

Gloriana's eyes burned a deep caramel as she continued to stare into Lin's eyes.

"You have great strength in your intent?"

"My intent is strong. My hold on it is unbreakable. But what—"

"You need only focus on your intent while holding my gaze. Your strength carries us both."

"I don't know you. Why would I even think about helping you?"

"Just look into my eyes and hold your intent. You may begin."

"No, I'm not doing anything like that."

Lin turned away and looked to her left, where the sun had breached the horizon and lit a long line in the sea toward the tower.

"I can teach you more of the magic. There is so much more, Lin Finity."

"I know too much already, that's for sure. I've learned all I want to learn."

Lin looked back down over the wall and saw that more of the broken structures had sunk below the waves.

"You are trying to fool yourself. In that you must fail. You cannot stop moving forward."

"What do you mean?"

"Learning of the magic is a wave of its own kind. It is a wave that lives in my intent and in yours. I ride that wave, and it leaves me here. Here I remain."

Lin snapped her head back to face Gloriana.

"Aren't you dead? Didn't you die centuries ago?"

"Death? Death is holding me even now, yet still, I exist. But I grow weary. Only your power can save me."

"You brought me here twice before, didn't you?"

"Yes."

"Why? Why did you show me those things? *How* did you show me all of that?"

"It is for you to know me and why I am doing what I do. Do you understand me, Lin Finity?"

Lin glanced at the rising sun then out over the ocean.

"Yeah, I think I do. I felt your frustration. I learned what it was like for you to hear God's answer. I felt your anger."

"Yes. You would be angry also. I arrange all of that to bring you to me."

"But I didn't just see it—I felt what you felt. How is any of that possible? That all happened so long ago."

"I tell you again: time is not what you believe it to be. If you can move between the Islands, you can find any Islands that your intent seeks to hold. Any Islands that are past. They persist even as the living continue across their centuries."

"What islands?"

Lin looked down from the tower at the unbroken expanse of water. "I don't see any islands. You're not making any sense."

"Islands of Time, Lin Finity. And no, I do not make sense. For you to be here, you must know that sense is weak. It is an empty promise. It survives only until it is challenged."

Lin looked again into unblinking eyes that glowed like molten caramel. A cold fear crept up on her as if sharp claws were reaching for the back of her neck, and she faced how lost she was in a fantasy world that didn't exist. So far from her home. So far from Jack and Taylor and Nomad and Gabby!

"But how could . . . I don't know what you're talking about . . . I shouldn't be—"

"You must leave. We speak again." Gloriana pointed toward the horizon directly out from the tower. "Go. Live again, Lin Finity."

Lin turned from the glow of Gloriana's eyes and looked out over the water. Just above the horizon, a black point appeared, and Lin could not look away. The dark dot grew into a larger circle, its edges racing to envelope her, and it pushed Gloriana and her world past her until she knew only an endless, empty night. Her breathing stopped, and she could feel nothing and think nothing. Then, her heartbeat vanished.

Without a thought, Lin fought to find the stillness inside her. There, she found her intent and her unbreakable hold on it.

She could do nothing but hold her intent in silence.

As centuries might have hurried past without her, Lin held fast to her intent.

* * *

A white point caught her attention, and it grew, dragging Lin's familiar world behind it. Her heart started up, and she felt the relief of being alive as she drew in a deep breath that carried the welcome aroma of pizza. She opened her eyes to see Gabriel staring at her with concern, and she found that she'd slumped back into the couch cushions. She stayed there.

"It happened again. I was—"

"Dead again, Lin."

"Gabby, I need to get stronger, or I'll never make it. I feel like I barely made it back."

"It's been only a minute or two. But I did check your pulse."

"Gone?"

"Gone."

"It was Gloriana again. She wants to come back. She said she needs me to bring her back."

Gabriel nodded but gave no response.

"She said she can't do it herself. She says she needs me to help her, but I felt like I barely got back myself. I don't think I can help her even if I wanted to."

"Where did she take you?"

"She said it was a memory of all that was left of her islands. She said she's been 'between the Islands.' What does that mean?"

Gabriel frowned but managed to reach for another slice.

"You will have to learn that for yourself. I can't help you with that yet."

"You don't know?"

Gabriel chewed for a few seconds before answering.

"I know of it. But my words might shape your understanding of it. You need to face it on your own first and know it in your own way. Later, we can talk."

"How do I stop her? You can tell me that much, can't you?"

"You're right—you need to be much stronger. I *can* help you with that."

Lin felt pieces of herself shifting about, rearranging themselves, and finding a new pattern. They all seemed to find positions that were acceptable, at least for a while, and Lin knew.

"I need to be on an island."

Gabriel finished chewing a large bite and swallowed.

"What do you mean?"

"I'm going back to St. Simons."

"Why?"

"I have no answer to that. But my mayhem first erupted there—on an island. And Gloriana, she spoke of her islands. You even told me that—that she'd created her own islands out in the ocean.

"And more importantly, she said she's been between the Islands of Time.

"God, Gabby, I need to get stronger. I hope I have enough time. Whatever the hell time really is."

Chapter 4 – Back To St. Simons

"Ben, this has to stop—I'm getting weaker every time. Just let me rest."

"We'll stop, I promise. But not yet. This fight tonight is the last, okay?"

"It's a lot of money, I know. Alright, I'll do it, but really, this is it."

Lee Turner collapsed into the worn hotel chair. They'd just arrived in Norfolk after a quiet drive in from Richmond. Ben Barlow's old pickup rattled all the way, and a working radio would have helped, but Ben had punched the life out of it weeks earlier. Lee still wore her short black leather jacket, and her straight black hair hung motionless after she closed her eyes.

"I never should have let you stop in Pittsburgh after we left the cabin. Just a quick match, you said. Easy money. I didn't realize what you had in mind. I wasn't even sure I could do it."

"You worked miracles in Philadelphia, Lee, when you healed Taylor and me. I knew you could do it again."

"But you don't seem to understand—that takes a lot out of me. I was already tired in Pittsburgh, and after you got the shit kicked out of you—"

"I only let that happen to raise the bets. I explained that to you."

"Sure, but you were really broken up, Ben. Lots of stuff."

"And I only asked you to fix some of it, remember? Just enough that I could get back in there and win."

"Right. Yeah, and then later, I had to fix it *all*. It's tiring, Ben, that's all I'm saying. I can't keep doing this."

He pulled off his flannel shirt and sat on the edge of the bed. Just the night before, he would have left blood everywhere. But now, he was perfect—not a scratch and no broken bones. He rubbed his hands over his bald head and leaned back on his elbows.

"And then in D.C. and again in Richmond—why, Ben? We have a big share of the cash that we got from The Shield, from that backpack full of it that Anna gave us. We don't need the extra money, but you had to fight again—twice. I swear I might not be able to help you next time. And when is your match? Eight hours from now?"

"Eight o'clock. It's a prime-time match. That's when all the sleazy characters come out and throw their money down."

"And then, that's the end of it, right?"

"Yeah, Lee. Just do your thing tonight."

Ben fell back into the stale blankets and dragged a pillow over his face. A minute later, his snoring filled the room, and Lee slipped out into the hallway, took out her phone, and kicked at the carpeting with the toe of her black snakeskin boot.

*　*　*

"Hi, Lee. Did you and Ben make it back to Georgia?"

"Oh God, Lin, no. And I need your help. Something's up with Ben. He's been fighting in bare-knuckle matches, and he's letting himself get banged up pretty good. Then, he has me heal him enough to finish and win the match."

"What? Why? He can't want the money that bad. He still has his cut, doesn't he?"

"Yeah, and I don't think it's just about the money. I don't know if I can keep doing this. I'm exhausted, and he's got a match tonight at eight. I can't talk him out of it. And if I don't at least try, God knows what will happen to him. He's tough, but there are a lot of tougher guys out there."

"Hard to believe, but yeah, Ben isn't always the biggest or meanest. So, where are you? You're not still in Pennsylvania, are you?"

"Norfolk. He just fought in Richmond last night. Saturday night was in D.C. After we left your cabin at St. Mary's, we only made it as far as Pittsburgh before he got this idea in his thick head."

"What are you going to do?"

"I have a bad feeling about this fight tonight. Ben said it'll be the last, but why the hell would I believe him? I don't know, I just thought maybe you'd have some advice."

"I can do better than give advice. Tell me the address, and I'll be there tonight for the fight. I've decided I need to get back to St. Simons anyway."

"Why? You just got back home about a week ago."

"There's some weird stuff going on. I'll explain better when I see you. It's almost noon, so by the time I throw some things together and get on the road, we should just make it in time. I'll see you then."

"Thanks, Lin. You'll be a big help; I know you will. I can't get through to him."

Lee recited the fight address to Lin, and they said their goodbyes.

*　*　*

"Gabby, that was Lee. She's kind of in some trouble. Something is going on with Ben. Funny how I just decided to head back to St. Simons, and Lee needs my help in Norfolk. It's on the way, so let's pack some things and get going."

"Now's a good time. You still have a lot of your mayhem converts here. You probably can't go back to work yet anyway."

Lin thought back to her first two converts, John and Tommy. They'd been converted before she'd gotten control of her mayhem, and they'd followed her to St. Simons Island. She remembered how impossible it had been to be around them. They'd been so infatuated and giggly, to the point where she could barely get away from them. If all the people she'd converted in Allentown when she'd healed Ben were still like that, there would be no way to go back. Not yet.

"Oh yeah, that's right. I'll call Dr. Grayson and see if I can get an extension. I have a feeling he'll be happy to do whatever I ask."

"Yes, just like a convert. Sweet Pets will manage without you a bit longer."

Gabriel smiled, and Lin nodded and disappeared to pack a bag.

"Jack," she said from the bedroom doorway. "Jack, get up. We have to get going."

He sat up on the bed and rubbed his eyes. Nomad continued to twitch.

"Going where? We just got here."

"St. Simons Island. You up for a road trip, Jack? Maybe we'll find a chilly hotel room there. How does that sound?"

Lin knew he had to remember that night nine days earlier in that cold hotel room with her. She'd been struggling to understand her power, which she'd buried when she was fifteen because it was too dangerous and uncontrollable. That night with Jack was the first time she'd stayed conscious while her mayhem rose up. And she took him with it, driving him mad with pleasure and nearly scaring him to death too.

He looked down at the floor as he dug around in his pants pocket until he found the engagement ring—the one he'd been trying to put on Lin's finger ever since the big scene in Allentown. He shook his head and let his breath out slowly.

"Lin, I . . ." He paused. "Lin, I'm really tired. I think I'll sit this one out."

She raised her eyebrows and stared at him before she could form a question.

"Really, Jack? You'd rather stay in Pennsylvania?"

"How long will you be gone?"

"I think only a couple of days. It'll be a short trip, I promise."

"Why are you going?"

"I can't give a good answer to that, Jack. This whole thing with me dying . . . I just need to get back to the Island. I don't know why."

"Yeah, you dying, that's . . ." He looked back down at the floor. "I need to look after my houses too. I could use a couple of days for that. And to rest. I'm really exhausted, Lin."

"Okay, Jack, you know what's best."

"Is Nomad going too?"

"It's probably better if he stays here. It might be too hot for him down there. Can you keep an eye on him?"

"Yes, of course. That'll be my workouts—carrying his food around."

She walked over and slipped her arms around his waist. Before kissing him, she looked into his adoring eyes and marveled at how he could keep up with her. All the times she'd used her mayhem on him might have sent any other man running for cover. But Jack stayed by her side with everything that life with her brought.

She felt tears working their way to the surface, but she squeezed her eyes shut, tilted her head up, and kissed him.

"My Cowgirl, you know I'd go to the ends of the Earth with you if you needed me to, don't you?"

"Okay, my Cowboy. That's a deal. But I don't want to go any farther than that."

* * *

"I'll ride in the back, Mom. Not a lot of room back there, but that's okay. And where did you ever get a car like this anyway? Why would anyone ever need to go that fast?"

"Sometimes, dear Taylor, a girl needs to move fast. Live a little dangerously. I like it."

"And what's with the license plate?"

"Oh, that's kind of like an inside joke. I'll tell you about it when we stop for a snack."

Lin closed Taylor's door and smiled—her girl's life was only beginning.

"Just be safe," said Jack, "and don't go too fast, alright?"

"I'll try to keep myself under control, but no guarantees."

"Just do your best." He gave her a small smile.

She looked over the roof of her Temt8tion.

"Gabby, you're coming too, aren't you?"

"Wouldn't miss it. I'd still like to talk more with Lee if we get a chance. She's quite remarkable."

"That's for sure. Okay, let's get—"

Lin saw a tiny black dot straight in front of her, drawing her eyes to it like a magnet. It raced toward her, and when it had nearly covered her, a point of light appeared at the same place. The darkness hurried past, and Lin's breaths froze in her chest as her thoughts and feelings left her. Even as she stared at the growing white light, she felt her heart silenced.

But only for an instant. The brightness soon covered her, and her heartbeat and the rest of her life returned in the world that the speeding whiteness had dragged with it.

She took a deep breath and started to collapse.

Chapter 5 – Some Crazy Fun

Jack caught her just as she started to tip.

"Lin, easy there. What's going on?"

"Nothing, Jack. Just maybe still a little tired."

She looked over at Gabriel, who only nodded and raised a hand to cover a barely noticeable smile.

Lin sank into her Temt8tion's molded leather seat and wiggled her behind deep into it. She felt her short black skirt ride up, and she glanced down with a grin at her bare legs ending in her favorite black heels. Gabriel took the passenger side. Jack slammed her door shut and tapped the car roof, and Lin blew him a kiss and squealed the tires as she backed her car to the road.

The scenery seemed to fly past like a slideshow in a dream as Gabriel sang along to all of the classic rock blasting from the radio. Taylor mostly slept in the back seat.

That girl needs to live a little, Lin told herself as she watched the dry pavement continue to flow under her powerful car. Any hint of rain had been left far behind.

"Okay, Taylor, wake up back there. We're in St. Simons, the place you've heard about from all my stories, but it probably doesn't even seem real to you—just some imaginary world.

"Gabriel, I bet you're hungry after that long drive, aren't you? Here's what I suggest: let's all get a good meal in the Village, and then, Taylor, we need to do some shopping. I know just the style for you. We can celebrate your recovery with a brand new wardrobe!"

"That sounds great, Mom. I already know I want some short skirts. Some really short skirts like you wear all the time."

"Oh, I don't know, Taylor—sounds like trouble. Do you think that's the best idea?"

"And heels. I want some really high heels, okay, Mom? It just seems wrong to wear a short skirt without high heels. You dress like that, and since when do you get in trouble?"

"Oh, Hon, the stories I could tell. Let's see what they have in the shops. Gabriel, it's a lot warmer here compared to icy Pennsylvania. How about some new clothes for you too?"

"That's an excellent idea, Lin. I'm sweating like a dog in this sweater. Like *your* dog, that big mutt. What's his name again?"

"His name? Oh my God . . . my dog's name. He's Nomad. Nomad! Why didn't we bring him?"

"Maybe because it's too hot?"

"Yeah, that must be it. Too hot for the big mutt. Maybe I'm too hot for Jack too," Lin said with a laugh and popped a button on her blouse.

Gabriel and Taylor laughed with her.

Lin picked out a crowded sidewalk cafe in the Village with umbrellas over the tables, and they all placed their orders.

"No hotcakes this time, Gabriel?"

"I don't even really like hotcakes. I don't know why I ate so many of them the other day. Just to keep you amused, I think. You need to laugh more, don't you think?"

"Well, as long as you get your fill, that's all that matters. And you're right—I need to laugh more. I do believe I need some crazy fun."

The food vanished as if it had never been there, and Lin ordered a round of cocktails. The three toasted and finished their drinks.

"Taylor, Honey, are you ready to shop yet?"

"Hell yeah, Mom. Let's go."

"I bet they have just the style you need right next door. I think you're right—you'd look best in a really, really short skirt and really, really high heels."

"Good, Mom, I can't wait!"

They all rose from their table, and Lin called over the young man who'd been waiting on them. She gave him a sly smile and looked him up and down as he approached.

"Young man, would you be an absolute sweetheart and save this table for us? We need to shop for just a minute, but we'll be back. Would you be a dear and do that for me?"

She looked him in the eye and held her chest out, stretching her thin blouse.

"Why, of course. Yes, yes, of course," he said, staring at Lin's generous cleavage.

She reached out to touch his cheek, and she leaned in close. When her red lips had closed the distance, almost brushing against his, she stared into his eyes with a smile and said, "You're the best!"

That boy must have forgotten how to blink, she thought as she took a few steps back and watched his smiling mouth hanging open. Then, she turned to leave, and she was just sure he was watching her long legs sticking her sharp heels into the patio's bricks.

The three took a short walk through an iron gate that squealed open for them, and instantly, they stood outside the trendy shop next door. Its large plate glass window displayed several mannequins dressed in summer fashions.

"Time for a special outfit, Taylor. But please, not like this boring crap in the window. Are you ready, Hon?"

"Yeah, Mom!"

In no time, Taylor had a short red skirt stretched around her trim hips, and her lean legs ended in a pair of short black boots with tall heels. She struck poses in front of the shop's mirror in a snug black tank top while flicking her hair back, and Lin could only hoot and whistle.

"Taylor, try on a tank a size smaller, okay? And Honey?"

"Yeah, Mom?"

"Lose the bra."

"Good idea, Mom!"

Taylor followed Lin's advice, and she continued her posing with the thin black material barely covering every curve and feature.

"Taylor, you look really hot in that coat of paint," Lin said with a snort. "You're going to attract all kinds of attention—I'm jealous! Doesn't she look hot, Gabriel?"

"Exactly so. She's definitely your daughter."

"She sure is. We're two hot women on the prowl and dressed like we mean business. This island doesn't stand a chance!"

They all tilted their heads back and laughed.

"Broken hearts or broken bones, right, Gabriel?"

"That's exactly right, Lin!"

She paid the expensive bill from her wad of cash, and they all stepped out into the hot sunshine.

"The world is yours, Taylor. What do you want most right now?"

"Mom, I want to see what kind of trouble I can find. I've been waiting a long time for this, and I sure am dressed for it! Don't wait for me because I probably won't see you until tomorrow. Forget that—not even tomorrow. Time for me to grow up, Mom."

"Oh, that's for sure. Go break some hearts, baby girl. Hey, why not take a cab down to Daytona? God knows the things that could happen to you there."

"I love that idea! But I'll just hitchhike instead."

"That's my girl."

"Shouldn't you give me some cash, Mom?"

"Honey, you have something they want more than money."

Taylor turned and strutted down the sidewalk with her hips swaying and her heels clicking. She'd taken only a dozen steps before she stopped and stretched down to tie a lace that was already tied. A white van saw the bait and pulled up. Its windowless door slid open, and Taylor got in.

"Ah, that girl, Gabriel. That might not be the safest thing, but oh, what the hell—I have other things on my mind."

"Exactly right, Lin."

She and Gabriel walked back to their table, and on the way, Lin hugged her server tight and kissed his cheek.

"You're sweet for saving the table, so I owe you. You'll have to figure out a way for me to pay you back. Why, I believe I'd do just about anything you can imagine."

She pulled her shoulders back and blew him a kiss. He blushed and hurried awkwardly into the kitchen.

After they sat back down, she blocked the sun with her hand and scanned along the other side of the street until her eyes fixed on something.

"Gabriel, why don't you get lost for a while too? You never know what kind of action you might find. And maybe think about getting a haircut, huh?"

She laughed at Gabriel and looked across Mallery Street to a row of bars mostly hidden in the night. A lone figure leaned against a cracked brick wall.

"Oh yeah, I see some unfinished business across the street. Maybe I'll see you later. Maybe not."

Lin stood and took another sip of the fresh cocktail her new young friend had brought over. She shook her long blond mane back onto the sheer white blouse that covered nothing but skin. With arms out to each side, she arched her back, straining the thin material already clinging to every tiny detail from the humidity. She popped open another button and started to pull her skirt down since it had slid up a little while sitting. But Gabriel had wise advice.

"Lin . . . be kind."

"You're right. Why on Earth would I ever pull my skirt back down? I don't think I have anything I need to hide, do I? Not from anyone."

"You certainly do not, Lin. Not from anyone at all."

She thought about how good her legs looked, smooth and bare in the hot sunshine.

"You know what I love, Gabriel? Showing everyone what a sweet, sinful treat I am. I love showing off everything I have to offer. That's *my* way of being kind."

"You always did like to show off," Gabriel said with a grin.

"So, why change now, you mean?"

"Yes, exactly. And you have your mayhem, and your intent can take anyone's magic. You'll never be in any real danger."

She ran her hands down her hips one more time.

"Oh, Gabriel, I told you I didn't want to use my powers anymore. And if I don't use them, with all the teasing I do, I could be in some real trouble. I'll be helpless and trying on some danger just like I'd slip on a skimpy nightie."

"No one slips on a nightie like you, Lin," Gabriel said and winked.

"You know what would feel even better? For me to tease my way into some danger *while* I'm wearing that tiny nightie."

"I do think you're onto something, Lin."

"If I draw a crowd, there will just have to be enough of me to go around."

Gabriel looked her in the eye and got a big grin.

"And if I'm a lucky girl, around *again*."

"Yes, Lin!"

"I'm kidding of course—I'm just a tease."

She downed the last of her cocktail and took her time popping open the rest of the buttons. The thin blouse mostly draped straight down, held away from her in two places which poked at the fine, almost transparent material.

She stretched again, almost opening her shirt completely. Then, she slid her hands down her hips and around behind her, feeling her smooth skin covered only by the thin cloth of her short skirt.

"Mm . . . I'm not too far from naked now, and I like it. Without my powers, I could be in some real trouble. It's not safe for a girl to be dressed like this."

"It's closer to 'undressed.'"

"Right, I'm sure not wearing much. But what the hell. Time to have some fun."

"Yes!"

"I just love showing off, Gabriel."

"That's for sure!"

Across hot road asphalt and between silent vehicles that had somehow frozen in place, Lin took long, graceful strides into the night. Her heels clacked, and her arms and open shirt swung around as she approached the fake bounty hunter still visible in the darkness in his white t-shirt—the man that she remembered had already tried to kill her once.

She felt the danger driving her heart rate higher, and she pushed aside any thought of her mayhem.

"Good to see you out of that old car of yours, tough guy."

"The car's gone, babe. You took it when you left me on Jericho. What brings you here?"

"After seeing you,"—she ran her hands up and down his muscular arms—"I swear, I can't remember."

He grabbed Lin's shoulders and pressed her back up against the cold brick wall. He released her only long enough to stretch her shirt to each side, and he pinned that to the wall too.

"Ooh . . ." She arched her back and took a deep breath as her heart pounded. Her tongue slid across her wet lips, and she felt a rush of electricity zip through her as she glanced down at her breasts in the brief headlights of a turning car.

"Oh, you like to play rough, that's for sure," she said as she placed her palms against his bare chest and spread her manicured fingers wide. From there, she slid her fingertips down over every muscle of his granite abdomen until they hooked the top of his belt.

"You like it rough if I remember right," he said.

"Yeah, rough is what I need, maybe because I'm so soft and smooth."

He looked down and said, "Yeah, that's for damn sure."

She wiggled her fingertips in farther.

"Still packing a pistol, stranger?"

"For a dangerous dame like you? I brought my biggest gun."

"You think you're gonna shoot that gun this time, fella?"

"Nothing's gonna stop me."

He moved one hand up to Lin's throat, and she looked up and parted her red lips.

"Can't you squeeze any harder than that, mister? You know I'm about to."

He did squeeze harder until Lin struggled to breathe as she was pressed against the cold fender of his old car on a lonely road northwest of Brunswick.

"You don't even remember my name, do you, honey?"

The trees all around them barely moved, and hot sunlight beamed through an open space above them.

"Sure, your name is Ivan. I bet this all looks pretty good, huh, Ivan?"

"Yeah, you look damn good. Just like last time."

"You didn't see just how sweet I am last time, poor boy. See anything you like?"

"I see a lot I like, babe. And I'm going to take it all."

"Take? Oh, you silly man. I like showing off, that's all. You don't get any."

"You're more than a show-off. You're cheap. You're easy."

"Wrong, tough guy. I just like being a tease."

"No, you're easy, and you'll do whatever I tell you."

"I don't seem to have much choice, do I?"

"No, you sure as hell don't."

"There's no one around to stop you, that's for sure. It's only you, me, and the trees out here."

He looked around quickly and repositioned his grip. Lin felt her heart pounding.

"But a girl like me, I'd show off for a crowd too."

"I bet you'd do a hell of a lot more than that for a crowd. I think you'd love to give it all to a crowd."

"If they're all as strong as you, big boy, I couldn't say no, could I?"

Lin felt his other hand reach up to her throat, and she had a fleeting image of what a crowd would expect of her. With her heart tapping out a hot rhythm, she let go of his belt.

"Mm . . ."—she slid her tongue along her lips—"I guess I'd have to do anything, anything at all."

She reached for the collar of her blouse, pulled it gently down over her shoulders, and let it drop onto the trunk of his old car. Her heart raced, and her mayhem was itching to break loose.

"That's better, isn't it?"

His blue eyes stared, and his grip tightened more. Lin felt her eyes begin to bulge out, and she slapped both hands onto his hard chest.

"You ain't getting away this time, but go ahead and try. Make it fun for me, bitch."

Lin felt her last breath dwindling inside as her thumping heart burned her last traces of oxygen. She pushed against his bare chest, even though she knew he was much too strong.

She noticed her mayhem coiled up like a spring just beneath her surface, always ready to rise up if needed. She resisted it, and she focused instead on how she was mostly undressed for a dangerous man, alone and helpless on a lonely road. And still a tease.

With her heart speeding as her air ran out, the thrill outweighed the danger. So, she ran her fingers back down to his belt, pulled his hips into her, and felt her breasts brushing against his solid chest. She felt the heat of his skin against her and his strong hands rough around her throat. Her behind squeezed into the cool metal of his car, and she was trapped there, wearing only a skirt and heels, with no chance of escape, and her heart beating a strong rhythm.

Unless she called her mayhem.

"You're so goddamn easy."

The words echoed through her, and she began to face that she really might be as easy as he said. Because she wished he'd stop choking her and start making her do things that an easy woman would do, things an easy woman like *her* would do.

His grip relaxed, but he kept his calloused hands around her throat. Lin took deep breaths while her heartbeat sounded inside her.

"You ready to do what I tell you?"

Lin nodded.

"You really are cheap, ain't you?"

Lin thought of her mayhem, pushed it aside again, and felt her heart beating hard in her bare chest pressed into his.

"Oh yeah, mister, I guess I am a cheap girl."

He dropped his hands down to his belt, and Lin knew it would be sexy to keep teasing him, so she reached down to the bottom hem of her skirt and began sliding it up.

"This won't save you. It's only buying you some time."

"I know."

He unbuckled, and Lin had pulled her skirt almost up to her waist.

"And you still want it?"

Keep teasing him, she told herself.

"God, yeah. Even more."

She knew he'd have her in only seconds, and she held her mayhem back.

She knew he'd strangle her after, too, and still, she pushed her mayhem aside. She knew she could wait until the very last second anyway.

He'd just grabbed the inside of her right thigh and began lifting her leg . . .

. . . and her mayhem erupted like a volcano from Hell, blasting green fire from her eyes.

"What the—"

Time stopped. And Ivan froze with it.

The world became a calm, flat surface, and Lin witnessed again the unidentifiable oceans of magic spinning mad patterns beneath it. Her hungers and cravings became lost in the infinity all around her, and she embraced the ecstasy of all that wondrous magic rushing into her, swelling her until she felt she might burst.

She looked into his caramel eyes and felt a powerful wave begin to rear up, ready to rush out and take him, to control him, to—

No, wait, she thought, Ivan didn't have caramel eyes! No, this isn't right!

Lin locked her eyes shut and blocked out the world—the world that now seemed crazy—and she found her intent in the stillness inside her.

She found her unbreakable hold on it, and she held it tight.

She didn't feel his hot skin pressed against hers, no cool metal against her thighs, and no hot sunshine.

In utter stillness and silence, Lin held her intent.

After an eternity in the darkness inside her closed eyelids, Lin witnessed a tiny point of light. It grew, racing toward her until it covered her, and she found that her eyes were already open.

As her life returned to her, she took a deep breath and started to collapse.

* * *

Jack caught her just as she started to tip.

"Lin, easy there. What's going on?"

"Oh, Jack! What is this? I'm still in Pennsylvania?"

Jack and Gabriel looked at each other. Tears leaked out of her eyes and began to streak down her cheeks.

"Yeah, of course. Where did you think we were?"

"Oh, Jack, that wasn't me! I'm not really like that!"

She held his arm with one hand while the other wiped at both eyes.

"Not like what?"

"I'm not that woman at all. Why would I act like that? I love you, Jack."

He only smiled and stared before finding his voice again.

"I love you too, Lin. More than you probably know."

She slipped her arms around his waist and hugged him in silence with her head on his shoulder. Her quiet sobs shook them both. Jack glanced over at Gabriel, who only looked down at the ground.

"Jack, just help me back into the house for a minute, okay?"

"Sure, Lin. Are you alright?"

"Yeah, I think. I just . . . I just want to change. It'll only take a few seconds."

Within a couple of minutes, they walked out of her house holding hands. Lin had traded her short skirt and tight blouse for a pair of jeans and a blue hooded sweatshirt. Her heels had been tossed aside for her black boots, and she'd tied her hair back in a ponytail.

"This is better, Jack. This is more comfortable for a long drive. Promise me you'll be around when I get back?"

"Of course, where else would I be? Hey, are you alright?"

"Just tired, Jack. I'll be fine."

She sank into her Temt8tion's black leather seat, and Gabriel took the passenger side. Jack slammed her door and pressed his palm against the glass. Lin returned it from inside, and they gazed into each other's eyes for a few seconds before Jack tapped the car roof and took a few steps back.

She turned toward Gabriel.

"Gabby, something just happened. Some kind of dream but more like a nightmare. Was I gone again?"

"It looked that way. You got pale, and your eyes closed. It only lasted a second, though."

"As soon as we can, we have to talk."

She carefully backed her Temt8tion to the road.

Chapter 6 – Lying Around Lying

After a short drive on the interstate, Taylor slipped her headphones down around her neck.

"I know you grew up in St. Simons, Mom, and I remember most of your stories. I'm so glad I feel better and we're traveling together. Just a few days ago, I was lying in the hospital dying. Lying. That's funny, Mom. I wasn't lying around lying. I was just lying. Get it?"

Gabriel glanced back to study Taylor for a second before turning to watch the approaching pavement.

"Taylor, your life is only going to get better now. Will you be happy to see Lee again?"

"Yeah, Mom. But I never want to be 'lying' around like that again, you know?"

Gabriel gave Lin a quick look before looking again out at the road.

"I do. I understand. Are you still tired?"

"You can tell, huh? I haven't slept much with you being dead and all. Once we get rolling, maybe I'll take a nap again."

The first raindrops began to strike the Temt8tion's windshield, and Lin set the wipers to swipe every couple of seconds.

"Oh, here we go again with the rain, Gabby. At least it isn't bad enough to blow down a cabin."

"Not yet, no."

"You scare me sometimes. You know that, don't you?"

"It can be a scary world, Lin."

* * *

After rolling past many cities and towns, Taylor had fallen asleep listening to her favorite music, and the rain had ended. Lin listened to her car's engine rumbling as it carried them south, and she struggled to find the words.

"I can't even explain what happened back there just before we left."

"You should try. Was it Gloriana again?"

"It must have been. Like before, when I was on the couch at home, some kind of emptiness took me, and I died. I felt it. Then, the world began again, and it felt like no time had passed. I was still standing in the same spot next to the car with everyone around me. But it was different. God, it was so different, only I didn't know it right away."

"Different how?"

"I was still me, but I was some kind of exaggerated, sleazy version of myself. I acted a little bit like me but to a ridiculous level. I can't really be like that, can I? Is that how people see me?"

"I doubt it. What else was it like?"

"I would never do all those things; I swear I wouldn't. I couldn't be like that, could I?"

"What things did you do? What were you like?"

"Oh God, I don't even want to get into it. I'm mostly upset about how I treated Taylor. I bought her new clothes and . . . oh, and we were in St. Simons. The drive went past like nothing. Then, we ate, and I bought Taylor new clothes, and I just sent her out into the world like I didn't care what happened to her. I dressed her up like a tease and sent her hitchhiking. Gabby, that's not me! How could I have done that?"

"You were here. Sure, you were probably dead for an instant, but you were standing by Jack the whole time. What else?"

"And Ivan was there. Ivan from Jericho Road when I killed Doc. I was coming on to him like a wild woman. I remember how I felt—I wanted only to be the biggest tease I could possibly be.

"Then, he started to strangle me, and I wasn't even worried about it. I knew I could summon my mayhem and take control of him again.

"But I didn't want to. I was enjoying being treated like that. I was excited by it. I knew I could destroy him with my mayhem, but I liked what was happening too much. He said I was cheap and easy, and I liked hearing it. And you know what? I really was cheap and easy.

"We were just about to . . . you know. Then, my mayhem rose up by itself. It protected me even when I was too stupid on my own. I was just about to send out a wave, and I was looking into his eyes, and . . ."

"Go on."

"Oh God, that wasn't Ivan. Now, I see. Somehow, that was Gloriana. It was all a trick. She'd told me before how to bring her back to this world. She said I needed to look into her eyes and use my intent, and that would bring us both back. I was looking into Ivan's eyes, and Gabby, I almost fell for it. But his eyes were Gloriana's eyes. So, I closed mine, and *then* I found my intent.

"And here I am."

"And you were only dead a second this time. It sounds like her ploy almost worked."

"It almost did. But the whole thing—it all felt so strange. None of us were acting right. And it was hot sunshine on one side of the street and night on the other."

"Like a dream?"

"Yeah. And then, we were on Jericho Road. I think she pulled things out of my memory, pieces of me, and she put them all together. But it didn't add up. What if she does a better job next time? I'd never know the difference. God, she's powerful."

"You were right before, Lin—you need to get stronger. And you will. I will stay with you and help."

"Thanks, Gabby. I think I need your help more now than I ever have before."

* * *

"I told you I would help, Tayo. I am glad your problems are not worse. A few broken bones. A concussion. You will be fine."

Even struggling with his injuries, Tayo Tersoo felt a familiar comfort at hearing Anna Andreyevna Kelgina's soft-spoken Russian accent. He glanced at her short skirt and heels and realized he never knew that she could dress that way. The years they'd spent together working with The Shield had forged his impressions of her. She'd worn stiff, formal suits every day, and her unimaginative hairstyle had neatly framed the large glasses she always wore. But now, her light brown hair fell softly to her shoulders, and he wondered if she'd switched to contact lenses. He registered a mental reminder to inquire about it soon.

"Many parts of my anatomy still hurt, Anna, but yes, I should heal at the expected rate. I won't be climbing trees for some time, though."

Tayo swung his leg off of the hospital bed, and the thick cast clunked on the floor. A nurse handed him his crutches, and he stood and tested his weight on the injured leg. He scowled and shifted to his good leg before sitting in the wheelchair the nurse had brought. Some of his black dreadlocks hung down over his forehead as he leaned into the seat.

"I will carry his bag," said Anna, and the nurse handed it to her. "And those sticks."

Anna took all of the items into her arms, and the nurse reached for the wheelchair's handles.

"Okay, Tayo, let us get you out to my car. Daria should have pulled it around front by now."

After a quick ride in the elevator and through the hospital corridors, Tayo took back his crutches and rose to stand next to Anna. The nurse retreated back through the automatic doors.

"It's still hard to believe, Anna—all the destruction Lin caused. I saw horrors around that cabin that I hope I can forget someday. I believe I will never stop fearing what she can do."

"And still you want to find her? Why, Tayo?"

"When I was in that tree and about to fire the rocket, I saw her eyes. Her bright, impossibly bright green eyes."

"I saw them more than once, and all it did was scare me. I do not believe she is evil like Wolfe said she had to be because she could use magic. I believe she is largely good. But she is a frightening thing. I do not want to see her again."

"I need to, but don't ask me why. I only know that my future involves her somehow. I must find her, Anna."

"Our work with The Shield is done. Wolfe is gone and so is his corporation. You watched Gabriel destroy him, did you not? Are you not afraid of these people?"

"Yes, but I must find her. Anna, that whole thing at Lin's cabin altered me. I tried to tell her back when you and Daria helped me go see her after Wolfe made me fire that goddamn rocket. There was so much I wanted to say, and I couldn't find the words. I mostly just felt awed by her."

"You were very broken up. How do you speak clearly with a concussion? You cannot even think in a straight line."

Tayo had been the lead investigator for The Shield, and he still hadn't come to terms with all the bizarre facts and coincidences he had discovered. How could parts of Lin's life have been so similar to stories from the distant past?

But none of that mattered compared to what he'd seen from up in a tree far from Lin's cabin while holding a rocket launcher. Lin had just destroyed the rest of The Shield's agents in ways too grisly for Tayo to comprehend. She'd stood there on the porch, a far distance away, and he could see her eyes glowing bright green. A blinding green. Lin's eyes had changed him.

"I'll recover from that, but still, I'm going to find Lin. Not for revenge. She could have killed me as easily as blinking her eyes. She let me live. She saw into my heart, Anna. I felt it. I only know that I must see her again. My life means nothing else to me now."

"You should just rest. That is what should mean something to you."

They'd made it to the sidewalk and saw Daria waiting in the car. She waved and shook back her thick black hair. A small black dog pawed at the glass of the passenger side window as they approached. She helped him into the back seat, and getting his tall frame inside took some effort. Anna held the top of his head so it wouldn't strike the frame, and she felt his hair soft against her palm.

"Where are we going, Mom?" said Daria.

"I do not even know, Daria. Where do you want to go, Tayo?"

"Let's locate Lin."

"You cannot be serious. You need to recover, do you not?"

"Sitting in the car will have to do. This is more important than anything in my life. Bigger than the Words of God. Please, if you and Daria don't have any pressing matters to address, can you drive me? I would drive myself, but this cast . . ."

"Yes, well, you cannot drive. That is obvious."

Anna turned to face Daria.

"Take I80 east. We are going to Lin's home. What we will do there, I cannot tell you a guess."

*　*　*

With their car humming along I80, Tayo had quickly drifted off to sleep.

"Mom, you seem back to normal. I mean, you were different for a while. What was going on? I've never seen you swearing before."

"Maybe it was just the stress of all of that. I do not know. Let us put that all behind us."

Except for the memory of Wolfe, thought Anna. She recalled the power he'd had over her and the things he'd made her do. The things she'd found herself willing to do.

She'd only been following her conscience, she'd thought. The voice in her mind had been a constant companion since she'd first met Lancaster Wolfe over twenty years earlier when she'd agreed to join The Shield. She'd believed it was her own conscience guiding her and helping her make choices. But the voice inside wasn't something natural at all.

And for the first time in twenty years, she felt that returning to Russia could be a real option. She'd joined The Shield to help in their quest to find someone that could read the Scroll, that ancient artifact that carried the Words of God. All that was in the past now. Lin had read the thing, and the melee that followed strained her sanity. But it was all over, and she was ready to face a new future without a voice in her head.

"Right, Mom, let's just forget about all the people that got killed. You saw the bodies around that cabin. God, what did she do to them? How was that even possible?"

"I do not understand the world any longer, Daria. Not after all that I have seen. I saw parts of a man sticking out of a tree trunk. I do not know if I want to be anywhere near Lin again. And are you not upset, Daria? You had to shoot Benson. I still do not understand why he would try to kill you."

"These are crazy times, Mom. We'll probably never figure all this out, so let's not even try."

Tayo awoke with a start and rummaged through his pockets until he'd found his phone. He punched a few numbers and held it up to his ear.

"It's Tayo. Get the boys together. I need your help. No, nothing like that. But I've sustained injuries, and I'll need assistance just getting around. No, I anticipate things will go easy. But if they go bad, they'll go bad in ways you can't imagine."

He paused and listened.

"You owe me, that's why. What do you—"

He paused again.

"No, I understand. You're unable, or unwilling, to honor your obligations. I've assisted you, and now—"

He held the phone away and stared at it before putting it away.

Anna shifted her dog to her lap and turned to look at him.

"Problems, Tayo?"

"Sometimes, friends are not friends at all. Just disappointments."

"You need help with something, is that it?"

"Yeah. Let's just get to Lin's. I'll figure this all out."

Anna turned back around and lifted the dog into her arms. She picked a few hairs off of her skirt and lowered the window to scatter them. Daria stared straight ahead at the highway, and no one spoke until they'd reached Lin's house.

* * *

"I feel no comfort being here. I would drop you here and ask you to walk the rest of the way, but you cannot. Daria, pull up near Lin's house, and Tayo, you get out and do whatever it is you think you should do."

"You do know what city we're in, don't you, Anna?"

"Yes. And I still do not understand it. It is very unsettling."

"It is very much unsettling. But it might be good, don't you think? Perhaps Lin is . . . I don't know . . . also someone special?"

"She is dangerous, that is all I know. Go, Tayo, and finish what you must do. We will not sit around here forever."

Tayo soon stood on the sidewalk in front of Lin's house with the rubber tips of his crutches planted firmly on the concrete. The house was dark and appeared deserted to him, and when he saw a woman walking out of the house next door with a dog, he hobbled over to meet her.

"Excuse me, but I was told to talk to Lin about adopting a puppy and that she could help point me in the right direction. But it looks like no one's home. I think I might have missed her."

"Oh, young man, she's off traveling again. I heard them all talking about going 'back down south,' but who knows where. I can take your name and number, and when she gets back, maybe she can call you?"

"No, thanks. I'll just wait until I can see her at Sweet Pets. This isn't a big rush. Thank you greatly for your help."

Within minutes, Daria had circled around, and they stopped to let him in.

"Well, you have found a dead end. Now, we can take you to your home. Tell us where, and we will drop you."

"I'm not going home. I'm going to see Lin. Anna, would you help me? I have no one else."

She looked at Daria, and Daria shrugged.

"Fine by me, Mom. Let's take him to Lin, and then, you and me, let's get the hell away from all of this."

"Where do you need to go, Tayo?"

"St. Simons Island."

Chapter 7 – The Moon Itself

"You got heart. I'll give you that."

Ben looked up from his hands and knees and turned his head to the left to give the blood a more direct path to the concrete floor.

"But your bones ain't gonna make it."

He took a quick step in and kicked the toe of his boot into Ben's exposed side. The dull thud reached every ear in the hushed warehouse before the crowd exploded in jeers and screams.

Ben let his head hang down and began to watch the thick puddle forming below him before his eye filled up and his world went red. He knew that he only had to drag himself back to his corner, and he'd be alright. One hand slipped and left a long streak as he began to crawl toward the sound of Lee's voice.

*   *   *

"We should probably get in there, don't you think?"

"Yes, after this song. He should be okay a few more minutes."

"Oh, Gabby, you and your classic rock. Does it make you feel you're going back in time?"

"Yes, but not too far back. Not like what Wolfe might have taught me."

Lin thought back to that day, still only three days in the past. The battle between Gabriel, the real Gabriel—the destroyer—and Lancaster Wolfe, the maniac that had pursued her to read the Words of God, still felt like a slowly healing wound. She looked at Gabriel and smiled, remembering again how many times she would have been lost on her own. But Gabriel had saved her from Wolfe and his army of demons, even the one that had singled her out. The one whose offers she might have accepted if the destroyer Gabriel hadn't come to her rescue.

Maybe the horror of that day had passed enough. It had become only vivid memories, not the stuff of nightmares. But what followed was something she still couldn't explain. And Gabriel wouldn't shed any light on it. She began to wonder if maybe it couldn't be explained.

"Yeah, maybe Wolfe could have given you something unbelievable, but I'd be gone. And Jack and Taylor too. And Nomad. I still can't understand how strong you are. You never falter."

"Oh no, Lin, sure I do. I'm not a saint."

Lin laughed and said, "No, you're something else, that's for sure."

*　*　*

"Come on, Ben, just get back to the corner, that's all you need to do."

Another kick landed in the same place. More ribs cracked, and even the weakest inhale was a bundle of knives thrust into his side. Ben curled himself up and waited for the next strike. But there were no more—only yelling and laughing and the sound of his opponent cussing while being shoved back to his own corner.

He stood weakly and walked toward Lee's voice, where he turned his head and spit blood at a bucket. He missed. He wiped at the eye that wasn't swollen shut and looked at Lee.

"It's bad this time, Lee."

"How bad?"

"A lot of breaks. I can't see. Hell, I can barely breathe."

"Sit down. We don't have much time."

"Do it all, Lee."

"That's not how this works. You know that."

"But I can't breathe," he said. "I can't beat this guy if I can't breathe. Or see."

"I can't pick and choose. You know that. All I can do is stop somewhere short of healing everything, and that should be enough to fix the ribs."

"No, don't stop this time. Do all of it. Everything, Lee."

"Ben, you know better. You know it won't end well."

"I don't care. I need to seriously kick this guy's ass. Come on, Lee, do it."

Ben sat on the stool with his back against the ropes and reached for his shoulders, and Lee reached through the ropes and placed her hands above both of his.

"Ben . . ."

"Do it. You're wasting time."

* * *

"When I first woke up—okay, I didn't just wake up, but you know what I mean. I felt like I couldn't deal with any of this. And I have to tell you, I still mostly feel that way. I've killed a lot of people. I know they would have killed us, so it's not like I murdered them or killed them for no reason. But I don't feel like ever using my powers again. Enough with the magic already!

"And I feel like I need all my strength to fight off Gloriana and whatever the hell is going on with that."

"You have every reason to be alarmed by that. I know I've been reluctant to discuss it with you, and there's a reason for that. Soon, though, we can talk about it."

"Let me guess—it's one of those things I have to fight through on my own?"

"Yes, but don't think that that makes it any easier for me."

"Everything seems easy for you. When those demons were attacking, you said that each one had a tempting offer for you. Like what? I can't even imagine."

"Think about it. I've been obsessed with food since I became real again. I ate so many blueberry hotcakes I thought I might split open.

That's what most of them tempted me with. And Lin, I gave each offer a delicious amount of consideration."

"Oh, Gabby, there's nothing bad about any of that. You're just enjoying being real again."

"Yes, but it's worse than that."

"What else?"

"One offer that I really had to fight myself over."

"What?"

"To be a rock star."

Lin laughed. "Oh yeah, well . . . you already have the hair."

"My desire wasn't just about *looking* like a rock star. I wanted the whole life. Everything you've heard about that life, I wanted it all. And to sing and play guitar very well too."

Gabriel stared out into the dark alley as the music offered its final notes.

"Okay, before the next one starts, it's time to leave the comfort of your Temt8tion."

* * *

Lee sighed and closed her eyes. Only seconds had passed before her eyes opened, and she grabbed the ropes to steady herself. She stepped back from the ring and held the folding chair tightly as she lowered herself onto it.

Ben took a deep breath and jumped to his feet. He grabbed the wet towel and wiped himself off everywhere he could reach, revealing perfect skin without even a scratch.

He slowly turned to face the opponent who had strutted to the center of the ring and stood with clenched fists and his chest puffed out.

Ben swung his arms to either side a few times and laughed before he patted both sides of his rib cage, staring directly at the man he would face once more. Tapping on his ribs wasn't enough. He pounded them hard. And he laughed more. His opponent's eyes grew wide as he took a step back.

Ben walked forward until he pressed up against the outstretched gloved hand of the referee, whose arms full of prison tattoos also carried a slimy coating of Ben's blood. Again, his opponent took a step back.

"What the hell, man . . ."

No trace of the fighter's laughter remained, only disbelief and fear in a cavernous, windowless room that had fallen quiet.

"Step forward for round seven, gentlemen."

"Somethin' ain't right. I felt his ribs breaking. And he was bleeding everywhere. What happened to that? What the hell is going on?"

"Step forward or quit. Make your choice."

Another man climbed into the ring, a man not dressed for fighting. He'd taken off his pin-striped jacket, and his stainless pistol was plain to see shining above his waistband. He dragged his fighter back another step and faced Ben and the referee.

"What the hell is this?" he said to the referee. He turned to face the crowd.

"How is this piece of shit even standing? This is cheating. I don't know how, but dammit, that man's a cheater. Or something worse. My man won.

"Now you," he said, pointing at Ben, "get your ass back to your corner." His other hand covered his revolver.

Ben stared coldly and took a step toward him.

The man pulled his piece.

* * *

"This isn't what I expected."

"No, Lin, I bet it isn't. What did you expect?"

"That I'd turn a few more heads," Lin said with a laugh. "But no one cares. They're all staring at Ben and that other guy in the ring."

"Never mind these people. You're quite attractive even in jeans and a sweatshirt."

"Oh yeah, I'm not wearing my usual stuff. And you know what? I'm done with getting attention like that. I don't need that kind of wardrobe anymore."

"No, you don't, but it served its purpose. Your blue beret still looks quite fashionable, though."

"Thanks, Gabby."

They stood on the cold concrete and made no attempt to push closer to the ring. The crowd began shouting and whistling at the sight of the man in the ring raising his gun to point at Ben.

"Will you use your powers one more time to help Ben?"

She broke her gaze into Gabriel's eyes and looked toward the fighters.

"Yes, but then, I'm done."

Lin knew what she needed to do, and her intent focused in an instant and found the magic inside her. Her intent opened the door to the spinning, chaotic magic, and her eyes began to close. She felt the magic flowing into her and filling her from head to toe. With all her senses opened wide, she saw infinity in every direction.

Before she stopped time, any one of the crowd could have turned to see the shiny green glowing of her eyes. But they didn't look, and she saw the world become a calm surface with unimaginable layers of churning magic below.

Then, Lin stopped time, and she felt no hurry as she took in a deep breath and held it. She felt the ecstasy of the magic streaming into her, creating her in every moment. The pressure inside reached a sweet, familiar level, as it always did, and she sharply exhaled.

It was as if the moon itself had crashed onto the calm surface of the world, and a gigantic wave rose up and rushed out from her, carrying her spirit with it. She allowed the wave to travel in every direction, affecting everyone in attendance. But she focused only on Ben and Lee.

She easily invaded the narrow space between Ben's spirit and his body—between his magic and his reality. With some dismay, Lin was reminded that she wasn't able to invade Lee—Lee was too strong for that. But Lin had other tools. Other abilities. And before she used any of that, she remembered that there was an easier way to get the task done.

With complete control over Ben, she caused him to step out of the ring so that he stood next to Lee. It took hardly any effort to make him scoop up Lee in his arms. He walked out through the frozen crowd, careful to not snag Lee's boots on anyone, and he kicked the door open. A quick walk through the deserted alley led them to Ben's truck parked behind a packed dumpster.

After both of them were seated and the doors closed, Lin returned to herself and allowed time to continue. There was silence at first as the crowd and the men in the ring felt the shock of having witnessed Ben and Lee disappear. They were there, the man had drawn his pistol, things were getting ugly, and in an instant, they had vanished.

Lin's eyes had returned to their normal shade of green, and she smiled at the successful operation. She brushed her hair back over her shoulders, and a look of relief joined the quiet strength in her eyes.

"That comes in pretty handy sometimes, Lin."

"And no 'broken bones' this time, Gabby."

"That's always good. But why with the breath again? You don't need that."

"Oh, that. I still like it. I like the way it feels."

"And why the wave through everyone? You lose your aim?" Gabriel said with a grin.

"No, that's just my gift to them. Even though they probably don't deserve it." And Lin smiled as she looked into Gabriel's peaceful brown eyes. "It won't last long. I made sure of that."

"That 'gift' means we better get going, don't you think?"

"Yeah, we better go. Things might get crazy in here, and they'll be looking for me too. And we came here to talk to Ben and Lee, not get swarmed by an infatuated crowd."

"Yes. Let's go."

* * *

With the engine fired up and echoing off the brick walls lining the filthy alley in a sinister corner of Norfolk, Ben and Lee didn't hear Lin and Gabriel approaching. Ben turned at the sound of Lin tapping on the window, and he cranked it down while he killed the engine.

"You really should get a new truck, Ben. They have power windows now, you know." And she gave him a big smile.

He returned the smile. "Yeah, I will. But a better house is first on the list. Fighting will help with that."

"You can do better. Just give some thought to what you want. You can do anything, Ben."

"Thanks, I do need to give it some thought. And soon. I probably shouldn't keep doing this." He pointed back at the warehouse entrance. "Not much of a way to spend a quiet Monday night, is it?"

"No, certainly not. And they'll be looking for you two. Oh, hey Lee. How have you been?"

"Hi, Lin. Doing fine, just tired now from healing Ben again. It's just you and Gabriel?"

"Taylor's sleeping in the car around the corner, but Jack's exhausted and stayed home. Nomad too. Taylor wanted to see you both, but she's got a very good reason for being tired. We should let her sleep."

Lee continued. "Ben and I make a pretty unique team, wouldn't you say?"

Lin and Lee shared a smile. They'd had plans to compare notes in more detail about their powers, but that was before Wolfe and his gang had launched their final, fatal attack. Lin had insisted that Ben and Lee leave before it got ugly.

"Yeah, you two work great together."

"You moved me around like a puppet," said Ben. "I'll never understand you. But thanks, it wasn't going well in there. Thank God I've gotten used to you doing that. Maybe it's from all the witchcraft from Lee," he said and turned to smile at her.

"Stop, Ben. You know it's not witchcraft."

Gabriel said, "It's because Lin healed you, Ben. Otherwise, you'd always be terrified of her."

"Oh, that makes sense," said Lin.

"And I didn't feel anything, Lin. I just appeared here in Ben's truck. Teach me that sometime, will you?"

"I will if I can. We're parked right around the corner. When you see us pull out, just fall in behind. Apparently, Gabby needs to eat again."

"Lin, if you don't mind, Ben and I are heading out. I'm exhausted and just want to get home already."

"I understand, Lee. You too, Ben? You need to get back?"

"Yeah, and I really am tired too."

"That's a hard way to earn a paycheck," said Lin. "But I admire your reasons for doing it. Does Luanne know what you're up to?"

"I called her, so she knows I'm fighting, but she doesn't know it's bare-knuckle. And she's happy for the cash I'll bring home and the thought of a better house. That old place is one good storm away from being scraped off the hill. Luanne deserves better."

"Yes, she does. She loves you, Ben."

"I know. But I didn't know it until a week ago in Allentown, when you . . . when that—"

"The main thing is that now you know. Your life will only get better. How about you, Lee? What else is going on with you?"

"Alex hasn't come back from that treatment center in Austin yet. Maybe he never will. And Alessa is doing fine. I called her earlier. But I do need to get back. I'm not going to keep doing this with Ben. He's fought in four different cities in four nights. As you can imagine, we can't stick around. If people saw him fully recovered the very next day, think of the chaos that would cause."

"Except tonight, huh?"

"Yeah, I guess we got carried away. I fixed him completely, not just some of it like usual. We knew there'd be problems, but not that bad. Not some psycho with a gun. We're lucky you made it here in time."

"My fast car helped, that's for sure."

"So, why are you going back to St. Simons?" said Lee.

"Oh God, there's some strange stuff going on in my life. Norfolk was on the way."

"You've had enough problems," said Ben. "Can we help?"

"I don't think so. After you left us in that cabin, Gabby and I finished off most of Lancaster Wolfe's group, and I thought we'd be fine after that. We probably should have killed all of them."

"Lin, choosing good is still the way to go."

Lin turned to glance over her shoulder at Gabriel.

"I know, Gabby. I'm just saying. Anyway, it's not about any of them. It's something I can't hardly understand myself."

"Is there any way we can help?" said Ben.

"Thanks, Ben, but I don't think anyone can help. It's something to do with those Words of God. Every time I spoke them, I felt something funny inside. And then, I don't know, I think I went back in time, and I saw things that happened back then. I felt what she felt."

"What who felt?" said Lee.

"The woman who put the Words into the Scroll. She wants my help. I'll deal with it. I'll figure it out. You two should get back to your lives. We'll talk again, I promise."

"We can help, Ben and I. We'll do whatever we can."

"No, I don't want either of you around this. Ben, just take care of Luanne. Lee, same thing with Alessa. I'll catch up with you two soon. And I need to be on an island. Don't ask me why, because I can't tell you. I just know I have to. I'm going back to St. Simons Island."

"We should all leave," said Gabriel. "I believe there's a great little diner a few blocks from here."

They all smiled, but Lin had the biggest one.

"Gabby, you really do want to eat again? I shouldn't think twice about it by now, but it still makes me laugh. Sometimes I think I can understand who you are or what you are. And other times, all I can do is shake my head and laugh."

"And you can do both of those things at the diner. Look."

Gabriel pointed at the chattering crowd exiting the warehouse.

"We'll catch up again, Lee. Safe travels, okay?"

Lin and Gabriel stepped back and watched Ben's old truck rattle away through the empty alley.

Chapter 8 – From Taylor's Eyes

After a quick drive through dark, deserted streets, Lin found a cheery diner boasting brightly lit windows and lodged between two looming brick monoliths. She parked beneath the single lamppost and killed the engine. Before opening her door, she reached back and shook Taylor awake.

"Where are we?"

"At a diner in Norfolk. How about some dinner?"

"Sounds good. I like your car, Mom. I wish I could drive it, but I can't."

"Yeah, I know. You didn't get to renew your license, you poor girl. Your life is about to take off, Hon, I just know it."

They climbed out, began the short walk to the entrance, and Lin clicked the locks over her shoulder. The few raindrops that had begun to fall tapped a rhythm on the cloth awning as Taylor pulled the door open and jangled the bells.

Lin and Taylor took one side of a booth and Gabriel the other. They drank coffee and studied the menus while Taylor sipped an iced tea and stared out into the drizzly evening.

"What looks good to you, Gabby?"

"Oh, Lin, you must know by now that it all looks good."

"Yeah, but you'll have to choose. Free will, right?"

The server appeared again and took everyone's orders before refilling the coffee and heading back to the kitchen.

"You probably shouldn't eat just French fries and apple pie. Even hotcakes would be better."

"You're right, of course. And I'll have those for dessert. A lot of them."

"You don't have to eat hotcakes just to keep me happy. You really like them?"

"Of course. Why wouldn't I?"

Lin's eyes smiled over the hot coffee she sipped.

"Taylor, you look exhausted," said Lin. "Let's just eat quick and find a place to stay."

"I am, Mom, but my mind is going like crazy. I have all this new energy, and I guess I'm not used to it. I just keep thinking about things. Did I tell you I want to be a writer? Words are amazing, Mom. It's fun even just looking at them."

"You'd be a wonderful author, Hon. What would you write about?"

"I don't even care. I just like words. Words are so—"

"The food's coming, Lin. I can see it," Gabriel said while watching Taylor.

The conversation held back as they feasted and sipped their coffee and tea. And when they'd all finished, Lin settled the bill, and they took another short drive in a steady rain to the nearest hotel. They checked into a room, walked in, and dropped their bags.

*　*　*

"Here we are again—a different hotel in a different town. At least we don't have Wolfe chasing after us anymore."

"Yes, Lin, but you still have a good share of concerns," said Gabriel.

"Yeah, Mom, what the heck is going on now? I'm still worried about you."

They'd all brought in their bags and switched on most of the lamps. The rain pounding against the window couldn't completely block the sound of wind whipping up and around the eaves.

"I'm fine, Hon. I tried to explain it to Gabriel, but it's a really weird thing. It would take a while to go through, and it's late. And Taylor, you're exhausted, aren't you? Why don't we all get some sleep and deal with it tomorrow?"

"You do look sleepy," said Gabriel. "You didn't sleep much when your mom was dead, did you?"

"Nope. It sucked with you being dead, Mom."

"Well, it wasn't exactly fun to be dead, you know. Okay then—off to bed. We'll get an early start in the morning and be in St. Simons before we know it."

Taylor claimed one side of the bed and crawled under the covers. Within minutes, Lin saw her slight twitching and heard her faint snoring.

* * *

"We have a few minutes. I need to tell you more of what happened right before we left my house."

"Yes, I imagine there's much more than what you said."

"That's for sure. How could Gloriana make all that happen? Did she create some twisted fantasy world and stick me in it?"

"That could be what happened. Remember, she was able to create islands out in the ocean using only her intent. She took the limitless magic that supports everything, and she made her own world out of it."

"I can't even imagine such power. But she got too weak, and it all fell apart, isn't that right?"

"Yes, her islands no longer exist. But we can't know how much power she has left."

"She seems to have plenty. That felt like a real world, but weird. Things about it were off, but I didn't know it. And the way I acted in that world. Did she make me act that way? I swear, I would never do all the things I did there."

"If you ever want to tell me more, Lin, know that I want to listen. I care a great deal about you."

"Oh, Gabby, I know you do. You've been my best friend for so long . . . since I was fifteen! I wouldn't be here today without you."

"I did tell you that you were important. You remember that, don't you?"

"Yeah, of course. You're going to ask me to go into the magic with you to fight evil. I'm just not that strong."

"You're getting stronger every day, though."

"Yes, I believe I am. But I'm also not that good. You are impossibly good. I could never be like you."

"You're changing all the time. Maybe you'll be strong enough and good enough someday? Maybe then, you'll want to join the war."

"Oh, I'm changing, that's for sure. You probably noticed one big change: my clothes. I'm done with the short skirts and spike heels. I know why I started dressing that way, and it helped me. I needed to break down some walls that I'd built inside myself. But I don't need that style anymore."

"Why now?"

"It's from that bizarre world I got pulled into, where Gloriana tried to trick me into helping her get back. I was such a demented, outlandish version of myself. Just thinking about it now makes me feel funny inside. I don't want to be like that. I know I'm *not* like that, and I never was. But I don't even want to look that way anymore."

"Your jeans and sweatshirt are quite a good style too, Lin. And you're right—you did need that style for a while, and it helped you. What you do now is entirely up to you."

"This is my new style. Well, at least until we get to St. Simons. If it's hot, maybe jeans and a sweatshirt don't make sense."

"Did you notice the change?"

"Yeah, I've changed my style. I just told you—"

"No, not that change."

"What are you talking about?"

"The rain stopped. And the wind."

"Oh yeah, that's good. It seems the weather's been following us from Pennsylvania. And don't tell me it's going to blow this hotel down, Gabby. It won't, will it?"

"No. Not now. Taylor's asleep."

Lin turned and stared at Gabriel with her mouth hanging open.

"What on Earth are you talking about now?"

"I believe she's become a Glyphin."

"A what? What the heck is that?"

"After we fought Wolfe and his army, you were exhausted, and you sat on the couch, but you could barely even sit up. You had Taylor on one side and Jack on the other. You do remember that, don't you?"

"Yeah, and I was talking to you, and then something crazy happened. Something with Gloriana, and she—"

"No. Before that."

"I remember Nomad's head was on my lap. His eyes were bloodshot from the waves of magic. And you were standing in front of me, and you—"

Lin froze and stared at Gabriel, then she quickly turned to look at Taylor, who still snored beneath the blankets.

"Yes, you do remember."

"And I asked you about that. You said maybe I was just tired. But it wasn't just because I was tired, was it?"

"No. I wanted to be sure. You really did see green light reflected in my eyes."

"And the green light, it was—"

"From Taylor's eyes."

Lin slumped farther into the couch as her mind raced out of control. Her daughter had powers over the magic too! She felt large pieces of herself shifting around inside, parts of her with no names, parts that couldn't be talked about and certainly not understood. They fell into a new arrangement, and she knew.

"My daughter wasn't only sick because of how I locked my powers away when I was fifteen. That didn't just give her a mysterious illness that no one could cure. She began her life inside a mother with power over the magic. My daughter has power over the magic too."

"Yes, Lin, but not like you. I believe she has the power of a Glyphin."

"And what exactly is that? I've never heard of that."

"No one has, not for many centuries. I began explaining it with a word on a pizza box."

"Yes, I remember. 'Sex' is what you wrote."

"It could be any word. I thought that was a good choice, don't you?"

"Oh, it got a reaction, that's for sure. But what's a Glyphin?"

"We talked about the different levels of comprehending a single word. Words are very important in our world, Lin. They're woven into our perception of everything. Using words links us to the world."

"Like a magic spell, you mean?"

"No, not at all. Your power over the magic has nothing to do with words. You must have noticed that."

"Yeah, of course. It's like a feeling but not really. I know that what I'm really doing is using my intent. Don't ask me to explain what it is. I just know mine is getting stronger every day. And God, the things I can do with it."

"And you don't use words for that."

"No, of course not."

"The way all of us use words gives us power to understand our world. And to shape it to some extent. The right words can change how we perceive everything around us."

"Okay, I guess you're saying a Glyphin can use words somehow? To do what?"

"The way they learned to use words was at higher levels than any normal person can. And when they do that, they're changing not only how they perceive things around them. They're actually changing part of the reality around them. For a beginner that hasn't learned any control, it most often affects the weather. That next level up in perceiving a word is linked to the Earth. Weather is the easiest thing to change, but a skilled Glyphin can cause earthquakes, volcano eruptions . . . things like that."

"Oh, you can't be serious. You know that sounds like nonsense, don't you?"

"After all you've seen of the magic that supports everything in this world, you still have doubts?"

Lin sat and stared before looking again at Taylor.

"Taylor's a Glyphin?"

"Yes. I'm sure of it now. When she's asleep, the weather is calm. When she's agitated, it rains and gets windy. When you were dead, she leveled your cabin. I'd say we should keep her happy. Or asleep."

Lin shook inside trying to comprehend what her best friend had just explained. Some kind of power that could control the weather? Taylor had that power?

"I know I'm strong, but sometimes I think this is all too much. Just a few days ago, I got control of my mayhem. I found such an unbreakable hold on my intent that I'll never lose it. And I've learned so much more about the magic. I saved Renato from an eternity of being a scroll—I turned him back into a man. I've turned concrete to water and metal to smoke. And it's exhausting.

"Now, I'm fighting some powerful queen from centuries ago. She seems to be able to take me whenever she wants. And that last time, I didn't even know I was gone. And I was insane in that world of hers.

"And now, you're telling me that my daughter has somehow become a Glyphin? Something no one has ever heard of?"

"Well, not recently . . ."

Lin got up and found the complimentary bottle of wine, which she quickly uncorked. She poured a glass, drank most of it, and refilled it almost to the top.

"Lin, this will all work out. It's—"

"Gabby, I just need a break. And don't tell me I just had one—being dead for three days is *not* a break," she said with a short laugh before taking a long drink.

"Perhaps we should just get some rest, then?"

"Yeah. Some rest."

Lin took slow steps to her side of the bed, where she pulled the covers down gently while watching Taylor. She'd brought the bottle and set it on the nightstand. Her emptied glass remained on the dresser near the couch.

Gabriel curled up on the couch and was soon fast asleep. Lin sat and stared at the wall and drank from the bottle.

*   *   *

"Does it really need to be that loud?"

"No, but it's a joy of life, Lin. You might have noticed that I have a lot of favorite songs."

"Yeah, Gabby. I'm seeing a lot of different sides of you lately."

The drive from Norfolk snaked through a lot of small towns plus empty back roads where Lin could open up her Temt8tion. The Oblivion Black paint caught sunlight and threw it toward her as she reveled in the road rushing under the powerful car's leading edge.

As the pavement sped past, she thought ahead to what might be leading her back to her childhood home—St. Simons Island. She remembered how it had felt when her power, her mayhem, had first erupted.

It was after three years of abuse by her Uncle Ray, which began shortly after he'd moved in with the family. Lin couldn't tell anyone because she knew Ray meant what he said—he'd stop paying, and her family would be out on the streets. But Lin smiled, even thinking about all that trauma, recalling that it never broke her. She'd focused all the strength and determination that a child could muster and never accepted the unfairness of the ordeal.

And it led to her mayhem, the unstoppable power that she couldn't control at first. After it had destroyed Ray, it lashed out again to protect her, gravely harming Ben. She'd seen only one option: locking it away deep inside herself, where it stayed out of sight and out of memory for over thirty years.

But it wouldn't remain inside forever. It rose up on its own only two weeks ago several times, injuring people badly. She had to understand it or let it destroy her and everyone close to her. And she did get control of it while being strangled by Ivan on a lonely Georgia road. She found her intent, and she got an unbreakable hold on it. Her mayhem would never be out of reach again.

And through it all, Lin had carried Gabriel within her. Not in a silent way, but as a friend. One that no one else could see. But Lin could see Gabriel. Or at least she thought so. She still didn't completely understand how that worked, but she knew it didn't matter. Gabriel was real again after she had chosen to heal Ben rather than kill him in an Allentown restaurant. Gabriel knew it was time for her to see things clearly.

Gabriel had been real ever since. And hungry too.

"Mom, are we there yet?" Taylor said with her headphones in her hand.

"Almost, Hon. Are you enjoying your music?"

"Yeah, Mom. It's relaxing. It's not slow stuff, but sometimes I fall asleep listening to it."

"Relaxing is good," said Gabriel. "You've been through a lot. Keep listening."

Chapter 9 – That's My Penance

"What's wrong?"

Ben put his phone back in his pocket and picked up his coffee mug. They'd driven as far as Augusta before stopping for food and drink. He looked into Lee's eyes without blinking.

"Luanne told me not to come home. She said she's had enough time to think it over, with me being gone, chasing after Lin, and getting into trouble. Not telling her what I was up to. Or where. It's over."

"I'm sorry. If you could see her, talk to her in person, maybe she'd reconsider. Why don't we finish the trip and give her another chance?"

Ben leaned back in his seat with his arms crossed as he stared up at the ceiling. He shook his head and looked back at Lee.

"No. She's right about wanting me gone. She's just got the wrong reasons, that's all."

"What do you mean?"

"She remembers the old me. Always drunk and violent . . . just a worthless bastard. She doesn't know who I am today."

"I know, Ben. Lin did something to you in Allentown, right? Is that what you mean? Explain it to her. Show her."

"Even you don't get it, Lee. Lin did fix me, that's true enough. But that 'fixing' kept going. When we left Lin's cabin, I remember telling Taylor that I had to make up for thirty years of shit that I handed Luanne."

"Right, so—"

"I handed a lot of shit to a lot of people. I've hurt so many people, and I need to make up for all of that. I see that now. Yeah, Lin fixed me—made me a better man. Too good of a man. I can't live with all I've done."

"You're not that man anymore. The past is gone, Ben."

"Is it gone? Is it ever really gone? I know you've wondered why I had to stop in Pittsburgh. You were right—we had plenty of cash with us. Only now do I get it—I need to be hurt and hurt bad. That's my penance. And I'm not done yet."

"You can't be serious. You want to get the shit kicked out of you? You want your bones broken? How the hell would that ever—"

"It's payback. I don't care if you understand or not. Just believe me, every time I got busted up and you fixed me, I felt like I'd paid some of my dues."

"And you need me to patch you up, that's what you're saying?"

"Either that, or I'll be dead soon. And that's fine too."

"You know, I think maybe you're tired from everything we've been through. Okay, you can't go home, at least not yet. And you're not going to fight in any more matches, are you?"

"No, I don't want to."

"Let's check into that motel next door. You get a good night's sleep and see how you feel about it all in the morning, okay?"

"Sure, why not. I got nowhere else to go. I don't know what my life is about. Who am I, Lee?"

*   *   *

When the door had slammed shut behind them and they'd dropped their bags on the floor, Ben turned to Lee and made a request as reasonably as he could.

"I can't just turn it off. And I ain't gonna be able to sleep unless you help. I'm begging you."

"Why the hell did you bring that—"

"Take this."

"I don't want it. Put the brick down, Ben."

As he held it out in his left hand for Lee, he placed his right hand flat on the dresser top.

"Take it and hit that hand as hard as you can. Do it, Lee."

"Ben, no. Stop it. This isn't the answer."

"I can't do it myself—that doesn't count. Come on, Lee."

Lee took the brick and saw tears begin to seep out of the big man's eyes. They showed a desperation and sadness that almost caused Lee to cry herself.

But there was no way in hell she was about to cry.

So, she slammed the brick down as hard as she could.

Ben didn't make a sound other than his bones splintering like wood under an axe. He wiped at his tears with his left hand, and his big red eyes looked into Lee's.

"Thanks. That helps. Now, can you fix it?"

Lee shook her head, sighed, and led Ben to the edge of the bed, where they both sat. She took his left hand in hers, and within seconds, Ben's eyes closed and he fell back onto the blankets. Seconds later, Lee's eyes closed too.

* * *

Lee returned to the special place she called home, a cheerful clearing of green grass in a tranquil valley with a brilliant blue sky above. A quick glance to the sky revealed her hot sun directly above her, not changing in intensity or location since the first time she'd gone there when she was but a child. Her severe congenital health problems couldn't be helped by any conventional means, and Lee realized at a young age that she alone bore the full responsibility for fixing herself. No one else could do it. And she knew that her only chance would come from within her.

Many years had passed in fruitless attempts to help herself in the unexplainable world she'd found. She'd tried many different things, none of them making sense to her, before she had a feeling that the stones she'd found there were key to her mission. So many arrangements she'd tried, none of them having any effect, until she found the right pattern only nine years ago. When she laid out her forty stones in a figure eight in the grass, everything that had been wrong with her became right. All illness and defects of any kind left her.

Gabriel had told her later that it wasn't a figure eight she was making—it was the symbol for infinity. She didn't care what it was called. When she had first set the stones correctly, it felt to her like countless scattered puzzle pieces instantly lined up and snapped into place. And every time she needed any help, even from eating a bag of donuts, she went there and fixed herself.

What she continued to do in her home prevented her from aging at all. She recalled that Lin had "renamed" her Lee Ternity, a more appropriate name than Lee Turner.

Lee saw that her stones were only a bit out of place. Probably from the lousy food she'd just eaten at the diner, she thought. So, she put them just where they needed to be, and she felt her health become perfect immediately.

But she remembered that she wasn't there just for herself. Ben needed help. She'd come there for Ben's benefit.

When she'd healed him before, he'd appeared in her home as a giant oak tree. She wondered briefly if that memory would dictate how she'd find him there this time. She looked up and saw again a single branch, dense with smaller twigs and leaves and blocking her sun. It came from beyond the edge of her clearing, and she turned and began her hike to find the oak. Every step took her into increasing darkness, and she felt her fatigue growing.

The weeds adjacent to the grass were tall and still, buzzing with unseen insects, and she parted them carefully and followed the branch. A few steps later, she reached the clearing she'd seen before, one with a low mat of thick ground cover and a massive oak tree anchored in the middle. No sunlight could reach the ground beneath it, and she felt almost too weak to advance any farther. So, she stood among the tall plants and studied the tree for any obvious problem.

It took only seconds for her to see the tree's affliction: a single, thin branch had coiled completely around the trunk, spiraling down to almost touch the ground. It appeared to be squeezing into the bark, digging itself into a trench. The tree was strangling itself.

Lee took one more step and felt like closing her eyes. She took another and felt her energy running out of her like a plug had been popped. With her eyes focused only on the very end of the branch, dug deep into the bark at the height of her knees, she walked into the complete shade of the mighty oak.

She stood a moment with her eyes closed, and only then did she hear the tree's soft crying. It sounded like only the wind as the tree slowly killed itself in that lonely landscape.

Lee forced her eyes to open, and she reached down for the branch. She worked her fingers around behind it and pulled, wanting only for it to release itself, and it responded without any real struggle. The very end now jutted out from the trunk, and it began to unwind on its own. It circled around the trunk, and she saw it gaining speed as it approached her. Somehow, she found the energy to crouch down and let it pass over her.

It continued to speed up on its second time around, and Lee barely had time to duck down as it whistled past inches above her. It slowed its travel and came to a stop before it reached her again. She looked up to see the branch solid and strong straight out high above the ground.

She saw that the grooves in the trunk had started to heal, and the wind sound, the tree's soft crying, had stopped.

But Lee had no strength to return to her stones. The darkness beneath the giant tree had sapped all of her strength. She had a quick thought that if she'd had the energy to cry, would it sound like the wind in that forsaken place? Would anyone come to help her? No, she realized. No one could help.

As she stood quietly with her eyes closed, she felt an arm reach around her waist. She opened her eyes only enough to see that the branch had looped all around her, and it began to lift her. Like an elephant might do, she thought, and she couldn't find the strength to even smile.

With eyes shut again, Lee soon felt her feet combing the tall weeds as she was carried through them, her head leaning to one side and her legs hanging loose and limp above the ground. The first patch of light from her sun warmed her, giving her renewed strength and hope. She opened her eyes and saw that she was near the grass of her home, mostly in the sun's healing light again, and her power and health increased rapidly.

The branch set her down gently, and Lee held it with both hands for a quiet moment as it waited for her to find her balance. Then, it unwound from her waist, and she watched it withdraw above the grass, over the tall weeds, and out of sight.

Feeling almost perfect again, Lee crouched down to set her stones in their exact, proper locations. Instantly, she felt every minute piece of herself snap into a flawless alignment. Lee Ternity again had perfect health. Knowing that her work there was done, she opened her eyes.

She found that she'd fallen onto her back on the soft blankets. Ben lay on his back next to her fast asleep with his left arm around her waist and his right across his chest. She looked at his hand, the one that she'd smashed only moments earlier, and saw that it was healed. It was perfect.

A moment later, Ben's eyes opened, and he turned to look at her. He stared at her a few seconds, pulled his right hand up to take a look, and laughed.

"Lee, you work miracles. I don't know how."

"Happy to help, Ben. But like I told you, that tires me out. I can only . . . I can . . ."

Her eyes closed as she slumped into the blankets and began a low snoring. Ben rolled to his side and held her waist with both arms, and he snuggled in as close as he could.

Chapter 10 – Took My Life

"Don't put on that old suit, Huff. That thing was out of style thirty years ago when you first started wearing it."

June Houghman looked her husband up and down with a frown. Her deep blue eyes matched her long-sleeved blouse, and her long silver hair bounced as she shook her head and stared at him with her hands in her jeans pockets.

"And why are you getting all dressed up? My Heaven, it's a Tuesday morning!"

"Oh, June Bug, I'm going down to the station. There's something exciting I need to look into."

Elias snugged up his tie and slipped on the vintage brown jacket. After checking his gray hair in the mirror, he turned to his wife.

"When you're retired, you should just stay put and keep me company. That's the whole point. What's the big deal down there that's got you all riled up?"

"Something from my past maybe, Bug. You don't remember, I'm sure you don't. How could you? It was over thirty years ago."

"What was?"

"Do you remember that case with a guy named Ray? I kind of hope you don't."

"No, I remember. He hurt himself real bad, right?"

"Yeah, then he hanged himself."

"That was a long time ago, Huff. He's been dead and buried forever."

"I know, I know. But the department is holding this guy named Ivan downtown before the feds come and pick him up. This might be my last chance to see him."

"And who the heck is Ivan?"

"Nobody. Nobody that I know anyway. But there's something strange going on with him. Maybe I'm getting senile, but the case reminds me of Ray. I just want to take a quick look. Maybe talk with him."

"I was hoping we'd have lunch in the Village today. Take care of your stuff and meet me, okay?"

"Sure, Bug, I'll text you when I wrap things up with Ivan. You going shopping too?"

"Always, Huff, always," she said with a grin.

Elias gave her a quick kiss and turned to leave.

* * *

"Huff! Can't you stay retired? What's with the fancy duds?"

Sam, Elias's former captain, fought to contain his smile.

"I can't stay away. You know that. And I wanted to see if this old suit still fits. It does, Sam."

"Yeah, you do look pretty sharp. What brings you here?"

"That guy named Ivan. I heard he's in pretty bad shape. Mentally. Any chance I can see him?"

"You have no official business here anymore. You do know that, right?"

"Can you put me on as an unpaid consultant or something? I think there's a slim possibility I can help with this case."

"Yeah, sure, that's easy enough. But why, Huff? Life on Brockinton getting a little slow for you?"

"God, no. Retirement is the best move I've ever made. Just set it up, okay? Get the paperwork going and get me in a room with Ivan."

"I'll do it, but then we're even, right?"

"Yeah, Sam. This is the last favor I'll ever call in."

* * *

Elias waited in a quiet room and looked at the empty chair across the table from him. Only a few minutes had passed before the door swung open. Two officers brought in a muscular man with neat short hair and wearing a shiny pair of cuffs, and they sat him across from Elias and chained him to the table. They handed Elias a folder and retreated, closing and locking the door behind them.

Ivan's blue eyes looked straight into Elias's forehead before darting to the side and then back to stare at Elias's chin. They jerked to the other side, then up at the ceiling, then at the wall above Elias's head.

"Who's there? Who . . . what do you want?" He pulled at the big hook in the center of the table, and Elias prayed the bolts in the floor would hold.

"Ivan Kotov? That's your name?"

Ivan yanked at the hook, clanging metal against metal.

"What happened to you, Ivan?"

"Witch!"

The sudden scream caused Elias to lean back and stare with his mouth open. Ivan kept jerking his cuffs and shaking the table.

"Don't let her . . . she's a witch! I have to get . . . I—"

"Okay, settle down, settle down. Do you know where you are?"

Ivan's lips trembled before he stopped his struggle, leaned forward, and covered his eyes with his hands.

"Who was she, Ivan?"

Ivan sat upright and shrieked at the ceiling, causing Elias to jump up and bump his chair backward to the floor.

Then, Ivan spoke softly.

"Beautiful. So, so, so beautiful . . ."

"What did she look like?"

Ivan grunted and said, "Took my life, took my life. Just took it." And he focused all of his energy on the metal ring that locked him to the table. Veins in his forearms swelled, and he ground his teeth while his eyes searched in every direction.

Elias leaned in with both hands on the table.

"Took my life. Just like that. Took it! How can—"

"Who—"

"Her eyes. I saw her eyes!"

"What about her eyes?"

"Bright! How . . . how could . . . witch took my life!"

"You're still alive, Ivan."

He left his cuffs alone and almost whispered, "She . . . she . . . gave it back." He sat calmly.

Elias waited a few seconds and said, "Was her hair—"

"Witch! WITCH!" he wailed and renewed his battle as tears streamed from his unseeing eyes.

Elias shook his head, backed to the door, and pounded on it with both fists.

*　*　*

"I could have told you that's what would happen," said Sam.

"What on Earth is wrong with him? Has psych evaluated him?"

"Yeah, they tried. That's about as coherent as he's been since we found him on Jericho Road."

"Does he remember anything of what happened?"

"Who the hell knows? The guy can barely form a sentence. I think what you heard is what's going on in his head all the time."

"And you have no leads on what happened? There was another guy there. Doc, right? And he was dead?"

"Yeah, and that was weird too. His heart had been crushed. Inside him. How the hell does that happen?"

"I'm going to do some poking around, Sam. If Ivan ever has anything real to say, can you let me know?"

"Yeah, of course. I'll wake you up from your nap on the couch." He gave Elias a big grin.

"It ain't like that, Sam."

Sam tilted his head.

"Well, not every day anyway." He returned Sam's smile.

"Oh, I almost forgot. There's more news you probably haven't heard," said Sam.

"Like what?"

"Steve Banning, the local pastor. He's missing. And so is the organist at his church. Some guy named Joel."

"Maybe they're traveling. Who reported them missing?"

"The church secretary. She's sure they're not gone for official business—there was nothing on Steve's calendar. And she said he'd never leave without any notice like that. I'm not saying their disappearance has anything to do with our buddy, Ivan. It's just something else weird going on."

"The Island hasn't been this weird in a long time, Sam. Over thirty years."

Chapter 11 – Splattering Of Red

"Find another way, Ben."

"I wish I could. There's no other way."

Lee had awakened first to find her arm around Ben while he slept peacefully. She could see his hand, the one she'd smashed earlier and that she'd healed. It looked fine, like she'd never crushed it with the brick he'd grabbed from the hotel's landscaping.

"No, there has to be. Let me up."

He rolled to one side, freeing her arm, and she rose and walked over to the dresser. She brushed her long black hair back over both shoulders and dropped her arms to her sides. Her chest expanded with a deep breath, and she held it with her eyes closed. She exhaled, opened her eyes, and turned to face him.

"You just did it again, didn't you? You fixed yourself all up?"

"I do it all the time. Did you know that Lin gave me a new name?"

"I don't even remember your old name."

"Turner. Lee Turner. But Lin changed it. Well, not legally anyway."

"To what?"

"Lee Ternity. What I do keeps me from aging. As far as I know, I can do this forever."

Ben sat up on the bed and stared a few seconds before speaking.

"How . . . how could you learn something like that? And how can Lin . . . she—"

"It's all about magic. Lin and I, we just figured some things out, that's all. I believe anyone can under the right circumstances if they try hard enough."

"I owe you and Lin so much. I can never repay you, either of you. But . . ."

"But what, Ben?"

"Are you witches?"

"If a witch is someone who figured out how to use magic, like Lin and I have, then yeah, that word's as good as any other."

"You're not ugly or scary, though. You're just . . . you're beautiful, Lee."

"Aw, thank you, Ben. You ain't so bad yourself. And I don't plan on breaking any more of your bones."

His face twisted into a scowl, and he looked to the floor.

"Then, somebody else will."

"No, Ben, that has to stop. I'm done with it. If you go out and fight again, whatever happens to you, it's all yours."

"But if you—"

"No. I'm not hurting you again."

He began to shake quietly, and a single tear crept down his cheek.

"You don't get it, Lee. How could you? Lin fixed me inside. Too much. Nobody should be that perfect inside. And now, I can't live with the memories of who I was and all that I've done. I've hurt so many people . . ."

Ben's eyes closed, sending new trails of tears out to collect under his chin, where they began to drip onto his lap.

"So, just be a good man from now on. Isn't that enough?"

"No. There has to be a reckoning, Lee. There's a price I have to pay, and by God, I'll pay it. I understand that it's not your problem. You have a life to live. A life of perfect health that will never end. I'm happy for you."

Lee had tears in her eyes, too, as she looked at the healed but still broken man sitting near her. She walked over and put a hand on his shoulder. He looked up with wet eyes, pleading without a word.

And she struck him across his cheek with her fist. A cut opened and blood trickled down, mixing with his tears. She struck him again and looked down at her knuckles. The skin had peeled back, and some of the blood on his face was hers. She took a deep breath and punched him again as hard as she could. And she knew that she could hit hard— she kept her muscles much stronger than most men. He spun away and fell into the bed covers.

She felt a new excitement grab her heart.

"Is that what you need, Ben? Does that help?"

She grabbed the lamp off of the dresser, yanked its cord out of the wall, and walked back to the man bleeding into the bed. She raised the lamp high and crashed its metal base down into his exposed ribs. She felt the bones break and allow the lamp to dig in. She hit him again. And again.

"Okay. Okay, Lee,"—he struggled to speak—"that's good for now."

She struck him again.

Ben curled up and lay motionless taking hit after hit. When Lee had had enough, she wiped the blood off of the lamp with her t-shirt and placed it back on the dresser. She stood looking down on him with her hands on her hips.

"And now, you want me to heal you, huh?"

He nodded, but he didn't move.

She lifted his head up and sat under him so that his bloody cheek rested on her lap. He looked into her eyes, shuddered at what he saw, and snapped them shut again.

"Give me your hand, Ben. Let me fix those nasty broken bones of yours."

*　*　*

"Did that help?"

"Yeah, Lee. Thanks. I don't know, but maybe I only need so much of that, and then I'll be done."

"I'll help you, Ben. I think I understand. I kind of enjoyed breaking your bones. Healing you felt different that time, even though you were still an oak."

"I was what?"

"Nothing."

"I don't get how you can heal like that. It's all fixed. I feel pretty good."

"Which means you're ready for more," she said before rising and walking to the dresser.

"I'm fixed, but that still isn't much fun. I'm not sure—"

Lee swung the lamp into the side of his head, and he slumped over. Fresh blood flowed from a deep gash, and his eyes remained open, but he didn't speak. She aimed and hit the lamp into the new cut, and his eyes closed. She struck his head three more times before dropping the lamp and lying down behind him.

Reaching over his unconscious, limp body, she got a grip on his left hand. In a few seconds, her eyes rolled up high and closed. Lee returned to her home.

*   *   *

Lee found her quiet field of lush grass in a peaceful valley beneath a crystal blue sky. She looked up at her old friend, the sun that never moved, and smiled. She was sure that her sun smiled back at her as its brilliant green light warmed her and nourished her.

She looked down at her stones arranged in a ragged figure eight, and she knew that Gabriel had been right about that—it was the symbol for infinity. Some of the stones had rolled away from their proper locations. Probably from the thrill of violence that had coursed through her only moments earlier, she realized with a grin.

A push here, a nudge there, and soon, all the stones were in their exact locations. Infinity. Lee felt her power and health snap into complete perfection. Then, she remembered why she'd returned: Ben was broken. She'd broken him again, and he needed her. He needed her to help him.

She looked up again at her sun and felt a confidence that she'd find Ben there in her home. She basked in her sun's heat and waited patiently.

When she felt her sun's warmth diminish, she knew that the healing would begin. She looked up and saw branches packed with leaves beginning to block her sun's light. Like before, she thought, remembering that Ben always appeared in her home as a giant oak tree. The first time, the tree's branches were pinned to the ground. It had weakened her greatly to help free the branch, and she recalled the tree's soft crying inside and how it had sounded like only the wind.

Lee began walking through the thick grass of her meadow and followed the tree branch like she had before. Through the tall weeds bordering her grassy field she hiked, again feeling weaker with every step. She began to feel an emptiness inside, right in the middle of her. Her weakness and emptiness increased the farther she walked, but she knew that she couldn't stop. She'd come there to heal him.

When she'd reached the edge of the patch of tall weeds, Lee again saw the massive, thick oak tree planted solidly and surrounded by low ground cover. The void in her middle grew as she walked farther into the tree's shade, but she ignored it and looked around to find the problem. And it was plain to see: a large, rough branch had been bent to the ground. It dropped down from the tree, almost touching the carpet of plants, and its outer branches struggled to reach up toward the sky.

There were no stones to roll aside to free the branch like the first time with the first oak. She looked around, feeling her emptiness growing, and decided that she needed to get closer. A few more steps brought her to the branch, near the part of it that grazed the ground below it. In nearly complete darkness, she felt a hollowness and hunger that was about to consume her.

She needed to rest. She knew it was her only hope.

Lee swung her right leg over the branch so that she faced the tree, and she sat and struggled to hold herself upright. She needed strength to help the tree, but she had none, so she leaned forward onto the branch and listened to the soft crying of the wind.

As she lay there completely still, too weak to move, she felt a sliver of her sun's light warm her back. It was so small that it barely had any effect. She didn't move. She just waited to see if the light would increase.

She felt the tiny patch of light begin to crawl up along her back toward her head. Its warmth brought new hope to her as she lay there too weak to return to her meadow. When she felt the warmth move beyond the top of her head, she wiggled her way up the branch to again feel the heat.

But the nourishing sunlight began retracing its path back down along her spine. So, she followed it—she shimmied herself along the branch, chasing the light. And again, the light moved up along her back, more quickly than the first time. She followed it again, and she noticed that her feet no longer touched the ground. The branch had begun to rise. Somehow, she was succeeding, and she knew that soon, the branch, and Ben, would be healed.

As Lee continued dragging herself in and out along the stout branch, the heat on her back increased, even while it guided her, urging her to keep moving. The heat grew as the branch raised itself higher until it was almost straight out high above the ground.

The heat on her back had become an inferno, and she felt the healing magic of it, the ecstasy that she now knew her sun could give her, the one that never moved high above her in her home.

Lee's emptiness had left her. She continued to move only to feel the revitalizing light of her sun.

When the branch was jutting out solid from the oak, the tree's soft crying, the sound of the wind, had stopped. Lee felt deep satisfaction at having healed Ben, and gratification from the flaming sun on her back, and she knew that's what the tree felt too.

She had no intention of stopping as the pleasure quickly rose so high that she feared she'd lose her mind, and she couldn't help but scream. Her howl wasn't limited by any breath inside her, and she felt it twisting and weaving itself in with a growing wave of wanton delight wracking her like some unknowable electricity. Abruptly, her cry stopped, and her eyes snapped open, returning her to her life.

She looked down to see Ben beneath her, his fearful eyes wild and staring into hers. They were both naked, and Lee straddled the big man as she continued to move back and forth, over and over along the memory of the branch.

The raw euphoria never stopped. She still felt her green sun burning into her, branding her with a boundless bliss like she'd never known before, and she fought to stay silent. She reached down and placed her hands on his chest, on the thick branch beneath her, and felt an explosion of green, a blaze of healing light from her sun. Waves of green rapture rolled through her as she healed the branch and drove Ben insane.

The endless ecstasy rolled through and then away from Lee, like an echo of a lover's voice down a long tunnel. When the last ripple had left, and there was only silence, she collapsed onto Ben's chest. Their sweat mingled, and he reached around to hold her.

Lee pushed herself back up and kept her hands on his chest. Ben held her hips and appeared ready to ask a question, but his open mouth said nothing. They looked at each other several moments before Lee freed herself and climbed off of the bed. Seconds later, she started her shower.

* * *

Lee raised her arms above her and spun around under the hot spray until all of her sweat and Ben's sweat had washed off, and she let the water hit her until the heat became overpowering. She turned it cooler and still felt the heat from the memory of her sun in her home. The sun that had burned so hot on her back just moments before.

She turned the water as cold as it would go and felt her skin tighten from it. She let the icy water rain down on her until she shivered and her teeth chattered. And then, she felt ready for more heat. More nourishing heat from her sun that never moved.

Lee grabbed the handle and jammed it off, stepped out of the stall, and dragged a towel across her wet skin in front of the mirror. As she looked at her eyes, fierce eyes that she didn't recognize, she also saw an unfamiliar smile. She wrapped the thick white towel around her and watched herself as she combed back her long hair, still wet and dripping onto the floor.

After hitting the switch to kill the fan, she strode back into the room. A quick glance told her that Ben was still on his back and covered by only the t-shirt she'd tossed over him. His eyes were open, and he stared at the ceiling, blinking only occasionally.

Before returning to the bed, she uncorked the free wine. In one hand, she clutched the blood-stained brick as she held the bottle up to her lips and drank half of it. She slammed the bottle down on the dresser and turned to Ben.

"Ben, it's good you're awake."

"Yeah, Lee, I'm awake. But I've been thinking. Maybe I've paid my dues. Maybe I've been beat up enough."

She left the wine uncorked and brought the brick to the bed. It left a few red smudges on her white towel as she held it close behind her. She stood looking down on him, and he looked away from the ceiling to focus on her eyes. While he cringed at the sight, Lee shook her head slowly as she remembered the ecstasy of her sun exploding for her in her home.

"I don't feel like I need—"

Lee crashed the brick into his face. She heard bones crunching and saw blood streaming out of his nose and a wide gash. He'd lost consciousness and couldn't resist, so she swept her leg over him to sit and tossed her towel to the floor. Again, she brought the brick down hard against his face. Ben never moved. His blood soaked into the sheets on both sides.

She struck his forehead and laughed at the dent she'd made. She gave him three more hits, remembering to use the brick's sharp corner, before she tossed it to the floor.

Seated atop the unrecognizable man, Lee looked up to see that the mirror above the headboard gave her a memorable view of herself. Her hair was still wet and hung straight down to each side of her breasts, which made obvious the thrill she felt. Her lean, muscular body carried a splattering of red drops, the larger ones trickling down and drawing long lines on her cheeks and chest. She looked down and took Ben's hands.

* * *

Lee returned to her home, the lush patch of green grass in a quiet meadow beneath a clear blue sky with a brilliant sun directly above her. She looked at her sun and nodded, remembering its power and welcoming the craving again awakening in her.

A quick look at her stones, her infinity symbol, showed them to be in perfect order. She didn't hesitate as she turned and began a quick walk to the oak tree. To Ben.

She saw the same branch looped down to a level just above the ground. She felt the emptiness inside, right in the middle of her. And she knew what she needed to do to help Ben and to quench her ravenous hunger.

* * *

Lee opened her eyes to see Ben unconscious beneath her. He'd been healed—there wasn't a mark to be seen. But she saw that her powers couldn't clean up the blood.

Fine, she thought, whatever it takes. A little blood isn't going to stop me.

She swung her leg off of him and picked up her towel. After throwing it over her shoulder and seeing again in the mirror all the speckles of red everywhere on her skin, she reached for the wine. She found that she liked watching herself wearing so much of Ben's blood and chugging from a bottle. When she'd emptied that, she headed for another shower.

The hot water flowed over her, rinsing her down and sending red spirals into the drain. She couldn't stop grinning. She basked in the water's heat until she couldn't take any more, then she turned it back to ice water. She felt her skin cool down and draw tight everywhere, and when she began shaking from the chills, she knew that she was ready for more.

Looking in the mirror again, Lee saw a new radiance and an unfamiliar smile. She combed back her long black hair and touched her smooth skin all over, ageless skin that stretched over solid muscles that she knew she'd have forever. She looked back into her eyes and nodded. It was time to visit Ben again.

She left the towel on the rack and sauntered out of the bathroom naked and dripping. She saw the wet brick on the floor, the empty wine bottle on the dresser, and the bloody bed. It was empty too.

Chapter 12 – Feeling A Need

After switching to I95 to make better time, Lin chose a more scenic ride on Golden Isles Parkway, followed by a short jaunt on Route 17. From there, she took a left on the Causeway which led to her childhood home, St. Simons Island. She reached behind her and shook Taylor's leg. Taylor pulled an earphone away and waited.

"We're almost there, Taylor. And it's warm! You never know this time of year."

"What's first, Mom? I'm kind of hungry. I'm not 'hangry' yet, though. That's a funny word, isn't it? Have you ever heard that word, Mom?"

Gabriel hurried to say, "What's your favorite food, Taylor? What meal makes you happy?"

"Oh, I think seafood. I've never had seafood right near the ocean. That would be my pick."

"Okay, let's head straight for the marina," said Lin. "One of my favorite spots is right there. They should be open by now."

"And the food is good, Lin?"

Lin turned to look at Gabriel with a big smile.

"The best, Gabby. The best.

"Taylor, I bet you're going to like it here. This will be your first experience of St. Simons Island. Nice and sunny today too. Looks like we've finally left all that rain behind."

"Good. I'm tired of all that rain. And I'm still kind of sleepy. I can't believe I slept most of the way here!"

"We'll get some lunch and maybe some coffee? That should get you going."

"Sometime today, can we stop at a store? I want to get a tablet to keep notes and ideas."

"What for, Hon?"

"It'll help me when I start seriously writing. I like words. They're funny sometimes. I can take down notes whenever I want, and then someday, put them all together and see what I get. 'Get' is a funny word too."

"What's funny about it?" said Gabriel.

"It means opposite things, kind of. You can use it to tell someone to leave. Or it could mean that you're receiving something. Things going, things coming. All in one word. At the same time. It's just amusing, that's all."

"How long have you thought about words like that?" said Gabriel.

"Only the last few days. Maybe I'm just exhausted, but I'm glad we're on your island, Mom."

Gabriel turned to look at Lin, but she only continued to pilot her car through the parking lot until she found a place to her liking.

She switched off the Temt8tion's big motor and stepped out onto asphalt beginning to warm in the South Georgia sun. She rubbed her boots into the hot surface as she turned to look over at the line of boats bobbing in the gently rolling water. A soft breeze caught her hair and lifted it off of her shoulders, and she took a deep breath and stretched her arms to each side.

"I like the way you dress now. But I think I like your skirts too. That was quite a style. Can I get—'get'—there's that word again! Can I get some new clothes?"

Gabriel stopped to observe Taylor while Lin spoke.

"Sure, Taylor, if that's what you want. You need a whole new wardrobe, that's for sure. Whatever styles you want. I'm just so happy that you're better now. Lee is amazing, isn't she?"

"It's so good to not feel sick anymore, Mom. And the sunshine—I love it. I don't want to think about how I was sick for so long. Let's go eat, and then . . . show me your island!"

The three walked into the restaurant with Gabriel watching Taylor closely. They found a table with a good view of the waterway, and Lin couldn't help but reminisce about being there just two weeks earlier with John and Tommy. What an ordeal that had been, she remembered. And she recalled with some amusement that she hadn't even figured out her mayhem then.

And she'd only recently learned from Gabriel why John and Tommy had adored her so much. It started when her mayhem rose up when she was being attacked by the pond near New Galilee. She'd blacked out, but her mayhem had made a real mess of the man accosting her. Davey was his name. The wave from her mayhem was what had affected John and Tommy. The explanation was so simple when Gabriel spelled it out.

That wave of magic from Lin closed the natural gap every human has between their bodies in the real world and their spirits in the magic. That gap was free will, and with it, humans are full of doubts and questions about their existence. But it also gives the ability to shape the extremely slow magic of the world.

No other living thing has free will, Gabriel had told her. Instead, they have a constant knowledge of God's presence in their lives. They feel a contentment no human can even comprehend.

Lin's wave of magic filled their gaps, and it took away all of their doubts. And since the wave came from Lin, they saw her, at least for a while, as God. They'd adored her to the point of driving her crazy.

"It's nearly lunchtime," Lin said to them, "so I'm having a drink with my lobster. Gabby, do you ever drink? I mean, alcohol . . . do you ever?"

"I haven't, but why not? If I'm going to be a rock star someday . . ."

"Oh yeah, that's right. Have one, at least." Lin smiled at her unbelievable friend.

"Me too, Mom. I'm twenty-three, and I haven't had a drink in years. Not long after I got old enough, I got too sick. I never had as much fun as all the other kids. I never got to—"

Gabriel cut in and said, "Taylor, we weren't going to think about those days so much, were we?"

"No, you're right, Gabriel. We're just going to have a good time."

Gabriel looked up and saw that the few thin clouds that had gathered above them had begun to break apart and drift to the west with the gentle ocean breezes.

* * *

Lin and Taylor still picked at the last of their lobster, and Gabriel feasted on a second plate of pasta. Lin took another sip of her gin and tonic, and she couldn't contain a grin as she watched Gabriel finish the cold beer. Taylor had decided on a glass of Merlot, and she seemed to be savoring every drop.

"Miss?"

Lin looked up.

"You were here a couple of weeks ago, I remember. You were with those guys that were kind of . . . they were—"

"They were goofy. And sloppy. You won't offend me, that's for sure. Yes, I was here. And?"

"Those same two guys, they were here yesterday. But they weren't so goofy anymore. I think they were looking for you."

Oh no, thought Lin. John and Tommy are on the Island? Looking for me?

"Thanks for the warning. I mean, thanks for letting me know. I'll keep an eye out for them."

"Lin," said Gabriel, "do we really need to be here? Are you sure there's a reason for you to be on an island? This island?"

"Yeah, Gabby, this is where I need to be. And John and Tommy, they're harmless. We'll probably never see them anyway."

"Who are John and Tommy, Mom?"

"When I was here two weeks ago, they were just a couple of guys I met. They thought they knew me from Pennsylvania. They're nice guys, Taylor, but they might not even be around here anymore."

The food was gone, the plates had been cleared, and Taylor had finished her first glass of wine.

"That was good. I like your island so far, Mom. Time to go shopping?"

"Soon. First, let's head down to Ocean Boulevard and get a couple of rooms or another suite. We won't be here long, I don't think, but there's no reason we can't have ocean views."

* * *

As they traveled down Kings Way and crossed over Mallery Street, Lin took in all the sights and sounds and scents, savoring being back on the Island. The far past, when she'd suffered the abuse of her Uncle Ray, was a memory that didn't need another look. And the more recent past was beginning to fade too.

They passed the hotel where Ben had attacked her less than two weeks earlier, and Lin felt not a trace of foreboding. Nothing like that would ever happen again. She looked for and found her mayhem waiting just beneath her surface, always ready to rise up and protect her. She looked in her Temt8tion's rearview mirror and let her eyes flash green for just an instant.

A quick check-in allowed them to find their suite, toss their bags onto one of the beds, and head back out. No need for the car, thought Lin, as they all began a leisurely walk toward the Village. When they passed the bar with the smiling neon sun in the window, she stopped and stared at it.

"What, Mom? Don't tell me you need another drink!" Taylor said with a grin.

"No, nothing like that, Hon. Just taking in the sights. It's good to be home."

* * *

Elias left the station endeavoring to put the pieces together. He doubted that Ivan's odd condition had anything to do with the priest and organist disappearing. How could it? But he couldn't dispute the coincidence of all of it happening on the same day. He wondered if there was a connection and whether he still had enough of his detective's skills to somehow figure it out.

Traffic was sparse on the Causeway, and he took a deep breath of the air beginning to play across the marshes. He branched off onto Demere and then took a left onto Brockinton to check at home. As he suspected, June's car was gone, and he knew that she'd be in the Village shopping and waiting on him to join her for lunch.

He texted her and immediately got a reply saying that she was at their favorite sidewalk cafe, and could he please hurry and join her. She was starving and couldn't wait all day.

That's my Bug, he thought with a smile.

* * *

Lin turned and looked across Mallery at the spot where she'd sat and had a panicky lunch while waiting for Ben to exit the bar, the one with the sun in the window. It seemed so far in the past with all that had happened since then. She made the decision to bring Gabriel and Taylor there, and if she could get the same seat as before, she'd take it.

"Before we do any serious shopping, do you mind if we sit a minute? Maybe have a cup of hot coffee? I just feel like soaking up the atmosphere for a while."

"Sounds like a good idea to me, Lin. I don't believe I've ever enjoyed this area in a *real* way. Whether you need to be on an island right now or not, this is still very nice."

"Yeah, Mom. I've really missed out on a lot, and I'm going to make up for all of that. Maybe I should get some makeup too? I can make up for things with new makeup. That's kind of funny, isn't it? Get it? And there's that word 'get' again too. See, Mom? Words are—"

"You know," Lin said quickly, "I think I'm going to have another drink. There's no need to drive, and it feels so good out here in the sunshine."

"Fantastic idea, Mom. Me too. Another glass of wine."

"Gabby, how about another beer?" said Lin.

Gabriel paused before answering.

"None for me, thanks. But if you're feeling a need to have another, you *are* on vacation."

"Well, you make a good point."

Lin looked up from the conversation and scanned the service entry, watching for a server to come out. The white door appeared very clean except for a single smudge near the middle of it. It must be a small spot of grease, she guessed, after considering all the hot food that passed through there.

But when she tried to look away, she couldn't. Her eyes could see only the black spot. And it began to grow. Not slowly. It raced until it covered her, and she froze solid. With no thoughts or feelings or breaths. And with no heartbeat.

Just as quickly, a single white dot appeared and grew and wrapped all around her. She'd had no time to find her intent. It had all happened in a single instant. She felt her heart beating and opened her eyes to see Gabriel and Taylor staring at her.

She took a deep breath and held the table to keep from falling from her chair.

Chapter 13 – That Mayhem Stuff

"Lin, don't tell me. Not again."

"Yeah, I'm afraid so. But it only lasted a second. Well, not a second. You know what I mean."

"You almost spilled your drink this time."

"As long as you don't spill mine, Mom."

Lin reached out to hold the chilled glass wet from the humidity, and she picked it up and downed what was left.

"God, I needed that."

Taylor picked up her wine glass and finished it all.

"It's up to you, Gabriel. Are you sure you don't need another beer?"

"Watching you two enjoying your drinks has made me reconsider. Yes, let's order another round."

Lin looked again at the white door to the kitchen, and at once, a server appeared and walked to their table. She ordered herself a double gin and tonic, a bottle of wine for Taylor, and a jumbo frosty mug of beer for Gabriel.

They held their glasses up for a toast before Lin downed half of hers, and Taylor chugged a full glass of wine. Lin shook her head with a grin as she watched Gabriel looking cross-eyed into the giant mug while gulping it nonstop until it was tipped all the way back and empty.

"You know, with this hot weather and being back on the Island again, I'm not so thrilled about wearing jeans. You two keep drinking, and I'll be right back."

Lin stood, swallowed the last of her drink, and walked out through the cafe's gate to the sidewalk. Trying on and buying the clothes in the boutique next door was a blur, and in no time, she returned.

Taylor and Gabriel and every other guest couldn't blink as Lin strutted slowly through the gate wearing the shortest of short black skirts. Her bare legs ended with high black heels strapped around her ankles. Her thin pink blouse stretched over nothing but her skin beneath it. She'd left many of the top buttons undone, and no one would be begging their imagination for help.

Before she sat, Lin called the server back to the table. The young man couldn't help but look all the way up and down her legs before his eyes became fixed on what her shirt was too thin to hide.

"Young man," she said, "be a darling and set us up with another round."

She flicked her hair back and flashed him a big smile. He looked up at her and grinned before turning to almost run to fulfill her request. She sat, giving her skirt a ride higher.

"I see you're back to your very stylish wardrobe, Lin."

"Yeah. Enough with the jeans and sweatshirts and clunky boots already. Legs like these shouldn't be locked away somewhere, should they, Gabriel?"

She ran her palms up and down her smooth thighs.

"Not in a kind world, Lin."

Gabriel raised the empty mug, and they clinked glasses.

"Mom, I wasn't sure you'd want me dressing that way. But you do, don't you?"

"Oh hell, Taylor, your legs are beautiful. Give the world a break and show them off a little."

"A little?"

"Okay, a lot, like I do. Everyone will want to see your legs too. I know—let's not wait. Let's get you all dolled up, okay?"

"Yeah, Mom, I really want to!"

Lin called the server over, and he walked up to her quickly with a big smile. She stood only inches from him, and with her heels, he had to look up to see her eyes.

"Young man. My dear, dear young man." With both hands, she held him by his shoulders. "We're going to step next door for just a second or two. I will be in your debt if you'd hold this table for us."

With her right hand, she reached out and held his chin.

"Would you be a sweetheart and keep it for us?"

She nodded his head while he smiled.

"Oh, I knew you would." She pulled him in for a hug, pressing his face where he'd been staring. She let him go, but he didn't move, so she gave Taylor a wink and pried him loose.

"And have another round for us when we get back, okay?"

He nodded.

She kissed his cheek and said, "Make that two rounds," and she kissed his other cheek.

She picked up her drink, and they walked back to the boutique next door.

"Well, that didn't take any time at all, Honey. Sure you can walk on those heels?"

"Gotta learn sometime, Mom."

Lin paid the clerk from her roll of crisp bills, and the women sauntered back to their table with Gabriel close behind.

"Mom, that server's cute. I think I want to go home with him."

"Oh, Baby, I thought I might keep him for myself," Lin said with a snicker.

"Right, Mom. As if you forgot about Jack."

"Who the hell is Jack?"

They all laughed and toasted again.

"Okay, Hon, you deserve to have some fun. But tease him for a while first. You know what I mean?"

"Oh, do I ever. I think I inherited that from you."

Taylor's new friend brought Lin another drink, which she quickly finished off. She tried to stand, but her heels might as well have been stilts, so she dropped back onto her seat.

"I think I need at least one . . . one more, Gabriel."

And another drink appeared in front of her. She picked it up and began slurping it down as she looked out at Mallery Street. A car cruised by slowly, and Lin's face turned into a sneer. She thought back over the last two weeks, and she knew without a doubt who it was: Davey. The guy that harassed her by the pond near New Galilee.

Ooh, he's still looking for trouble, she thought.

"Gabriel, I see some trouble I need . . . that I should . . . to finish off once and for all."

"You can barely walk. Maybe you should just sit awhile."

"Nonsense, you goofball. I'm going to get my Tem . . . Tem . . . my car, and I'm gonna give that bastard more than he . . . than I . . . you know. After I finish this drink."

"Yeah, you really need it," Gabriel said and snickered.

"Oh, I need . . . you know . . . something, Gabriel. When I'm looking . . . look this sexy, I want booze too."

"Yeah, go have some fun. You do have your mayhem, so you'll never be in any real danger."

"I know . . . that mayhem stuff is . . . that's kinda awesome. I'm o . . . okay with using that . . . again."

Lin stood and held onto the table. She slid her left hand around on the wet glass until she'd hooked her drink, and she leaned over to hold it still with her lips, smiling because she knew that her skirt was inching way up. She kept the glass pressed to her smile as she stood and downed almost all of it. Some of it dribbled down her chin, where it dripped off to form a thin trickle between her breasts.

"Ooh . . . that's cold, Gabriel. But you know . . . I kinda like it."

She sat down and leaned back in her seat. After picking out the largest ice cube, she tilted the glass and poured the last of the drink onto her chest.

"Hell of a show, Lin."

"Damn right, goofball," she said as she rubbed the ice around on her skin with her right hand. She slid it under her blouse and swirled it in tight circles before repeating it on her other side with her left hand.

"Mm . . . cold is good. Those . . . they like it," she said with a laugh and a snort.

"Damn right, Lin."

She rose from her seat, applied some lip gloss, and staggered out to her car, which had appeared in the road right in front of the cafe.

After fumbling with the handle, she swung the door wide. A passing tow truck hit its brakes and blared its horn, and she swore and flipped off the driver. Once she was in the plush interior of her Temt8tion, Lin let out a deep sigh and popped another button to better rub the wet skin between her breasts.

A voice from the passenger seat stopped her. "That looks damn good."

She turned to look. A man with short blond hair and a smiling, clean-shaven face gazed back at her.

"Davey, what the hell . . . I thought that was you, but—"

"I knew you'd remember me. Here's your second chance to treat me right."

"Well, if you would . . . you know . . . treat me like a lady, maybe—" Davey laughed.

"You ain't no lady. No lady dresses like that."

"These clothes? Nonsense. This is just . . . this is how—"

"You were such a tease back in PA. You still are. Time for you to deliver."

"Nonsense. I'm just . . . just gonna drive."

Lin smirked and jammed her lip gloss into the steering column several times.

"You're not going anywhere. Not with how much booze you sucked down."

She tossed it over her shoulder and flicked her hair back.

"I like booze," she said before she turned to him and smiled. "And boy do I love to—"

"Yeah, that's obvious. Everything else too. Now, get out of that car and keep me company."

Lin saw him through the narrow opening above her window.

"Come on. I have a bottle of whiskey. I know you want that."

Her eyes followed a meandering path down the long sleeve of his white shirt to see a mostly-full bottle. He unscrewed the cap and took a drink.

"Well, now you're talking my . . . that language."

She felt her mayhem swirling just beneath her surface, and she left it there. It was time to do some real teasing, she knew. And get a few thrills.

Definitely have a drink.

Lin stepped out of her car and began weaving toward Davey as he sat against the hood of his car. She felt her heels stabbing into the gravel and heard the cattail stalks rattling from the chill wind crawling across the pond. But her eyes locked onto the whiskey bottle in his hand, drawing her in like a beacon.

"Sure, Davey boy. I'm coming just for you. And your . . . that booze."

"Good. You know, you're just about out of that shirt."

"Oh yeah, I love losing that . . . these clothes. It's what I do. I'm a . . . such a tease."

Lin took more choppy steps until she stood with her legs outside of his, and his khakis felt warm against her skin. She felt him trying to spread his legs, coaxing hers apart, so she unstuck her heels, stepped them out farther, and poked them back into the loose stones. Her skirt began its journey higher up her thighs.

"Close enough for you? And that . . . that whiskey?"

She gave him a smile and brushed her hair back before she reached out, took the bottle from him, and tipped it back for a generous swallow.

"Kiss me, honey."

"Whoa, big fella. I'm a tease, that's . . . that's all, and I . . . I have a boyfriend."

"You don't care about him. And I bet he'd be happy to share you, wouldn't he?"

"May . . . maybe he . . . he might. Because I have more . . . I have plenty for—"

"And you, you'd like to be passed all around, wouldn't you?"

"Well, I . . . I never thought . . . but maybe I—"

"You're way more than just a tease, aren't you?"

She hit the bottle again.

"Maybe I might be . . . more than a . . . that."

"Yeah, I can tell by the looks of you. You're loose. You're cheap."

"What did . . . did you call me?"

"I said you're cheap. You don't just look cheap—you *are* cheap."

"Well, I never thought I . . . I mean, maybe I *am*."

She licked her lips and started to lean in to kiss him when a distant memory crept closer.

"Hold up, big boy. I'm starting to remember some . . . something about you, and—"

"You're drunk. You don't remember anything."

"Nonsense, goofball. I just . . . I'm just—"

"You're drunk, and you're cheap."

"Oh, I think I might be cheap . . . I think . . . but I'm not that . . . I didn't drink . . . I mean—"

"Damn, the things you're going to do. You're too drunk to argue."

"No, because I . . . I'm just—"

He laid his hands on her shoulders and began sliding her blouse down along her arms. Lin felt the sheer cloth gliding over her skin, and she sighed and stopped protesting. She straightened her arms down at her sides and wiggled her shoulders to help, but she stayed careful to not tip the bottle.

"Yeah, don't fight it. You like being undressed, don't you?"

She pulled her shoulders back farther and said, "Mm . . . yeah. Especially when I don't have a choice."

"You don't."

"Oh, mister, I always have . . . some choices. But I do like being . . . getting naked."

"Out here, even? Where anyone can see?"

"Why, you got your . . . your gang with you?" Lin said with a smirk. "You wish."

Lin licked her lips again and smiled.

"Mm . . . do I ever. A gang would be . . . I think I'd love to . . . I mean a cheap girl like me would—"

He slid her blouse down some more.

"Let's get you out of that shirt. Sound good?"

"Well, if I have to . . ."

"I insist."

Lin stopped to look down with a grin at how close she was to being exposed.

He pulled the thin material down more until a single button twisted on frayed threads, and only the edging of the cloth hung up in two places.

She knew it would need a final tug, and she felt a mild jolt at being so close.

She looked back into his eyes, smiled, and said, "Uh-oh . . . just about there."

He got a grip on her blouse on each side.

"Last chance to say no."

"If I'm so cheap, and . . . and I can't stop you, then—"

He gave her top a strong yank and left it bunched around her waist as she bounced free, and they settled out in the open air. Her wrists were wrapped up in it, and she felt the cold breezes caress her.

"Mm . . . that's better," she said. "Out there for ev . . . everyone to see."

Lin took a deep breath and pulled her left arm free, which caused a jiggle, just as she wanted. She passed the bottle to her left and snapped her right arm out of the shirt, causing them both to shake around. With her right hand, she swept her mane back and held it up. She lifted the bottle to her lips and took another hit. Then, she held the bottle out to her side and glanced back down with a satisfied grin.

His wide eyes stared from inches away.

"Look . . . the cold air . . . that's—"

"Beautiful. You like getting naked for strangers, don't you?"

"Oh, do I ever."

"Maybe you're more than just cheap."

Lin's heart sped up.

"Oh, you might . . . might be right. Maybe I am . . . am more than that. I love getting naked for any . . . any . . ."

"Anyone?"

"Yeah. That."

"And you're going to do exactly what I tell you, right?"

"Well, I have no choice," she said and felt excitement flowing like electricity, "so I guess I should do . . . I will do . . . any . . ."

"Anything?"

"Anyone. I'll do anything . . . with anyone."

"God, what a tramp."

Lin felt her heart jump, and she giggled.

"Oh, you know . . . that sounds good. I want . . . I want to be a tramp, and—"

"You want more than just a kiss, don't you?"

He nudged her legs a bit farther apart, and Lin felt her heels settle in deep.

"Oh, maybe. Maybe I do . . . I bet . . . I mean—"

"If you don't pull that skirt up, I will."

Lin wondered if she'd remembered to wear anything under her skirt, but she figured they might both get a nice surprise.

With a big grin, she pulled the skirt up to her waist and twisted it together with her blouse. She looked back up at him and froze.

"No, wait. I remember now."

She slapped her hands flat on his bare chest, which she found to be much more muscular than she remembered, and she fought to push herself away, but her legs were spread too wide. He stood the bottle on the hood, grabbed the clothing around her waist like a belt, and jerked her into him, pushing her arms up over his shoulders and sending her heart rate higher. Her heels had dug into the loose gravel, and she couldn't take a step back.

She knew it was time to use her mayhem, but she felt the cool air on her bare breasts as they rubbed across his hot chest. She searched again, found her intent, and also felt her clothes around her waist, holding her tight like a rope. She tried again to focus—she needed her mayhem!—but all she could remember was that she might be a tramp, just like he said.

"And I'm not sorry at all . . . about . . . what happened . . . what I did . . ."

But she laced her arms around his neck.

She thought of her mayhem again, and she also imagined how she'd look to anyone that might be watching, if there did happen to be a crowd. She wished there was a crowd to see her now—stripped down, drunk, and probably looking damn sexy.

Her heart sped up. Her mayhem stayed down.

"Don't fight me, tramp. You can't."

Lin felt his strong hold on the rope around her waist, and she knew that she couldn't get away unless she used her mayhem. But she couldn't focus the last time she'd looked, so she relaxed and quit fighting. She left her heels deep in the gravel.

"That's better. You ready to do what I say?"

"Uh-huh."

"Just like a tramp."

"Mm-hmm. Yup." She felt her heart pounding.

He reached back for the bottle and held it to her lips.

"Go ahead. Suck down some more."

Lin opened her lips for the bottle and tipped her head back. She swallowed as much as he poured, not losing a drop, and he put the bottle back behind him on the hood.

She didn't make a move as he let go of her blouse and grabbed her wrists. And she didn't resist as he pulled them around behind her and held them there. Her breasts were poking into his solid chest, and her heart raced.

She thought again of her mayhem since that was her only hope of escape. Without it, she knew that she was helpless, and she'd have to do everything he wanted. And since her mayhem was acting kind of funny, maybe that wouldn't be so bad. She thought she might really like what was coming next.

"Not much stop . . . stop . . . in the way now," she said with a grin and two glazed green eyes.

Lin heard two car doors open, and another two men stepped out onto the gravel. They stayed near their doors and stared with eager smiles.

"After I'm done with you, those two clowns are going to take their turns. A tramp like you wouldn't mind that, would you?"

Lin smiled and shook her head. She grinned at each of the men, then looked back at Davey, and without a thought or desire, her mayhem began to rise. It was back!

But I won't be needing that just yet, she thought.

"You don't know any of us, and I bet you like it that way."

Lin nodded again and smiled.

"You do . . . do have a gang . . . for me. I bet I'd . . . I'd like strangers to . . . to—"

"Just what a girl like you needs, right?"

"Mm . . . yeah. I think I've always want . . . wanted a gang. 'Cause there's plenty for . . . for everyone."

The two men walked around and stood on each side of her. Each grabbed one of her wrists, and they held them at the small of her back. Davey let go and laughed. The one to her right kept pulling at her thin elastic strap and letting it snap back against her skin. The one to her left grabbed all of her hair. She gasped and felt her heart pounding as Davey reached back for the bottle.

When he held it near, she opened her mouth and wrapped her red lips tight around it. She felt a tug on her hair, and the bottle followed as she looked straight up at two moons wobbling in the sky.

Davey poured.

Lin swallowed.

He tossed the empty bottle back onto the car with a rattle.

God, this is fun, Lin thought. But since my mayhem is back, maybe I can make it even more fun . . .

"You know, Davey boy oh boy, I'm not as help . . . helpless as you . . . you might—"

"Yeah, right. Look at you, you tramp. In about two seconds, you're losing this,"—he snapped her elastic onto her belly—"and then you're getting exactly what you need. From all of us."

Lin looked down to see only a small piece of thin cloth still covering her.

"Oh, I do need it. That's for sure. And boy, do I want it. From all . . . all of you."

She laughed and snorted.

"But first . . . let me . . . let me show *you* something."

She had only a hazy, blurry intention of it, and her mayhem still rose up like an exploding star. Her eyes blazed a vivid green. She knew they did because that's what they do. But it felt more like blue. Or maybe purple?

But time didn't stop. Davey was still looking right into her eyes, and his face was twisting and sagging like a melting clown mask, and his eyes were about ready to spring out, and he was probably going to scream because he'd just taken a really deep breath, and—

Then, time finally stalled and coasted to a stop.

Lin cackled as the magic began rushing into her, and she gazed at a world that had become a still, beautiful surface, one that tipped first to the left . . . then to the right . . . then back to the—

Well, that's a funny thing, she thought as she glanced at the chaotic magic swirling beneath her, magic that flowed into her, then back out, then way, way inside, then out just a small bit, then—

Oh, what the hell! she thought as she focused on Davey's magic, a glob of magic that glowed and seemed to resemble him, but it looked like it might be laughing. Or maybe crying. Can magic cry? she wondered.

But she knew it was time to have some fun. Just for kicks. And then, good old Davey could give her exactly what she needed. What a tramp like her needed. Hell, she wouldn't even have to move.

She scanned Davey's spirit, and it looked like it was his, but there was also something else hanging around. A couple of something elses. Oh . . . the car! Maybe that's the car's magic? It was just metal and plastic and junk, so there wouldn't be any glowing going on. And she remembered that she'd thought she'd seen the magic of a stone glowing once. When was that? Was that her? Oh well, doesn't matter, not when—what's that, the magic of the whiskey bottle? Yeah, it sure is. So, that's the magic of an empty whiskey bottle. Not nearly as magical as a *full* whiskey bottle, she knew, as she chuckled and shook her head. It looked fun, like something meant to be passed around. Just like her! But what about that bottle . . . she reached out and grabbed its magic, lifted it up, twirled it around . . . just had some fun with it. And when she was done, and she'd lost interest and had already turned away, she gave it a toss back into some kind of magic somewhere . . . wherever it came from. It didn't matter.

Why did she ever come here anyway? Oh yeah. She wanted Davey to see her green eyes burning up. Maybe even scare him. That way, she knew, he'd know that she knew that she really was a tramp, and he'd know it, too, like she knew it, but she knew it even more than he knew it because she was done fighting him, even though she could. Because she had magic and mayhem. And stuff.

Lin got jerked back into her own body, and the world returned to its normal state. But it still tipped a little to the left . . .

Time lurched and hiccupped to a start.

And Davey screamed like all the souls in Hell had joined a rock band.

Through watery eyes, Lin saw Davey's anguished melting-clown-mask face staring at his right arm, and she looked to see the bottom three inches of the whiskey bottle on one side of his upper arm and the open mouth of it poking out the other side. She felt the hands on her wrists and hair begin to shake.

Lin laughed while Davey continued to scream.

"Oops! Good thing it was em . . . empty, huh?"

"What the goddamn hell did you do? How . . . how did—"

"Sorry, Davey boy. That . . . that was magic . . . or something and—"

"Fix it!"

"Okay. Okay, *okay*!"

She fought hard to stop laughing and then gave him a serious look.

"And then, you . . . you finish that . . . what you were doing."

She gave him an exaggerated wink.

Lin managed to focus her intent, time shuddered to a stop, and everything bounced around inside her like a buoy in a tempest. But she scraped it together and made it work, and she saw magic, and maybe it was the bottle's magic? She didn't know, but she gave it a yank to fix Davey, returned to her own body, and gave time a shove to get it clicking and clacking down its tracks.

She felt the hands holding her hair and left wrist release her, and she turned to see a headless body folding up on itself on the cold gravel as its grinning head rolled into the weeds. She looked to her right to see the other guy, the one snapping her, which she liked, kicking up gravel and making a quick exit.

"Oh, Davey . . . I'm . . . I'm so sorry . . . about your gang . . . I didn't . . ."

She turned to look at him. He couldn't even scream, but his face was making a valiant effort.

We can still make this work, she thought, and she forced her mayhem back down. It was time to be a tramp. That didn't take much focus at all. It was the easiest thing ever.

She hitched a thumb in the corpse's direction.

"Forget about him, Davey boy."

She shook her head and smiled.

"Oh yeah, and . . . and that bottle there."

He continued to stare at her with his face knotted up.

"That one," she said and pointed at it. "*That* bottle."

He still stared, so she said, "Oh, nev . . . never mind."

Davey's face let go of its silent scream, and his breath leaked out like a tire going flat. He looked at the bottle embedded in his arm, then he turned to look right in front of him at all the soft, warm nakedness she was offering him . . . only inches away.

Lin looked into his scared but still excited eyes as she clamped down on her mayhem and tried to bury it. Her heart pounded a happy beat at being stripped and sexy and drunk and pretending to be helpless for a gang that had her surrounded. Except for the dead guy, she reminded herself. And the one that probably crapped himself while running off. Okay, not really a gang anymore.

But she couldn't stop it—her mayhem began to rise up anyway. She saw the world slowly turning into a calm, flat surface, and she began to see infinity in most directions. But it was slow going, a tipsy version of her mayhem, and she looked down to see Davey working his belt loose.

"I don't know what else you are, but you are one fine looking tramp," he said as he bumped her legs a bit farther apart. She looked down with a grin at how wide her legs had spread, and her heart thumped as he began to unzip.

"Mm-hmm," she said with a nod. "We're still, you know . . . let's—"

"I don't need those losers. You don't want to get away, do you?"

Lin shook her head and said, "Nope. Uh-uh. I ain't going nowhere."

She smiled and tried to ignore the bottle blended through his arm. And the steaming corpse to her left.

But her eyes became blinding green explosions, shocking him back into silence.

Time wasn't fooling around—it stopped right away.

No! she thought. Not yet!

The magic rushed into her and just began to flow back out in a massive wave as she stared into his caramel eyes.

Then, a solitary sober thought stood apart from the inebriated crowd and shouted:

"Caramel eyes! No, Lin! No intent while staring into caramel eyes!"

Her heart pounded, and she looked away from his eyes and down at how close he was to taking her, and how her skirt was up around her waist and totally out of the way, with only a tiny garment to pull to one side, and she smiled a sloppy smile and looked back up into his eyes, knowing that he was just about to—

"Pay attention, Lin! You're looking into caramel eyes! That's not a good thing!"

Her heart skipped a beat, and she thought about cussing, but she shut her glowing eyes and pulled back her mayhem.

Then, she found the stillness inside, and there, she grabbed her intent.

She no longer felt gravel pulling at her heels, no cool breeze touching all of her exposed skin, and no alcohol craziness either.

Not daring to open her eyes again, she held her intent in silence.

For how long, she couldn't know . . . in timeless emptiness, she held her intent.

The tiniest point of light appeared, and Lin locked onto it. It grew and raced toward her, dragging a world with it. When it had covered her completely, her life returned. She took a deep breath and smelled the welcome aromas of the cafe.

*   *   *

Lin became aware of her arms being held gently, but she was in no hurry to open her eyes. Until she heard her name.

"Lin," said Gabriel. "Lin, are you okay?"

"Mom, please tell me you're okay."

She felt the first raindrops hitting her and heard their muffled splatting on the umbrella.

She dared to open her eyes and saw that she was sitting at the table with Taylor and Gabriel. She looked down and saw that she still wore jeans, and she felt her sweatshirt warm and beginning to soak up rain. She quickly looked over at the white door and watched it nervously for several seconds, grateful that no black dot appeared.

"I think I'm okay."

"Mom, were you dead again?"

116

The rain became steady, and the wind began peeling napkins off of the tables. Lin leaned over the table and out of the rain.

"Oh, Taylor, I don't understand this. I'm not that kind of woman, Hon. I swear I'm not."

"What kind of woman, Mom?"

"How could I be like that? I don't think I'm like that, am I? I'd never do those things."

"Just don't be dead anymore, okay?"

"Taylor, she's fine. Nothing happened to her."

Taylor continued to watch Lin closely and reached out for another sip of her wine. The rain lessened as they crowded under the table's umbrella. Lin crossed her arms and held her sweatshirt tightly in each hand as she frowned down at her empty drink glass.

"Lin, no matter what you saw, you're back with us again. It's just us, Lin. You're alright."

"Maybe another drink will help, Mom. I'll call the server if—"

"No! I mean no thanks, Honey. I've had quite enough."

Chapter 14 – Like God's Heartbeat

"Okay, Mom, if you're sure you're not going to die on us, can we do some shopping already?"

"Sure thing, Hon. But I want to call Jack first. It'll just take a minute."

Lin took out her phone and walked to stand near the cafe's wrought iron gate. She rang Jack's number and held the railing tightly.

"Lin! Hi, how are things going?"

"Oh, Jack . . ."

"Are you alright? What's going on?"

"I love you, Jack. I just had to tell you. I don't want to be dead. I just want to live my life with you."

"I love you too. And that's what I want most—to live my life with you. You're the only Cowgirl I'll ever want."

"Oh, my Cowboy, that sounds wonderful. I need you, Jack."

"I'm right here. I can't wait to see you again. Will you be back—"

"Can you get on a plane right now? Nomad will be fine, just—"

"Just leave him a mountain of food?" Jack said before laughing.

"Yeah. That's for sure. Leave that sweet fluffy boy a mountain of food. I love him too, Jack."

"I know you do. He's such a good dog. And the way he looks at me sometimes, I'm not sure he's just a dog. You know what I mean?"

"Yes, I sure do. He's special. I'll text his sitter, and he'll be fine. Can you get down here, Jack? Just for a day or two, and then we'll all head back to Pennsylvania."

"I'll pack a few things, drop Nomad at your house, and catch the first flight I can. I'll text you when I hit the Island, alright? Are you sure you're okay?"

"I'll be fine. I can't wait, Jack. See you soon."

Lin ended the call and walked back to their table.

* * *

"Mom, is Jack okay?"

"Jack's fine, Honey. I asked him to join us, and he's flying down."

"He should have come down to begin with."

"I know, Hon. I thought so too."

"What about Nomad?"

"Nomad will be fine. We'll all be heading back soon, and I know I'm going to hug that big boy until he can't stand it anymore."

Taylor sat back and smiled, and Gabriel nodded.

"Now, young lady, you need some new clothes, don't you?"

"Yeah, Mom, let's go shopping."

Under a clearing sky, Lin left a few large bills on the table, and they walked through the gate. The quaint shop next door had posed a few mannequins in the window, and they stopped to look.

"That's not for me, Mom. I want more style than that."

"Stylish but still tasteful, I hope?"

"Yeah, something comfortable. When we get home, we can shop for skirts and stuff like that."

A half-hour later, they all walked back out onto the sidewalk. Lin wore khaki shorts to just above her knees, a loose peach-colored blouse, and nearly flat white sandals. Taylor's burgundy shorts were a bit shorter, and she wore a baggy white t-shirt and white sandals with wedge heels. Gabriel continued to wear jeans, but the boots were replaced by sandals and the sweater by a blue t-shirt.

With sunny skies above, they resumed their walk.

"Well, the weather sure has improved. It got a little rough there for a while."

"Yes, Lin. It's alarming how quickly the skies can change."

They both looked at Taylor, who stood outside a gift shop taking in all the curious items displayed in the window. Lin looked up to see the business's name.

"The Magic Island. Gabby, do you see that?"

"That's quite remarkable. Shall we go in?"

After a few minutes of walking through the aisles and examining all of the items, Lin approached the woman behind the counter.

"Quite a nice place you have here."

"It's for sale, sweetie, if you're interested."

"Oh, I don't think so. We're just visiting and leaving soon. But I really like the name of the place. Did you come up with that?"

"I guess you could say that. Someone told me that name in a dream. I liked it, and voila—there it is." She poked a thumb over her shoulder at the sign on the wall behind her.

"Well, thank you for the time. Very nice shop!"

Lin felt they should have been polite and bought something, but she made a mental note to stop back in before leaving for home.

Outside again, they all felt the South Georgia heat ramping up. But Lin still wanted a hot coffee, and the idea sounded good to Taylor and Gabriel too. Soon, they all had their hot drinks in paper cups and continued their walk.

"Does anyone else feel like sitting in that park awhile? It's such a beautiful day, don't you think?"

"I love it here, Mom, but I think I want to walk around some more. This is probably boring to you since you've lived here, and you just visited here a couple of weeks ago."

"Oh, there's nothing boring about any of this, Hon. But sure, take a walk."

"Okay, I'll see you around. Don't die again, okay?"

"I'll be fine, Hon. Enjoy your walk."

Taylor turned and began walking back toward the shops and restaurants of the Village.

"Gabby, care to sit a while?"

"Yes, Lin, that sounds like a very good idea. Did Gloriana take you again just now?"

"Yeah, she sure did. It was a different world than before, but still crazy. Really crazy."

"Crazy how?"

"Oh, I'm not sure I even want to get into it. Maybe later, okay?"

"Okay, Lin."

They took seats at an empty picnic table and watched Taylor blending in with the tourists and locals.

"I can't tell you how happy that makes me. Just seeing Taylor healthy and walking around. Such a simple thing—walking. She hasn't been able to for so long. Lee healed her. Lee made that possible."

"Lee is quite a remarkable person, Lin. Did she tell you much about her 'home?'"

"Enough. It's a peaceful valley under a blue sky and a bright sun. She rearranges stones there to make a figure eight, and that heals her. It even keeps her from aging."

"Has she talked about the sun and what color it is?"

"No, I just assumed that—"

"I think it must be green."

"She sees a green sun? Why would she imagine something like that?"

"Oh, Lin, that's not her imagination. What color are your eyes when you're using your mayhem?"

"That sun of hers—it's magic? That's why it's green?"

"Exactly. She's found a place where she can tap into that infinite supply of life-giving magic. Quite remarkable."

"And what about Taylor? How could she be a Glyphin? And what exactly *is* a Glyphin?"

"Ah, yes, let's talk about Glyphins. When I wrote the word on the pizza box, you almost immediately wondered about my intentions for writing that particular word."

"I'm still wondering," Lin said and shook her head with a smile. Gabriel smiled too.

"No need to wonder, Lin. I just wanted to get your attention. I think I did."

"Oh, that's for sure."

"You perceived that word at a high level. You didn't just see a word and know its meaning. You didn't see it and know that it's a word but not know its meaning. You didn't see only letters and not the word. You didn't see the markings and not know that you saw letters. And so on . . ."

"Yeah, because no one lives like that."

"And I told you there are even higher ways of perceiving a word. That's what Glyphins can do."

"Okay, but how?"

"The next level up is making it a double word. We read words left to right, and we understand them. A Glyphin sees the word plus its mirror image right after it with a space in between. I shouldn't say a mirror image, though—that's not right. It's the word spelled the same way, but it's read backwards.

"They are able to focus on the space in between the word on the left and the other on the right. They can perceive both at the same time. They read the word left to right and at the same time its twin right to left. There's no meaning for that second word. It's like a ghost image of a word. An unknowable thought. They don't try to understand that one.

"When they read both, one is a nonsense, meaningless version of the other. One's a word with meaning, and one's a word that can't be comprehended. Both blend together in the empty space, and that focuses their power. When they do it right, and they focus on the empty space, they grab onto something that ordinarily can't be touched.

"For most beginning Glyphins, that usually means some part of the weather around them. I don't know why, Lin. That's just how it works. Maybe it's because the air is mostly what we touch first in the world. And when they do that, whatever they're feeling gets twisted in with the weather. It changes the weather for better or worse. Usually worse."

Lin sat in silence, so Gabriel continued.

"Remember that everything is connected to the magic. Every tiniest thing you can perceive is supported by unlimited magic feeding it from every direction from inside and outside. Making it real. Allowing it to exist one more moment.

"Weather is no different. It's a collection of real things in the world, organized and following a pattern. A Glyphin taps into the magic of the pattern that makes it real. They can affect the weather."

Lin sat speechless, staring at her best friend for over thirty years explaining yet another unknown act of power over the magic.

"Will we ever run out of new things for me to try to understand?"

"No."

"But for you, I mean, you—"

"No, Lin, I'll never run out either. The magic is endless. You know that. How that magic can be used is endless too."

Lin sat back against the table and looked up at the sunny sky that held only a few puffy clouds drifting past, carried inland by the ocean breezes.

"So, let me get this right," she said while still looking at the sky. "Taylor is happy right now?"

"Yes, Lin, and we should try to keep her that way. At least until she can get control of her power."

"Can you help her with that?"

"I'm not sure I can. This is an ancient power. I know of it, but not the details of how it's used."

"And why is my daughter a Glyphin?"

"It's probably not a random coincidence. I think it's from those Words of God that were recorded on the Messenger Scroll, which was really Renato. I believe the very Words themselves carried magic put there by the powers of a Glyphin."

"The Words of God were all about the weather? That can't be—"

"No, Lin, playing with the weather is for beginners. Those Words were tainted by a very powerful practitioner, and it wasn't about the weather. When Renato spoke the Words to you, you didn't feel anything. When you thought about the Words, nothing happened. Only when you spoke the Words did the Glyphin power affect you."

"You're right. I felt it every time I spoke the Words. You didn't know? You couldn't stop me? I should have left those Words unspoken."

"Yes. I'm sorry, but I didn't know. I don't know everything, remember?"

They shared a brief smile before Lin continued.

"So, what was that magic meant to do?"

"Open a door."

"Oh God, Gabby. Yeah, it did that. Just speaking the Words gave that queen a direct route to me. Whatever else she is, she must be a Glyphin too."

"Yes. And there's something else that's clear now too."

"What's that?"

"We wondered why reading the Scroll's message was made to be so difficult. It was set up so that no ordinary person could even look at the Scroll without losing their mind. I'm sorry that I never even considered this possibility.

"That queen didn't care about anyone reading the Words of God. I don't even know now whether those were really the Words of God or not. The whole point was for someone with power over the magic, such as you, to know the Words. To speak them. Only someone with power like you can bring Gloriana back, like she's been trying to trick you into doing."

"That all makes sense. That was like a message in a bottle. The Scroll, Renato, all the Words of God—she was sending out a lifeline, not knowing if anyone like me would ever find it."

"It took many centuries, but it worked. It's quite an act of power, wouldn't you say?"

"I can barely comprehend that kind of power. Where is she? How could she still be around and coming after me like this?"

"You've been taken there two more times already. It's a good time to discuss it.

"She told you she was 'between the Islands.' She was referring to the Islands of Time. You and I, and everyone and everything, exist on those Islands. It's been a long time since I've journeyed into the spaces in between. We're not meant to go there, Lin."

"What do you mean we're on the Islands?"

"It's like so many things that we find impossible to fit into words, but I'll try. We live from moment to moment. To us, it seems continuous, but you know that can't be true."

"I don't know any such thing, Gabby. There are no empty moments in what I experience."

"Think about infinity, Lin. Now, divide a second in half. Divide one of the halves, and keep dividing it an infinite number of times. Is it so hard to believe that at some point, time can't be divided any further? That smallest bit of time . . . that's an Island of Time. The smallest instant you or anyone else can perceive, even what can be registered by powerful instruments, is made up of more Islands than can ever be counted. We don't see the spaces in between. We're not made to do that."

"We can't see the spaces in between? Why not?"

"Each Island is like a flash of light, and they're so close together that all we see is the light. There's darkness in between, but we don't see it. We focus on those moments of light, and we string them together so they seem uninterrupted. We're built to see the light and not the dark. We live only on the Islands of Time."

"And Gloriana escaped into those spaces in between?"

"She died. That's the definition of death—you're no longer on the Islands."

"But she didn't die, Gabby. How?"

"Her intent is still so strong that she's been able to survive there. It's hard to conceive of such strength. I believe she voluntarily traveled into those spaces in between—she died—while she still had a very strong intent. She's been there for centuries, quietly holding onto that intent. Waiting."

"For me."

"Yes."

"And she's a Glyphin."

"Yes."

"Taylor too."

"Yes, but not as strong."

"Oh, strong enough to destroy the cabin at St. Mary's, though."

"Yes."

"Do you know how Taylor got that power?"

"Not for sure, but she was healed at about the same time you first spoke the Words."

"And she naturally picked it up somehow?"

"I believe so. Maybe from you speaking the Words."

"Why are there Islands of Time, Gabby? Why is everything set up that way?"

"I believe that's the way God wants it. There can be no other explanation."

"I don't get it. I really don't."

"Think of the Islands as coming from God. Like God's heartbeat, Lin. We all live in each precious heartbeat of God."

"And what's in between?"

"Horrors that can't be imagined. Every type of thing that brings death and decay. Emptiness. The absence of anything good or even evil."

"But there's evil in the magic, right?"

"Yes, there sure is. Evil is a part of life. But the magic that you're learning so much about exists only on the Islands. What's in between is even more incomprehensible."

"And we're surround by that? All through our lives?"

"Not really surrounded. For each of us, when we pass between the Islands of Time, we're passing through that Godless emptiness. One or more of the things that brings death and decay finds us. It comes to know us. It latches onto us each time we pass through. And it works at us, picking away at us until we can't continue any longer.

"But for most of us, survival there isn't an option. Our magic—our spirits—exist only on the Islands. It is only our intent that passes through there. When we can go no further, we return to the magic. The endless, infinite magic that exists only on the Islands."

"Gloriana is dead, then?"

"Yes. And no."

"When I was dead, that's what happened to me too?"

"Yes. And you held onto your intent long enough to get back. Don't ever lose your hold on your intent, Lin."

"I won't. No matter what. But when Gloriana pulled me between the Islands, I felt like I was living a life. A crazy life, but still . . . a life. How could she do that?"

"Perhaps you'll get the chance to ask her."

Chapter 15 – Into The Magic

"Maybe we should head back to the Village and see what Taylor's up to."

"Good idea, Lin. I can appreciate how she must feel to have her life back."

"I bet you can. I still can't believe how patient you are. You stayed with me for over thirty years, protecting me and guiding me, and now, you're real again. I can tell how much you're enjoying it."

"Yes, I certainly am. And I enjoyed those three decades too. Please don't ever think that was a bother for me."

"And I know why you were sent. My power. It's so rare. The last time anyone has seen it was twenty centuries ago. And I know you want me to help fight the war against evil in the magic, but I don't know if I'll ever be ready to commit to something like that."

"Just live your life, Lin. See where it takes you. You don't need to make a decision yet. Except maybe where we're going to get a cup of coffee next."

"Yes, I can decide that. Let's start walking, and we'll see—oh no, Gabby. Do you see what I see?"

Gabriel turned to look where Lin was staring.

"Yes. Your first two converts."

"Yeah, those two. They really are here on my island."

"And since we're going that way, would you care to say hello to them?"

"What would I say? What do they think of me now? I know they're not converts anymore."

"I bet you're curious, aren't you? Let's take a walk. They did journey here just in the hopes of finding you."

* * *

Elias pulled right back out of his driveway and headed for the Village. Within minutes, he'd driven his old car down Mallery and past their favorite cafe, where he saw June seated in the patio area under a large umbrella that held back the brilliant mid-day sun.

And across the street he saw something that scattered his thoughts and replaced them with long-forgotten recollections. Chills climbed up his spine like a mountaineer on a rope despite the day's growing heat. He remembered that he was in a moving car—one that he was driving—and he turned to see a high truck bumper about to peel back his car's hood. He slammed his brakes, and the squealing tires brought him to a dead stop.

Before his heart had time to react, he turned his head and saw Lin Finnerty gazing in his direction. He felt sure it was her. He'd done some research and found her online, and he also knew that she'd changed her name to Lin Finity. And she was back. Back on his island. With a companion who had long, wavy brown hair.

He gave his car some careful gas to pull around the truck, and after accepting with a nod and a smile a few swear words from the driver he'd almost hit, he traveled a couple of blocks and parked.

* * *

John saw Lin first. He flashed a genuine smile, but it was nowhere near what he'd offered two weeks earlier when he was Lin's convert. He elbowed Tommy, spilling his drink on the sidewalk, and Tommy got a smile that was big but fell short of insane.

Together, they crossed Mallery Street, patiently waiting and dodging traffic until they'd made it to Lin and Gabriel.

"I knew we'd find you, Lin," said John. "We've been looking for you."

You should be looking for your head, Lin thought with a laugh to herself. It was grinning when it rolled into the weeds.

"Yes, we sure have," said Tommy.

No, you were running away, she thought. And why were you snapping the strap of my undies?

"You guys. Again. What are you doing in St. Simons?"

"Besides it being a nice place to visit, you mean? We were hoping to somehow see you again. I can't believe our good luck. Hi Lin, it's good to see you again."

"Very good," said Tommy with a grin.

"But you two have lives to live, don't you? Don't you have jobs? And Tommy, what about your family?"

"I'm back with my family. I love them very much. I always did, and still, I remember not caring whether I saw them again or not."

"Same thing with my job, Lin. I like my job. I'm not a bum. But I didn't care. Not a bit."

"And what is it that you want?"

"How about an answer for starters."

"What's your question?"

"How? How did that all happen?" said John.

"Well, I'm not sure I can explain that. Maybe I just have a very strong personality?"

"She does," said Gabriel. "She can have that kind of effect."

"And who are you, if you don't mind me asking?" said Tommy.

"Just a friend. A good friend of Lin's."

"Okay, here it is, Lin," said John. "We want to feel that way again. We thought if we could find you, somehow it could happen. Can it?"

"Guys, I don't think that's a good idea. Didn't your lives kind of fall apart there for a while?"

"Yeah," Tommy said, "but we didn't care. I've never felt that way before. I want that again."

"Look, I think you two should head back home. I'm on vacation. A real vacation this time. I can't have you guys tagging along after me like last time."

"But we helped you with that big guy at your reunion," said Tommy.

"Yes, you did. Thanks for that."

"I know you don't owe us, but I really wish you believed you did," said John in a perfectly reasonable voice.

Lin turned to look at Gabriel, whose head was shaking slowly.

* * *

Elias froze on the sidewalk against a brick wall baked by the sun. He felt the heat rising off of the concrete as he stared at Lin and her friend talking with two other strangers. She hadn't looked over, none of them had, and Elias kept his back to the wall and forced himself to look around and not gawk in Lin's direction.

But he memorized the faces of Lin's three companions. Decades of police work gave him an ability to lock those images away. And he knew his next move would be to scan their database and see what that might turn up.

He continued to watch, and to him, it seemed like the two men were asking Lin for something. Their gestures showed that they were relaxed and at ease around her as if they knew her. But they wanted something from her too.

* * *

John continued. "Look, Lin, you won't have to worry about us bugging you. I've thought through this, and here's my plan. We're going to take a bus north later today. I'll tell you the time and place. Whatever you did before, please do it again right before we get on the bus."

"We'll be gone for good," said Tommy.

Lin looked for Gabriel's advice again, and Gabriel's response was the same.

"You guys. I don't know what to do with you two. Tell me when you're leaving, and I'll think about it. That's the best I can offer you."

John and Tommy got huge smiles, and John scribbled some information on a business card. Lin saw that he was an engineer for a company in the Cleveland area. A logical man, she thought. Ordinarily. Without her mayhem converting him.

She tucked the card in her pocket.

"Thanks, Lin," said John. "Either way, we're leaving. We really do want to keep our lives. But we know now that something is missing."

John continued to look into Lin's eyes.

"Something huge."

John's mouth moved, but he remained silent for a few seconds.

"Please show up, and you'll never see us again," he said without a smile.

They turned and walked down the sidewalk, and Lin marveled at the sight of them voluntarily leaving her, something they'd never do as converts.

"Gabby, that was weird."

"I hope you're not seriously considering their request."

"I've done a lot of damage and killed a lot of people. I know they were bad people, but still, wouldn't it help for me to do some good?"

"I understand your intentions, Lin. But it might be better to find other ways to do good in the world."

"I know, like when I healed Ben. Is that what you mean?"

"Yes."

"And how much good is enough? The Words of God said everyone that tries to find God will be with God after their time is through. That is, if those really were the Words of God."

"The Words didn't say how much, though, Lin."

"I killed Doc. I see now that maybe I didn't have to kill him. I know there's some good in it, though, because he'll never hurt any innocent people again. But how much good would I have to do to make up for that?"

"It's impossible to know."

"I told Wolfe I'd go out and preach a message of hope. But how could I? People would ask the same question, and all I could say would be, 'Duh . . . I dunno.' Wow, some message of hope."

"Maybe all anyone can do is consider their own lives and do as much good as they can."

"I feel like I'm basically good, mostly from your influence. But also from being dead. The two times Gloriana tried to trick me into bringing her back, they changed me. I know it wasn't real—not like any of this is. But still, I saw such a twisted version of myself that I don't ever want to be that person. I don't even want to come close."

Lin stopped herself for a moment, then added another comment.

"It's kind of fascinating to think about all that, though."

"Do you think about those experiences often?"

"Oh, not often, I guess. But yeah, I do go through the memories. There's some entertainment value there. But that doesn't matter. What matters is that I'm always trying to become a better person."

"All of us should try to improve as we go through life. When we didn't have the Words of God, we talked about trying to always do good, even if we don't know of any reward for it. No guarantees."

"Yeah, and that hasn't changed. I will choose good, Gabby. I can feel that it's right no matter what it gets me."

"And you're still getting stronger, aren't you?"

"Yes, I really am. Except when I'm dead."

Lin and Gabriel shared their smiles and took seats on a sidewalk bench.

"Who knows, maybe we can just sit here, and Taylor will find us?"

* * *

"I knew I'd seen those faces before."

"What are you getting into now, Huff?" said Sam.

After having lunch with June, Elias headed straight back to the police station. He sat at his old desk and looked through recent case files on the laptop. It didn't take long before he'd come across reports from the fight that had blown up at Lin's reunion less than two weeks earlier. It was considered an unresolved case because they'd never learned the identity of the large man at the center of it all, the one who'd gone through the resort security like they were frail children. But the two men who'd been questioned—the police knew all about them. And they were back. And talking to Lin. Lin Finity now, Elias reminded himself.

"I'm just chasing down some clues here, Sam. Don't mind me."

He read more of the report and found that an unidentified blond woman had been involved, too, but she'd skipped out before the police arrived. That could have been only one person, concluded Elias.

After closing the report, he visited Ivan's cell. He looked in on a man staring at the wall and occasionally trembling. An outrageous idea bubbled to the surface, and he knew what he had to do.

*   *   *

"Yes, you really have continued to get stronger, Lin. I think now might be a good time to show you something."

"Really? I'm still kind of reeling from dying. That's almost impossible to deal with. It's not at all like going into the magic. No amount of strength helps in that space in between the Islands of Time."

"Do you remember how you got there? What did you experience?"

"Each time, I see a black dot. And no matter how hard I try, I can't look away from it. The spot keeps growing, like it's racing toward me. When it covers me, I can't breathe anymore. I can't think, and I have no feelings. All I have is my heartbeat. Then, that stops too. I'm just frozen . . . nowhere. There's no way to do anything about it."

"Yes, because you're no longer alive. There's no magic there. The only thing left is your intent. If your intent weren't so strong, you wouldn't be aware of anything, and you sure wouldn't remember it."

"But what is that black dot, Gabby? And then, the white dot that brings me back?"

"Somehow, you managed to change your speed so that you experience every wave, every Island of Time, as they wash through you. Each wave, each Island, brings you life. But when you're in between, there's no life."

"There doesn't seem to be anything. But there are things there, aren't there?"

"Yes. Things that are best left alone. We can't help but travel past them every time we move between the Islands. But to seek them out . . . that's madness."

"Not the same kind of madness as in the magic, though, right?"

"No. Going between the Islands is the madness of suicide. It's not the same as too many realities all at once that a mind can't understand, like in the magic. It's very dangerous. Unless, of course, you have an unbreakable hold on your intent."

"Which I do."

"Yes, so you survive because you're strong enough. And I believe you have enough strength that I can show you something. We talked about it before. Something that could never be explained to you because you'd have to experience it."

"I remember. What every living creature feels except for humans. That's what you mean, isn't it?"

"Yes. But only for a very brief instant, Lin. Staying there too long could cripple you."

"Like broken bones, Gabby?" Lin said with a laugh.

"No, like a broken spirit. You might not be able to accept being alive as a human again."

"Well then, let's not stay too long. What do I need to do?"

"We must go into the magic. From there, I will guide you."

"Okay, let's go."

"First, let's take a walk between these buildings."

"Why?"

"It might be upsetting for the locals to see us vanish."

Lin could only stare at Gabriel, trying to form a question, and Gabriel turned and began walking. So, she followed, and they walked down a narrow alley until they were behind a large garbage container.

She watched as Gabriel's eyes changed from their natural brown to a rich, glowing green. She felt her own eyes glowing, too, and when Gabriel's eyes closed, she closed hers as well.

The whipping force, which Lin had felt every time they'd journeyed into the magic, never ceased to surprise her. It grabbed her and pulled her to an impossible height far above the Earth, where she felt that she lingered, anticipating the fall. Together, they dove through the sky and traveled through the border into the magic. And like so many times before, she felt the confusion of her senses: she could smell colors, hear flavors, and she gazed at her heartbeats tumbling over a cliff and dividing into dozens of pieces that danced and laughed as they fell.

In an instant, they were through, and Lin came to a stop with Gabriel in the churning madness of the magic.

Chapter 16 – To Just Be

Lin felt lost in the swirling chaotic magic, and she squeezed Gabriel's hand to keep from being abandoned there. After sensing that she would be safe with Gabriel, she looked for her intent deep within the stillness inside her. She found her unbreakable hold on it, and her concerns about losing her way left her. Her intent would always keep her safe there, so she released Gabriel's hand. And she reminded herself that they didn't really have hands anymore.

Gabriel led the way, and Lin followed closely behind. Through endless fields of magic they traveled, around mountains of it, with memories and ideas and feelings crashing into them from every direction, and every one of her senses overlapping with every other. It was total madness, and she had learned to not try to make sense of it because there was none to be found. The magic, she now understood, was outside of her mind. And to journey there, her mind must be left behind.

They had become two insignificant specks in a maelstrom of magic that wove unknowable patterns. All around them, writhing shapes crashed and frolicked, weaving complex designs that few would ever see.

Gabriel began to rise to a surface, and Lin followed. She saw a collection of spirits all moving in unison. Each had its own magic, but they seemed to move as one. In some way, she felt a tug from Gabriel moving her spirit, and they closed in on two members of the speedy group.

Lin relaxed and accepted a feeling of falling but without any fear, as her senses all found their own places again. She felt a joining. A becoming.

A beginning like birth.

With her left eye, Lin saw Gabriel's smooth gray body swimming beside her, a large unblinking eye looking into her own. With her right eye, she saw infinite blue—an endless world within an even larger world. She felt a refreshing coolness against all of her skin, caressing her as she worked her powerful muscles, each thrust up and down of her tail speeding her alongside her best friend.

They swam among dozens of others, all watching each other and watching out for each other, as they moved like a conscious cloud toward Lin's next meal: a school of small fish darting about but remaining part of a single grouping. She thought that the school resembled a giant drop of some thicker fluid that had spilled into the sea and was being squeezed and shaped by unseen currents.

"Not far now," a voice told her.

Lin felt the hunger that drove her onward, and she flicked her tail more quickly.

"You are swift and sure."

Lin glanced at Gabriel then focused ahead.

"They understand. Just as you would."

Lin swept her wide tail up and down as she raced along with Gabriel.

"Remember that I am with them to their last moments, as I will be with you. Forever we will remain together."

The cool water seemed to fly past.

"The sun is wondrous today."

Lin could see sunlight close above her. She skimmed above the waves, drawing in enough precious oxygen to continue the hunt before she cut back down through the waves to her place beside Gabriel. Gabriel angled up and dove into the air before sinking back down beside her and dragging a string of bubbles.

They swam, and they watched to each side with the cool blue world supporting them, providing food, and giving them protection. It was their home, and they knew exactly how to be what they were. What they were meant to be. What God wanted them to be.

"I am with you."

Lin felt her tail launching her forward with every stroke.

"I am always with you."

Lin knew without any doubts what she was. And that she was never alone.

"I am here."

She tried to remember being human, but it seemed too far away. It had never been real. The memory was but a splash of saltwater swept behind by her vigorously pulsing tail.

"Feel the water. Feel your body. Feel the life you have been given."

As they neared the small fish, Lin felt an abrupt pull. She knew that Gabriel was bringing her back to something, back to some other place. But her best friend was also ending her life, killing her as she swam through her cool blue world.

A quick journey through uncountable layers of magic ended with a sharp leap through the barrier, and even as she could see the alley around them, Lin felt herself thrown high above the clouds. They lingered there before plunging to the world. She opened her eyes to see Gabriel's eyes opening too, showing the last traces of bright green.

Gabriel smiled and waited for her to speak.

"That was . . . that was profound. I felt it. I heard God's words, Gabby. Not a lot, but enough. Can we go back? Right now?"

"That's not a good idea, Lin. Just keep that as a memory for now."

"Just a few minutes more, okay? I've never felt . . . I mean, that was . . . just take me back—"

"Lin, look around you."

Lin's eyes continued to plead silently.

"Really, Lin. Look at everything."

She broke her gaze at Gabriel and looked first at the brick wall on their side, then the weathered wood plank siding across the alley, then down the alley toward Mallery. Crowds walked past the alley's entry in both directions and across the street, some looking in shop windows, some eating and drinking as they moved about. She heard their laughter and conversations and the sounds of traffic. Her eyes touched all of the bright colors, and her breaths brought her a menu of tempting scents from the restaurants.

Following Gabriel's pointing finger, Lin looked up above the shops across Mallery and saw the dazzling sun lazily flaming its path across a bright blue sky. Only a few brave, puffy white clouds attempted to interfere with its work.

A look back to Gabriel showed the deep love that she always saw in those eyes. A love that had saved her over three decades ago. And power. Such power and strength and goodness. All devoted to her.

She began to relax at feeling the comfort of Gabriel's protection and love. But her smile yielded to hot tears building up and beginning to spill out.

And she remembered the tiny part of the life she had just shared with a creature she'll never meet, in a sea she'll never touch. How it felt to have no doubts. To just be. To be what God wanted. Only what God—

"Lin, look at me."

She found that she'd been staring down and frowning at the dirty pavement on which they stood, totally unaware of her surroundings.

"Lin."

She looked into Gabriel's eyes. Gabriel's arms were out with palms turned up.

"This is *our* world, Lin. *This* is the life you have been given. Remember the other life that you shared, but do not let it take you."

"It's all I can think of, Gabby. If I could just go back, just for—"

"No, Lin. Coming back took almost all of your strength. It wasn't easy to pull you away. When you're much stronger, you'll be able to experience it again. Not now."

Lin could do nothing but stare into Gabriel's eyes, and she couldn't stop the tears running down her cheeks.

"Taylor should be around somewhere, don't you think?"

"Yeah, Gabby. Probably."

She wiped at her tears with the back of her hand.

"And soon, Jack will be here, won't he?"

She continued to gaze into Gabriel's big brown eyes.

"It'll be good to see Jack. I . . . I wanted him to come with us."

Another tear rolled down her cheek, and she caught it on a fingertip.

"Do you feel the hot sunshine, Lin?

She nodded.

"Do you feel the light breezes across your cheek and playing with your hair?"

"Yes. It really is beautiful here, Gabby."

"How about if we start walking?"

"Okay."

They began the short walk back toward Mallery, and Lin's gaze fell again to the asphalt.

"Before we find Taylor, can you tell me your favorite things about Nomad?"

Lin looked up into Gabriel's eyes.

"Oh, that could take a while," Lin said with a soft laugh between quiet sobs. "There are so many things I love about him. Nomad is—"

She stopped and grabbed Gabriel's arm, and they both stood in the unopposed sunshine warming the sidewalk.

"Oh, you're good, Gabby. You're really good. I think I'll be okay. And I'll never forget what I felt there in that other life. Really, I'll be okay."

"I know you will, Lin. The lives *we* have been given are also quite beautiful. Sometimes, we need to remind ourselves."

* * *

Gabriel pointed out a vacant bench under a sprawling live oak, and they sat.

"This world really is beautiful too. But how did you take me there? How does that work?"

"It's all intent, Lin. With enough strength, our intent can accomplish far more than we can ever understand. If we needed to wait for our minds to know things first, we'd get nothing done."

"Why did you pick that place and those lives?"

"I didn't."

"But how . . . how did—"

"Your intent pointed out a good direction for you. I'd guess where we went had some meaning to you?"

Lin nodded her head in silence before she spoke.

"Yeah, Gabby. From my childhood. Is that why it affected me so much?"

"No. You'd feel that no matter what life you shared, with any living thing other than humans."

She leaned back and gazed up at the sky.

"Do you feel okay?"

"Yeah, I do. The sunshine feels good on my legs, even though I'm not showing my entire legs to any stranger that wanders past."

"Dressing that way did serve a purpose, though. You'd repressed so much of yourself when you locked your powers away. You were only fifteen, Lin. What else could you do? You didn't have the strength then to deal with it."

"And then, you showed up, and you kept me company. All those years, Gabby. You really are an—"

"Look, Lin. There's Taylor across the street."

"Why on Earth did she buy a black hat? Heck, I can see it all the way from here."

"Lin, she isn't . . ."

Gabriel's words fell into a well and vanished. Lin stared at Taylor's black hat, which was mostly just a small point from being so far away, and she found that she couldn't look anywhere else. In an angry rush, the blackness attacked her, and she felt every piece of her life freeze solid in an emptiness without beginning or end.

Chapter 17 – Pretty Damn Powerful

No measurable time had passed before light sped toward Lin and covered her, and she could feel and think again. Her heart began a steady beat, and she took a deep breath and held onto the bench with both hands.

She opened her eyes to see Taylor standing before her. And she noted with relief that Taylor was wearing the same clothes she'd had on when she'd left for her walk around the Village.

"Are you okay, Lin?" said Gabriel. "You looked a little faint there for just a second."

"I'm fine. I think Gloriana tried to get me again. But you're right about me getting stronger. It didn't work this time. Taylor, how was your walk?"

"Oh, Mom, just walking feels so good. I can't ever thank Lee enough for healing me. When can we see her again?"

"I have no idea. All I know right now is that it's so hot out here."

Lin began rolling her shorts up and exposing her thighs to the hot sun.

"You should do the same, Hon. Get some daylight on those pretty legs of yours. You'll be happier, and God knows,"—she paused to wink at Gabriel —"we need to keep you happy."

"Okay, Mom, you're right."

She rolled her shorts up as high as they could go.

"We just look silly, Taylor. Let's get some real clothes."

They were still close to the boutique with the sexy clothing, and no time had passed before both women strode out in short black skirts and spiky black heels. Lin's thin orange blouse and Taylor's purple one accomplished little more than changing their skin color.

"You really are happier like that, aren't you, Lin?" said Gabriel.

"You know it, Gabriel. I tried being boring, and guess what—it didn't take!"

She ran her hands down her thighs and pulled her shoulders back, stretching the thin material covering nothing but her skin. She let out a playful moan as she slid her hands around behind her, where she gave her round bottom a squeeze.

"This is the real me. No reason I should bury that like I did with my mayhem, is there?"

"Nope—bad idea, Lin."

"And my legs, Gabriel. I know they look pretty damn delicious like this, bare and stretched out for the world to see."

"The world can be crappy, but it does deserve some happiness, Lin."

"See, you get me, Gabriel. Taylor, do you get me?"

"Oh yeah, I do, Mom. I think I'm just another version of you."

Taylor ran her hands down her hips until she found the hem of her skirt. She folded up the bottom all around and smoothed it out.

"Looking good, baby girl. Let's get a few drinks and see what the world has to offer."

"I'll drink at least as much as you, Mom. I want to get crazy!"

"Now, there's a plan I can slide up next to and squeeze real tight."

"Tight's the word, Mom. The world doesn't stand a chance!"

With heels clicking on the hot pavement, Taylor led the way, and her hips bounced as she offered smiles to everyone she passed. Lin followed close behind, grinning at seeing so much of her daughter on display. They found seats near the sidewalk, and Lin stretched again and twirled around, swinging her long blond hair back over her shoulders.

When the young server approached them, Lin sat quickly and pulled him down onto her lap. With one hand on his leg and the other rubbing his back, she said, "You sweet, sweet young thing. There are two very thirsty ladies here that need your attention." She gave him a big smile.

"I can bring you whatever you want. Maybe a—"

Lin hurried one manicured fingertip to his lips and silenced him.

"Of course, you'll bring me whatever I want. That's your job. But tell me . . . would you *do* whatever I want?"

His lips wanted to form words, so Lin moved her finger to his chin.

"I . . . I mean . . . yeah, I think so—"

She pinned his lips shut again.

"Because I'm sure I'd do whatever you wanted. Doesn't that sound nice?"

She held his chin and nodded his head. She let go, and he continued to nod.

"Good boy. Bring a double gin and tonic for me and a bottle of Merlot for this beautiful girl."

She pushed her chest out farther.

"And think about what *you* might like, okay? Use your imagination."

He stared at her cleavage. Lin let him go, and he stood.

"I . . . I . . . I'll get you what you want. Real quick!"

Lin blew him a kiss, and when he turned to leave, Taylor smacked his behind.

"We're off to a good start, Hon. I like how you rolled your skirt up. Me too."

Lin stood and began slowly peeling her skirt up her thighs. She made several neat folds, and more than just a hint of her underwear could be seen.

The drinks arrived, and Taylor stood to greet her new friend. After he set the drinks down, she wrapped her arms around his waist and reached down to get a solid hold on his backside. He seemed to have no aversion to kissing her. When she released him, she spun him around to face the kitchen and smacked his behind again.

"A toast, Mom. Me and you, showing the world how it's done."

"Down the hatch."

They chugged their drinks, and Lin waved for another round.

"Mom, after this next one, I'm heading out. I've never just put myself out there, you know what I mean?"

"Oh, do I ever. Go give the world a taste. Hell, give them more than they can handle. I won't wait up for you."

After downing most of the bottle, Taylor began weaving toward the gate, and she turned when Lin called to her.

"Hey, roll it up a little more. Show those legs, Baby."

Taylor rolled her skirt up another fold and disappeared around the corner.

"Oh, my, my . . . that girl. She has no idea how much trouble she's going to find. And she's going to love it, Gabriel."

"I do believe she will, Lin. She's definitely your daughter."

"Yeah, that's for sure." Lin waved for another drink.

"I need some trouble too. I know just the kind of trouble I want, Gabriel, and I can handle lots of it. I'm pretty damn powerful."

"Pretty damn drunk too."

"Getting there," she said with a smirk, chugged her drink, and whistled for another.

"I can find infinity and damn, the things I can do. You get what I'm saying?"

"I sure do. You can destroy just about anyone. And you'll never stop being a tease, will you?"

"With legs like these, oh, hell no. And I'm thinking legs like these were made for more than just teasing. One more drink, then I'll take a hike myself. I love showing everything off."

"You do have a lot to show off, Lin."

Lin quickly swallowed her new drink, smacked the server's behind, and strutted out through the gate. She immediately saw a blazing neon sun across Mallery, and it seemed to be laughing at her. She knew that she couldn't let a stupid sun get away with that.

Before taking another step, she popped the top button on her blouse, showing more of what was barely hidden under the thin material. She popped another, spread her arms to each side, and arched her back.

The buttons held as the cloth strained against her bare skin. Lin looked down and laughed.

I can fix that, she thought, as she unbuttoned the entire blouse. Without the buttons holding it together, it spread open enough to show uninterrupted skin from her chin down between her breasts and over her belly all the way to the top band of her skirt. And she began a casual stroll toward the bar.

A tall, rough-looking bald man wearing a black t-shirt with a skull and crossbones on it stepped out from the dark doorway. She knew in an instant that it wasn't the neon sun that irritated her. It was that man. He needed his ass kicked, and she knew that she was just the woman to do it.

But first, some teasing would be fun, she thought. And she reminded herself that she could push anything as far as she wanted, and if she needed it, her mayhem would always rescue her. So, why stop with just the teasing? Why not have whatever fun she feels like having? Maybe even find some thrilling new feelings . . .

"Hey, big fella, you looking for trouble?"

"I wasn't, but,"—he looked her up and down—"it looks like you're offering."

"Oh, I do have some sweet things to offer. That's for damn sure."

"Gimme a better look. Pull that shirt open."

She complied without hesitation, carefully holding each edge and spreading the blouse wide open. Nothing blocked the view, and Lin grinned, happy to have them out for the world to see. And happy knowing she had his full attention.

"See anything you like?"

"That's really good what you got there," he said. "You just like putting it all out there for anyone, don't you?"

"Oh yeah, and I'm not just for show. Mm . . . the things I'll do if I have to . . ."

"I have no doubt." He looked down at her tiny skirt.

"See anything else you like, big fella?"

"Hell, yeah. Why stop? Lose the skirt too."

"Oh, you mean this silly little thing?"

She began sliding it down, twisting her hips around and working the material over her behind. The top band had made it down to her knees, and she stopped and put her hands on her hips.

"Is this what you had in mind? Why, anyone can see my underwear now."

"That bit of cloth? It ain't hiding much."

Lin stretched it up tight with both hands and said, "It sure isn't. What do you think of that, big fella?"

"That's a damn sight, right there."

"Oh, big boy, I'm a sight all over."

She lifted her blouse above her waist, spun all the way around, and gave her hips a couple of shakes.

"That's good. Real good. Really nice ass. Now, all the way with the skirt."

"Oh, like this?"

She shimmied her skirt until it fell around her heels. She carefully lifted each shoe out and kicked it off into the street, where it got caught up in the wheel well of a passing tour bus. Lin waved to the flashing cameras.

"Now, lose the shirt too."

"If you insist."

She backed up a few steps to be nearer the bed. One of her sharp heels caught in the carpet, and she almost stumbled.

"Okay, I'll do what you say, tough guy."

Something about the man enjoying her strip show finally filtered into her thoughts. She knew the man. She'd seen him before, right there in St. Simons. But where?

Lin lifted her shirt over her shoulders and began gliding it down her back. She shook her arms and let it drop behind her, and she stood there in the dim light wearing only her underwear and heels. She brushed her hair back over her shoulders to not block the view. Her heart tapped a healthy beat.

"Mm . . . that's much better," she said and looked into his eyes while giving him a big smile.

"Like the show so far, fella?"

She remembered his name, but she couldn't recall any more. And she wondered if it mattered who he was—she knew that she liked standing there wearing mostly nothing. Teasing him.

"That's good. Just keep doing what I tell you. You remember me now, don't you?"

Lin backed up until she bumped into the bed, and she felt its blanket cool against her skin. She looked up into his eyes.

"Oh, I remember your name now, mister. Your name is Len."

"Ben."

"Ben. Yeah, Ben. Where do I know you from, Ben?"

"You'll remember."

She looked into his eyes and hooked her thumbs in the thin elastic circling her waist.

"I'm just about naked now. You like having a stripped-down girl in your room?"

He grinned and said, "I do."

Lin laughed and thought about Jack saying those two words someday. But not today. No, not today.

She remembered her mayhem and knew she'd be using it soon. She looked inside and found it waiting patiently.

Not yet, she thought. She knew that she wanted to have some fun first.

She stopped smiling and shook her head enough that her bare breasts swayed.

"Oh, maybe I should leave. It's been fun, but I should go."

He still hadn't looked back up at her eyes when he spoke.

"Don't make me mad, bitch. You owe me a free show."

Lin felt her heart beating strong in her chest. She glanced at the door and faked a worried expression.

"Okay, no need to get mad. I won't leave."

Oh God, she thought, I sure am some kind of tease. I'm just about naked now and locked in a room with a dangerous man. Without my mayhem, I'd be so helpless . . .

"Course you ain't leaving. 'Cause you're so goddamn cheap."

Lin felt a jolt rush through her. Some unknown parts of her began shifting around inside. She looked for her mayhem and found it, but she left it alone.

"Well, I do love getting naked, so maybe I am cheap."

She took a quick look down from his eyes.

"You like what you see."

"Yeah. You'll find out just how much."

"I'm sure you'll make me, stranger."

He stared intently but not at her eyes. Lin stood there wearing only her underwear and heels, slowly rotating back and forth for him, and she craved the mild electricity running through her. Despite being so vulnerable. Despite the danger.

More pieces of her jostled around, seeking a new pattern. They found new places, and Lin knew: the excitement was *because* she was in danger. She felt an undeniable urge to be stripped and in danger, so she pushed her mayhem further back.

"I must be cheap. I bet I look pretty damn cheap right now."

Lin felt her heart pounding a strong beat, and she waited for whatever would come next.

"You'll do more than just look cheap. Get down on your knees."

She felt her heart leap again, and she could barely resist kneeling. Her mayhem swirled just beneath her surface, ready to save her, but a tempting new hunger told her what she needed first.

"Oh, I don't think so, mister. No way am I—"

A quick backhand across her right cheek spun her around, and she held herself up with two hands on the cool blanket.

"Stand up."

Lin stood and felt her mayhem about to pop loose, but she held it back. She knew that he could hit way harder than that, so obviously, he didn't want to hurt her. He was just taking what he wanted, and she liked his way of asking. Her favorite new appetite compelled her to get asked again.

"What kind of woman do you think—"

He struck her again, and when she turned to face him, he reached out and held her chin in a solid grip.

"Not so powerful anymore, are you?"

She felt the fresh stinging on her cheek, fought to hide her smile, and tried to shake her head.

"I know what kind of woman you are. Do you want to get on your knees for me?"

He nodded her head several times and let her go. She faked a worried look and continued to nod on her own, and he stepped back to enjoy the sight.

"Okay, okay, I'll do it."

"Answer my question."

"Yes, I sure do want to get on my knees."

And then, she thought, right after you see how close you are, maybe I'll summon my mayhem and destroy you.

"For who? Answer the goddamn question."

"Yes, I want to get on my knees for you."

Lin dropped her knees onto the carpet and felt her breasts bounce softly. A couple of the larger pieces inside locked into a new place, a place that felt so right, like they finally found where they belonged. She made sure her back was straight and her shoulders were pulled back, and she let out a deep sigh.

"Like this?"

She shook her hair back, looked up at him, and knew she could destroy him anytime.

"Yeah, just like that. You look damn good like that."

She knew that she looked good on her knees, and she liked hearing it. Soon, she told herself.

"What's next, big fella?"

"You do what I tell you."

She fought to not give him a smile.

"I don't have a choice now, not stripped and on my knees for you. Pretty helpless, ain't I?"

"Damn right, you're helpless, and that's the way you like it."

She felt her heart beating all through her.

"Hmm . . . maybe I do like being helpless."

"You like being on your knees, too, don't you?"

She felt a sharp desire to go ahead and say exactly what she felt.

"Oh, I sure do like it. I think I was made to kneel and do whatever I'm told."

"Yeah, that's exactly the kind of woman you are. And after I'm done with you, it's payback time."

She swept her hair back again.

"Payback? Why, what do—"

"When we were fifteen, Lin. What you did to me. First, I'm gonna give you what a tramp like you needs."

"I'll probably have to pretend I enjoy—"

"Then, I'm gonna mess *you* up. I don't have any fancy magic powers, but I can sure break you up good."

Lin glanced one last time at the door and felt her mayhem waiting. But the hunger inside turned her head toward the man standing near. She felt her heart pounding a solid beat.

"You don't have to hit me again—I'll do what you tell me."

"I'll hit you if I feel like it."

"Can't stop you, that's for sure."

Lin fought to contain her smile.

"Damn right, you can't. Come closer."

"On my knees?"

"Hell yeah, on your knees."

Lin's excitement jumped up, knowing that without her mayhem, she was helpless and had no choice. And she wondered if she might be something more than just cheap because her mayhem was a fading memory.

After she'd moved one knee forward on the carpet, she heard Ben.

"Even when we were kids, Lin, just by the looks of you, I knew you'd end up a total tramp."

Lin felt her heart bouncing like crazy, and bigger pieces scrambled about inside her.

"What am I, Ben?"

"You're stripped down and on your knees in a hotel room. You're a tramp."

She'd heard him just fine.

"I'm a what?"

"A tramp. You act classy, but you ain't. You're just a cheap tramp."

She knew that her mayhem could wait a while longer. Maybe a long while.

"Admit it."

She knew that she could destroy him anytime, but still . . . he sure was right.

"Oh, God yeah. I really am, ain't I? I mean . . . look at me. You knew? I didn't even know."

Lin's heart raced, and she reached down for her thighs as she looked up into his eyes.

"The way you dress and strut around? Everybody knows it."

"I sure do dress cheap and strut around, don't I?"

"You must want everyone to know it."

"Everyone?"

"Everyone but your boyfriend."

"Jack loves me."

"What would he think if he saw you now?"

Lin frowned and looked away a few seconds. She felt only a few small pieces still tumbling about. She barely remembered anything about any kind of mayhem. Instead, a relieved smile took over and she let out a big sigh.

"He'd finally see that his girlfriend is really just a tramp."

"And he wouldn't love you anymore."

"No, he sure as hell wouldn't."

"And still, look what you're about to do. You look pretty damn eager too."

Lin's heart rate spiked. Most of the moving pieces settled into a tight arrangement.

"Oh, God yeah. I wouldn't care if he was watching. I want him to see what a tramp I am. I don't have a choice anyway, do I?"

"Hell, no. Don't do as you're told, and I'll keep slapping you around. I think you like that too."

She felt an odd heat squirming through her.

"Mm . . . maybe I do."

Lin didn't feel too many parts moving around inside. Almost all had settled where they wanted to be. The last few fell into their places and locked solid. She knew that they wouldn't be moving again, and she liked them just exactly where they were. She liked who she was and what she was: just a tramp. Stripped, helpless, and on her knees in a stranger's hotel room.

She had no memory of her mayhem.

"Yeah, you're right—I do like it. A tramp like me needs to be slapped," she said. Then, with a deep sigh, she reached out and unbuckled his belt. His zipper was tight, and it took some effort, but eventually, she handled it.

With her heart racing and a peculiar need compelling her, Lin looked up again and said, "Maybe I should just leave—"

He smacked her across her left cheek, but she didn't turn away, and she didn't let go. She only savored the fresh stinging, shook her hair back, and faced straight ahead.

When Ben said, "Yep, you're done talking now, tramp," only Lin's eyes turned up.

* * *

Lin felt the sudden explosion as her mayhem shot out like a geyser from Hell, and Ben couldn't possibly have been quick enough. Her intent stopped time, and everything froze in place, including Ben. Her eyes filled with green fire, and his stared helplessly. She'd invaded him and taken his life.

The world all around her had become a beautiful, tranquil surface, and boundless rivers of magic flowed beneath it in every direction. Her eyes continued to glow, and she felt infinity unrolling to every horizon.

Damn that mayhem, she thought. Why couldn't it wait just a bit longer?

She rocked back up onto her heels and stood. She knew that Ben didn't have a chance. She was drunk and almost naked in a hotel room with him, and her mayhem still flew out in a gigantic wave and took control of him.

She took a few steps back and turned his eyes down to look at the breasts she held in her hands.

"Oh, poor Ben. Didn't really get all you wanted, did you? Now that I know what a tramp I really am, I'll strip and share all of this every chance I get. With everyone but you."

With her hands back on her hips, Lin watched with satisfaction as Ben's terror settled in. She considered silencing him but decided she'd rather hear him begging for mercy in the strange, silent way of a life taken by her mayhem. Mercy that she'd never give.

Ben was locked in place and completely helpless, and there was no need to rush. Lin considered her options before remembering that he'd threatened to break her bones. Silly, stupid man, she thought, and she broke all of his ribs one at a time.

She heard his silent shrieks as she snapped each bone. Then, she went through and cracked them all again. His shrieking had turned into sobbing, but she didn't care. He didn't beg, but she wouldn't have cared about that either.

"You want to break my bones, huh? Try this," she said, and she intended that both of his arms pull out of their sockets. Ben couldn't move, but tears streamed down his cheeks.

"Had enough, big man? How about this, just for fun?"

She shattered each of his kneecaps, but he didn't fall to the carpeting. He couldn't. Lin was holding him in place, just a puppet to suffer her retribution.

She walked up to him and caused his eyes to look down to hers. She saw the insanity she'd caused by unleashing all that pain on him.

She put her silky blouse back on and took her time buttoning it up half-way, leaving plenty for the crippled man to see. She traced tight circles each side with her manicured fingers.

"These really are pretty luscious, aren't they, Ben? A tramp like me, I won't be just showing them off. I can't wait to let anyone at all enjoy them . . . anywhere and anytime."

She snapped all of his leg bones as she continued to stare into his eyes.

"If you survive, be sure to tell Jack what a tramp his girlfriend is," she said and broke his back.

"I want him to know." She broke his neck and allowed his head to slump to the side.

"Better yet, I'll make sure he sees me in action sometime soon." She broke his left arm.

"I bet all his friends will be happy to give me a try." She broke his right arm.

His tears still poured out, but his eyes softened and turned to a normal shade of green. Not a glowing green—he had no power—just a pretty green. And he had hair now. Cute blond hair. Lin almost reached out and brushed the hair back since Taylor's bones were all broken, and she couldn't do it herself.

Taylor!

"Mom," said Taylor's voice, "it hurts so bad. Why, Mom?"

The silent shrieking became silent sobbing as Taylor was held in place with most of her bones broken.

"Taylor, I never . . . I can fix you, Taylor. I can fix all of it. I'm so sorry!"

"I'm sorry about the storms. I didn't mean it."

"Oh, Honey, it's okay. I can help!"

"It's too late. I think you murdered me, Mom."

Her eyes started to close.

"No! Taylor, hang on! Look at me! Keep looking at me! I can fix this!"

Lin found her intent where she always does, hidden within the stillness inside her. As she looked into her broken daughter's eyes, she got a solid grip on her intent. She knew that she needed to work quickly. She found Taylor's magic and wrapped her arms around it. She felt it flowing into her, creating her anew in every moment.

But what to do now? She didn't know how to fix a damaged body. She felt a panic begin to rise as she looked into the sad, desperate, caramel eyes of her only daughter, the girl she'd just destroyed, breaking every—

Caramel eyes! Lin felt a shock wave blast through her. Her daughter remained frozen in front of her, trapped by her mayhem, but her eyes . . . Taylor's eyes were not caramel!

Lin closed her own eyes and locked a tight hold on her intent. The darkness overwhelmed her, and she died. No thoughts or feelings or beating heart.

She focused and held onto her intent in silence, knowing nothing but the stillness within her.

For what might have been centuries slipping past, she held her intent and waited.

A pinpoint of light raced toward her, forcing her old life back around her and chasing away the one she'd just lived.

* * *

Raindrops on her shoulders and two hands shaking her prompted Lin to open her eyes. She looked directly into Taylor's eyes, which offered an endless flow of tears.

"Stop dying, Mom! I can't take this anymore!"

The wind picked up, flapping umbrellas and pulling over tables at the cafe near the bench where Gabriel had taken Lin. Thunder exploded above them, and tourists scattered in every direction, screaming and dragging their children to the nearest shelter.

Lin took deep breaths, but she found it impossible to form any words as giant pieces scrambled inside her. Gabriel took the lead.

"Taylor, your mom is fine. Look, she's looking right at you."

Gabriel put an arm around Taylor, and her frantic tears became only sad tears. While Lin struggled to speak and fought to rearrange her moving parts, Taylor's tears stopped altogether.

"I just wish you would stop, Mom."

Lin held her life in a familiar order and found she could speak again.

"Me too, Hon."

Taylor leaned in and hugged her for several seconds as Gabriel watched quietly.

"I really am okay, Taylor. I don't think that will happen again. Are you okay?"

"Better. But still, it's just too much."

The wind dwindled, and the rain became a barely noticeable drizzle.

"Sit beside me, my dear daughter."

Taylor sat.

"Tell me what you think of Nomad."

"Nomad, Mom?"

Lin looked up at Gabriel, who smiled back at her.

"Yeah, what do you think of that big boy? He's pretty special, don't you think?"

"Oh my God, Mom, he's the sweetest fluffiest boy ever. I try to hug him, and I can't, not completely. His mane is so thick!"

The rain stopped, the clouds broke, and patches of sunlight crept along the pavement.

"And he eats a lot. Did you notice that?"

"He eats a *crazy* amount! But that's because he's so big. He's not a hog or anything. He's just a really, really big boy, Mom."

"And he's strong, wouldn't you say?"

In full sunlight, and with steam rising from the sidewalk, Lin sat on the wet bench with an arm around her daughter.

A daughter with no broken bones.

And eyes of green.

Chapter 18 – A Little Advice

Lin, Gabriel, and Taylor took the short walk back to their hotel suite. On the way, Lin gave a sideways glance to the bar's neon sun, and she felt a warmth inside. She knew what had just happened, and she knew it was upsetting, but she felt stronger for it. And it hadn't worked. Gloriana wasn't able to trick her.

But she also knew that something about her had changed while she was in that dream. Something inside.

"Taylor, Jack will probably be here soon. If you think you might need a nap, now might be a good time."

"I'm still tired, Mom, but I sure feel good. I feel so healthy now. But no matter how healthy I am, I know I need to sleep too. The last couple of days, with you . . . when you were—"

"It's been a rough couple of days for all of us, Hon. I might even lie down in a while myself. Why don't you get going on your nap? Later on, we'll probably all go out for dinner with Jack. And before you know it, we'll all be back home. Sound good?"

"Real good, Mom. Okay, off to bed . . ."

Within minutes, Taylor had burrowed beneath the blankets in a cool bedroom. Occasional twitches and snores told them that she'd fallen asleep.

*　*　*

"Gabby, that was the worst . . . I don't even know what to call it. 'Episode,' maybe? That Queen Gloriana—she can't get the worlds right. I know she's powerful. God, she's powerful. But she can't completely fool me."

"What happened this time? You were only out—"

"Dead, you mean?"

"Yes, you were only dead for about a minute."

"Oh, it seemed a lot longer to me. These worlds seem to be building on each other. The first time, I was just trashy. Way, way more than just the clothes I wore. And the second time, I was cheap and a lush too. I drank so much that I couldn't control my powers at all. It was a disaster, and all I did was laugh about it."

"And this time was worse, you said?"

"Yeah, way worse. I was trashy, drunk, *and* violent. Now, I don't ever want to hurt anyone again. Not even if I think they deserve it. What if I'm wrong? How bad would that be to destroy someone by mistake? I can't just say, 'Oh, sorry about all those broken bones.'"

"So, what was it like?"

"Okay. I was cheap again. And a drunk again. And I was happy breaking every bone in Ben's body."

"Ben? Why Ben?"

"Who knows? Ask Gloriana. But it was Ben, and he talked about hurting me, and wow, did I go crazy on him."

"There was a time when you thought he deserved that."

"And if he would have stayed the old Ben, maybe it wouldn't have been so bad. But he didn't stay Ben. After I broke most of his bones, I saw that it was really Taylor. Can you imagine how that felt? My daughter was dying, and she was begging me to fix her. I can't, Gabby, I'm not Lee. Lee can do that, but I can't. I was watching my daughter die, and I couldn't help her, and she was begging for me to help, but I—"

"Lin, it's okay now. What else happened?"

Lin took a deep breath and let it out.

"And then, I saw it."

"What?"

"Gloriana's eyes. Again, Gloriana's eyes. It was another big trick."

"And you didn't fall for it."

"No way. I closed my eyes, and I held onto my intent. I can always find that Gabby, you know that. And I kept holding onto it. It seemed like forever, but there was nothing else I could do. Then, I felt the rain and Taylor shaking me. I opened my eyes, and I was back."

"And now, you don't want to hurt anyone?"

"I will do absolutely everything else I possibly can first. Even those Shield agents at the cabin when they were coming after us. Did I have to kill them? I don't know now. Maybe I could have tried something else."

"They were coming to kill you and everyone you care about."

"But I didn't even try anything else. I don't like Gloriana's crazy fake worlds, but I'm learning from each of them. In spite of her.

"But you know, I must be getting stronger because even though this one was the worst, I'm not that upset about it. In some odd way, aside from hurting Taylor, of course, it was fun how I was acting. Kind of exciting."

Lin paused and looked away from Gabriel with a smile.

"But I'm stronger now. I know I am. And I'm a better person."

"I believe that, Lin."

"And there was something else about this time. I felt . . . I don't know, kind of funny. Like I was becoming a different person. Or a different version of myself. And in that world, I wanted to be that other Lin. I remember how it felt. I still kind of feel it. Shouldn't I be more upset about it? It seems kind of amusing in a way."

"It's probably best if you don't dwell on it. It sounds like she can't fool you anymore."

"I really hope that's the end of it. She has to run out of power sometime, doesn't she? You know what, though? I wouldn't mind too much if she sent me back to any of those worlds just for fun, especially the last one. I was different, Gabby. So different. I know it's all fake, and it wasn't really me, but it sure was a thrill to be nothing but a—"

A rapid knocking at the door quieted Lin, and she rose to answer it. And at the sight of the man still holding his knuckles out, over thirty years shook themselves loose, and Lin felt fifteen again.

* * *

"Is this some kind of joke?"

"No, it's not a joke. Why do you ask that?"

"You're wearing the same suit."

"So, you do remember me?"

"You and the suit. Not your name."

"I remember your name, Lin. And it's Finity now, right?"

"That's me. You stopped by for a visit?"

"Sort of. I was hoping we could talk a little."

"And just how did you find me here?"

"Oh, Lin, I've been a cop a long time," he said with a warm smile.

"Are you still with the police?"

"Yes. Not full-time anymore, but yes, I'm with the police."

"And what is it you want to talk about? Ray?"

"Ah, I was wondering if you even remembered all that. But I wasn't going to ask."

"Yeah, of course, I remember. That was a nightmare."

"For Ray, yeah, a big nightmare."

"For everyone. I'm sorry, what is your name?"

"Elias Houghman. Everyone just calls me Huff, though."

"Okay, Huff. Ray was a long time ago. What's on your mind?"

"May I come in? Standing in the hall just feels a little strange."

"Oh, of course. Pardon me. Please, come in."

"Huff, this is Gabriel. Gabby, Huff."

They nodded to each other.

"There have been some strange things going on here in St. Simons. I'm trying to look into all that, but I have to admit that I happened to see you when I was driving down Mallery. It just brought back a lot of memories, and it made me wonder how things have turned out for you. That was a lot of trauma for a young girl."

"It was more trauma than you can probably imagine. It hasn't always been easy, but I'm doing fine. Have you been well? You're still a detective?"

"Technically, I'm retired. I'm just doing a little consulting for the department."

"Looking into strange things, you said."

"Yes. Perhaps we should talk more in private?"

He gestured toward Gabriel.

"Gabby's my best friend. We don't keep secrets."

"Well, sure. Okay, then. There have been some unexplained, violent happenings around here. Plus some disappearances. A couple of weeks ago, we found a guy known as Doc dead on a road northwest of here. His buddy wasn't dead, but it seems maybe he wishes he was."

"That's pretty horrible. How could I possibly help you with that?"

"Probably you can't. I mostly wanted to see how you're getting on these days, and excuse me, but I tend to babble about whatever I'm working on."

"No, that's fine. There's more than just that incident?"

"Yeah, the local priest is missing. So is the church organist. They disappeared the same day we found Doc and his buddy."

"Are those things related in some way?"

"I believe they are."

"How?"

"I have no idea, but I've learned to trust my gut. And it's screaming at me that this is all twisted up together."

"Well, I wish you the best of luck. Detective work sounds like quite a challenge."

"Yes, that it is."

He turned and walked toward the door, and after pulling it in, he stopped.

"You know, Lin, it would be much appreciated if you could stop down at the station sometime. I have more questions, and it's a habit I can't shake: I feel more professional on my home turf."

"I really don't know how I could be of any help."

"Most likely you can't. But it would still be nice if we could have a little chat. I'd like you to see Ivan too."

"Ivan? One of your cop buddies?"

"No, he's the thug that was with Doc. We have him in a cell."

"Why would you want me to see him?"

"I just wonder what your opinion of him might be. Tomorrow, okay? Let's not make this a big deal. It's not serious like that. Just come on down, and we'll talk a little."

"Sure. Okay."

"It's been very good seeing you again, Lin."

With that, he turned, and Lin and Gabriel listened to his steps fading as he neared the stairs at the end of the hall.

Lin closed the door, latched it, and leaned her back against it.

"Gabby, I can't be anywhere near Ivan."

* * *

Lin plopped down on the couch next to Gabriel, and she said again, "I can't go there. Ivan would go nuts with me in the same room as him."

"Yes, he certainly would. When you used your mayhem, you terrified him more than anything possibly could. He'll never get over that."

"That's for sure. So, what am I supposed to do? Sure, I could go down there and kill everyone, but I'm not doing that. I can't just leave town. He's a cop—he'd find me back in Pennsylvania."

"No, you sure can't run either."

"Gabby, a little advice here?"

"Lin, we've talked many times about how you face adversity, and you become stronger for it. You don't back down, and because of that, because of who you are, you learn so much."

"Oh, come on, don't make me walk into a building full of cops and try to figure this out."

"There might be a way . . ."

"Now, you're just messing with me. You are, aren't you?"

"Yes. I can't help it sometimes. It's one of my weaknesses."

"What? You don't have any weaknesses."

"Okay, just this one. But there is a way. It's not easy, but I think you can do it."

"Please, don't tell me I have to hurt anyone. I'm not doing that. I'd rather take my chances with Ivan going crazy when I get close enough."

"No, you won't have to hurt anyone. If you stopped time, everything would stop, and you could do things from there, right?"

"You're testing me; I know you are. Gabby, I can't stop time. It just seems that way because I'm in the magic. I'm outside of time."

"That's correct. And from there, you can silence Ivan, can't you?"

"Yes, but that won't help. As soon as I let time start back up—okay, after I come back from the magic—things will go right back to normal. Probably no one would even know that anything happened. I need for Huff to be alive like he normally is and see me next to Ivan with nothing happening. That's what I have to figure out how to do."

"There's a way to send out a wave of your mayhem to control Ivan or anyone else and never stop time. You only affect that one individual. Or two or more if you're strong enough and focused enough."

"How is that even possible? Either I stop time or I don't, right?"

"You must split your focus so that part of your magic rushes into your target's narrow space, and part of your magic stays with you. And the world continues."

"You know, when you put it like that, it does seem possible. But how? How do I learn that?"

"Intent, Lin. Like so many things. Maybe everything. It's all about your intent. You must intend for that to happen. And your intent must be strong enough to hold yourself and your target at the same time."

"Wait a minute. You've done this?"

"Well, no, but I know of a man—"

"Gabby! I don't have time for some theory about sending out waves, doing new things that no one has ever done before."

"I didn't say no one has ever—"

"But you're not telling me anything I can use! I need some advice for right now. I'm going to be face to face with Ivan soon, and he's going to flip out unless I can control him somehow."

"You could always do it the hard way, Lin. You can use many, many waves instead of just one."

"What does that mean? What are you talking about?"

"When you use your mayhem, and you take control of someone, they're done. They can't do anything except what you make them do. Have you noticed that when you release someone, they don't instantly scream or run or do anything?"

"I guess. But it doesn't take long, and then they're screaming and running and everything else. How does that help?"

"You need to send out a wave and take control of Ivan. Then, you can release him and let time resume. And again, quickly, before Ivan can take any significant action, send out another wave. Ivan will never be free of your mayhem. And to everyone else, there's no change in time."

"That's it? That would work?"

"Yes, but—"

"But what?"

"Ivan will appear a little, um, strange to them. He'll seem locked up, like he's having seizures. He won't be able to respond to them in any way. If you go back and forth quickly enough, he'll never be free of your mayhem."

Lin shook her head and smiled at her best friend revealing obscure practices of her power over the magic.

"The best of both worlds, Lin."

"And that can work?"

"Well, in theory . . ."

"You've never done this?"

"Well no, but I heard of a—"

"Gabby, I'm doomed. I don't know if I can pull that off. I don't know if anyone can."

"We'll find out tomorrow. I'm sure you'll be fine, Lin," Gabriel said with a smile.

Lin shook her head and stared at her unbelievable best friend.

Chapter 19 – What Matters Most

Lin received the text while staring at Gabriel and contemplating her looming challenge: how to control Ivan while surrounded by the police. Her frown gave way to a smile.

"Gabby, that was Jack. He just got to the Island, and I sent him the address here. Are you ready for a nice dinner out?"

"You know me, Lin. I'm always ready for dinner. Or lunch . . ."

Lin got a big smile.

". . . or breakfast, or a snack, or—"

"Yeah, I know. Man, do I know. And I understand too. I still can't believe how you could be so patient to stay with me like that for over three decades."

"Compared to fighting evil in the magic? Oh, Lin, it's been easy. Always remember that it was a joy to be with you. It still is."

"I hope so. I'll worry about what to do with Ivan soon. But right now, I just want to see Jack."

Lin walked in and stood near Taylor's bed, listening to the low snoring.

"Taylor." She shook her softly. "Taylor, how about getting up?"

Taylor peeked up through eyes barely open.

"Jack's going to be here soon, and we're going to take him out for dinner. Would you like to go too?"

Taylor stretched and yawned before she answered. "Yeah, Mom, of course. I like Jack. I'm glad he's coming. He should have come with us."

"I know, Hon. It's just a lot for him, you know?"

"Yeah, I get it. Alright, I'm going to take a quick shower."

She threw the blankets aside, marched into the restroom, and closed the door. Seconds later, Lin heard the shower start up.

* * *

By the time Taylor's long shower had ended, Lin heard a knocking on the hotel room door.

Oh no, she thought, please don't be Huff again.

She pulled the door in and saw Jack smiling at her with a bouquet of flowers.

"Oh, my Cowboy. You brought me flowers, Jack?"

"My sweet Cowgirl, yes, I brought you flowers."

Without stepping into the room, Jack reached out and took her left hand. He held it up and kissed it before he wrapped it around his waist. Lin reached her other arm around him and turned her head up for a kiss.

She pulled away and looked into his eyes, feeling relief and a warmth inside at seeing that no effect of her mayhem lingered. He'd been through so much with her, she knew, and still, he was always there for her. That alone was some kind of magic, she thought.

"Jack, come on in. Taylor's not quite ready yet, but soon we can all get something to eat. Sound okay?"

"Yeah, of course. That sounds great. Hi, Gabriel."

"Hi, Jack. It's good that you could travel here."

"I should have come with you right from the start, Lin," he said, turning back to face her. "It's just . . . with how I feel about you . . . it seemed like too much."

"Because I kept dying on you, Jack? Yeah, that *is* too much. I'm sorry, Jack."

She took two steps toward him and reached around for a hug. He held her tight, and they rocked each other gently for several moments.

Before letting her go, he said, "And now, here we are—back in St. Simons. I'm not even going to ask why. Holding you is what matters most."

"Aw, Jack, you're too good to me."

"Well, I love you, Cowgirl."

"You must, Cowboy! And I love you too."

She gave him a final squeeze and released him. Taylor's shower ended, and the blow dryer began a high whine.

"We need to eat, Jack. What are you in the mood for?"

"Anything. How about just some burgers and fries?"

"Perfect. When Taylor's done, I'm going to take a few minutes, and then we can go."

Jack looked over at Gabriel, who only smiled and shrugged.

* * *

Being early for dinner, the restaurant in the Village had only a scattering of diners, all lost in their own meals and conversations.

"Jack, I should try to explain more to you. You too, Taylor. I don't always understand what's happening either. Especially that whole dying thing."

"I'd be happy enough if that never happened again, whether you explain it or not," said Jack.

"Me too, Mom. Just the thought of you being dead, it's—"

"Taylor," said Gabriel. "Your mom is fine, and I bet you're hungry, aren't you?"

"Yeah, I really am hungry. And I feel so good, Gabriel. I still don't know how Lee did that. But you know what? I guess I don't really care either."

"That's wonderful, Hon. I think you're right—maybe it doesn't matter. But I need to tell you both what I can about what I'm going through. Taylor, don't let yourself get upset, okay? Promise me?"

"I promise, Mom. I'll think about happy things. Not about dying. Or even lying. That's still a funny word because—"

"Taylor," said Gabriel, "look, the server's coming."

"About time. I'm starving!"

170

The server took their orders and left. Gabriel ordered a salad and fries and the rest ordered hamburgers. When Lin ordered an iced tea, Jack's eyes opened wide, but he waited to ask her.

"No cocktail, Lin?"

"Not for me, Jack. I'm done with alcohol. It's part of what I want to talk to you about. You probably noticed I'm dressed a lot different too."

"Yeah, you sure are. But damn, you're still absolutely gorgeous. It doesn't matter what you wear."

"I agree, Mom. I like the short skirts and heels, but I like this too."

"And you're probably wondering why, right?"

Jack and Taylor nodded.

"That Scroll, the one The Shield wanted me to read—it was more than just a scroll. It was created with magic, and even the Words themselves were filled with magic. Every time I spoke any of the Words, it changed me inside, but I didn't know what was happening. It was all a setup to get someone like me, someone with these kinds of powers, to speak the Words. And when I did, it was as if I'd opened up a door."

Gabriel listened quietly with no change in expression. Jack and Taylor stared and hung on Lin's every word.

"The woman that recorded the Words—well, that's another story, isn't it, Gabby?"

Gabriel only nodded.

"Anyway, that's not the point. The thing is, she's still out there in a way that's impossible to describe. And she needs help to come back to this world. I'm the first person in twenty centuries with enough power to help her. She's desperate for me to save her, and she's trying all kinds of nasty tricks.

"That's what's happening when you think I'm dead."

Gabriel's head moved from side to side slowly.

"Okay, when I *am* dead. She's taken me somewhere, and while I'm there, in this world, I really am dead. But you don't have to worry, either of you. She doesn't want to kill me. She can't. I'm her only hope, you see? She needs me alive, and even though she might keep trying to trick me into helping her, she'd never kill me.

"Jack, you should just ask whatever it is you're thinking."

"I feel like I should be shocked by what's going on. But for some reason, I'm not. And I'm okay with it. I only know that I love you, and no matter what you're going through, I will always be by your side. If you let me . . ."

"Oh, Jack," Lin brushed at a fresh tear on her cheek. "Of course, I'll let you. I love you too, Jack."

"Me too, Mom. Thanks for explaining all about how you're dying all the time. Since Lee healed me back in Philadelphia, I've seen so much that I can't explain. But I accept it. I'll try not to be scared of you dying anymore. But Mom, please don't. Don't do that anymore, okay?"

"I'll try not to, Hon. But the rest of what I want to explain is how this is all affecting me. You noticed I got rid of the skirts and heels."

"And you're still stunning," Jack said with a big grin.

"Thanks, Jack. That's so good to hear. Anyway, every time that woman . . . oh, her name's Gloriana. Every time Gloriana has tried to fool me into helping her, I've learned things about myself. Things I probably should have seen on my own. I'm glad I can turn her attacks into something positive."

"What else, Mom? Besides the clothes?"

"I see now that I don't need any alcohol. Okay, I guess I never really needed it. But it was something that I'd do, and I don't feel any desire for it now, especially with all the power I have. That makes sense, doesn't it?"

They nodded.

"I need to be as clear as possible. I can't be going around making dumb mistakes."

"Same here, Lin. I'm with you on that," said Jack.

"Not me, Mom. I don't have some crazy power that I have to control."

Lin and Gabriel exchanged a quick glance.

"Sure, Taylor, have a drink if you want. You too, Jack. There's no real harm. I just know that it's not for me anymore."

"There's more, isn't there, Lin?" said Gabriel.

"Yeah, probably the most important. I don't want to hurt anyone again, even if I think they deserve it. Like those Shield agents coming after us at the cabin, they—"

"You saved our lives. They would have killed all of us."

"I know, Jack. Yeah, they would have. But could I have tried something else? Did I even look for any other options?"

"Like what, Mom? What would you want me to do if someone was trying to kill me?"

"Oh, Hon, you should do whatever you can. But I question now, deep in my heart, whether I had to destroy them."

* * *

Satisfied that she'd explained her situation well enough for Jack and Taylor, Lin dug into her meal with an unexpected enthusiasm. So did the rest of them, and soon, it had all been consumed and the plates cleared.

Lin looked at Jack, and they held each other's gaze as long as possible. Taylor must have noticed.

"Mom, that was good. The Village is such a cool place, I think I just want to wander around and check everything out. I'll meet you back at the hotel later, okay?"

"That sounds like a very good plan. Here's some cash—that'll make it even more fun, don't you think?"

Taylor accepted the thin stack of bills and smiled. She wiped across her lips with the napkin one more time and dropped it on the table.

"Thanks, Mom. See you later."

"Lin, I like Taylor's idea. I don't care about the shops so much, but what about ice cream? I don't think I've ever tried that."

"Here, Gabby, you'll need some money too. And I know you'll find the most delightful ice cream ever here in the Village. Chocolate is the best if you ask me. We'll see you later too?"

"Much later," Gabriel said with a big smile.

Gabriel left for a walk through the Village, and Lin and Jack were alone.

"Jack, why don't we take a walk ourselves?"

She reached out to place her hand over his. He looked into her eyes, and she spoke her desires silently, with only the smile she gave him.

They rose hand in hand and headed for the hotel.

Chapter 20 – Loving Each Other

Twenty steps from the door, Jack spun Lin around and lifted her into his arms. She reached around his neck and pulled herself up to kiss him. She looked down only long enough to swipe the room key, and he kicked the door open. Without letting her go, he leaned into the door to shut it more quickly, and she reached up to set the latch.

Lin had left the curtains closed and set the air conditioning on high before they'd left for dinner. While they were gone, the room had become exactly what she wanted it to be: cool and dark. And very private.

Jack set her down on the bed so that she sat right on the end. He looked down on her as she smiled up at him, and he took note of her jeans and t-shirt and even her sneakers with white footie socks visible above the top.

He leaned down and gave her a kiss before dropping to his knees between her legs. With a big smile, he sat back on his heels and began to loosen her shoes. One at a time, he tossed them across the room, one of them striking the mirror on the dresser. They both laughed before they looked into each other's eyes with only the remnants of their grins.

Still sitting back, he reached out and slowly unclasped her thin belt, slid it out through the loops, and tossed it across the room. He looked down to be sure he didn't miss and found the top button of her jeans. They both watched as he undid every button and pulled at the top of her pants, working it as low as he could with Lin still sitting on the bed.

With a contented sigh, Lin stood, and Jack rose to his knees. He continued to pull down, and she wiggled her hips to help the denim over her curves. When he had the pants halfway down her thighs, Lin let out a low moan and pulled his face toward her. Jack moaned, too, as he reached around and held her from behind.

He breathed her in as he held her while on his knees, and when neither could remain patient any longer, he yanked her pants to the floor. Lin let go a short laugh and stepped out, kicking her pants to the side. Jack never let go as his hands still held her tight, and he stood and lifted her up. She wrapped her legs around his waist. Their laughter had stopped.

From there, with her arms around his neck, they kissed. A long, deep kiss. Still holding her lips against his own, he set her on the bed, where she leaned back into the soft bed coverings and pulled him down with her.

Jack had to break the kiss, but only long enough to sit her up and lift her t-shirt up above her, where it held her long blond hair a few seconds until it all spilled onto her shoulders. He tossed away her remaining garments, and she lay there wearing only her tiny white socks.

She nudged him over onto his back and undressed him quickly, all the while looking into his eyes. The ceiling fan above them moved the cool air around, chilling Lin, and Jack smiled at her noticeable response. She knew that he'd want a much closer look.

She swung her leg over him so that her knees were pressed against his sides, and she leaned into him, showing him what the cold air had done. She looked up and bit her lip as Jack tried to help, eagerly giving her the touch she wanted. She barely breathed as she accepted his attention, and she moved only from one side to the other. Slowly. Taking their time.

Lin couldn't help but notice Jack's eagerness for her as she straddled him in their cold oasis. She pulled away from his lips, and she heard his playful disappointment. But she gave his hungry mouth something else he desired—her own. She kissed him deep with their tongues twisting and wrapping together.

When Lin pulled back from the kiss to look into his eyes in the dim light of the room, she heard him say, "Whatever you want, my sweet Cowgirl."

Lin felt her mayhem wanting to rise up, but she knew that it wasn't needed. Not this time. She reached around behind her as she rose up onto her knees. She saw the longing and the sweet anguish in Jack's eyes, and she sat back down all the way until she felt Jack's hard muscles warm against her skin.

She began to move very slowly. Giving her Cowboy the exact magic he needed. That he craved. That would keep him coming back for more.

When he let out a deep breath and smiled at her, she gave him more, and she began to rise and fall above him. She felt her breasts bounce down each time then quickly back up. And Jack held her near her ankles, never letting go of her socks.

Lin felt the magic of her natural powers, the first ones God had given her, and she knew that they were enough for her and Jack. The magic of their joining washed through her, and she lost any thought of using her mayhem in any way. She remembered the feeling of ecstasy she'd get when her mayhem was rising, and all the magic of the world flowed into her.

And it struck her like an explosion: she felt that same pleasure, just her and Jack, just as a woman and a man loving each other.

The wave began to hit them both at the same time, and Lin's motions became slow and deliberate as she brought each of them, together, to a place that left them without any awareness of themselves, and only a sea of ecstasy whose unstoppable currents carried them away.

* * *

After a long embrace, they pulled the covers up over themselves to block the cool breeze from the ceiling fan.

Jack kissed her and said, "Lin, my God, that was amazing. I loved you before, you must know that. But now it's even more . . . I can't even tell you—"

"Jack, I know. I feel the same way. But there's something important I have to tell you."

His eyes opened wide, and he waited for whatever she would say next.

"Taylor and Gabby, Jack. They could come back at any time."

"Oh, shit. Yeah, of course!"

While Lin laughed softly, Jack crawled out from the warmth of their bed and quickly got dressed. Then, he unlatched the door and switched the lights on higher.

"Don't stop, Jack," she said with a big smile as she pointed at her clothes thrown all over the room.

"Oh, right," he said and straightened up the chaos their amorous encounter had caused, throwing her jeans and t-shirt onto the bed. She rolled down the blankets long enough to slip on her clothing and retreated back under the covers.

"And I'll just have a seat right here," he said as he dropped himself onto the couch. "I can make myself do this because I have to. This time. You know I'd never want to let you go."

"Yeah, me too. I'll always need a Cowboy, Jack. Are you up for the job?"

"Yeah. Absolutely. Just give me a minute or two, alright?"

Lin laughed.

"Or with a little bit of magic, Jack . . ."

"You could do that?"

Lin's mind raced back to her recent dream worlds, and she thought of the possibilities her powers could bring. A few pieces inside felt like they were about to move. Soon, she told herself, she'd let them go and see where they ended up.

They continued to look into each other's eyes as their relaxed laughter filled the quiet room.

A soft knock on the door told them they'd made the best use of the short time they'd been given. The door swung in, and Taylor and Gabriel walked into the room.

Chapter 21 – It's Downright Magical

Under a strengthening morning sun, Gabriel led them all straight to a diner in the Village. Plates of food sat before them, including a mountainous stack of blueberry hotcakes in front of Gabriel.

Lin shook her head and smiled.

"Here we go again. I know that's only the first stack. I just wonder how many more?"

"No one can possibly know that, Lin. I can guarantee you at least one more pile. After that . . . well, we'll just have to see."

Lin sipped her coffee and caught Jack's eye. The twinkle she saw there made her smile, and the deep love there too warmed her inside.

"So, Mom, what are we doing in St. Simons? You've explained a lot to us but not that. Why are we here?"

"I can't explain that, Hon. I'm learning to follow my feelings. Or my intuition. I don't know what it is, but this is where I need to be."

"And that doesn't sound mysterious at all . . ."

"Sorry, Taylor. We'll head back soon, I'm sure of that too. But from here, I need to go to the police station."

"The police? What for?"

"You all know that I spent some of my childhood here, and we didn't move back to Pennsylvania until I'd finished high school, right? Well, something horrible happened when I was only fifteen. It was my uncle Ray. He hurt himself really bad, and not long after, he killed himself."

"God, Mom."

"There was a nice police detective that looked into all that, and yesterday when I was in the Village, he recognized me. He just wants to catch up a little and see how things have turned out for me."

"But that was over thirty years ago. Why would he still care?"

"He's a nice guy, Taylor. I remember at least that much about him. It won't hurt for me to stop in and say hi. Don't you have some more shopping to do anyway? You still don't have enough clothes."

"Sure, Mom. The Village is a cool place. I'll just hang out with Jack and Gabriel."

* * *

"Hi. I'm Lin. I'm here to see Huff."

"Hi, Lin. I'm Sam. Why don't you have a seat right over there. Huff just called, and he's on his way in."

Lin sat and looked around the plain room at the desks covered with papers and file folders, some with uniformed officers studying their computer screens. A ringing phone went unanswered, and the donut box on a table seemed to attract a crowd of coffee cups. She took a deep breath and wondered just what was about to happen.

Before she could give it much more thought, Elias arrived and walked up to her.

"Hi, Lin, I'm glad you could make it. Come on, let's walk down to my old office. You know I'm retired, but Sam set me up to get in there again. It feels good, just like slipping on this old suit of mine."

"The suit still looks good. Funny how that made an impression on me, even as a kid."

"And you're not a kid anymore, are you? Wow, more than thirty years has passed since then."

Elias took a seat behind the crowded desktop, and Lin sat in one of the guest chairs.

"I'm just trying to square some things up, Lin. I told you about the homicide victim, Doc, and—"

"It's a homicide, then?"

"Oh yeah, no doubt. Something strange happened to his heart. The Medical Examiner couldn't explain it, but it sure wasn't natural causes. And his buddy, Ivan—we have no idea what's going on with that guy. He seems to have lost his mind. I tried talking to him yesterday, and I couldn't get anywhere."

"And you somehow think I can help? How?"

"No, nothing like that. I mostly just wanted to run some things by you. It's a comfort talking with you. I think I can understand what you went through when you were just a teenager. It's good to see that you've moved past that."

"Well, yeah, I had to."

"It's just that I know you visited the church right before the priest,"—he glanced down at a paper in his hand—"Father Steve is his name. Before he disappeared. His organist is gone too."

"I did visit the church, and I had a nice chat with Father Steve. He was a big help to my family back then. Do you have any leads on where he went?"

"No, nothing at all. Not yet, anyway. If there's foul play involved, we might not get a positive ID back for a while. I was just wondering if he mentioned anything to you. Did he seem nervous? Was he acting funny at all?"

"Not when I talked with him. He seemed just like I remembered him. Except older, of course. And I only saw Father Steve, not the organist. Do you think they left together?"

"We have no idea, Lin. We'll have to wait and see if any reports come our way. In the meantime, about Ivan. It's the damnedest thing, Lin. The man keeps ranting about a witch. He said a beautiful witch took his life."

"He's dead, then? How could that be?"

"No, he's alive. He said she gave it back. It's about the strangest thing I've ever seen. And you know that I've seen some alarming things."

Lin looked down, remembering exactly what she'd done to Ray.

"Yeah, I heard about it. I'm glad I was in the other room."

"Good for you. That's nothing anyone should ever see."

"So, Huff, I don't see how I can help you with any of this. You're the detective, and I'm just a veterinarian's assistant."

"And a bounty hunter."

Lin stopped and stared at him. Elias waited.

"Not recently, that's for sure. I think I'm giving up that part-time job."

"The thing is, Lin, Ivan and Doc were on the run. A bail bonds guy,"—Elias looked through the papers—"named Arnie, he turned up dead too. Burned to a crisp along with his building. He's the guy that would have assigned a bounty hunter to go after these cons."

Lin shrugged and waited for Elias to continue.

"But if he did, we'll never know. Dead men don't talk much."

"That's for sure."

Lin felt her heart rate inching up. He was getting close. Too close. She looked for her mayhem and found it boiling just beneath her surface, ready to rise up and protect her if she needed it.

"Were you working for Arnie, Lin?"

She needed it.

In an instant, Lin's intent stopped time. Elias, the office, and all of the world around her became a calm surface. And beneath the surface, as she had witnessed so many times before, endless mountains of magic shifted and twirled, crashing into each other, breaking apart, rejoining, and flowing together like rivers.

With a deep breath, she felt all of that incomprehensible magic funneling into her, swelling her to the point of bursting. When she felt she could take no more, when the ecstasy of all that magic took away all of her doubts, she saw how easy it could be.

Her goal was never to harm Elias or even to make him a convert. She only needed him to stop caring. To forget about her and what she might have done. What she *did* do, she corrected herself. He only needed to be happy on his own.

Before exhaling, Lin observed all of the magic outside of herself. The magic she'd taken inside still swirled in impossible patterns, filling her with a pleasure and confidence that she could never take for granted. But she reached for the magic outside herself. Not Elias's magic—just the boundless magic of the world, the magic that supported and created everything in every moment.

While focusing on Elias's spirit, she dragged just a small part of the world's magic, one tiny handful, she thought, and guided it into the narrow gap between Elias's body and his spirit. Between his reality and his magic. And though she left her mayhem at a high level, she remembered to extinguish the green light in her eyes before allowing time to continue.

"Ah . . ." was all Elias said, and he leaned back and closed his eyes.

"Are you okay, Huff?"

He opened his eyes and smiled.

"Never better. What a fantastic day to be alive. The world is such a beautiful place, Lin."

"Won't argue with that. It's downright magical. Weren't you asking me something?"

Lin fought her urge to smile.

"Oh yeah, I guess I was. Something about some dead guy named Arnie. But you know what, Lin? He's dead!"

Elias laughed out loud as he continued to lean back in his seat. He kicked the chair back and forth and picked up his feet to let it spin all the way around.

As Lin listened to his laughter, and while she felt the boldness, the lack of any doubts while using her mayhem, she prodded him again.

"And you wanted me to see someone? Do you remember that, Huff?"

"Oh, that. Yeah, some loser named Ivan. We're going to lock him up tight in a cage, Lin, and he can scream about witches all he wants. Who cares?"

"I'll see him if you want me to, Huff. He's already crazy, right? What's the worst that could happen?"

Elias continued to laugh until he finally said, "Oh, my dear, you were a treasure when you were fifteen. I could tell. Such an adorable kid. And now, damn, you're a beautiful woman that probably has better things to do than hang around here with some old fart."

"So, you want me to leave?"

"You can go anytime you want, Lin Finity. But if you want to see Ivan, that deadbeat is right down the hall."

"Sure, let's take a peek. I have time," she said, feeling no threat from anyone or anything and wanting to see if he'd match the Ivan in her dream.

"I'll just get Sam to come with us. He's got the key. Come on."

Oh no, thought Lin. Should she do the same to Sam? And how many others? Or should she try what Gabriel had suggested—to jump from wave to wave, keeping Ivan locked down and helpless while everyone around them believed they lived an uninterrupted life?

Sam joined them for the short walk to a locked door with only a small window covered by a tight metal screen. Sam turned the key in the heavy lock, and Lin walked in. She saw Ivan handcuffed and seated in a plain wooden chair. His eyes moved, but they couldn't find her. She saw his mouth curling up into what promised to be a gut-wrenching scream, and she sent out her first wave.

The world stopped. She knew that the world really didn't stop— she was only in the magic and outside of time—but it seemed that way. Everything became a still surface, and Lin rejoiced in seeing massive layers of magic tumbling all over each other below them.

Lin had taken control of Ivan just like she'd done mere days earlier—the first time she had consciously started her mayhem. She felt the terror settle into an already tormented man while she held him helpless in his seat. She even wiped the scowl off of his face. He was no closer to screaming than before she'd entered his cell.

She let time resume.

"Lin—" said Elias, and she sent out another wave. The tiny beginnings of Ivan's scream were smoothed out as he sat there in the grasp of Lin's mayhem. She studied his muscular arms and took a moment to imagine him without his shirt.

Time started.

"—this—" Another wave, and Lin reset Ivan as before. She knew he certainly could overpower her and trap her tight against his old car, especially if she were mostly naked and balancing on her heels. She could almost feel the cool metal against her skin and his rough hands around her throat.

She let time resume.

"—is—" A quick wave, invading Ivan again and increasing his terror but keeping him almost motionless. And Lin thought of taking the time and sitting on his lap because she knew she had forever. With his eyes only inches away, she could lift her t-shirt up and off and lay it across his shoulder. Then, it would be only the bra covering her as she focused his eyes in just the right places. And she could just slip that off, too, and wrap it around his neck. She could reach his chained hands up to hold her, and she could pull him in closer and closer until he'd finally feel that the terrifying witch was also soft and smooth and warm and—

She shook those silly dream world thoughts out of her head and got back to the plan.

Lin continued to cycle through wave after wave, easily pinning Ivan to his seat and keeping him quiet. Flooding him with terror, which he had no hope to express. And weakening herself every time.

"—Ivan." Elias paused and looked at the man who sat perfectly still, showing only an occasional twitch. Even his eyes remained pointed at the floor, never looking up.

"So, that's Ivan, huh, Huff?"

"Yeah, and it's crazy, but I thought he'd have more to say," said Elias, with an eternity between each word he spoke and between each thought in his mind.

"Hell, I've never seen him sit so still. I thought you might rile him up some, but you seem to calm him down."

"He does seem pretty content to sit still like that. Perhaps he can't find the words?"

"Will you look at that? He's just twitching like he's having seizures or something. Damnedest thing."

All three watched Ivan for several seconds as Lin stopped and started time over and over.

"Yeah, and who cares anyway? Okay, Sam, we've seen enough."

Elias turned to look at Lin and said, "Lin, what's wrong? You look tired as heck."

"Yeah, I am kind of tired, Huff," she said as she continued to send out waves.

They all exited the cell, and Sam made sure the door was locked. Lin noted when they were inside that the walls must be soundproofed because the ringing phones and office noises had vanished. When they'd made it back down the hall, she stopped her rapid waves and released Ivan completely.

Lin heard the screams, but only because she was listening for them. She couldn't hide her faint smile as she shook Elias's hand.

"I know we met at a traumatic time, Huff, but I'm glad we were able to talk again."

"Same here, Lin. It's made me so happy just spending some time with you. I can't explain it, but I like it."

"Good luck with your case. You're a good detective, I can tell. You'll figure it out."

"Or maybe I'll just go back to retirement and forget all about this nonsense. You know, that's sounding like a really good idea. I'm heading for home right now. I'm going to grab that June Bug of mine and show her just how much I care."

"I'm sure you will, Huff. Goodbye."

Lin walked out of the station with a big grin, and at the first bench she found, she collapsed and lay on her side. She managed to curl her legs up onto the warm wood planks, and with her eyes closed, she breathed and fought to remain conscious.

Chapter 22 – Everything Crashes Together

"Lin. Lin, wake up."

She felt a warm hand gently holding her shoulder and shaking her. She opened her eyes and sat up.

"Oh, I didn't even know I was out."

"At least you weren't dead," Gabriel said with a smile.

"Yeah, not this time. But oh God, Gabby, I was so tired after that."

"After what?"

"Learning new things is pretty cool, but when will I ever be strong enough to do all this?"

"All what?"

Gabriel took a seat next to her, and they both paused a few seconds to watch the tourists and locals passing by.

"I'll tell you about the easy thing first. I don't know why I never thought of it before. Converts. I can do the same thing, and they're kind of converted, but they don't care about me. The magic didn't come from me."

Gabriel's eyes opened wide and stared at Lin before they looked back out to the sidewalk and road.

"You figured that out?"

"You knew about it? But you didn't tell me?"

"It's not without risk, Lin."

"What risk? All I did was—"

"Take some magic from somewhere? You didn't create new magic, did you?"

"No, I can't. I mean, I—"

"That small bit of magic came from somewhere."

Lin turned to stare at Gabriel.

"Or someone. Was anyone screaming?"

Lin shook her head and looked back toward Mallery.

"No, I think everyone was okay."

"Perhaps a coffee mug disappeared, then. Better than someone's hand. Or head."

"God, I hope that's all that happened. Okay, I'll be more careful next—"

"It's also a dangerous thing to do, Lin."

"Wait. If I'm careful, and a mug vanishes, what's the big deal? I just made Huff one of the happiest guys around. And from what he was saying, pretty soon, his wife will be pretty damn happy too."

"Yes, and it's a huge temptation knowing that you can do it many times with many people."

Lin felt a flinch inside. Just a gentle tremor. She pushed it aside.

"I only did it to him because I needed to. I *really* needed to. The walls were closing in on me, Gabby."

"And now, you don't plan to go around making everyone happy?"

"There's a part of me that does want to make a lot of people happy. Whatever it takes. Is that so bad?"

"I never said bad. Dangerous."

Lin took a deep breath and continued to watch the traffic.

"Dangerous, huh? But it's so easy, and it made such a difference in his life. Yeah, I do want to keep doing that. I didn't even have time to think about that yet. I barely made it to this bench after what else I just did."

"Before we talk about that, Lin, let's finish on that convert business."

"Okay, tell me, then . . . what's the downside?"

"It's as simple as this: people are meant to live as they were created. If they can get strong enough to find the magic on their own, like you have, that's fine too. But if you make someone overly content, you've changed the path of their lives. Can you be sure it's a good path?"

"What could be wrong with Huff being happier and more content?"

"There are countless possibilities, Lin."

"One. Just tell me one. Because he's happier now than he's ever been."

"Let's suppose his wife tells him she thinks the brakes in her car are going bad, and she asks him to take it for service. Ordinarily, he'd probably get to it quickly because he'd be concerned about her safety. But if he's as content as he is now, would he bother? Would he be so content with life that he'd let it go another day? Or longer?"

"I think he loves his wife. I don't think—"

"And we don't know. Do you want that responsibility?"

Lin took a deep breath and let it out slowly.

"It's never easy, is it, Gabby? I'm just realizing that I don't ever want to hurt anyone again. And now, I think what I'm learning here is that I can't make people happy either?"

"You can make people happy, Lin. A lot of people, if you wish. Just do it as Lin."

She felt something shift around inside, but she focused only on the conversation.

"So . . . John and Tommy? I can't hit them with even a tiny wave? Help them out just a little?"

"What do you think?"

"I think if I see them, Lin Finity will have to be enough."

"Lin Finity is more than enough. I think Jack would agree."

"Well, yeah, Jack sure would."

"And Nomad too."

"Yes, of course. Nomad too."

"Just being Lin is enough. What else did you learn?"

"Okay, my back was against the wall in there. I made Huff happy, and that should have been enough. But he decided to bring another guy named Sam with us to see Ivan. I didn't think it would be smart to convert both of them like that. And I didn't know what I was going to do. I only knew that if I got in the same room with Ivan, he'd start screaming about witches. These guys aren't dumb, Gabby. They'd know."

"And you figured out something else? You didn't take my suggestion and try to hold Ivan without stopping time?"

"No, I didn't think I could pull that off. So, I *did* stop time, and I took control of Ivan. He was just starting to scream, but I put his mouth back where it was. Then, I released him and let time go again. But only long enough for Huff to say one word."

"Then, you stopped time and took Ivan again?"

"Yes, over and over. It worked, but it went on too long. How long was I asleep on this bench? I don't even know. And I'm still tired. But it worked."

"And now, you're exhausted. My way would have been easier."

"Yeah, I believe you. Next time. If there ever is a next time. But Gabby, I'm still . . . really . . ."

She leaned into Gabriel's shoulder, and they sat in the warm sunshine falling all over Mallery Street.

* * *

"How long was I out?"

"Not long. About ten minutes."

"Where are Jack and Taylor?"

"They didn't know when you'd get back, so Jack went with Taylor for more shopping. I think Taylor's happy about that."

Lin looked up at the clear blue sky.

"I guess I'll always know what mood my daughter is in."

"At least until she can get control of her power. We should talk to her about it soon."

"Yeah, you're right. With all she's seen already, I don't think it'll bother her much. She'll just think it's cool. The hard part will be for her to not play with it."

"Exactly right, Lin. It will be a huge temptation for her if she's angry about something, or even if she's happy. I believe it would be great fun to create a storm and send it around like a pet."

191

"So, that's how it works, like you told me before? A Glyphin takes two words and does things, and that focuses their power?"

"Yes. That's how it starts anyway."

"And the second word is nonsense, right?"

"Yes, it has to be. They're mixing something their mind can understand with something that can't be understood. And they both crash together in the space in between."

"And when they crash, that's when things happen?"

"Yes, usually out-of-control things."

"So, they take a word, they imagine another one, one that doesn't make sense, and—"

"That's when they use only two words, Lin."

"Oh, you can't be serious. What else?"

"They can put one above, pointed down. They can put another one below, pointed up, with the same empty space in the middle."

"And they read all of them at the same time?"

"It takes a stronger Glyphin to do that, but yes. Many people sense that words are related to power in some way, but they make the mistake of thinking the words themselves can have power. They can't. It's all about finding the power inside us."

"There's more, isn't there? I know the magic is boundless. I've seen that so many times. There's got to be more, I'm sure of it."

"Yes. There's always more. Infinity, Lin. A good Glyphin can do all that with nonsense words from even more directions. And that's just using their eyes. A very strong Glyphin will see a bunch of words—half of them real and the other half nonsense—and in a visual way, they perceive all of that. They can also, at the same time, pull in sounds from around them. The sounds follow the words, and everything collides in the empty space."

"But the sounds are real, not like the nonsense words, right?"

"Some of them, yes. Just as there are words with no meaning, there are sounds that contain only silence. Glyphins find those, too, and pair them with sounds that can be heard. Everything crashes together."

"That sounds crazy: 'sounds that contain only silence?'"

"You're saying that you've never heard one?"

Gabriel smiled and waited.

"No, of course, I haven't."

"Yes, they *are* hard to find. But a Glyphin can find them and use them."

"I bet there's still more. More than just nonsense words and sounds with no sound."

"There's no end to what they can pull into that space. Just like you, they are limited only by how much power they have. What I've told you about is all I've ever heard. But I wouldn't be surprised if they could bring other things into the mix: an odor and another with no scent, a memory plus one that never happened, a moment in time and one outside of time, a—"

"Gabby. That last thing you said. About time. That sounds like the Islands and the spaces in between. Maybe that's what Gloriana used on the Words of God? And somehow, that caught me up in it? That led her to me?"

"Lin, you amaze me so often. Yes, that's quite possible."

"God. And Taylor's a Glyphin."

"Yes."

"Let's keep her happy until you can help her. You *can* help her, can't you?"

"Not too much. But I will try."

Lin let out a deep breath and stared straight ahead. Gabriel remained silent as they watched cars and pedestrians with an occasional glance to the sky from each of them.

* * *

"How'd it go at the station, Huff?"

"I guess it went okay, Bug. But you know what? It doesn't really matter. I'm retired, and I shouldn't be wasting any more time with any of that. That's not important," Elias said with a smile.

"I'm glad to hear that! You've paid your dues. Let Sam and the rest of them handle it. They'll manage without you."

"What a wonderful world, huh, June? The sun's shining, we have the rest of the day to ourselves, and there's only one thing on my mind."

"What's that, Huff?"

Elias walked toward her and slipped his arms around her waist. June's eyes opened wide, but she wrapped her arms around his neck as he pulled her up tight against him.

"Oh Huff, what the—"

He kissed her again, like he hadn't in years, before he picked her up and carried her to the bedroom, where Elias had no doubts. And before long, and for a long, loving morning, neither did an ecstatic June.

*　*　*

"Taylor becoming a Glyphin . . . that's all because of Gloriana and those Words of God?"

"Whatever else Gloriana was, she—"

"Is, Gabby."

"*Is* . . . she is also a Glyphin. A very powerful one. She was able to imprint magic onto those Words. Those Words were aimed at someone with power over the magic. That's why she made the Scroll so that it would destroy anyone else."

"How could anyone even come up with a plan like that? She didn't know if anyone like me would ever come along. How could she? And she ended up between the Islands of Time, waiting for God knows how long?"

"She probably didn't see any other choice. We might not like what she's done and all the problems she's caused, but we can still admire her power."

"It makes sense. Well, okay . . . none of it makes 'sense,' but you know what I mean. It wasn't until I spoke the Words that I felt a change. Hearing them from Renato didn't do anything. Thinking about them didn't either."

"All those other things that Glyphins focus on—the extra words and everything else, all the unknowable things—somehow, she attached it all to each Word. When you spoke the Words, because of your powers, you did what a Glyphin would do without even knowing it was happening. And she made it all focus on you, not the weather."

"Can I fix it? Undo what the Words did to me?"

"Yes, I believe so. But I don't know how. She created a path to you. You two are connected."

"What's the harm in me helping her? All she said she wants is to live again on the Islands of Time like the rest of us."

"That would take enormous strength, Lin. You're probably strong enough, but there might be other risks that we can't imagine."

"If she's going to keep coming after me, maybe I have no choice but to try."

"You may be right. Or maybe she'll get too weak from trying to drag you in there, and you'll never hear from her again."

Lin paused and shook her head slowly.

"That sounds kind of sad, Gabby. I don't believe she'd want to hurt me. Why would she? She can't take my power, can she?"

"No, she can't. No one can. But do we want her here with us?"

Lin couldn't answer, so they both sat in silence, and after a short time, they rose and began walking.

* * *

When they'd reached the Magic Island gift shop, Lin stopped and studied the items displayed behind the plate glass window. Gabriel stopped with her.

"Gabby, she can't fool me. She's tried three times, and she's failed three times. I've decided that if she sets me up like that again, I'll just enjoy the ride. I won't even let it upset me."

"That's very wise, Lin. Just like when you were twelve, you face your battles and you get stronger. You've gotten stronger from Gloriana's attacks, haven't you?"

"Oh, that's for sure. And not just stronger—I've learned things too. Things about myself. I know that if she tries anything again, I'll learn even more. She's wasting her time."

"I wonder if she can feel the door, that connection between you, starting to close?"

"Could she? The more I learn, the more that keeps coming at me— things I can't understand."

"Like that jewel?"

Lin looked in the direction Gabriel pointed and saw a large burgundy jewel resting on a small pillow.

"That reminds me of the one you showed me in the magic. The one that had a color I can't remember because it doesn't exist here. But I know that color. I'm looking right at it."

"Do you feel like anything unusual is going on? Or does everything seem normal?"

"Normal. This is normal. Gabby, I know I'm not—" Lin stopped abruptly.

"What is it?"

"Gabby . . . not Gabriel. That's it!"

Gabriel only stared and waited.

"When Gloriana took me and tried to trick me, I was calling you Gabriel. I never do that. She never got that detail right. If I ever find myself calling you Gabriel, I'll know I'm somewhere else."

"It's good that her power isn't greater, Lin. I believe you've gotten past a point where she can trick you again."

Lin smiled and said, "Yeah, you're right. Let's go find Jack."

She turned and looked up at the sunny sky.

"And my dear young Glyphin."

Chapter 23 – A First Lesson

Lin and Gabriel continued their walk until they'd reached the small park near the pier. Lin saw that there were only a few open spaces along the rails, and she remembered standing there only days before, staring out at the sea. So many mysteries lay waiting beneath all that water, she'd observed. And she knew that she was the same.

Since then, she'd found her mysteries. She'd embraced them and continued to learn about them. Her mayhem was first: that ability to see infinity all around and endless, unknowable magic below before sending out a wave that could take control of people. She knew that there was no flat surface of the world—Gabriel had convinced her of that. But she still liked the way her mind showed it to her, in a way that she could understand.

After using her mayhem many times, she'd found herself in more danger and in situations that her mayhem couldn't fix. And she'd learned how to use the magic of anything or anyone. It was tiring to take a thing's magic and change it, but she knew that she could do it if there was a need.

She hoped there would never again be a need.

"Jack, is that seat taken?" She pointed at the picnic table bench next to him and smiled.

"I hope so, Cowgirl."

Lin's heart sped up at seeing his big brown eyes showing what was in his heart. And he was just her Cowboy. With all that she'd put him through, he was still Jack, and he was still by her side. That really is some kind of magic, she thought.

She took a seat and pressed up against him, and Gabriel sat next to Taylor.

"How'd it go with that guy, Mom? That detective?"

"Oh, we had a very nice chat, Hon. I must admit, it was a little uncomfortable there for a while. He's someone from a past that I don't want to think too much about."

"I'm not going to pry, Mom. But if you ever want to talk about anything, I'd love to hear all of it."

"You're a sweet girl, Taylor. We'll find time for that, I promise."

"Maybe this is a good time, Lin."

"Good time for what?"

"A first lesson?"

"Oh, I don't know, Gabby."

She stared into Gabriel's eyes and ignored the questioning looks from Taylor and Jack. Gabriel didn't look away and waited for an answer.

"Maybe it can't wait, though. Is that what you're thinking?"

"Yes. We all know what can happen. We all saw it. Well, not you, Lin."

"Yeah. It's still hard to believe, though."

"We can go to St. Mary's if you'd like. Try to find the pieces."

Taylor said, "Yeah, Mom. That storm was incredible. We barely made it out of there. But you, you were already dead, so . . ."

Taylor's smile had faded, and she'd closed her eyes. Lin immediately felt the patch of sunlight on her arm dwindle. A look at the sky confirmed her fears.

"But Taylor, I'm fine now. And we should talk about that storm."

"What's the point?" said Jack. "I know you had insurance. It'll get rebuilt."

"It's more than that, Jack. It's about Taylor."

Lin turned to look into Taylor's eyes.

"What, Mom?"

"You caused that storm," said Gabriel.

Taylor's eyes stretched open as she looked at Gabriel then back at Lin.

"What do you mean? You can't blame that on me!"

"It's not blaming, Hon. You've seen that I have powers. All we're saying is—"

"What? What are you saying?"

"—is that you have powers too."

All four sat in silence with three pairs of eyes focused on Taylor.

"But it's okay, Hon. It's nothing to worry—"

"I have powers too?" Taylor beamed a huge smile.

"You're not upset?" said Lin.

"Oh, heck no, Mom. I can control the weather? That's my power?"

Gabriel said, "Yes, but right now you're not controlling it. Without control, it can be very dangerous."

Taylor's smile faded again as she said, "Mom, you're saying I destroyed your cabin? That I almost killed all of us? Well, the ones that were still alive . . ."

"Okay, Taylor. I really am sorry I was dead. And don't worry about the cabin—that's not the point. Gabriel wants to talk to you about your power."

Lin noticed Jack staring calmly at them, listening to every word with no reaction.

"Jack, are you okay?"

"Yeah, I really am, Lin. There's magic, I can't argue with that. And you have such powers . . . like I can't even imagine. Why would I be surprised that your daughter, your own flesh and blood, has powers too?"

"Oh, Jack. You're the best. How do you put up with all this?"

"Easy. I love you."

"I love you too, Jack." She leaned in for a quick kiss.

"What is this power, Mom? Gabriel? Am I some kind of witch?"

"You are a Glyphin," said Gabriel. "It's a person who can do magical things, mostly using just words. I've noticed that you're very interested in words lately."

"I really am. At the cabin, I started thinking about pigeons. Not pigeons, just the word 'pigeon.' It's a funny word."

"Why were you thinking about that word?" said Gabriel.

Taylor closed her eyes and tipped her head down.

"Because Mom was dead, and I was sad. And I couldn't help but think about how much time I'd spent in hospitals, watching pigeons outside the window. Wishing I could be outside. Wishing I could fly away too. I spent so many endless days alone just wishing I could fly away. And it all made me angry. Just thinking about it now—"

A sharp thunderclap echoed around the Village and through the park's live oaks. There were cries of surprise, and people began running for cover.

"Taylor. Look at your mom. She's right there. She's fine."

Taylor looked up from the table and held Lin's gaze.

"You really are okay, Mom. I won't think about all that right now."

Lin felt the sunshine again on her shoulders and watched it warming the wooden tabletop.

"What did you just do?" said Gabriel.

"In my mind, I saw the word 'pigeon,' and I played with it, Gabriel. That's all."

"Played how?"

"I just looked at all the letters—the way the word is spelled. Did I tell you guys I want to be an author someday? I know I told Jack—"

"Yes, you wanted to get a tablet for that, Hon. That's wonderful. But what else did you do with the word?"

"Nothing. Well, it was some kind of feeling, like a game with words. For each one, I saw what order the letters were in, and I thought about them going the opposite way. Then, I saw them in different orders, like the first letter followed by the third, then the second, then the fourth. I was just playing, Gabriel."

"And you saw those other words one at a time?"

"No, it was all at once. All of the words. There were lots of them, Gabriel, and altogether they made a shape. Some kind of . . . something."

"And?"

"And it felt like I was holding that something. That shape was like a bubble, maybe? I was squeezing it between the palms of my hands, and . . . oh, it would sound crazy."

"Keep going," said Gabriel. "You should suspect by now that nothing you could say would surprise us."

"Yeah, you're right about that! Well, it's my hands, but it's not my hands. One hand feels normal and natural . . . that one makes sense. It's just my hand. The other hand . . . I don't know. I don't understand what it is. I try not to think about it."

Taylor shook her head quickly and looked away.

"Why not, Hon?"

She turned and looked into Lin's eyes.

"Because that one doesn't make any sense at all. It could be anything. I'm not even sure it's mine, you know? It would probably scare me if I thought about it much," Taylor said with a quick shiver.

Lin and Gabriel exchanged a long look, and Lin turned back to Taylor.

"And what do you do?" said Lin.

"When I read all the funny words, it happens real fast. My hand and that other hand thing squeeze that shape, and it pops. It's like a little explosion. And Mom, it feels good. It feels really good. It's hard to stop."

"And *that* is what you must learn to control," said Gabriel.

"But it's so fun. I just think of any word, and—"

"And you can destroy a cabin. Or many other things."

"I didn't mean that, Gabriel. Really. I can't believe I caused all of that. See? Here I go again. The word 'caused' is a strange one too. There's no 'z' in it, just—"

"Don't, Hon. Try to stop."

"Or better yet," said Gabriel, "think about the ocean. Look out at the sea, at a point far out near the horizon. Can you do that?"

Taylor looked past Lin and Jack and stared calmly.

"Keep looking at the ocean. Think about all that water and how empty it is. No boats and no airplanes up above."

Taylor kept staring.

"Look at the horizon and think of your word. Whatever word you think is funny. Play with the word, Taylor. Play with it and focus on the ocean."

Taylor continued to stare, and Lin and Jack and Gabriel all saw her eyes take on a barely-noticeable green glow. The glow increased quickly into a flash, and then it was gone. Gabriel looked over Lin's shoulder toward the ocean.

When Gabriel pointed, Lin turned to see a thick bank of dark clouds far out over the water. Bony fingers of lightning clawed through the clouds, and moments later, they all heard the thunder rumbling in over the waves.

Lin looked back at Taylor and saw the same odd smile as she'd seen at the cabin. She'd seen green light reflected in Gabriel's eyes, but by the time she'd turned to look, Taylor's eyes were no longer glowing. But she'd smiled in a way Lin had never seen before.

And shortly after seeing Taylor staring at the wall of the cabin, Lin had been taken by Gloriana. She'd died. And Taylor had summoned a storm that continued to grow until they'd had to leave, and it flattened the cabin.

"It's important to know how to stop it too, Taylor."

"How, Gabriel? And I don't see why. That storm isn't hurting anyone. Why can't we just let it go now? Let it be like any other storm?"

"That particular storm might be harmless. But the next one might not. Can you make it stop?"

"I can barely believe I made it start. How the heck would I make it stop?"

"I don't know. This is an ancient knowledge that the world hasn't seen in centuries."

"So, I should just let it go then."

"Let's try to fix it, Taylor. Try to push that word, whatever word you played with, completely out of your mind. As if you never knew that word. Like it never existed."

Taylor's face took on a serious expression, then it turned to a look of indifference. She appeared completely calm, as if nothing odd had ever happened.

"I did something, Mom. I found something . . . inside."

Lin turned to see the clouds still a thick roll, but they were lighter, and the lightning had stopped.

"What did you find, Hon?"

"A quiet place. A place where everything was completely still. Even the world around me seemed to be getting still."

Lin looked at Gabriel, and Gabriel smiled.

"You found the stillness inside you, Hon. That helped."

"Can you try harder, Taylor?" said Gabriel.

"You guys, this is tiring. Look at it. It's better than it was."

Lin sighed while watching the puffy clouds drift northward.

Jack reached out and took Lin's hand.

"Lin, I feel lucky to know all of you. Your powers scared me at first, but now, I'm more used to them. I accept it all. Taylor's powers too."

"Oh, Jack. You're wonderful. We're all lucky to have you too."

"But this is also pretty damn tiring. I'd like to go back to the room and lie down for a while."

"It's been a tiring day for all of us. Gabby, we can order room service if you're hungry again."

"Exactly right, Lin. I'll eat while the rest of you rest."

"While the 'rest' of you 'rest,'" Taylor said with a big smile. "I'm not playing with it, but it's funny. You all have to admit that."

Everyone stared at Taylor and waited.

"You guys, I got this. I'm not starting anything. What did you say I was again?"

"A Glyphin," said Lin.

"And I'm your daughter too, Mom. Let's not forget that, okay?"

Chapter 24 – Fringes Of Something

"I should never have volunteered for this, Tayo."

"Me neither," Daria said while looking at the crippled man in the backseat.

"I can't thank you enough. Both of you. The logistics of arranging other travel would be challenging and less enjoyable. Perhaps you have questions for her too?"

Daria held Ozzy, and they both looked at Anna, who only stared out at Interstate 95 as she drove them south to St. Simons Island.

"No, and I still do not understand your obsession with the woman, Lin Finity. She is like some kind of monster, is she not?"

"No, Anna, she's not a monster. You've seen her eyes too. I don't understand why that affected me the way it has. I've wondered if the wavelength of the green light from her eyes matched some minute structure of my eyes but not yours. I'll do some more research on that later."

"Maybe you are just being foolish. Have you considered that? You are a logical man, and the logical conclusion is to run far from her."

"Aw, she's not that bad, Mom. You talk like you don't like her, but look at you. You've started dressing like her. And it looks good."

Anna blushed and forced her eyes to stay on the highway, but she couldn't deny Daria's claim. She'd traded in her drab, professional suit with its knee-length skirt for a tighter, much shorter skirt. Her jacket had been replaced with a thin, low-cut sweater, and her modest footwear had been cast aside. She knew she'd need more practice on her new heels.

"Well, Daria, I can like her style and still know that she is a monster, can I not?"

"Sure, Mom. Whatever you say. You'll probably start swearing again too," Daria said with a laugh.

"Goddamnit, Daria. Like that, you mean?"

And Anna laughed too.

"Yeah, Mom. Just like that."

"Goddamnit, Tayo, why must you go find that goddamn monster, Lin Finity? She is like a thing from Hell, and—"

"Okay, Mom. We get it. You don't have to swear every time you open your mouth."

Anna looked over at her daughter and her dog, and they shared a quick smile before she looked back at the road.

"I doubt that I can explain it adequately, Anna. When I was in that tree, about to launch the rocket at Lin's cabin, I saw her eyes glowing. It was from far away—I don't know the exact distance. I should have brought the range finder—"

"Yes, you should have brought it to help with the launch of the rocket, Tayo."

"I will never make that error again because I will never send more rockets after anyone. But it was a substantial distance, and I could see how bright her eyes were shining. I felt it. I didn't just see it. That's a consequential distinction, even though I don't understand it clearly. I felt something, and I saw a new path for my life. My future lies beyond the green light shining from Lin Finity's eyes."

Anna looked again at Daria before looking back at the approaching highway and speaking.

"Tayo, are you becoming a poet? Or a philosopher of some variety?"

"Maybe. Maybe, Anna. I know I'm not making sense."

"It's probably the pain pills," Daria said with a smirk.

Tayo said no more, and they continued their trek to South Georgia in silence.

* * *

"We will be in Georgia soon," said Anna. "Daria, you will not want those big black boots any longer."

Daria looked down at her boots far below the hem of her short camouflage dress.

"Yeah, probably not. But it's still a good look. Benson liked it too."

"We never discussed Benson. I still do not understand why he would try to kill you."

"I told you, Mom, he went crazy. I think he was probably always crazy."

"He did seem a bit off at some times."

"And Wolfe. What the hell was the deal with that guy?"

"Oh, Daria, he was more of a monster than that Lin Finity. I am glad he is gone. I know now that he had me under some odd kind of spell or something."

"What the hell is going on, Mom? I mean, all the things we've seen. What kind of world is this?"

"It's a world full of magic, Daria," Tayo said from the backseat as the car continued to speed south.

"But I never thought magic was—"

"It's real," said Tayo. "I've devoted my life to logic and rationality. I'm still rational, and I still think clearly. But I know now that I exist on the fringes of . . . something. And I'm looking at a world that I no longer understand. I need to revise my perceptions of the world. Somehow, I must continue to use my logic and apply it to a world that's . . . a world that's really—"

"Magic," said Anna. "So has proclaimed Tayo the philosopher."

* * *

"You have been here before, Tayo. Tell me where to drive this car," said Anna.

"Turn left right here. This is the Causeway into St. Simons Island. When I was here investigating Doc and Ivan, I never went to the Island. But this is the correct route."

"And where is Jericho Road? That is where you conducted an investigation, is it not?"

"That's northwest of Brunswick. We can take a ride up there if you'd like. The unusual growth in the area where Lin used her power might still be visible."

"There is no need. We will take you to the Island, and then you are on your own. Daria and I will not stay."

"Mom, where are we going to go, anyway? You can't really be thinking about going back to Russia, can you?"

"I do think about it, Daria. But no, I am not going back."

"Let's just stay here awhile. I need a vacation, and there's no place I need to be."

"We can stay for a time, Daria. Tayo, you can barely move around without our help. I do not know why you want to see Lin Finity again. She is a monster that can—"

"And now, you're dressing like her, Mom," Daria said before beginning to laugh.

Anna felt her skirt tight around her hips and her sweater even tighter. A smug smile was her only reply as she continued to drive over the Causeway with Ozzy's snout poking out of the passenger side window.

* * *

After crossing the Causeway and turning left on Demere, Tayo directed Anna to a motel off to the left.

"There's a pool, Mom, and they allow pets. Let's stop at this one, okay?"

"Very well, Daria. Tayo, I will drop you at the front and park the car."

While they still stood in the hallway outside their rooms, Anna said, "Tayo, you are on your own. We no longer have any kind of mission. Daria and I are here only to enjoy ourselves after all that has happened."

"You have been very kind to me, Anna. I'd like to explain to you in more detail why I feel I must see Lin. But I can't—I'm not following my logic anymore."

"There is no need to explain. You go do whatever you think you must, but leave us out of it. Do you understand, Tayo?"

"Yes, of course, I understand. And you can leave anytime you want. I'll be able to get around the Island somehow. I don't know how long I'll remain here."

Anna scoffed and said, "Or even why you are here."

Chapter 25 – Countless Sharp Teeth

Taylor was the first to walk into their suite, and she immediately slid open the glass doors and stepped onto the balcony. She looked out at the clear skies over the ocean and turned to smile back at them. Jack set their take-out lunch bags on the table, and Lin and Gabriel sank into the couch.

"I like that sky, Mom. I want sunny skies."

"Oh, that's good, Hon. No storms, at least for a while, okay?"

"Sure, Mom." She turned back to face the sea with her hands on the rail.

"You should eat, Honey," Lin said as Jack rummaged through the kitchen for plates.

"I will, Mom. There's just something about the ocean, you know?"

"Oh, that's for sure, Hon."

Taylor left her balcony view, sat at the small table, and poked through her bag until she'd found her sandwich. Jack took the remaining bags, plopped down in a seat near the couch, and passed everyone their orders.

Still chewing his last bite, Jack said, "Lin, you look tired. And I didn't get a chance to ask. Are you done with the police now?"

"Yeah, Jack, everything is perfectly fine. But I am tired, that's for sure."

"Take the bed, then. You could use a nap. I'm going to hit the couch if you guys give me some room."

Lin and Gabriel stood, and so did Jack.

Lin said, "That's a good—"

She fell silent at seeing a black dot appear on Jack's forehead. She could see his eyes questioning her as she stared in silence. She felt thin trickles of tears leak out.

"Lin, are you—"

She heard no more. The night rushed toward her and blocked out the world. Her breaths had stopped. All feelings and thoughts had vanished. She was alone in an endless night with only the sound of her heart.

Then, it stopped too.

Lin found her intent. It wasn't a thought. It wasn't a feeling. It wasn't even a memory of anything. It was just her intent, deep within the stillness inside her, and her hold on it was unbreakable. She held her intent in silence. In timeless patience.

After what could have been an eternity, a single point of light drew her attention. She couldn't look away as the light began racing toward her, dragging some other world with it.

* * *

"Mom?" Taylor said as she saw Lin begin to collapse.

Jack reached for her and held her as they both slumped to the carpet, where he sat with her in his arms. Her eyes were open, but they didn't move. Jack felt no breathing. He reached up to check for a pulse, and his anguished look answered Taylor's next question.

Beyond Taylor, Jack saw clouds gathering on the horizon.

"Taylor, keep thinking about the ocean. Far out on the ocean," Gabriel said.

Taylor bit her lip as a tear drew a wet path down her cheek.

"Mom's dead again, isn't she?"

"Yes, but remember that she'll be fine. She'll be okay. If you can't stop playing with words, remember to think about the ocean too."

"I don't know, Gabriel. I do *not* like Mom being dead."

The clouds over the sea swelled, and the wind around the hotel picked up. A steady rain began.

"Taylor, you must try . . ."

* * *

A world wrapped around her, and she felt her heart begin a steady beat. Thoughts and feelings returned, and she took a deep breath of ocean air. But Lin knew that she was no longer in her hotel room. She knew that she was a corpse there, and she was on a different kind of island with Gloriana.

Lin looked out over the ocean and turned to her right, where she saw a sun sinking below the waves. She looked straight out and up and saw a full moon, lonely and brightening as the sky's darkness took hold. Before looking to her left, she spoke.

"Why am I here?"

"I speak with you. I ask that you listen."

Lin turned to see Gloriana staring at her with big caramel eyes. Her wild brown hair coiled down past her shoulders, and she wore a gown the color of cinnamon. She stood like a statue of graceful granite, fit, yet feminine, and with no sign of weakness. Her eyes glowed softly.

"What is it you want?"

"I want what I want as countless centuries are counted. To return to the Islands of Time."

"You seem quite powerful. What's stopping you?"

"My power for the Islands is gone. I have only this,"—she raised her arms to each side—"that I create in the emptiness. And I lose that too."

"And you need me to help you get back?"

"Yes."

They both looked back out over the ocean as the waves bounced the moon's reflection about. A fresh breeze from the south came directly toward them from over the water and lifted their hair.

"This isn't so bad. Can't you be happy here?"

"I exist in a dream of my own creation. I create a place, but it is not real. I can create happiness too. But it is not real either."

"It's better than being dead, though. You've had more life than probably anyone ever has."

"And I want more. That is why I sent the Words to you."

"The Words of God? You weren't happy with God's answer."

"No, I am not. I must return to God. But not now. My life is a gift. I keep it."

"There's no shame in dying."

"Do you want to die?"

"No, of course not. But we have no choice. We—"

"You are wrong, Lin Finity. You can do what I do. And you end up here, as I am."

"As you are? You mean trapped? Miserable?"

"Alive. Somehow, still alive in these godforsaken spaces in between."

"This doesn't look all that bad."

Gloriana turned to look into Lin's eyes, and Lin thought she saw the beginning of a smile beneath bright glowing caramel.

"See behind this world I intend."

Gloriana pointed over the water.

"Look, Lin Finity . . ."

A familiar black dot appeared, framed by the moon's shattered reflection. It grew until it had swallowed Lin, and her lungs became solid. Her feelings all perished. Her mind became stone. Her heart stopped, and a silent scream wracked her as countless sharp teeth ripped into her flesh.

* * *

"I'm trying, Gabriel. I really am."

They all watched the narrow trees around the hotel become a row of snapping whips as the wind increased. The sky above the Island had grown dark, and automatic lights around the hotel switched on.

"Taylor, your mom will be fine," said Jack. "You've seen this before. None of us like it, but believe me, she'll be okay."

"I believe you, Jack. But I don't like it. I don't like it at all. I don't want my mom to be dead."

Rain sprayed in through the glass doors, and Jack rushed to slide them shut. Fat drops continued to pelt the glass as the wind lifted one of the chairs from the balcony, chattered it against the railing, and tumbled it away. They saw a transformer on a pole outside shoot out sparks with a loud pop, and the room went dark. Sirens howled up and down the coast.

"I *don't* want Mom dead."

* * *

The scream echoed silently through her as she fought to find her intent. While her skin was chewed and taken away in chunks, as the ghastly claws found her bones and dug into them, Lin looked for the stillness inside her. In that quiet place, her intent waited. She held it with a grip that would never weaken, even as she felt her body eaten away.

In utter darkness, with only pain instead of a beating heart, Lin held her intent.

In the absolute silence unbroken by her silent scream, she held her intent.

For how many centuries, she couldn't count . . . she held her intent.

Until a white spot expanded and sped over her, and she opened her eyes.

* * *

"Mom! I knew you'd make it back!"

Lin saw their faces in the dark room and felt the floor vibrating under her. She saw Taylor smiling through her tears, and she saw Jack's frown and wet eyes.

Poor Jack, she thought. He's been through so much with me!

"Yes, Taylor, I'm back. You can quit being a Glyphin now."

She gave Taylor a hopeful smile.

"Okay, Mom, I'll try. I didn't want to do any of that—it just happened. All I could think about was that you were dead again. It was like a reflex, Mom."

The wind continued to pound rain into the glass doors, and the other balcony chair danced without its partner before leaping and spinning around the building.

"Taylor, find your stillness," said Gabriel. "The stillness inside you. Find that. Quickly, if you can."

Taylor took a deep breath and looked out toward the ocean, which couldn't be seen through the heavy rain. She put her hands on her hips and shook her hair back. Lin saw a very slight smile advance across her face. The rain against the doors slowed then stopped, but it continued to fall straight into the ocean a short distance from the shore.

"Maybe I'll let it rain for a while. What do you think, Gabriel?"

"I think you're learning a remarkable amount of control. But perhaps it's better to let the skies clear, don't you think?"

"You're probably right. Okay."

Taylor took another deep breath and stared calmly out toward the ocean. Sunlight broke through the clouds, poking sharp rays onto sparkling patches on the calm sea. Less than a minute later, the rain had stopped, the wind had ceased, and the clouds began drifting inland.

"Nice job, Hon. You're becoming quite a Glyphin. But really, if I die again, remember that I'll be okay."

"I'll try, Mom. I kind of liked those chairs."

She gave Lin a weary smile.

"Magic is tiring."

"I know, Hon. For me too."

"I'm still exhausted from the last few days too. I'm just going to bed."

"Rest will do you good, Honey. Sweet dreams, I hope?"

"Okay. I can try anyway."

Taylor stumbled into a cool bedroom and snuggled under the bed's thick blanket. Lin took a look and closed her door.

*　*　*

"Lin, I gave up trying to understand you. And now, Taylor too. But I don't need to understand. My job is to accept you. I know that now. And I do. Hey, there's those two words I like," he said with a grin.

"I like those two words too, Jack." She returned his smile. "We'll have to talk about that sometime, okay? But right now, you look like you need to crash. You were tired before, and now, you should give yourself a break."

"Alright, Lin. For now." He gave her another grin. "I really am tired."

Jack plopped onto the couch and pulled a thin blanket over himself. Within seconds, his eyes closed, and he began a contented snoring.

*　*　*

"We need to talk."

"You were definitely dead again, Lin."

"Yeah, I know. How long?"

"Long enough for Taylor to stir up that storm, and it continued to grow. I'm glad you came back when you did. It was only about five minutes this time."

"Gabby, I didn't go to some crazy version of my life, thank God. I was back on the tower with Gloriana. She still wants to come back here. She's getting weaker, and she probably can't keep that up forever."

"She's survived there for countless centuries. That alone is a miracle. I'm not surprised that even she can't continue like that forever."

"I wanted to ask her about Taylor and about the Words and all that Glyphin stuff, but I never got the chance. I made the mistake of telling her that the tower and the world she created for herself were pretty nice. And she showed me what's behind it. What it's really like between the Islands of Time."

"You went there, Lin? And you made it back?"

"Yeah, I went there. It was the most awful thing I could imagine. Worse. But still, I found my intent. It felt like centuries must have passed as I held onto my intent. I'll never let go of my intent, Gabby, I promise you that."

"So, you know now."

"I was there, and I felt it, but I don't know what it means. Do you?"

"Yes, I do know. It's like I started to tell you before, but now that you've been there, you'll understand it better. All manner of death is present there. Well, that's not accurate. All manner of *things* that bring death to you."

"I felt sharp teeth biting me everywhere. It's like a bunch of wild animals, you mean?"

"I don't think so. But that's how you interpreted it this time."

"I hope there isn't a next time, that's for sure."

"Every possible ailment or disease is there, Lin. Those things have no place in these Islands of Time. Where we live is in God's world."

"But people everywhere have all kinds of sickness. What do you mean that it's not here with us?"

"We pass through that emptiness as we move from Island to Island. Each of us attracts something there. Sometimes more than one thing. Those things get to know us. They wait for us to pass through again. And when we do, you could say that they take another bite."

"That's what kills us? It's all from passing between the Islands?"

"Yes, death and old age too. The natural path for every living thing is to weaken and die. And everything else, every bit of order or pattern, it all descends into disarray from passing between the Islands."

"But there's new life here too, right? Otherwise, everything would just die, and that would be the end of it."

"Yes, God continually brings new life. It comes from the magic, which exists only on the Islands of Time. That is the miracle of life."

"There's no magic in between?"

"No. You must have seen that."

"But there's intent. I still found my intent."

"Yes, you did. Very few can."

"And that's all Gloriana has left? Just her intent?"

"And enough power to hold it. In that empty wasteland with all kinds of things biting her."

"But Gabby, the other times I passed through there to get to her tower, I never felt any of that. And it always seemed like centuries. How can that be?"

"It might have seemed you were in between for a long time, but it must have been brief. Just an instant. Not enough time for anything to find you."

Lin turned to gaze out at the ocean and tried to feel herself passing from Island to Island and subject to God knows what in between. All she could observe was a continuous existence on the Islands, in the reality of her own life, and all the challenges that life brought her.

"Do you know how crazy the last couple of weeks have been for me?"

"I do, Lin. Even though it's difficult and you're tired, you're getting stronger all the time. And you're learning so much."

"Will things ever even out for me? First, it was my mayhem erupting on its own until I got control of it. Then, Wolfe and The Shield came after me. I learned some new things because of that, but after we'd fought Wolfe and the rest of them, I was exhausted."

"Yes, you were very tired and weak."

"It would have been nice to take a little break, you know? But right away, Gloriana took me. I was dead for three days, Gabby!"

"Yes, and that wasn't enjoyable for anyone."

"Now, I'm back, and Taylor's a Glyphin. And Gloriana is still after me. Maybe if I just give in and help her come back, then I can get on with my life."

"What kind of life, Lin?"

"One without short skirts and heels. Really. One where I don't drink either, except maybe a sip of wine once in a while. And no violence. If I have to use the magic, I'll find a better way."

"That's all good. What else?"

"I swear, I want a life with Jack and Taylor. And Nomad, of course. I miss that sweet fluffy boy, Gabby. I want to get back home soon. I can have all kinds of power, and I can still live a normal life. I know I can. Really."

"You don't have to convince me, Lin."

She continued studying the ocean in silence.

Chapter 26 – Just For Fun

Lin listened to Jack's gentle snoring and couldn't hide her smile.

"Gabby, Jack is more amazing every day. How can he possibly put up with all this?"

"He's very strong, Lin, but he has no power over the magic. His strength comes from his love for you. And for Nomad. And I think maybe for Taylor now too."

"Thank God he doesn't have power over the magic too. It's just love."

"Might love be a form of magic too?"

Lin stopped and stared into Gabriel's eyes. Before she could speak, Gabriel glanced at Jack then turned back to Lin.

"You might not believe this, but I'm hungry again."

"How could I not believe that?"

They shared a quiet laugh.

"I'm going out for a couple of hours but not to a restaurant this time. I'm going straight to that bakery we passed in the Village. I hope they're open this late. I think I'll try at least one of everything."

With a big grin, Gabriel turned and left the room. Lin walked to the door and latched it.

*　*　*

Lin stood over Jack as he lay sleeping, studying him with a smile while shaking her head.

What an amazing man, she thought as she reached out to touch him. But she pulled her hand back.

My life is unexplainable, she thought, and still, Jack stands by me. He's never stopped loving me.

She watched him a few moments before holding his shoulder and shaking him awake.

"Jack. Jack, wake up. We're alone. Gabby left, and Taylor's sleeping in the other bedroom."

He sat up, pushed aside the blanket, and rubbed his face.

"We're really alone? For how long?"

"I think a couple of hours, but I latched the door just in case. Oh, Jack, I hope I'm finally getting back on track."

She gave him a playful smile and felt small pieces of herself begin to move about inside.

"Sometimes, I feel like a new woman."

"You sure are a—"

"I'm a what, Jack?" Lin said with a grin and her eyes wide open.

"A beautiful woman, of course. What did you think?"

"Nothing. That's what I wanted to hear. That whole ordeal with the Scroll and the Words of God was exhausting. And you might think being dead is restful, but it wasn't. That was quite upsetting. And that queen, she took me several times and tried to trick me into helping her."

"You haven't told me much about that. How bad was it?"

"You know, Jack, it was upsetting at first because I was in a world where I wasn't myself, and I was acting crazy like I'd never do in real life. But now, I know that it was all like a game. And I can think back to all of it, and since I know it wasn't real, it's more amusing than anything. It was kind of fun being different for a while."

A few more pieces shifted around inside.

"I have no idea what you mean. Is it something you can tell me about?"

She looked into his loving eyes, and she thought back to what a tease, what a wild woman she'd been in those worlds Gloriana had created. How it had felt when all the shifting pieces inside locked into place. What it was like to live as a different Lin.

And from somewhere deep inside, an idea took root and grew until Lin knew the only way she wanted to answer Jack's questions.

It'll be just for fun, she told herself.

"Telling you wouldn't do it, Jack. Not well enough. I can show you, though. I think maybe you'll like that better anyway."

"I will?"

"Yep. Me too."

She smiled and raised her eyebrows twice.

"Say yes, Jack. I'll make sure you don't regret it."

"Alright, I'm curious. I have no idea what you're talking about."

"Just remember, it isn't the real me, okay, Jack? It's just a fun way to show you?"

She felt a few small pieces inside slipping around.

"Uh . . . sure. Alright."

"Just give me a minute or two."

She kissed him, got up from the couch, and disappeared into the bathroom, and the shower ran for only a couple of minutes. Jack caught a flash of her wrapped in a towel as she sped into the other bedroom and closed the door.

He shrugged, shook his head, and got busy clearing up the plates, piling them all onto the counter near the sink. After the place had been straightened up, he dimmed the lights and took a seat on the couch.

* * *

As Lin reached for the special outfit that she'd packed when she still thought Jack would travel with them, she allowed a few memories from Gloriana's worlds to visit. She found herself standing in front of Davey after he'd pulled her pink blouse down so low it would need a strong tug to uncover her. And she remembered him yanking it down to her waist. How good it felt for her breasts to bounce free, out in the open for anyone to see. And how far he'd kicked her legs apart, her heels digging in and preventing her from escaping. And then, there were two more strangers eager to take their turns with her. Surrounded, naked, helpless, and—

Lin shook her head to chase the memories aside, but the smile never left her.

That's just some crazy make-believe world, she told herself.

She continued to dress herself up while unidentifiable parts of her moved around inside with each new item she added.

* * *

Several minutes later, Lin let out a deep breath and opened her bedroom door. She knew the weak light from behind her showed Jack her silhouette as she leaned her back against the door frame. Her thin blouse clung to every detail, with the most prominent features impossible to miss, and she turned to be sure he had a good look at both. She wore a tight, short skirt that covered little of her bare thighs. Her legs ended in black heels that were high and jabbed into the carpeting. She held a full wine glass in her hand.

"Lin, that's wine? You're—"

She held a hand up to cut him off. She swept her long hair back over her shoulder and raised the glass. While staring into Jack's eyes, she downed half of it, lowered the glass, and licked across her lips.

"I'm already not wearing much, Jack. And after a drink or two, a girl like me?"

Jack grinned but didn't say anything.

"I always end up naked, mister."

She began a slow walk toward him, and he began to rise up from the couch. But she'd already closed the distance, and with a hand on his shoulder, she tipped him back onto the cushions. She stepped in close to the couch with one heel on each side of his legs, and when he reached for her hips, she brushed his hands aside.

"Look but don't touch, fella. But look all you want."

He gazed up with a big grin as she popped another button of her blouse then took a big swallow of her wine. She ran her left hand down along her thigh to the bottom of her skirt and began pulling it up. When she'd gotten as close as she could to showing him what, if anything, she wore beneath it, she stopped, tipped the glass back, and emptied it.

When she looked down, she saw that he was leaning in close, but he'd managed to keep his hands to himself. He looked about ready to speak, so she pressed a manicured fingertip to his lips.

"Shh . . . big fella. Straighten my skirt out for me before I take a little stroll for you."

His hands shook as he grabbed her skirt at each side and carefully pulled it down over her thighs while Lin rested her hands on her hips. When he'd finished, he pulled his hands back and looked up at her smiling down at him.

"Before I go, I believe this shirt is hiding too much of me. Whatever should I do? Oh, I know."

With one hand, she opened the remaining buttons from the top to the bottom. She pulled the material to each side, far enough to give him a nearly complete view, but keeping two important details still hidden. She ran her fingertips down between her breasts, all the way down to her navel and to the top of her skirt.

Then, she turned, shook her hair back over her shoulders, and began a slow strut back into the bedroom. Jack found the courage to stand and follow a few steps behind her. With her blouse so close to opening completely, she leaned against the dresser and raised the wine bottle to her lips.

"I better keep my lips tight around it, don't you think? You wouldn't want me to spill even a drop."

She tipped it up high, chugging a few good swallows.

"Bet that was a sight. Give you any ideas, big fella?"

Jack grinned, nodded, and said, "Oh, hell yeah."

She put the bottle on the dresser and looked down from his eyes.

"You look like you might want something from me, stranger."

She looked back up into his eyes. Jack only stared back as if he were hypnotized.

"Mm . . . I know what you need. You need to watch me get these clothes off so I can be a bad, bad girl—for anyone that might be watching. I know I'll have to do anything they tell me."

Jack's smile grew as he continued to stare.

"I bet you want me to keep these heels on, but you probably want this blouse out of the way."

Looking him in the eye, she held the fabric in each hand, and Jack couldn't look away from her breasts barely out of his sight.

"They're almost out for anyone to see."

Jack continued to stare.

"And for anyone to touch."

The sheer cloth pulled back farther until the two things she knew mattered most to Jack at that moment were just behind the edges of the cloth. So close to popping out in the open.

"I think I'd rather lose this skirt first. I want to be mostly naked when I share those."

Jack stared with a silly grin.

"Then, I'm afraid I'll have to share every part of me."

"Oh my God . . ." Jack whispered.

"Oh dear . . . am I wearing panties? The kind of woman I am, probably not. But I don't think you'll let me stop now."

Jack stared at her skirt as she rubbed her way down her sides to the top band. Her manicured fingers slipped inside, and she wiggled her hips as she worked the stretchy material down over her hips and her behind. He stared at Lin's belly as a thin strand of elastic came into view first. It rose up around her hips, and when her skirt continued its descent along her thighs, he saw an almost transparent, very small triangle of white cloth conforming to every detail.

"Oh, that doesn't really cover much, does it, tough guy?"

"No, it sure doesn't," he said with a big smile.

"Yeah, you do like that, stranger," she said with another glance down.

"Almost there, big fella. I just love having an audience watch me get naked. Here's a view you might like."

Jack kept smiling, and Lin turned away and continued to work the tight skirt down her thighs. It dropped to the floor around her heels, and she stepped each foot out and kicked it aside.

"That's better," she said as she stood before him in heels, an unbuttoned shirt about to open up, and a tiny piece of thin cloth.

She ran her hands back up her thighs, over her behind, then up her sides.

"Just a few more little things, mister."

She reached up and held her breasts through the thin cloth.

"These are always welcome when I share them. And I always share them. Mm . . . I just love showing them off."

She held the bottom of the blouse and pulled it straight down, making more obvious two parts of her driving Jack crazy. He could see the curves of her breasts and all the way down to her thin panties. He took one more look down along every inch of her legs, then down to her heels, sharp and sticking into the carpet.

He looked back into her eyes.

"Why, I'm almost naked now. I'm sure I couldn't stop anyone from doing whatever they wanted with me."

She arched her back and stretched her blouse straight down again. Jack couldn't find any words.

"And I'm afraid I'd have to do every naughty, nasty thing anyone wants me to do. I wouldn't have a choice, would I, mister?"

She licked across her lips and shook her hair back. Jack started shaking.

"You might as well take what you want, big fella. Before everyone else does."

With a deep growl, Jack moved in and reached around her waist, and Lin wrapped her arms around his neck. His hands immediately squeezed her behind, and they found each other's lips. He kissed her long and deep as his hands moved along her back, up under her blouse.

Lin reached for her shirt up near its collar and pulled it down slowly over her shoulders. She spread it open and dropped it behind her, covering Jack's hands and trapping her own. She managed to pull him in close so that he could feel her hot and poking against his chest.

They resumed their deep kiss, and then she pulled her hands free. She hooked her thumbs under the thin elastic stretched around her hips.

"If I were to lose my panties, I couldn't stop anyone. I'd be naked and helpless, stranger."

Jack tossed her blouse back over his shoulder and dropped to his knees. Lin reached out and played with his hair and said, "Do you want me naked and helpless, mister?"

She watched as Jack nodded and reverently began pulling her panties down. She moaned and wiggled her hips slowly until he'd moved the snug elastic half-way down her thighs. His hands returned to her behind, and he looked up at her. Lin felt a few more unknown pieces shifting inside as she gazed at the natural madness in his eyes.

"Oh no, what are you going to make me do, tough guy?"

Jack stood and lifted her into his strong arms. Her long blond hair hung down, and she smiled up at him, wearing only her heels and thin panties tight around her thighs.

He laid her on the bed and reached down with one hand to finish undressing her. Their lips met, and Lin fought to keep from laughing at how she'd nearly driven him insane.

But she didn't laugh and neither did he. And a savage, wanton magic filled the room as Jack's madness savored everything Lin had offered.

* * *

They collapsed onto the sheets, both covered in sweat, and Jack pulled her close for another long, deep kiss.

"Lin . . . oh my God."

"Mm . . . that was good, mister."

"Is that what you wanted to show me? About your weird dreams? You were like that?"

"That was a good start, big fella. A girl like me? Once I lose my clothes, I'm always ready for more. I just can't say no."

"Oh, you're such a—"

"I'm a what, stranger?"

Lin stared and waited for him to finish.

"A tease. You're such a tease."

"Hmm. I sure am a tease, mister."

Lin intended her mayhem, and Jack only smiled at the green fire in her eyes before time stopped, and infinity expanded all around her. The world became a tranquil surface, and she saw complex rivers of magic flowing in every direction below it. She took a deep breath, held it long enough to get a rush of pleasure from it, then released a thin stream of magic into Jack.

Just a part of Jack.

And she let time resume.

"Oh God, Lin, you really can do that?" he said as he looked down then back into her eyes.

Lin lay back against the pillows and reached up to hold her breasts. She slid her tongue along her lips and said, "Looks like you still need something from me, tough guy. I'm naked and helpless, and you can do anything you can imagine."

Jack raised himself up on his elbow and felt the renewed passion the magic had given him. Lin reached down and rubbed the outsides of her thighs and said, "I sure can't stop you, stranger."

He didn't disappoint her. More magic, natural and overpowering, filled the quiet room. After loving her every way he could, he placed his hands on the sheets to each side of her. He held himself above her, kissing her lips, her cheeks, her neck and ears, and Lin felt the sheets rubbing beneath her. She ran her hands up his muscular arms, over his strong shoulders, and down his back to hold his trim waist. She tipped her head back and let out a soft moan.

He dropped onto his side next to her, and his eyes showed a fatigue and a satisfaction that Lin had never seen before.

Although he still hadn't caught his breath, he grinned when he saw Lin's eyes begin a soft green glow.

"Oh, Lin, I don't know—"

"I sure am a bad girl, fella."

She let out a low moan, and he watched as she reached down to the insides of her thighs.

"And I sure am naked and helpless."

She moved her hands up, fingertips gliding along her soft, smooth skin, caressing everything along the way until she reached her breasts. She swirled her manicured fingertips around in tight circles while she looked him in the eye. One finger continued until it found her lips, and she held it tight.

Lin looked down with a smile and saw that her magic hadn't missed. She pulled her finger out and said, "There's no way I can stop you, mister."

Chapter 27 – You Were Dead

After Lin had finally put her powers aside and allowed a content but exhausted Jack to collapse, she'd slipped out of bed and put on her pajamas and white footie socks. Back under the covers, they spent the night in each other's arms, even though Jack mostly resembled a dead man. As the sun began to wedge its way into their quiet room, he awoke, pulled her close against him, and kissed her.

"Welcome back, Jack," she said with a smile. "Looks like it was your turn to play dead. I checked a couple of times to be sure you were breathing. You never heard Gabby come back, did you?"

"No, not at all. My God, Lin, I'm still tired. You are the most beautiful, most incredible woman ever. I knew you were sexy, but damn. Whew . . ."

He let out a deep sigh and rolled onto his back, but his right arm remained around her waist.

"Jack, before you ask, I want to tell you that was not what my dreams were like. I never actually did anything with anybody."

"But you were sexy like that?"

"Yeah, Jack, I was such a tease. But I didn't choose those worlds."

"So, it was like watching a movie?"

"No, not really. My feelings mostly matched what I was doing. I wanted to do everything I did."

"So, you liked what you were doing?"

Lin paused and bit her lip as she looked into Jack's eyes. He waited for an answer.

"I think that must have been part of the trick, Jack. To make me feel like that too. She took parts of my memory, I think, and she tried to create a world with it. It was all exaggerated and crazy—not like the real me."

"But still, you must have been really sexy."

He gave her a quick kiss.

"Jack, I was a total tease. That woman—that other me—would be a tease for anyone."

Jack got a big smile.

"Well, you did totally enjoy your short skirts and heels. That's a little bit of teasing."

Lin coughed.

"Well, okay. Yeah, I guess I was a little bit of a tease. But nowhere close to that other me."

"I'd never want you to be like that. But how you were last night? God . . ."

"You liked me being a tease for you, Jack?"

"Hell yeah, and I know it was just for fun. God, that was good."

"So, I could do that again? I could play like that again?"

She held her breath and waited.

"Oh, hell yeah. You're good at it."

Lin let out a big sigh.

"Good, because I liked being like that for you. I liked pretending I was the other me."

"You couldn't have enjoyed it as much as I did."

"I don't know, Jack. I feel like I can play that part even better next time."

"I can't imagine how."

"I can," she said as a few memories raced through her and were gone.

He reached down along her long pajama pants, feeling her strong thighs before she brought her knees up, and he continued until he'd found her socks. He squeezed her feet and played with her toes before he slid her pants up and massaged her calves.

"But this Lin is really sexy too. Maybe even more sexy."

He reached back up around her waist, she straightened out her legs, and he squeezed her close for a deep kiss.

"It makes you seem completely innocent. But sometimes, you're not innocent at all."

"Oh, I think you might be right about that, Jack."

His hands got a grip on the elastic band at the waistline of her pajamas.

"Jack," she said between kisses, "everyone's here. Maybe we shouldn't."

Jack had already started pulling at her pajama pants, and they were halfway down her behind, which he rubbed and squeezed while he kissed her neck and ears.

"Of course, I suppose we could be very quiet, Cowboy . . ."

He worked her pants down just a little bit more, and she turned her back to him. He gave her his full attention and kissed and nibbled the back of her neck as his own powers gave Lin a smiling, but hushed, start to her day.

* * *

"Maybe you should get me dressed, Cowboy. Can you stand to cover me back up?"

"I think I can do it. It'll be hard, though," he said as he slid her pajama bottoms back up to her waist.

"Funny guy," she said with a grin.

Lin rolled over, wrapped her arms around him, and kissed him several times.

"Taylor will be up soon. Why don't we get dressed—really dressed—and head out for some coffee?"

He kissed her and said, "Coffee sounds good, but I'll drink it black. I've already had more sugar than any man deserves."

"Oh, Jack." She nuzzled in and hugged him tight. Then, she smacked his behind as well as she could beneath the thick blanket.

"Okay, big fella," she said with a smile. "Get moving."

They both dressed quickly and crept quietly out of the room. The sun was just beginning to venture across a clear blue sky, and the pavement was dry and clean from the storm no one had forecast. A short walk hand-in-hand brought them to Lin's new favorite coffee shop in the Village.

"That bench looks perfect, Jack. Over there under the awning. It's going to be a hot one today."

Seated up against each other, Jack drank half of his coffee and looked down at Lin's knees.

"I love your new style. Don't get me wrong—the other wardrobe was like another kind of power you have. Really hot. But there's something even hotter about you now. Those shorts, I mean . . . just . . . wow. You've never looked better."

Lin laughed and said, "You know, Jack, it might be just because you know what's under the clothes, no matter what I wear."

Jack smiled and nodded and said, "And I absolutely love every inch of what I know is under there. And I bet you're more comfortable dressed like this, right?"

"Yeah, it's a different kind of comfort. But it's nice dressing up too. And I still can if I feel like it. If I'm feeling like a bad girl," she said and gave him a big smile. "I think maybe I'm really—"

Lin stopped and looked across Mallery.

"Oh no, Jack. Don't look. Oh, too late. They saw us."

John and Tommy smiled and waved and began the walk across the street toward them. They still wore reasonable smiles as they stood only several feet from her. John was the first to speak.

"Hi, Lin. It's really good to see you again."

"Yeah, it really is," said Tommy.

"You guys. You're stalking me now?"

"No, Lin, I don't ever want to bother you. I was only hoping to see you one more time. I have a good job back in Cleveland, and I'm not about to give that up."

"And I love my family," said Tommy. "I'm just trying to understand what happened. I've never felt so happy in my life, and I have no idea why."

"I was a different man for almost a week. And then . . . poof . . . back to how I was before. I miss it," said John.

"Remember me?"

Jack stood to greet the two men who had ignored him completely.

"Oh yeah, I remember you. From the reunion," said John. "Hi."

"You guys aren't planning on bothering my Lin, are you?"

"No, not a chance," said Tommy.

"No, we just . . . hell, I don't know what we want," said John.

"I know what you want. You want to feel that again like you did before. Isn't that right?"

John got a big smile.

"Yeah, whatever it was. It was real, wasn't it?"

"It was real," Lin said. "You guys, I think what I have is like a strong aura. It can affect you if you're close enough at the right time."

"Like when Davey got messed up?" said Tommy.

"Yes, exactly like that. When are you guys leaving?"

John glanced at his watch and said, "Our bus leaves in about thirty minutes two blocks from here. We need to get going if we're going to catch it."

"You guys did help me at the reunion. You were both very brave."

"I remember, Lin. I would have died for you, and I didn't even know you," said John.

"And you're both going back to your lives?"

Jack looked from the two guys to Lin and back at the two guys.

"Yeah, I'm definitely going back," said John.

"Me too."

"Okay. Close your eyes."

They closed their eyes.

Lin intended her mayhem, and the world around her became a calm surface, beautiful and still. She knew it still moved, but it was so dreadfully slow that it could barely be noticed. Beneath the frozen world, limitless layers of magic flowed in every direction, creating mad patterns that would never be repeated.

She drew in a deep breath and felt the magic flowing into her, expanding her, filling her to every corner. And she remembered the drunken dream, when the magic didn't just flow into her—it had acted weird, moving in *and* out. Lin observed the timeless streams of magic billowing up from the endless depths, and she wondered if she could slow the magic down. If she could cause the timeless river of it to slow and maybe even stop.

She intended the magic to slow, and she felt it hold a moment, then it began to withdraw. She still saw the world as a calm surface as the magic spilled from her back into the churning, chaotic fields below. As the magic left her, she tightened her grip on her intent, and she felt the magic of the world slow even further.

As the last traces of magic left her, and she had no concern for John or Tommy or Jack motionless beside her, Lin saw a single black dot appear directly in front of her. Her eyes locked on it, and she couldn't turn away. The point grew, racing toward her, dragging an empty blackness with it until it covered her.

Lin couldn't breathe. She couldn't think, and she couldn't feel.

Then, her heart stopped.

She found herself alone in the spaces between the Islands of Time. If she could have panicked, she might have, but she held her intent with her unbreakable hold on it. She held her intent in the stillness within her, and when things began to bite, and when things began to claw at her, she intended her return to the Islands.

It was just a tiny white spot appearing where her world had disappeared, how many lifetimes ago she couldn't guess. It grew and raced toward her, dragging her world with it. Soon, it had covered her.

After her heart began a steady beat, Lin could feel relief and could think about what she'd felt in those vast empty spaces between the Islands. She took a deep breath and opened her eyes to the world.

* * *

Lin found herself slumped against Jack on the bench. She could feel him shaking as he held her tight. He was speaking or mumbling, she noticed. No, he was praying. Jack was asking God for help. For her life.

"Jack," she said without moving. "I'm okay, Jack."

He fell silent and tightened his hold on her. She felt his hands warm against her, and she began to shiver. Jack rubbed up and down her arm and continued to keep her close.

"Thank God, Lin. Are you sure you're alright?"

Lin sat up straight, and he kept one arm around her. She touched her own bare leg and felt that it was cold. She noticed the abundant daylight and clear skies.

"Taylor didn't know this time, did she?"

"No, we've been sitting here for a while. I'm sure she's fine—see the sky?" Jack gave her a weak laugh. "But I haven't seen her or Gabriel."

"Where are John and Tommy? They were standing right there."

"Oh, Lin, they got scared and left. I told them you'd been blacking out, and they should probably go catch their bus. They're well on their way back to Cleveland by now."

"How long, Jack?"

"About four hours. I really have to use a restroom," he said and laughed softly.

"Jack, thanks for staying with me. I'm sorry I put you through that."

"That woman, Gloriana, she took you again?"

"No," Lin said as she stretched her arms forward. "That was pretty awesome, Jack. I did that. I did that all on my own."

"You did what? You killed yourself? Is that really something to be happy about?"

"Well, when you put it that way, no. But Jack, it wasn't Gloriana this time. I don't know if I can explain it to you, but I traveled there on my own. And I found my way back."

"It took you four hours, though. You're still cold. You were dead."

"But I'm not afraid of it anymore. She can't scare me anymore, Jack. This is good!"

"It might not scare you, but what about the rest of us? Those two guys, they got pretty pale, and they kind of ran to catch their bus. They were happy to be leaving."

"Good, I can forget about them. They're not important."

"I was scared too. I knew you'd come back, but still, I sat here with a dead Lin for four hours. It's not fun, Lin."

"But you love me, don't you, Jack?"

He smiled and took a deep breath.

"Yeah, I love you. Dead or alive."

He pulled her into him, and she wrapped an arm around his waist. And they sat there only a few minutes before Jack said, "Lin, I really need to go. We can warm you up later."

"Okay, Jack. I have to go now too. I guess being dead doesn't really stop all that."

* * *

A hurried walk brought Lin and Jack back to their suite at the hotel. Gabriel had found the two chairs Taylor's storm had whisked away and placed them back on their balcony. Taylor lay across the bed with her headphones on. Jack walked straight into the restroom before greeting anyone.

"Lin, you're back. That was a long walk for you and Jack."

Lin glanced over to see that Taylor wasn't listening.

"Gabby, I was dead again. For about four hours. Jack sat with me the whole time."

"Lin, I'm sorry to hear that. Gloriana should be—"

"No, it wasn't her. I found the way in myself. How to get between the Islands of Time. Now, if I talk to Gloriana again, it will be on my terms. She's not pulling my strings anymore."

"Lin, you astound me so often. You're learning incredible things without anyone helping at all. When we have more time, tell me how you did it."

"You think you might want to go there again? I felt things starting to bite at me. It's not a good place."

"No, I have no desire to go there. But I'd like to know how you do it, and I bet you want to tell me," Gabriel said and smiled.

"Yes, I certainly do. Soon, I'd like to tell you—"

Lin's phone rang in her pocket just as Jack joined them, and she took it out to see who was calling.

"Hi, Lee."

"Hi, Lin. I'm back home in Jacksonville. I just wanted to see how things are going for you."

"Oh, it's interesting, that's for sure. All kinds of crazy stuff going on, like usual. How are you? How's Ben?"

"I'm fine, but Ben took off."

"Back to Luanne, probably."

"I don't think so. She dumped him."

"She did? After he's become a good guy again?"

"She never knew it. She got tired of the old Ben. Gave him a call. Ended it just like that."

"So, you're back home. How are—"

"Quit staring at me, Alessa, you're giving me the creeps! I'm on the phone! Sorry, Lin."

"Is everything okay?"

"That girl's just getting weird, that's all. It's worse with Alex gone."

"I'm surprised. Did she miss you? Is that the problem?"

"Forget about her. Look, I just wanted to check in to see how you were. But with this crap at home, I'm dumping her back at her grandma's and coming up to the Island. I'll see you tomorrow morning."

"No, don't. I won't be here. I'm leaving for home in the morning."

"Fine, Lin. Keep in touch."

Lee ended the call.

Lin held the phone away and looked at it before sliding it back into her pocket.

"Well, that was weird. Something's going on with Lee."

"And we're leaving, Lin? You're done with St. Simons?"

"Yes. I didn't know why I came here, Gabby, until just a little while ago. I didn't plan it, but I've tied up some loose ends here. John and Tommy have seen enough. They won't think I'm special anymore. I'm some woman that blacked out on a sidewalk bench. That'll be their last memory of me, and they'll be happy to get back to their lives and forget about me.

"Ivan was a problem waiting to happen too. That detective wouldn't have stopped. He would have put the pieces together and tracked me down. Even if I hadn't hit him with that convert magic, he saw me in the same room with Ivan, and he didn't go crazy, like Huff probably thought he would. Huff is back in his life, too, and he doesn't care about the case at all.

"And most importantly, I've learned how to travel between the Islands of Time. I can't explain it, but it seems I needed to be here for that. I've done that. I can do it again if I want."

Lin saw that Taylor had slipped her headphones down around her neck.

"But all I want is to go home. I miss Nomad."

"We're going home, Mom? Already?"

"Yeah, Hon, tomorrow morning. It's been fun, but I miss Nomad too much. Don't you?"

"Oh yeah, I sure do. He's such a good boy. And we got to shop and hang out for a while. And I got to whip up a monster storm because I'm a Glyphin." She paused to smile at Gabriel. "Let's go home."

Lin just shook her head and smiled at Taylor, a girl who had been ill for so long. But now she's cured—Lee cured her—and she might even have her powers under better control, Lin hoped.

"Mom, I almost got worried you were gone so long. Is everything okay?"

"Yeah, Hon, everything is good. And yes, I'm still alive. Have you two had enough to eat?"

"We had a good breakfast, Lin. And Taylor and I have had a good talk."

"About me being a Glyphin, Mom. Who would have thought any of that could be possible? Just a couple of days ago, I was sick and lying . . . uh-oh, Gabriel . . . there's that word again—'lying.'"

"And you don't have to think about it, do you, Taylor? You can let it go?"

"Yeah, I can let it go because I'm happy we're going home. And I won't want it to rain on Nomad. I can't even imagine drying all that fur. Or even trying! Uh-oh, Gabriel: lying, drying, and trying!"

A loud thunderclap sounded directly above them.

"Taylor," said Lin, "maybe caffeine isn't the best idea."

"You're right, Mom. I'm kind of buzzed up and a little out of control. But look, the skies are still clear. I'm learning. I'm really learning."

"Thanks, Hon. It takes some effort, that's for sure."

She gave her daughter a big smile.

"Okay, I'm hungry. How about the rest of you? I know a fantastic little diner . . ."

Chapter 28 – That Eye Thing

They found Lin's favorite diner in the Village, and Taylor pointed at an open corner booth. Lin and Jack took one side and Gabriel and Taylor the other. They'd started on their drinks and were waiting for the meals to arrive.

Lin's phone rang, and she slipped it out of her pocket. She saw who it was and frowned.

"Oh God, I almost forgot about those people." She clicked to answer.

"Anna? Why are you calling me?"

"I am sorry for bothering you, Lin. I do not want to. I do not want anything to do with you."

"Okay, then why are you bugging me?"

"It is for Tayo. He feels some need to see you."

"Well, I don't feel any need to see him. He shot a rocket at me, Anna. He's lucky I didn't kill him."

"He knows that. And he was not lying—he really did not want to kill you."

"So, now he wants to see me? Why?"

"We are on St. Simons Island. He will have to explain himself. I cannot."

"You and Tayo are here?"

"And Daria too."

"Really? All of you?"

"Oh, and Ozzy too."

"We won't be here much longer. I don't have any time to waste with—"

"Please, Lin. I know you do not owe me. But I did give you the Telling. And you know that Wolfe had me under a spell of some type."

"Yeah, that's all true, but—"

"Can you speak with him for just a minute or more? Then, Daria and I will leave for good. I have seen too much. Helping Tayo one last time is all I can do, and then I am done."

"Fine. We're at a little diner across from the bakery on Mallery. We're sitting there finishing up. But make it quick. We'll be done and leaving soon."

"Thank you, Lin. We will all be there in only several minutes."

The call ended, and Lin looked at the three curious faces.

"Just one more thing to deal with. I'll talk to this guy, and then we're done with all of them."

"More loose ends, Lin?"

"It would seem so. I guess another round of coffee is in order. Decaf, Taylor."

"Okay, Mom. You know, I don't really like storms all that much myself."

* * *

Out through the glass, Lin saw a well-dressed woman with stylish brown hair standing near the bakery. Lin shook her head in surprise at seeing her short skirt and heels, and she felt like laughing, but she only ran her hands over her own plain shorts. Next to her was Daria, with her thick black hair laying across her shoulders and wearing tight jeans and a t-shirt. Tayo wore his black and white striped shirt and long khakis. Daria helped the crippled man, and Anna toted her dog.

"I hoped I'd never see any of you people again."

Anna, Ozzy, and Daria stared at Lin with big eyes, but Tayo looked at the floor.

"Lin, I am sorry, but I had to see you again. Your eyes, Lin. They changed me."

"It's just green light. You need to get on with your life. Forget all of what you saw."

"I'm trying to forget the horrible things I saw. But I'll never forget your eyes. Lin, I know now. I know there is something I must do for you."

"What are you talking about? You sound like a lunatic."

"I don't know what I'm talking about. You're correct."

"And you," said Lin. "What are you doing? Copying my old style?"

"It is a good look, Lin. And it was time for a change. I do not want to be like you, though. You scare me."

"Me too," said Daria. "You scare the crap out of me. The things you did around that cabin? My God, what the hell kind of a—"

"You're both pissing me off. Is that a good idea?"

The two women got silent and looked down, but Tayo looked into Lin's eyes. So did the dog.

"You won't see any green light there. Is that what you want, Tayo?"

"No, I don't need that again. That's not why I'm—"

"This is your last chance, and I don't mean that I'm going to destroy you. Although I could, that's for sure. I mean that I'm leaving, and if you have some reason for seeing me, get to the point."

Lin stared at Tayo and waited.

"I am offering to assist you, Lin. If you ever need me, I will come. I'll do whatever you need."

"That's it? You came to Georgia for that?"

"I don't understand it either." Tayo again looked at the floor.

"Anna, you and Daria are done now, right? I expect you two to stay out of my life."

Lin let her eyes flash an intense green.

They both took a step back and Daria grabbed Anna's arm, but she also reached into her back pocket and took out her phone.

"Just do that eye thing again, just for a second, okay?" And she began to raise her phone up for a photo.

Lin stopped time. Without a conscious thought, she'd gotten a solid hold on her intent, froze the world in an instant, and saw infinity in every direction. And the world again became a calm, flat surface that moved so slowly that no one could ever notice. But she did—she saw that it was magic too. The world of reality was just impossibly slow magic.

Her glowing green eyes scanned everyone and everything before focusing on Daria's phone and its magic. Some part of Lin reached out for the phone's magic, and she held it, feeling it flowing continuously, bringing its existence fresh in every moment. She saw that Daria's palm was mostly facing up, holding the phone, and Lin knew that she didn't want to hurt the girl. She could plant Daria's head halfway into the wall. She could sink her to her throat into the concrete and dirt beneath the diner's floor. Or she could even take her completely and set her gently in the tree outside the diner fifty feet above the sidewalk.

But it was time for fun, she realized. More of a prank. And that might be scary enough anyway.

Lin looked for and found a vision of the breakfast she'd just finished. The omelet was tasty and covered in hot cheese, the potatoes were just the right amount of crispy, and the hotcakes were sweet and fluffy, reminding her of Nomad. But what she needed was the image of the syrup. That thick, sweet syrup that poured so slowly and stuck to whatever it touched. Just thick, sticky, gooey syrup, pouring and flowing, flowing and dripping, dripping and drizzling, drizzling and—

She gave the magic of Daria's phone a quick squeeze and released her intent. The glow in her eyes faded some, but the light remained, even after she'd let time resume. She wanted Daria to get a good look at her glowing eyes before she looked down at her hand.

Daria's phone was gone, and her hand held only maple syrup. The thick mess oozed down between her fingers onto her jeans and boots. She stared at the slop in her hand, and her face locked into a silent scream.

With her eyes three times their normal size, she turned to Anna and said, "Let's get the hell out of here, Mom!"

"Yes, Daria, we must go!" With her voice shaking, she turned to Lin and said, "Thank you for being kind. Goodbye forever, Lin!"

They turned and began walking toward the door, each holding one of Tayo's arms and mostly dragging him, with Daria leaving a trail of syrup drops. Lin noticed most the sound of Anna's heels striking the diner's tile floor on her way out, and the feel of her own sneakers kept her from smiling at the mirth of what she'd just done. Within seconds, they were gone, as if they'd never been there, and Lin slumped back into their booth.

"That was weird, Mom, but I'm glad you didn't hurt anyone. Can we get out of here now?"

Lin's eyes remained closed for several moments before she opened them and answered.

"Yes, Taylor, of course." She paused and closed her eyes. "Gabby, I feel like I tied up two loose ends but opened a new one. What's going on with that Tayo guy?"

"He's not a convert, Lin, but you've had a profound effect on him. Perhaps it wouldn't hurt to remember him. And maybe someday, you just might need help with something."

"I can't imagine how."

"Neither can I."

$$* \quad * \quad *$$

"Daria, you almost got us all slaughtered. All for a goddamn photograph."

"Okay, Mom, you don't have to start swearing again. Sorry, I couldn't resist."

"And Tayo, you have squandered a large portion of my time."

"I'm sorry you feel that way, Anna, but I don't share that opinion. I needed to see Lin again, and you have helped me greatly. Thank you."

They'd found Anna's car in the lot several blocks away, and they'd begun their long drive north.

"You live in Baltimore, Tayo? I will drop you where you need to be."

"Yes, Baltimore. Thanks, Anna. And you too, Daria."

"Hey, I'm just along for the ride. Maybe I'll get back to modeling when we get back. I never should have bothered working with The Shield. But Mom, that was some crazy time, wasn't it?"

"It is all behind us, Daria. I am happy that for sure we can all go back to normal lives beginning now."

* * *

After Lin had regained her energy, they all enjoyed an uneventful afternoon of walking through the Village shopping and sightseeing and ended up back in their suite.

"Room service, anyone?" Gabriel said.

"Oh yeah, please," said Lin. "I'm tired, and I need food. This hasn't been the best vacation, but we're all together. That counts for a lot."

"Except for Nomad, Mom. I miss him too."

"We'll be home soon enough. Maybe we'll have sunny weather in Pennsylvania, Taylor?"

"That's funny, Mom. As long as I don't get too 'hangry.' Remember that word? It's already not even a word, not a real one. Even before I start playing with it."

"Which you don't need to do?" said Gabriel.

"Yeah. Not right now anyway, because we're getting room service!"

* * *

After Taylor had expressed an urgent need for seafood, everyone agreed that would be the best for them too. Lin savored every morsel of her lobster with a tall glass of iced tea. She picked at tiny bits remaining on her plate and tried to keep an eye on Taylor, but she mostly watched Jack.

His wavy brown hair almost touched his shoulders, which strained against his thin t-shirt. His solid chest muscles flexed every time he reached his fork out, and his arms looked unnecessarily strong for snatching up morsels of fish and baked potato.

And when he looked up and caught her gazing at him, she saw the calm strength and acceptance that he'd developed over the last couple of weeks. He'd been through so much with her—being terrified of her, being her convert, and losing his will when she'd played with him like a puppet. And staying by her side when she was dead . . . for three days.

She watched as the plates emptied and knew that she needed to be alone with him. Gabriel would have to leave, and Taylor could retreat to one of the bedrooms. Then, alone with Jack, the possibilities were endless, like the magic that supported all of them and everything else.

"That was very good, Lin. Of all the magical things in the world, perhaps room service is one of the best," Gabriel said with a big grin.

"Yeah, Mom, that was good. What time are we leaving tomorrow?"

"Early would be best, Hon. We should have time to grab a quick breakfast, and I have one errand to run. But after that, it's back home for us."

"I'm ready to go back. I really do miss Nomad."

"We all do, Taylor," said Jack. "Do you think he misses us?"

"Oh yeah, I'm sure of it, Jack."

"Especially at mealtime?"

Jack smiled at Lin. Taylor turned to look at Lin too.

"When is it not his mealtime?" she said with a big grin.

"Okay, you two. He's a big boy, we all know that."

"It's late, Mom. I'm done. I'll take that small bedroom, okay?"

"That's a great idea, Taylor."

Taylor got up and kissed Lin's cheek before retreating to her bedroom and closing the door.

"Let's hope she goes right to sleep. Right, Lin?" Gabriel said.

"If there's a problem, we'll know about it, that's for sure."

"I'll take that chance and wander the streets awhile. I have a taste for ice cream again, and if the weather stays pleasant, I'll be gone for some time."

"That sounds good, Gabby. I'll leave the door unlocked, so come back whenever."

Gabriel departed, and Lin looked back to Jack and the smile he offered her. What a magical life they shared together, she thought.

And she remembered the joy she'd felt when Gabriel had taken her to swim along with the other lives. In some ocean she'd never find, moving through water she'd never touch. She felt the challenge of her current life as she remembered that brief frolic.

"Jack, we're alone again. You can't possibly guess what I'm thinking."

"Hold that thought, Cowgirl. I just want to grab a quick shower, alright? What a crazy day this has been."

"That's for sure. Okay, Jack, get moving," she said and smacked his behind.

"Okay, alright. I'm going!"

Chapter 29 – Desperation Of Silence

Five minutes later, the shower stopped, and a few minutes after that, Jack opened the door and let the humid air roll out. Lin had changed into an orange bikini and leaned against the wall across from the bathroom door. She gave him a smile.

"Oh my God, Lin. You're gorgeous."

"Aw, thanks, Jack. You wear a towel pretty well yourself."

Jack's hair was still wet and in need of combing, and he wore only a fresh white towel. Without another word, Lin took his hand and led him to the bed. She turned him and pushed down on his shoulders until he sat, and she stood in front of him, running her hands through his hair. Her bikini left little for him to imagine, and her coconut lotion was only part of the reason he took deep breaths of her.

She climbed up and knelt against him, and he reached around to get a good hold of her. She eased herself down onto his lap and looked into his big brown eyes.

"Jack, I'm still pretty tired from that magic business with the phone, but I'd like to try something. Kind of a little adventure. What do you think?"

She ran her fingers up from behind his ears until they were all buried in his wavy brown hair. He looked at her and smiled, and she could see his soul behind his moistening eyes, aching for her, willing to do whatever she had in mind. She fought to not laugh from relief at not seeing any fear or senseless convert adoration.

"Yes, yes, Lin, anything. Something like before? You know we can play that game anytime at all."

He gave her a big smile, and she felt his intentions beneath her. A few memories of being a tease in Gloriana's dreams raced through her, and she let them pass.

"Oh, Jack, we'll definitely play that way again. You like the bad Lin, I can tell. And I'm not sure I can stop myself anyway. But this is something different."

"Anything you want, my sweet girl."

Lin welcomed his answer, but she'd already felt his growing eagerness. Still holding his head in her hands, she leaned in and kissed him in a slow deep way, with her tongue touching his and guiding it from one side to the other. His enthusiasm increased, and she broke from his lips to laugh once before she swung her leg away to sit next to him on the bed.

Jack let out a low whine, a very good imitation of Nomad, but his smile showed not a trace of dissatisfaction.

"I liked you on my lap. You must have noticed."

"Oh, I noticed. Hold that thought, Jack." She pulled him down with her onto the cool blanket.

They lay side-by-side with Jack's arms around her waist and hers around his neck, and a soft green glow lit her eyes. Jack flinched only slightly at seeing Lin's power rise up, but she kissed him again, and most parts of his hard body melted and molded to her soft curves.

Lin felt her mayhem rising, and she focused her intent on the magic inside her with a simple goal: to take Jack with her to live what she'd experienced earlier—for each of them to merge with another of Earth's creatures. To see life through their eyes. Together.

The door to the twisting, crashing magic opened up, and Lin felt it all flowing into her, swelling her with a pleasure that carried such a sweet, unbearable pressure. She took a deep breath and held it, pressed her lips against Jack's again, and looked into his eyes. She held her objective lightly, knowing that her intent would find a way. She saw the acceptance and love in his eyes, and her own green light reflected, and she backed her lips away as she slowly released the breath.

A gentle ripple rushed from her as her spirit swept up Jack's, and they both traveled to a place Lin hadn't chosen and would never in her lifetime find.

* * *

She sensed a brief and rapid falling followed by a settling in. An arriving. A feeling of belonging. She noticed first her quick breathing.

Lin felt the warmth of soft bedding under her and all around. And she felt Jack pressed tight against her. Her eyes were closed, and her head was pressed into his warm chest, but she could feel him breathing rapidly, and his heart beat a tempo of five beats per second. Maybe more.

Lin knew they weren't Words that came to her, but they felt like Words.

"Open your eyes and see."

After a few fast blinks, her eyes opened, and she saw only fine, perfect white feathers packed tight and vibrating with Jack's rapid pulse. Looking down, she saw her own orange beak with the point buried in his feathers.

"Look to the sky."

She rotated her head and looked up to see slivers of a golden world beyond layers of branches thick with leaves. Lin felt their nest riding the easy swaying of a sturdy branch.

"Soon, you will go to the sky. Your wings will take you there."

Lin felt her own young heart pick up its pace with a longing to launch into that limitless expanse.

"You belong in the sky. But there are dangers there. Remember that trees are your home."

Jack awoke and looked up at the sky then back at Lin. They pressed farther into each other, but Lin kept her gaze on the sky. She felt her delicate legs warm and curled up beneath her.

"You have much to learn. I will tell you all you need to know."

Lin studied all the branches which wove a tapestry above her and around her. The leaves shivered as the branches moved with the light wind, and she could almost feel her claws wrapped tight around the nearest twig while she looked ahead to one higher up, and the one after, each one taking her closer to the sky.

"Always be aware of everything around you. Do you hear that sound getting louder? It does not slow or speed up. Only humans move about like that."

The footsteps grew louder beneath the nest, and Lin felt her heart beating more quickly.

"You are high above the ground, and most humans will only ignore you. Wait. Listen. Stay still."

The regular plodding of shoes on the sidewalk grew softer as the solitary person out for a jog had passed the nest.

Lin turned to look into Jack's eyes and into the baby bird's eyes. She could see that it was Jack, and it was a bird too—her intent had succeeded in bringing them both to that nest, in a tree in a place she'd never find. She wanted to laugh, but she couldn't.

"Your mother will return soon. She will feed you. She will care for you until you can care for yourself."

Lin flexed her legs and curled them tighter beneath their feathers. She shook her wings and felt them puff up fluffy and warm.

"Never worry when you think you are alone. I am here. I am always with you."

Lin felt human tears that her eyes couldn't cry as she twitched her growing wings and pressed her beak back into Jack's feathers. He fluttered, and his wing ended up over her, causing her need for tears to increase.

"I am here. I am always with you."

Then, Lin's intent began to fight inside her with the goal she'd set for herself and for Jack. She remembered that they needed to return. But to what? What other life is there than to be in a nest with Jack? Two new birds ready for their first flight. What other life could there possibly be?

"I will never leave you."

I want to stay here, she thought. I need to stay here. Where everything makes sense. Where I have no doubts. This is my life.

"I am with you."

She felt her intent begin to drag her away from her life, away from the Words that kept her safe, the Words that told her in every moment that she was cared for and loved. Her intent would try to take her someplace she couldn't remember, a world that no longer existed.

"I am here."

The twigs and leaves beneath her, the warmth of Jack's feathers against her own, his heartbeat sounding through her, the clear sky above, beckoning her tiny heart, all began to fall away as Lin's intent struggled to return her, to bring her and Jack back to some other place. To a life that had already become a forgotten dream.

"You are never alone."

But Lin's hold on her intent was unbreakable, even in the life of a young bird high up in a nest on a branch rocking gently beneath a tempting sky. She felt her intent's tight grip ripping her from her life, stealing her away from all she knew. From all she wanted.

"You will always have me with you."

Lin felt her death approaching, drawing nearer to take her from her life. Her speedy heartbeat blended with Jack's—two racing hearts longing for the sky.

Both about to die.

"I am with you. Always."

Just as she felt death come to her and Jack, she heard one last time, "I am here. I am always with you . . ."

And then, the Words spoke no more.

* * *

Lin felt the softness of their bed and her own heart beating a regular, familiar pace. She waited and listened, but no more Words came to her.

She opened her eyes and saw Jack's face pressed against hers, and he felt warm in the room's cool air. He awoke, too, and they lay there looking at each other in silence.

Though groggy from their travels, they found each other. They found their connection. And they moved slowly, skin against skin, tangled together under the covers. And they loved each other as humans in a slow, steady, powerful way.

Lin's tears streamed down to one side as she looked into Jack's eyes. She eased her way on top of him, never slowing, never breaking their bond. And she felt consumed by the tragedy of being separate. By the desperation of silence.

They finished that way—Jack not remembering any of their journey, and Lin feeling her heart beating slowly and sadly while her tears dripped hot onto Jack's chest. When they had answered each other's needs, she pulled him to his side, where they lay entwined.

Lin struggled to contain her sobbing, but she couldn't remain completely silent. Jack held her tightly as she loved and regretted being there with him, knowing what she didn't know before: what every other living thing knows with their every breath.

"Shh. I'm here, Lin. I'm here."

Her tears continued to flow as Jack held her close and gently kissed her forehead.

"I'm here with you, Cowgirl. It's okay. I will always be here."

After many tears had fallen, Lin's crying ended, and she breathed deeply as she slept in his arms.

Only then did Jack's words stop too.

* * *

Lin awoke slowly in Jack's arms. He hadn't slept, but he'd pulled the blanket up over them both and held her against him.

"Oh, Jack, it's good here in your arms. I couldn't answer, but I heard you. I love you, Jack."

"I love you too, Lin. Do you feel alright?"

"I feel better now."

"I don't know what happened. I lost track of time, and then we were together. My God, Lin, that was powerful. I don't know why, but I felt sad. And I've never seen you so sad."

"You don't remember, Jack? Where we went?"

"No. We went somewhere?"

"Oh, it's probably better that you don't remember. It made me sad that we had to come back, that's all."

"Alright, you must know I'm confused. Where did we go?"

"We lived different lives, but only for a moment or two. I still feel the sadness of leaving those lives that we shared. I'm glad you don't feel that too."

He continued to hold her close, and he asked no more. She wiped at her eyes one last time.

"Fly Jack fly fly fly."

Jack laughed softly and whispered, "What?"

Lin shook her head, blinked three times quickly, and said, "You should get dressed and get over on that couch, Jack."

"How about if I just hold you a few minutes first, alright?"

Jack's arms held her tight, and he touched her all over very softly, hugging her closer and rubbing their skin together. His hands ended at the small of her back, and he squeezed her into him as he kissed her. A long, deep kiss. He pulled away and smiled.

"Alright, that'll have to do. For now." He gave her another kiss before he stood and began to get dressed.

Lin lay naked under the blankets watching him, and she said, "Jack, this bed was our nest. We nested, you and I."

Jack stopped buttoning his shirt and tilted his head to one side. He saw Lin's green eyes wet with fresh tears, but he smiled and said, "I pray I may always nest with you."

Chapter 30 – Quite The Badass

"Coffee will help, Jack," Taylor said as they all settled in for a last breakfast before leaving the Island.

"It always does," said Jack. "No sugar in mine, though."

He smiled when Lin squeezed his leg under the table.

"So do hotcakes," said Gabriel. "Blueberry are the best. Two stacks at least."

"Oh, Gabby," Lin said without letting Jack go. "Again with the hotcakes?"

She shook her head with a smile and picked up her menu with both hands. Gabriel returned her smile, and without looking away from her, pointed at the window.

"Lee's here."

Lee stood peeking in through the glass with both hands blocking out the daylight. Lin waved her in, and the hostess dragged a chair up to the end of their booth.

"Hey, Lee, you made it. How are things at home?"

"I had to get out of there. Alessa is impossible to deal with. And Ben took off too. I might as well spend some time here on the Island."

"How is Alessa impossible?" said Lin. "She's okay, isn't she? From the magic?"

"Maybe too okay. She's like a little saint or an angel or something. Who could ever live with something like that?"

"Oh, it's probably not that hard to do," Lin said as she glanced at Gabriel. "Why is that a problem? Would you rather she be more difficult?"

"Yeah, maybe. Being nice is just stupid. I know I'm done taking crap from anyone."

"I don't get it. Who's giving you crap? Ben?"

"Oh, that Ben. He was using me, but that's done. If any using is going to happen, I'll be doing it."

Lin looked at Jack, then Gabriel, then back at Lee.

"Do you want some breakfast, Lee?"

"No, I just ate a box of fudge walking up here."

Jack looked again at Lee's lean, muscular body and shook his head.

"Thanks for the text. I never would have found you in this place."

Lin took her final bite and washed it down with the last of her coffee.

"Why don't you all just sit tight while I run a last-minute errand. Lee, care to join me?"

Lin stood to leave. Lee gazed up at her a second.

"Sure, why not."

Lee stood, and they both walked out onto the sidewalk.

* * *

"What's going on, Lee? I can tell something's up."

Lee hesitated as they walked through the Village, which was beginning to warm under a clear blue sky.

"I've discovered something, Lin. It was one thing to heal myself nine years ago. That was cool, and I keep fixing myself all the time. I deserve that name you gave me—'Lee Ternity.' But after I healed Ben and Taylor, I don't know. There's a whole world of amusing possibilities now."

They'd made it only a half-block from the diner, and Lin grabbed Lee's arm and stopped her.

"Like what, Lee? What's going on with you?"

Lee paused again and looked up and down the street.

"I need someone to use. Someone to take to my home. I want to beat the shit out of some guy, any guy, and take him to my home. I'll heal him, and physically, he'll be fine, like Ben was. I healed him up perfect. And that asshole took off anyway. He—"

"What did you do to Ben?"

"Like I just said. I beat the shit out of him. And when I healed him . . . Lin, it was the best sex I've ever had. My sun exploded all over me. I've never felt anything like that, and I'm damn sure going to do it again."

Lin could only stare at her new friend who had healed her daughter just days ago. And she saw the new coldness in her eyes.

Power over the magic changes everyone, she realized.

"No, Lee, you can't go around hurting people and healing them just for your own pleasure."

"Sure I can, and I will. Think you can follow me around and stop me?"

"I think you better just leave. Go home and think this through. You'll see this isn't the way."

"Oh, you are so wrong, Lin. You have no idea how good it is to mix sex with magic."

Lin felt something begin to squirm inside, then a hand on her shoulder. She turned to see Jack smiling at her.

"Oh, Jack, what's going on?"

"I just wanted to check on you. Hi, Lee. Everything okay here?"

Lee took a step toward him and said, "Jack will do just fine," and she reached for him with her left and pulled back her right fist.

Without a thought, Lin's intent immediately stopped time. The world became a flat, motionless surface, and Jack and Lee were frozen with it. Endless tides and waves of magic tumbled beneath them as she watched infinity roll out to every horizon.

As the magic swirled and raced into her, Lin remembered that she couldn't invade Lee. Lee was too strong since she'd taken control of her own gap, that narrow space between her spirit and her body.

But Lin knew that she could find Lee's magic, and her intent took her there. She saw a single dark streak mixed in with the green glow of Lee's spirit. It wasn't a wound, and it wasn't from an evil traveler tagging along. Lin knew that it was there by choice. Lee had chosen a darker direction for herself.

Could Lee's spirit be healed like she'd done with Ben in that Allentown restaurant? Lin tried to replace the darkness with fresh light, with fresh magic that she carefully took from the soil around the nearby potted tree. But it didn't work. The darkness in Lee's spirit hadn't been imposed on her. She'd chosen it, and she'd have to correct it herself, Lin knew.

She remembered that Lee was only an instant from striking Jack and dragging him off to her home, and she wrapped her arms around Lee's magic. She felt it flowing into her, creating her anew in every moment. She knew one reliable option was squeezing her magic and ending her life. But she remembered the friendship they'd shared, and she remembered, too, the pitfalls and temptations of using power over the magic.

Instead of destroying her, Lin gathered up her magic and carried it to the end of the street, where she turned her to face away from her and Jack. Lin's intent brought her back to her own body, and she let time resume.

Lin watched the confusion Lee faced as she suddenly found herself in a different place, alone on a street corner. She'd been reaching for Jack, and in an instant, she'd been relocated down the street. She spun around to see Lin and Jack watching her.

"Lin," said Jack. "What the hell—"

"Hold on a second, Jack," she said as they saw Lee walking back toward them. "We're not done yet."

"Stop, Lee. Right there."

Lee stopped five paces from them.

"I can do this all day, Lee. Or worse. Trust me—'worse' will change you forever."

"Then, I'll find someone else if I have to. Jack wouldn't mind, would you, Jack?"

"I think you better do what Lin wants."

Lee stared at them a few seconds and turned and began walking away.

"Lin, what the hell was that?"

She held him around his waist and laid her head on his shoulder. With closed eyes, she said, "Jack, keep watching her. Tell me if she comes back. I need to rest a second."

Ten seconds later, she squeezed him tighter and looked up for a kiss.

"You feel better? What was—"

"That tires me out a little, that's all."

She gave him another kiss and took a step back.

"You know she has some powers, Jack. She's losing control of herself. She wanted to try her new game with you, and it's not a game you'd like."

"I should be shocked at what just happened. Lee vanished and reappeared down the street. That's just a fact of our lives now, isn't it?"

"Yeah, Jack. That and other things too."

She reached around his waist and waited for another kiss. Jack smiled and kissed her in the morning sunlight as the Village came to life around them.

"Am I going to have problems with her?"

"No, I'm sure you won't. You just happened to be standing next to her. And besides, I can be quite the badass, Jack."

He held her hips and looked around behind her with a big smile.

"Yeah, that and every other part of you."

"You like me bad, Jack? 'Cause I think I want to be a really bad girl."

"You like being a tease, don't you?"

"Mm-hmm . . ."

She reached up around his neck and pulled him in for a kiss.

"Come on, let's head back, alright?"

She squeezed him tight and said, "Yeah, we have to get going. I still have to run one errand before we leave. I'll catch up with you back at the diner, okay?"

"Sure thing. See you in a few," he said and began walking away.

* * *

Lin turned away from Jack and watched Lee putting distance between them, and she decided to stare at Lee's black hair. From that distance, it was quickly becoming just a spot of darkness. Like a black dot.

Some of the fatigue from just using Lee's magic weighed on her, but the time still seemed right. It was time to give it another try, but with the hope that it would be quick, not four hours like before. She realized that when she'd tried it before, she'd had no thought at all of how long she should be gone.

Leaning her shoulder into the brick wall, Lin found her intent. Time stopped, and she saw the calm surface of the world and endless spinning magic below. When the magic started to flow into her, her intent slowed it down. Magic flowed back out of her, and she felt herself slowing as it left her. Finally, she'd slowed it enough, and the black dot began racing toward her.

It covered her, and when her breathing stopped and her thoughts and feelings left her, she waited for her heart to stop too. And it did stop.

In the stillness within her, Lin held her intent with her unbreakable hold on it.

A pinpoint of light raced toward her, wrapping a world around her. Her heart started, thoughts and feelings returned, and she took a deep breath of air high above an ocean on a tower made of stone.

Lin didn't turn to face her right. She only looked out at the water as it carried a shattered version of the moon that looked down from a sky without stars.

"Hello, Gloriana."

"Lin Finity. You travel between the Islands on your own."

"Yes. Somehow, I learned that."

"You are taught that. The times I take you from the Islands, you learn to navigate those seas of magic."

Lin turned to look at Gloriana, and she looked back at Lin. Her caramel eyes showed her weariness, and Lin felt a tear gathering as she considered the centuries she'd spent holding onto her intent in an empty nightmare full of things that bit and clawed and fought to destroy her.

"Your strength is almost gone, Gloriana. I can tell. You don't have any power over me."

"I cannot reach into the Islands again. My hope lies with you."

They both turned to look out over dark waters with crests of waves lit by dim moonlight.

"Your islands, the world you created long ago, are gone as if they never existed. They live only in legends."

"Yes. Everyone I love is gone. Everyone I know."

"Soon, you won't have the ocean. And your tower will be gone too."

"There is only darkness waiting for me."

"And still, you won't let go? Aren't you tired?"

"I am more tired than you can know, Lin Finity."

"Then, why?"

"Life is such a gift, even when I am lost in darkness between the Islands of Time. I will never let it go. It will take much to wrest it from me."

Lin felt a tear begin to roll down her cheek as she glanced up at the silent moon. It looked down on them without any interest—two powerful travelers on a tower that didn't exist. Lin knew that the moon could wait forever and wondered if Gloriana could too.

Then, she remembered that it wasn't a real moon anyway.

"I must go."

"I am not a legend, Lin Finity. When you see darkness, remember that I am there."

Fresh tears wet Lin's eyes as she looked inside herself, even as she stared at the moon above them. She found the stillness within her, and she felt her strong hold on her intent, a hold that would only let go if she allowed it. And she knew that she never would. Just as Gloriana never would.

With her unyielding grip on her intent, Lin gazed out over Gloriana's ocean. The familiar black dot appeared on the horizon, and she waited as it rushed toward her. It buried her, and everything stopped. She was alone in the darkness without even a heartbeat, holding on to her intent.

A racing white light pulled Lin's own world around her, and her life returned. She found that she still leaned against the cool bricks, and she knew that only a fraction of a second had passed.

She stood up straight and began walking through the Village. She needed to finish an errand before joining Jack, Taylor, and Gabriel and leaving for home.

* * *

"Gabby, I'm going to do it. I haven't done it since I left Allentown after I cured Ben."

"I won't try to talk you out of it, Lin. You could use a little fun, don't you think?"

They'd all settled into Lin's Temt8tion, with Taylor and Jack in the backseat and Gabriel up front with Lin. She thought about Gabriel's last comment: that she could use a little fun. And she remembered her brief life as a bird with Jack. The sadness of returning still draped over her, dulling the happiness of her real life.

And she also remembered the wild night she'd spent with Jack. She felt a heat inside recalling how it had felt to relive the outlandish worlds Gloriana had spun to try to trick her. She'd played that part, and it almost drove Jack insane. And her too. That wouldn't be the last time they'd play that way, she told herself. She knew that she could barely wait to play that role again.

"Everyone's ready to go? Taylor, say goodbye to St. Simons Island."

"Goodbye, Island," Taylor said and laughed. "And keep your crazy storms!"

"Yes, that's a good idea," said Gabriel. "We can leave those storms here. I'm ready to go too, Lin."

"Let's go," said Jack. "There's a gigantic starving boy waiting for us."

All four of them watched the tiny lights lined up along the centerline of her car's Oblivion Black hood. The engine rumbled and waited only for the command from Lin's sneaker.

Lin pressed the pedal to the floor, and the tires screamed and spun like mad until they began to dig into the pavement. Three of the lamps lit, then a fourth joined them. Three more lit and the eighth one too. As they felt themselves thrust back into their seats, they saw all ten lights shining, and amid loud cheering, Lin backed off of the gas. One by one, they all dimmed, and Lin settled in at her cruising speed. She knew that no one would be passing her.

* * *

After some pavement had passed under Lin's powerful car, Taylor had reinstalled her headphones, and occasional off-tune humming could be heard above the Temt8tion's rumble. Gabriel reached for the stereo, and classic rock drowned out both Taylor and the engine.

Lin glanced quickly in back to see that Jack had dozed off. She looked over at Gabriel and smiled before staring back out at the freeway rushing toward them. And she thought about how so many pieces of her life were finding comfortable places—an arrangement that worked.

Taylor had been healed, and even though she was a Glyphin, Gabriel had helped her to get some control over it. Lin knew that she'd need to keep an eye on her, but Taylor would be okay. She probably wouldn't destroy their home.

Jack loved her more than ever, and she him. She felt the freedom of him loving her innocent and being a tease too. She could be anything for him, with or without her powers.

But mostly, she wanted to be a tease. Or worse. Like she was in the memories from Gloriana's fake worlds. All the thoughts that kept sneaking up on her. And the memories that seemed so real. She knew what she had become in that hotel room. And she remembered liking it.

But she pushed those thoughts aside. They were just dreams, and she knew that they'd soon be forgotten.

And so many loose ends were probably out of her life. She felt some regret that Lee had chosen a darker path. But that was her own doing, and Lin knew that she didn't have to be part of it. Lee would have to find her own way.

Anna had turned into some kind of fan club, dressing up the way Lin used to feel was necessary. But it was an improvement over the drab suits she'd worn as Assistant Director of The Shield. She and Daria could take their dog and go their own way now without Lancaster Wolfe's interference.

And what about Tayo? she wondered. His sincerity and dedication were obvious, but what would he do with the curious effect Lin had had on him? Would she ever need his help? Lin couldn't imagine how. Tayo, too, would have to find his own way after all they'd been through.

She remembered who she was driving home to see: Nomad. Her sweet fluffy boy. She wanted nothing more than to snuggle with him on the couch. She couldn't wait to play their game at the door too. She wondered if she'd have the patience to win this time. Would she break down first and call to him? Or would he bark first?

And she couldn't forget her unfinished business with Gloriana. She was out there, or back there, or wherever and whenever she was. Alone in the darkness and locked onto her own intent. Lin knew that she was Gloriana's only hope. Should she really consider helping her get back? Could that ever work out? The plan she'd just thought up seemed like a good one. Maybe Gabriel would have some advice.

Gabriel. What of Gabriel? Did she still need help and guidance? Or had she moved beyond all that to where she was ready to face life on her own?

A sadder life than before, she reminded herself, as she remembered her existence in a simple nest in a life without doubts.

Magic will sort it all out, she told herself as she piloted her Temt8tion north. Back to home.

Chapter 31 – Covered With Barnacles

Lin glanced over and saw Gabriel's mouth hanging open, adding more snoring to Taylor's coming from the backseat. Jack slept silently with his head tipped against the window. She switched off the stereo and listened to the big engine purr for several minutes, then she shook Gabriel awake.

"Uh . . . okay, Lin. I'm awake. Are we there yet?"

"No, not yet, Gabby. But I want to talk to you about something important."

"Yes, of course. I will always help you if you need it. What's going on?"

"I traveled between the Islands of Time again."

"On your own?"

"Yes. After I talked with Lee, I did it right there on the sidewalk. It only took a second, and—"

"You do know that it's difficult to control that, don't you?"

"How long I've been gone, you mean?"

"Yes. A few seconds one time. Three days another time. A century next time? All it takes is one mistake."

"No, you can't be serious. I could be dead for a hundred years?"

"Okay, I'm exaggerating. But a day or two isn't out of the question. What are you doing?"

"Gloriana isn't a bad person. She really can't get back on her own. She put the last of her power into me by trying to get me to help her. That's what those outrageous episodes were all about. She tried to trick me a few times, but now, she's too weak."

"And you believe you should help her?"

"I'm thinking about it, that's for sure."

"And if you were able to bring her here, what then? You saved Renato from being a scroll for countless centuries, and do you remember the anguish he felt?"

"This is different. Renato didn't have any powers. He never could have adapted to a new world. I believe Gloriana could. She's already survived so long. I can't even imagine how she can have such a strong hold on her intent."

"As do you."

"Oh, I don't know. Not like that. And I'd never be able to create worlds like she does. She created those islands of hers out in the ocean, remember? Hey, like when I took some magic for that cop, where did Gloriana take that magic from to make the islands?"

"We may never know, Lin. I'd guess the ocean. No one would ever miss it."

"That's for sure. So, she took the boundless magic supporting everything, and with just her intent, she created islands. I still can't comprehend that."

"And what did it get her?"

"A long life for one thing. The stories she could tell, Gabby. And teach. I wonder what she could teach too? Hey, she knows all about Glyphins. She could probably help Taylor, don't you think?"

"You sound like you're making all sorts of plans to have some ancient queen as your next gal pal."

"Well, when you put it like that . . ."

Lin watched the road approaching and diving under her car's leading edge and listened to the big engine rumbling.

"She and I are connected. When I spoke the Words of God, whatever Glyphin magic she mixed into them affected me. I'm not sure I can just walk away from that."

"You seem very determined, Lin, so we should discuss the dangers. It's not as easy as picking her up and flying her to the present time."

"What do you mean? I've been there a couple of times, and the last time, it was completely on my own. It took hardly any effort."

"Think of a new ship dropped into the water for the first time."

"Oh, here we go, Gabby. Okay, I'm thinking of a big shiny boat."

"That's right. You're exactly right, Lin. It's shiny. It hasn't been in the water. Now, think of one that's been at the bottom of the ocean for a long, long time."

"Oh, well, that's different. It's got barnacles and seaweed and God knows what else sticking to it."

Lin turned to look at Gabriel, who only stared back at her and shrugged. Lin looked back at the highway.

"Gloriana's covered with barnacles?"

"In a manner of speaking. I'm sure she looks quite beautiful, though. The barnacles from the spaces in between the Islands are hard to see, but she's probably attracted a few."

"Things trying to kill her? That's what you mean?"

"Yes."

"All the more reason to help her out, right?"

"Can you deal with her barnacles? Do you know how to save her from them? Should you really bring them into this world?"

"Aren't there already tons of things trying to kill us all the time?"

"Yes, between the Islands of Time. When we pass through, we're fair game for them. It would be an abomination to somehow bring one into the world."

"Is that even possible? Can that happen?"

"I don't know, Lin. Perhaps we shouldn't find out."

*   *   *

"Okay, everyone," Lin said as she raced her Temt8tion along the off-ramp. "It's late—why don't we stop for the night? I think we all need a break."

"Sounds good to me," said Jack. "You're probably overdue for a speeding ticket anyway."

"Oh, Jack, do you think I'd ever let anyone write me up?"

"You'd use your powers for something like that?"

"No, probably not. But I could, that's for sure."

"There are much, much better uses for your powers."

"Mm-hmm. Oh yeah, Jack." She smiled at him in the rearview mirror.

Lin pulled her Temt8tion into a spot close to the hotel's office and switched off the big engine. All four doors opened and shut, and Lin clicked to lock it up. A quick walk brought them to the desk, and the weary clerk looked up from a comic book.

"We'd like a suite for the night."

"We only have one left, and it's three bedrooms."

"That's fine—we'll take it."

"Sure. Checkout is before ten." He handed Lin the key.

While walking to the room, Taylor said, "Mom, I just remembered—you never told me about your license plate."

"Oh, that. Okay, Hon, let's just wait until we get home and get more time to talk."

"'Get' and 'get,' huh, Mom?"

"They're just words, Taylor, and they're—"

"I know, Gabriel, I know! I'm just saying."

They walked into a large suite, and after dropping their bags, Lin said, "How does room service sound?"

"Lin, that is an excellent idea," said Gabriel. "I pray they serve breakfast even at this time."

"Oh Gabby, you haven't had enough hotcakes? Yes, I'm sure they do. And here you go again—praying for food."

They shared a smile as only friends for three decades could, and Lin phoned in their orders. Jack left for a quick shower, and Gabriel flipped through TV channels while slouched deep into the couch. Taylor stared out at a sky which discarded daylight by the second.

*　*　*

Jack had just dressed and rejoined them when a rapping on the door signaled that the meal had arrived. Everyone picked through the cart that was wheeled in, searched for their orders, and sat down for the feast. Taylor finished first and stretched with a big yawn.

"Okay, I'm done. I'm still tired from . . . you know, Mom, when you were—"

"Sorry, Hon. You're probably tired from all your Glyphin stuff too. Using the magic is tiring for me too. Gabby,"—Lin turned toward Gabriel—"when you did all that destroying of Wolfe and his minions, did that tire you out? Does it affect you that way too?"

"It did in the beginning—it was exhausting for me as well. After many centuries of practice, well, it's gotten easier."

"Centuries?"

"Centuries for the world, but for me? No, I have only one lifetime. You will gain strength, Lin. And Taylor, you will as well. It will come quickly."

"I hope so, Gabriel. That is, if I keep causing storms. I do need to learn how to control that."

"You will, Hon. For now, though, maybe a good night's sleep is the best thing. Before long, we'll see that sweet fluffy boy again."

"Nomad's the best, Mom. Okay, I'm done. See you all in the morning."

"Good night, Honey. Jack, you look pretty tired too."

"Yeah, I am. I'll take one of the rooms. You're probably going to sit up and talk awhile, right?"

Lin turned to look at Gabriel and smiled. She turned back to Jack and nodded, saying, "Yeah, Jack. There's something on my mind. See you soon?"

Jack held her gaze and hesitated until Lin said, "At breakfast?"

He gave her another smile, stepped closer for a kiss, and said, "Alright, Lin. Breakfast sounds good. Have a good night."

* * *

With Jack and Taylor each in a bedroom with closed doors, Lin joined Gabriel on the couch. She took the remote and muted the cartoons before saying, "Gabby, if you have a second or two, I'm wondering about the whole Glyphin thing."

"You want to become a Glyphin."

She stared for a few seconds with her eyes wide and said, "How did you know? Yeah, of course, I do."

"The magic will draw you along, Lin. It's no surprise that you're interested in Glyphin powers too."

"That's kind of what Gloriana said. She said, 'learning of the magic is a wave of its own kind.' She was right. I guess she'd know, huh?"

"She more than almost anyone, yes."

"So, I can learn to do what Taylor does?"

"Yes. And more."

"There's more that you didn't tell me?"

"Infinity, Lin. There is always more. But don't you have enough going on right now?"

"Oh, I sure do. It's just the end of the day, and we'll all be home soon, and I'm thinking about things, that's all."

"You're not determined to become a Glyphin right here in this hotel room?"

Lin laughed and said, "No, I don't have the energy for that now anyway. Just wondering."

"Well, then I can tell you this: when a Glyphin uses words, they tap into a dangerous power. But there's something they can use that's more devastating. I'm surprised you haven't thought of it yet on your own."

"Maybe I'm too distracted, Gabby? Just tell me so I don't stay up all night thinking about it, okay?"

"Yes, Lin, I can tell you. I only ask that you don't even hint of it to Taylor. Someday when she has enough control, maybe, but not now."

"Sure, that makes sense. What else can they use?"

"Numbers."

Lin stared and shook her head slowly while she thought of how that could work.

"Numbers? But if a Glyphin reads numbers backwards, like with a word, it's still just a number, right? It's not some unknowable thing like a word read the wrong way."

"That's true for ordinary numbers. But there are other numbers, Lin, ones that have been banished from all knowledge because of how Glyphins used them. They have been purged from all records, and anyone that spoke of them was eliminated. Those were harsh times, but I can't disagree with their goals. All memory of those types of numbers has been lost."

"Except for you, you mean?"

"Yes."

"Aren't you worried someone will come after you too?"

Gabriel laughed and said, "No, Lin, no one can harm me anymore. And there's probably only one other that knows about them."

"Gloriana, right?"

"Yes."

"And I'm supposed to sleep now, wondering just what the heck you're talking about?"

"You can count sheep," Gabriel said with a big grin.

"That's funny—forgetting about numbers by counting. You're really funny sometimes."

They shared a long smile, and Lin said, "You're not going to tell me more than that, are you?"

"No, I'm sorry, Lin. It's a knowledge that's best left alone. And soon, you'll be home with Nomad, and that's a good thing, isn't it?"

"It really is. You're right—I have so much else to focus on, including Nomad. I don't need to know about those forgotten magical numbers."

"Oh, Lin, you know they're not magical. When you learn of them, you'll see they're only forgotten, nothing more. It's what Glyphins can do with them—that's the concern."

"This is all tiring."

"Yes, I know."

"Goodnight, Gabby." Lin rose from the couch. "You're staying up?"

"Yes, that small penguin is lost in a blizzard. I'd like to see him find his way."

Lin picked up the remote, pointed it, and set the volume higher. She shook her head with a smile and said, "See you in the morning."

* * *

Their journey came to an end with Lin clicking her garage door opener. The door went up, she drove the car in, and its deep rumbling echoed around the garage until she killed the engine. She clicked to close the door and let out a long sigh.

"It's good to be home, Mom. I like that game you said you play with Nomad. I want to try it this time."

"Sure, Hon, give it a go. He's pretty stubborn, though. It won't be easy."

Taylor opened her door and began to climb out.

"Oh, Taylor, close your door extra hard. The more noise you make, the better."

Taylor slammed it and walked up to the door to the house. She started to raise her hand toward the doorknob, but she pulled it back. Instead, she leaned in close, putting her ear near the door to listen. Lin, Jack, and Gabriel remained in the car, all trying not to laugh.

Again, Taylor reached for the door.

"Patience, Taylor," Lin said under her breath.

Several minutes of silence passed before they all heard a single deep, "Woof!"

Taylor pushed the door in a few inches, and a huge red snout jammed into the opening, and Nomad's thick mane pushed the door open wide. He reached up for Taylor's shoulders and licked her face clean, stopping only long enough to look up and bark once before he continued welcoming her home.

"Okay, I think it's safe now."

They all got out of the car, and Nomad rushed past Taylor and pounced on Lin. She held his thick arms and moved them to her shoulders, and from there, Nomad showed that he'd saved plenty of affection for her too.

"Oh, Nomad, my sweet fluffy boy! Okay, big boy, let me get the luggage."

Lin pried herself free and popped the trunk. She and Jack gathered up their few bags, and they all walked into the kitchen. Nomad helped Lin focus on the important things by nosing his empty bowl across the floor.

"Nomad, I know the sitter must have fed you. You ate it all?"

"I think I'm rested up enough to shovel a few tons," said Jack.

The sound of Jack pouring the bag of chunks into the metal bowl filled the quiet house, followed quickly by loud crunching.

"He really eats a lot, Mom! Look at him!"

Over the sound of chewing and the bowl being pushed around, Lin tried to be heard.

"Yeah, he really does. He's such a good boy."

"I'm going to take a shower, Mom. It's good to be home. It's good to be home with you."

She left Nomad to give Lin a long hug, and when she turned to go for her shower, Lin wiped at her eyes. Jack stood next to Nomad and played with his ears.

"And I'm going to head home for a few minutes to check on things. I'll be back soon, alright?"

"Sure, Jack. We'll have some dinner."

He kissed her and left through the front door.

"So many things are going well. I don't want to ruin anything. I really don't."

"But you can't leave Gloriana where she is, can you?"

"I have to talk to her again. At least talk, Gabby. If nothing else, I need to ask her about the Words and what speaking them did to me."

"Maybe all that did was open a door for her. A way to reach out to you. It might not have changed you at all."

"I can hope. That's why I need to talk to her again."

"And that's it, you'll just talk?"

"I won't try to save her. I should go right now while Taylor's in the shower."

"And if you're dead again for more than a couple of minutes?"

Lin crossed her arms and stared at Gabriel. She let out a deep breath.

"Taylor has some control, Lin, but not much. This house,"—Gabriel paused to look around the room—"probably isn't as strong as your cabin. I mean, as your cabin was."

"Okay, it can wait I guess."

"She's already been waiting a long time."

"Yeah, I know. Another day wouldn't hurt. She can't tell time anyway."

Chapter 32 – Witches Having Fun

Lin's phone chimed, and she looked to see a text from Jack. She opened it and found a poem, his rhyming attempt at telling her of losing his mind for his Cowgirl tease. Lin smiled and texted him back with a reminder that his very bad girl missed him.

"Gabby, Jack will be here soon. I hate to even ask this, but I have to. What are your plans?"

They sat on the couch listening to Taylor's shower in the next room. Nomad had finished and came to rest his massive head on Gabriel's knees.

"Since you've already learned to travel between the Islands, you probably don't need me. I believe you can help Taylor more than I can too. For her, it's not about the Glyphin business. It's more about controlling herself and not letting words drag her down that path."

"What you're saying is that you're leaving?"

"Soon. I must return to my war, Lin. That's what I have become. I live to fight evil in the magic."

"Can't you let the rest of them fight? Why does it always have to be you?"

"It takes a lot of us. No one ever sees what we do, but if we stopped, the cruelty and suffering in the world would become unbearable."

Gabriel held Lin's gaze, and she could feel tears beginning to force their way out. Gabriel and others fought that war in the timeless magic, keeping evil at bay. She couldn't imagine the goodness and strength that Gabriel possessed.

And she couldn't imagine a life without Gabriel.

"Even though you've been real only a couple of weeks, that war has gone on without you for over thirty years. And besides, aren't you doing good things while you're here too?"

"You're very convincing, Lin. And I've enjoyed being with you more than you'll ever know. But I know what's waiting for me. And I know what I am."

"A destroyer?"

"Yes."

"One that likes blueberry hotcakes?"

"Yes, that too."

"And cookies and cake and—"

"Yes, Lin, it's all good. I could keep eating until—"

"Until you finally get to be a rock star?"

Lin's tears had been replaced by laughter, and Gabriel joined her.

"Yes. I never should have told you that."

"So, you still want that, don't you?"

Gabriel paused to nod as the laughter dwindled.

"Maybe the next time around, Lin."

Lin sighed and turned to look out the window at her neighborhood bathed in fading daylight under clear skies.

* * *

The sound of a blow drier whining lasted a few minutes, and Taylor walked out to join them. She'd changed into jeans and a long-sleeved blouse, and her old hiking boots from her closet still fit.

"Mom, you know what? I've never learned anything about cooking. Show me something, okay? Let's hang out."

She took Lin's hand, and before they left the room, Lin said, "Gabby, since you're not going anywhere, not for a while, maybe watch some TV with Nomad?"

She tossed Gabriel the remote, and Nomad saw the opportunity to claim the rest of the couch. Lin flashed them both a smile as they left for the kitchen.

277

"I don't even care what it is, Mom. Let's just make something."

"Okay, but just a second."

She reached into the pantry and pushed boxes aside until she'd found what she needed. She poked her head into the living room.

"Gabby. Here." And she tossed in a box of crackers. "Dinner won't be for a while."

"Ah, thanks, Lin. It's a small box, but thanks."

Gabriel gave her a big smile while Nomad looked only at the crackers.

* * *

"Let's start with something simple, Hon. Fill that pot up with water and get it boiling. Then, dump some spaghetti in there to boil while we heat up this pasta sauce."

With everything cooking, and while Lin straightened up the counter, Taylor began.

"So . . . Mom. What the heck is going on? How is all of this happening?"

"Oh, Taylor, I don't know if we have time for everything. How about if I give you the quick version for now?"

"Sure, Mom."

"It starts with things I didn't want to tell you about. I didn't even know it when you were asking because I had some of the memories buried in me. Just looking in that direction confused me and scared me. I couldn't tell you anything. I really couldn't."

"Anything about what?"

"Honey, I was abused when I was a twelve-year-old girl. And it lasted for about three years."

"Oh my God, Mom, that's horrible. No wonder that caused so much of a problem for us. I never should have asked you—"

"No, Taylor, it wasn't your fault. It was my uncle Ray's fault. He gets all the blame."

"I hope he's still in jail somewhere, the perv."

"Honey, he's dead. He's the one that hurt himself and then killed himself. That's what stopped the abuse."

Lin knew that she couldn't go any further than that.

"Well, good. He deserves worse than just prison. Are you alright from all that?"

"You've seen all the things I can do. It's all because of that abuse and how I struggled against it. I never gave up, and I wanted nothing more than to find a way to make him stop. And one day, somehow, I guess I did."

"You used magic on him?"

"That's probably the easiest way to explain it. Yeah, magic. But I buried my powers along with those memories of what I'd done to him because I couldn't deal with any of it. And then, a little over two weeks ago, my powers started up again."

"Oh, wow, that must have been exciting!"

"No, Taylor, it's not like witches having fun in the movies. It was pretty damn scary, and I had to fight a huge battle to get control of it. But I did."

"And now you can do all kinds of stuff. And I'm your daughter. I'm a Glyphin. It's pretty cool, Mom."

"One thing I've learned, Hon, is that we have to be very careful with it. Things don't always go the way we plan."

"Oh. Sorry about your cabin."

"That's okay. No one got hurt."

"Oh, and before we forget again. Your license plate says 'BH OR BB.' What's that all about?"

"That stands for 'broken hearts or broken bones.'"

"And what does that mean?"

"When I was a little girl, my mom—"

"Grandma?"

"Yes, grandma used to always tell me that I shouldn't go around breaking anyone's heart. I was young, and I guess I didn't really understand what she meant. But when I got a little older, I started to realize that I did look pretty cute. And you know what? I learned real quick that I didn't mind breaking hearts. At least young teenage hearts anyway.

"God, Taylor, this is hard to go through too. I didn't understand this either until a couple of weeks ago, even though I've been saying that for a long time."

"It's okay, Mom. You don't have to tell me. Maybe some other—"

"No, Honey, it's okay. No more secrets.

"In the years leading up to my uncle abusing me, I felt good about being cute. It made life fun, you know? And I didn't make the connection at the time, but that cuteness probably helped lead to that bastard doing what he did. I felt guilty about it, and that's something that I'd blocked out too.

"So, right away, I wanted to make him stop, but I couldn't. No, you know what? I wanted to hurt him. I wanted him hurt real bad. That's where the 'broken bones' part of it came from. I wanted nothing more than to destroy him."

"Which you did, right?"

"Yeah. Oh yeah, I sure did. And somehow, in my mind, those two things—breaking hearts and breaking bones—got stuck together. It was almost like a mantra in the back of my mind. Anytime I hurt someone, or if I did break their heart in any way, that phrase would echo inside me. I think it helped keep all that crap buried so I never had to really look at it."

"But it's not buried anymore, and you still say it, don't you?"

"I sure do. I understand myself and my past now. But that phrase— it's just such a part of me. Even if you don't know my story, it still sounds pretty cool, doesn't it?"

"Yeah, Mom, it really does. I don't want to live through all the stuff you have, but I wish I had my own cool saying like that."

"Oh, Honey, you *have* been through a lot. And since you're a Glyphin, every word can be special to you. 'Broken hearts or broken bones' will never conjure up a storm."

"Nope, you'll have to leave that to me."

Taylor looked away from Lin and stared until she found a smile and turned back to her.

"I think I'll pick 'Lying Around Lying' for myself. And not because I want to tell lies."

"Why, then?"

"Because one just means laying around, which I did for so long in hospital beds. I never told you how that felt most of the time. I was alone so much, Mom, and I used to watch the birds outside the window. They seemed to show up wherever I was, and I wished I could fly away like they could."

"Oh, Hon, I'm sorry you went through all that. I'll make sure you never feel all alone again, okay?"

Taylor got a big smile and said, "Thanks, Mom. It's good to be home."

"Okay, so what does the second 'lying' mean?"

"Because when I do the Glyphin thing, the second word, the one I play with—it's fake. It's not a real word. It's like a lie."

"I like it, Hon. Soon, maybe you can have your own license plate on your own car?"

"Mom, I'd love that!"

"Hang on a second."

Lin walked over and peeked around the corner. She saw Gabriel and Nomad staring at the TV. Gabriel was taking turns feeding crackers to both of them. She shook her head and turned back into the kitchen.

"And who's Gabriel?"

"Honey, this might be the hardest thing for you to accept. When my powers first showed up, I couldn't handle it. I felt like it wrecked me. Really, I thought I was done. Gabby was sent to protect me and watch over me. Gabby has been around ever since."

"You've known Gabriel since you were what . . . fifteen? Mom, that's amazing!"

"Gabby's amazing, Hon. There's so much more to Gabby than what you see if you peek around the corner. The Gabby that's watching

TV and giving Nomad crackers. God, Hon, there's so much more to Gabby."

"So, Gabriel is what I think?"

"Yeah, Hon."

"I don't know why, Mom, but none of this is hard for me to accept. I guess I kind of always felt that magic was real. And especially now since I can do that Glyphin stuff with words. Even Gabriel being here doesn't surprise me."

"But you have real good control of your power, don't you, Taylor?"

"I think so. Yeah. Probably."

"Okay, I hope so. Jack will be here soon, and this food is almost done. See, nothing to it."

"Couldn't you just use magic, Mom?"

Taylor gave Lin a big grin.

"You know, I've never even thought of that. Let's save that for another time." And she smiled right back.

*　*　*

At the knocking on the door, Lin left and found Jack on the porch waiting to be invited in.

"Jack, just walk in, okay? Dinner's almost ready."

She turned to lead the way, and he reached out and hooked the back pocket of her jeans. He gave her a tug, and she spun around into his arms. He reached around her and squeezed her tight as their lips met.

"Oh, is that what's on your mind, tough guy?"

"Yep. You read the poem, didn't you?"

"Mm . . . I'm still a bad girl, Jack. Maybe that's the real me."

She gave him a mischievous grin, took his hand, and led him into the house.

"Hi, Taylor."

"Hi, Jack."

He took a seat at the table in the kitchen.

"What's cooking? It smells good."

"Spaghetti. I cooked it. I hope it's alright."

"It'll be perfect. I smell garlic bread too."

"Yeah, almost done."

Lin took a step into the living room, and Gabriel and Nomad continued to stare at the TV.

"Hey. You two. Dinner's ready."

"That's good, Lin. We're hungry."

Lin gave them both a look.

"Really, we're still hungry."

*　*　*

Four took their seats, and one stood over a cavernous polished bowl. Nomad's big eyes looked at everyone else's, but they'd begun their dinners, and he'd have to wait.

But not for long. Jack got back up to shake the heavy bag into the bowl. The crunching began immediately.

In between forkfuls, Taylor said, "Jack, do you think I'm dangerous?"

"Well, you're still learning. The spaghetti isn't that bad. With more practice, you—"

"No, Jack. I know you're just being funny. I mean the storms. What I do with the weather."

"Hey, I like a good storm once in a while. What do you think about it?"

"I can control the weather, Jack. It's the coolest thing!"

"Hon, controlling it is the hard part, right? We need to find a way for you to control it."

"Yeah, I know. It isn't easy. I'm not sure I'll ever be able to."

Jack looked at Taylor then back at Lin. His loaded fork waited halfway to his open mouth. He gave a glance at Gabriel, who only shrugged and smiled.

"We're quite a bunch, aren't we, Jack?" Taylor said with a grin.

"Just when I think I'm starting to get used to things, Lin, then something like—"

"Oh, Jack. Compared to everything else, is having a Glyphin around really that big of a deal?"

Jack's spaghetti found its destination, and he chewed with a growing smile.

"I love you guys. All of you."

He paused for another quick glance at Gabriel.

"You too, Nomad," he said in a louder voice over the crunching.

He looked at Lin. "I love your big dog, Lin."

"Jack, you're wonderful. We didn't ask for this. Well, no, that's not true. I guess I did kind of hope for it in some desperate way. But I never would have guessed."

"And Taylor, since she's your daughter, she inherited some of it?"

"Maybe," said Gabriel. "But we think it might have come along with the Words of God. They affected Lin, and maybe they affected Taylor too. But she was already special. She began her life in someone special."

Jack looked back to Lin and said, "Yeah. God yeah, she's special."

He reached into his pants pocket and found the engagement ring. The one he'd been carrying around for a couple of weeks. He left it in his pocket.

"Lin, I'm glad things have settled down. I think they've settled down, haven't they?"

"I hope so, Jack. Yeah, for the most part."

"That's good because I need to finish up that project house. Did I tell you the foundation has some problems now too? We're getting close to December, and digging around out there won't be much fun. But I need to get down below the frost line. Taylor, can you guess how deep that is?"

"No, I have no idea, Jack. But I'm going to go listen to some music. In *my* room."

She gave Lin a big smile.

"You guys have fun talking about dirt and stuff."

With that, Taylor got up to leave, but she stopped herself and said, "Mom, call me when you're all done, and I'll help clean it up."

"Okay, Taylor. Thanks, I'll let you know. Enjoy your music. In *your* room."

Lin turned to Jack.

"Well, that's all very good, Jack. I know you—"

"Don't care about it. I don't. But it worked. I wanted to get a chance to ask you something."

"What, Jack?"

Jack held the ring in his pocket. He gave Gabriel a quick look, smiled, and let it go.

"Are you done dying? I can take a lot. I know I can. But that, Lin . . ."

"You never have to worry, Jack. I've always come back, haven't I?"

"But the first time you were gone—dead—for three days. And where's your cabin now?"

"That shouldn't happen again. I know what I'm doing now."

"It's hard to understand—what exactly are you doing?"

"It's kind of like going back in time, but not really. Gloriana is still there. She's trapped. She wants me to help bring her back. I'm the only one that can do it."

"But it's not your problem, right? Things seem to be evening out. Maybe you can just let her do the best she can on her own?"

Lin looked to Gabriel, who only shrugged and continued poking at the spaghetti.

"The thing is, Jack, I need her help. She's a Glyphin too. Plus, whatever else she knows. She can probably tell Taylor exactly how to control herself. I'm worried that we're only one upset daughter away from this house blowing down too."

Jack paused and stared at her before responding.

"You make a good point. Is there any other way to communicate with her? Like a séance or something?"

Jack broke out a big smile.

"That's funny, Jack. You're a real funny guy."

She smiled while gazing into his big brown eyes.

"Okay, I think I understand. One more time, then that's it? And you won't be dead long, right?"

"Jack, after you left me on the sidewalk in St. Simons, I did that. I did the dead thing, and I talked to Gloriana. I wasn't even out for a second. When I decided to come back, I did."

"Why don't you try it right now before I lose my stomach for it? Can you? Right now?"

"Okay. Yeah, let's get it over with. Gabby, I'll be back before you can take another bite."

"Yes, and be careful. Remember the barnacles, Lin."

While looking into Jack's questioning eyes, Lin intended her mayhem, and the room and Jack and Gabriel and the rest of the world became a still, beautiful surface. Below the world, clouds of magic swelled and blended with each other, swirling in mad patterns. She took a deep breath and felt the magic begin to flow into her and rush pleasure to every cell.

And she slowed the magic down until it hit her in waves. She felt a wave drain out of her, followed by a moment of emptiness. Another wave of magic hit and slowed further, so slow she felt that she barely existed. The wave passed, and no more followed.

A single black dot appeared before her, and her eyes locked onto it. It raced toward her, dragging complete night along with it. It covered her, and she could no longer breathe. Her thoughts ground to a stop, and her feelings were gone. There was only the sound of her heart beating.

Then, it stopped.

* * *

"It's been thirty seconds, Gabriel," Jack said as he shook Lin's arm lightly.

She slumped forward onto the table, and her forehead clunked softly on the tablecloth.

"We must give her time, Jack. She'll be fine."

"You don't know that. She should have been back by now. What if—"

Jack turned to see Taylor standing in the doorway with her earphones around her neck.

An angry thunderclap shook the house, and the first heavy raindrops began to fall.

Chapter 33 – A Fever Inside

Lin was locked in a frozen night with nothing but her intent. She held it tight and waited, not knowing if centuries were passing her by. Not able to even think the question.

A pinpoint of light appeared, and she focused on it. It grew slowly and blocked the darkness before expanding all at once and covering her. She felt her heart begin a comfortable rhythm, and thoughts and feelings returned. She took a deep breath as she looked out over an ocean.

To her left, Lin could see a sun beginning to break the horizon. She looked down at the stone floor then over the edge, and she saw no tower supporting it—only empty air and waves a dizzying distance below. She looked to her right and found the caramel eyes she knew were beside her.

"Gloriana."

"Lin Finity."

"I can't stay long."

"You know your words contain no sense."

Lin shrugged and looked back at the bouncing waves.

"You know what I mean. I don't belong here."

"No living thing belongs here."

They both watched the ocean dance.

"I have a daughter. She's a Glyphin now."

"Yes. From the Words. The Words carry magic, Lin Finity."

"Yeah, I get that. You aimed that at me."

"Or one that is like you. You are rare."

"It's been two-thousand years since the last. You asked him for help too, didn't you?"

"Yes. But he offers no help. He has his own mission."

They didn't speak for what could have been seconds or centuries.

"I need your help. An answer. How does a Glyphin control her power?"

"Is there destruction?"

"Yes. She can't control it. How can she do that?"

"The answer brings little comfort."

"Well, I've come this far."

"Far?"

"You know what I mean. I'd like to hear your answer."

"Practice."

Lin turned to face Gloriana. She saw her wild brown hair blowing around lightly near her shoulders. Her gown looked new, and Lin realized that all of it was new. And none of it was real. Only Gloriana's intent was real.

"She can start small at a time when she is not angry. Let her begin something tiny, and since she is not upset, she can end it with ease."

"That's pretty simple. That's it? That would work?"

"Yes. Is that all you wish to know?"

"No. One other thing. What did the Words of God do to me?"

"The Words are not from God. No human can hear God's Words. They are my words. I ask a question, and the world gives me the answer I already know to be true."

"Then, why the whole thing with a Scroll and Renato?"

"You know Renato? You are very strong."

"But why all that?"

"The Scroll causes others to seek one like you. Like a net cast into the approaching centuries, the Scroll finds you."

"You knew all that would happen?"

"I cannot know. Only hope."

Lin felt a trembling inside. Taylor. And Jack and Gabby. She had to get back. She'd heard enough.

"You are not compelled. The Scroll is my hope. I continue to wait if I must. I am glad to know you, Lin Finity."

"The Scroll is gone. I returned Renato to his human form. There isn't a net out there anymore trying to catch someone like me."

Gloriana looked down at the stone floor. Minutes passed. Or months.

"I understand. Then, I must ask you again. Bring me back to the Islands of Time. I have no strength to do it myself."

"If I don't, what will become of you?"

"I hold my intent. Eternity resumes when you live again."

Lin shook deep inside at Gloriana's strength and determination, but she looked for and found her own stillness. She found the intent deep inside her, and she held it in silence. After an immeasurable time, a black dot began racing toward her. No breathing, and no thoughts or feelings. No beating heart.

In complete emptiness, Lin held her intent.

She felt the first teeth find her. The first sharp claws.

She quietly held her intent.

*　*　*

"No. No, Jack. Gabriel, how could you let her? And I don't mean 'letter,' that thing you stick in the mail. And that doesn't mean 'male,' like Nomad's a boy. 'Nomad' is the funniest word ever. Who names a dog that and locks him in a house?"

Wind whipped rain into the dining room window and chattered it up and down the roof of Lin's house. The gutters began overflowing and spilled over all along their lengths. A blinding flash of lightning and a quick boom took out the lights. In the next flash, Taylor could be seen staring at Lin, who was slumped over the table dead.

"Taylor," said Gabriel. "It's going to be okay. We've seen this before, haven't we?"

290

"And *we* have hated it every time, Gabriel! I don't want my Mom to be,"—she took a deep breath—"DEAD!" Another loud boom shook the house. The green flash of her eyes cut through the darkness.

Jack stood up and put an arm around her, and she shoved it away.

"No, Jack. You go get her. Both of you. Wherever she went, you two, go get her. I swear . . ."

Sirens wailed from every direction.

"And what if I did swear? Those are some fun words. You want me to play with swear words, Gabriel?"

"Taylor, you don't want to hurt anyone, do you?" said Gabriel.

"No. But I don't want a dead mother either."

Lightning flashed, and thunder boomed.

"We'll figure this out, I'm sure of it," said Jack.

Nomad poked his big nose into one of Taylor's hands, and she raised both arms and crossed them. With illumination from a continuous stream of lightning, Nomad could be seen standing up and placing his paws on the table. His snout was level with Taylor's face, and he turned to look at her.

"Not now, Nomad. Just go hide somewhere."

He reached for her shoulder, found a solid place to hold, and turned to place his other paw on Taylor's other shoulder. Jack found the flashlight on his phone, and the room lit up. Jack and Gabriel stared in silence.

Taylor uncrossed her arms and dropped them to her sides.

"Stop it, Nomad." She turned her head to face Jack.

"Jack, you shouldn't have—"

Nomad reached a massive paw out for Taylor's cheek and gently turned her to face him. She looked into his eyes and saw his big calm eyes looking first at her left eye, then her right, then back again.

She reached up and placed her hands over his paws and continued to gaze into his eyes.

Taylor nodded twice, took a deep breath and closed her eyes, and she didn't let go of him. The lightning stopped, and the wind calmed, but heavy rains continued to fall.

"I don't want to hurt anyone. Especially Nomad."

"That's good, Taylor," said Jack. "He's probably kind of scared right now."

She looked into the quiet dog's eyes. He rarely blinked as he continued to gaze calmly into her teary eyes.

The rain lessened, but it still cascaded out over the gutters.

"Can you imagine drying all that fur, Taylor?" said Jack.

Taylor laughed.

"No, Jack. That would be impossible."

"And what if his food got all wet? What then?"

"He'd starve. Real quick. Jack, I can only stop this so much."

The rain lessened but remained steady.

"I know you're trying to help. Both of you. Nomad too."

Nomad licked her face a few times and dropped to the floor with a thud. He stayed near, and Taylor rubbed his head and played with his ears.

"It's like a fever inside. I can cool it down some, but I can't put out the fire. Not while my mom is dead." And at that word, more lightning flashed.

"She's not really dead. Come on, we know that. Your mom, she just . . . I don't know, but she's fine. I know she is. We've seen this before."

"I'm trying, Jack. I'm really, really trying."

*　*　*

After an unknowable amount of time, a point of light appeared before Lin. Her attention fastened to it and wouldn't let it go. It raced toward her, stretching out and dragging a world behind it. When no more darkness could be seen, she felt her heart welcoming her back to life. Feelings and thoughts returned, and she took a deep breath.

It smelled like an old tablecloth. She opened her eyes and saw mostly darkness until Jack turned his phone toward her.

"Lin, oh my God! You're back!" said Jack.

"I never doubted you, Lin," said Gabriel.

She sat up and tried to look around the room. She felt Taylor wrap her arms around her and begin crying into her shoulder.

"Mom, you were dead again. Please stop doing that!"

Taylor laughed and cried at the same time.

The rain continued.

"Okay, Hon. I'm back. You can stop the rain, okay?"

"I can't, Mom. I'm never going to get used to you dying all the time. Let it rain . . ."

Lin looked out and saw that, though the rain continued, the lightning and thunder had ceased. A few seconds later, the lights flickered and stayed on.

"Okay, Honey."

She hugged her close.

"Let it rain."

*   *   *

With the recliner tipped back and her headphones on, it wasn't long before Taylor's slippers stopped bouncing, and her head tipped to the side. Lin planted herself up against Jack on the couch, and Gabriel took the other chair.

"Okay, that can't be good," Lin said while pointing at her living room window.

The drops on the glass no longer pulled together to run down in streams. Instead, they froze against the window and sparkled from the glow of the streetlights.

Jack checked his phone and relayed the bad news.

"Yeah, the temperature's dropping. The forecast says way below freezing tonight."

"I told Taylor to let the rain keep going because I thought she'd tire out eventually. I remember that every time she fell asleep, whatever she was doing stopped. Not this time."

"You were right about it tiring her out, I think," said Gabriel. "She's using the magic. I've never heard about Glyphins getting tired, but that's probably how it works."

"So, how come the rain didn't stop?"

"I don't understand it. Maybe she can maintain that while she sleeps. But that might not be the biggest problem."

"That's right," said Jack. "Snow. That's going to be our problem next."

Nomad jumped onto the couch next to Jack, nuzzled his neck a few seconds, then lay down across both of them.

"What was that all about with Nomad, Gabriel?" said Jack. "He wasn't exactly acting like a dog."

"He's very protective—that's nothing new. He knew Taylor was upset."

Lin and Jack stared back at Gabriel while she scratched Nomad's back and Jack fiddled with his floppy ears.

"Gloriana gave me some advice."

"That's why you had to die, Lin? To go chat with that woman?"

"Yeah, but it was an important chat. I asked her how a Glyphin can learn to control their power. She said 'practice.'"

"It looks like she's getting plenty of that."

"Oh, not like this, Jack. Taylor started all this because of the strong emotions she was feeling. Gloriana said she needs to start something small when she's not upset at all."

"Just a little storm for fun?" Jack said with a grin.

"Something like that, yeah. And then, since she doesn't really care about it, or she has no need for it, she'd have an easier time stopping it."

"Makes sense," Jack said before he pried himself out from under the heavy dog and walked to the window. "But what do we do about this?"

"We start shoveling, Jack," Lin said with a tired smile.

He walked back to her, leaned over Nomad, and gave her a kiss.

"You're right—it's not that bad. It's just snow."

"For now," said Gabriel.

"You're scaring me again, Gabby. You must know that."

Gabriel only shrugged.

* * *

Jack stared out into the dark, and Lin and Gabriel waited for his weather update.

"I've never seen it snow so hard. It's almost knee-deep already."

"Gabby, you're not leaving. You can't, right? And I don't mean because of the snow."

"No, I'm not leaving, Lin. And when I do, you know the weather won't matter."

"I need help with Taylor. Can you stay at least until we figure that out?"

"Yes, I'll stay, but I don't know what else to tell her. I suspect Gloriana didn't tell you all she knows."

"Oh, that's for sure. 'Practice,' she said. It can't be that easy. It probably has something to do with the words she used too."

"I believe that's right."

"Alright, so no one's going anywhere for a while. Lin, you have a lot of food packed away, right?"

"Oh, Jack. No, not as much as I'd like to have. I've been busy the last couple of weeks."

"Hell yeah, you've been busy."

Jack shook his head and smiled.

"We should be fine. There's always Nomad's food."

Nomad turned to look at Lin, and he stared for several seconds before turning back around and laying his head down.

The smile left Lin's face.

"I have to go again."

Jack and Gabriel froze and stared at her.

"No, Lin, you can't. You saw what happened last time."

"Jack, it's already snowing. Does that look like it's about to stop? And look at Taylor, sleeping like a baby over there. And still—"

"I don't believe she'll tell you, Lin. This might all be part of her plan."

"Oh God, I didn't even consider that. That's pretty diabolical."

"Yes. And she's had many lifetimes to plan this out."

"She won't tell me unless I bring her back? Is that what you're saying?"

"Maybe."

"She knew someone would become a Glyphin and cause something like this?"

"I believe it's possible."

"Then, I have to bring her back, Gabby. I thought I wanted to anyway, even before this." She pointed at the blizzard hitting the glass.

"Maybe it'll stop soon," said Jack. "There's no need to rush back, is there? Can't you wait awhile and see how the storm goes?"

"It's really piling up, Jack. By morning, the house might be covered."

"Let's take that chance, alright? Let's see how it looks in the morning."

"I can't fix any of this with its magic. There's too much."

"And I can't—"

"I know, you can't either. You can't interfere with peoples' lives."

"This is a good plan, Lin. Jack, if you carry Taylor to bed, I'll sleep on the couch. If Nomad allows me enough room."

Jack lifted Taylor out of her recliner, and Lin pulled down the blankets on her bed. After they'd tucked her in, they paused to look out her bedroom window. All they could see was white with a couple of dim glows that Lin thought must be streetlights.

They closed the door and stood in the hall. He reached around her waist from behind and pulled her close. Her hair was off to one side and hanging down past her shoulder in front of her. He found her neck and began kissing her.

"Oh, Jack. That's sweet."

She felt his muscular arms holding her, and she moved only to confirm his strength.

"Sweet is nice, Jack. But does a bad girl deserve something a bit different?"

He spun her around and squeezed her tight, gave her a big kiss, and they broke to smile in the near darkness.

"Sweet, bad, anything . . . you're my Cowgirl." He kissed her again.

"And you'll have to at least start out in the guest room, don't you think?"

"Yeah, it's where I finish that matters." He gave her a big grin.

"Your work might never be finished, Jack. Not with a girl like me."

"You do like acting like a bad girl, don't you?"

Vivid recollections of her dreams crept into her, and they didn't rush back out. A sharp memory grabbed her, and Lin felt she was naked and on her knees in a hotel room. She shook her head and answered.

"Who says I'm acting, Jack?"

He growled and lifted her in his hug, kissing her while her bare feet kicked high above the floor. He put her down and said, "You probably have to talk about some kind of magic stuff, right?"

"I probably should, yeah. I need some advice about all that's going on. You don't mind, do you?"

"No, it's fine. I'll shovel some food into the dog's giant bowl and go take a shower."

"Oh, Jack." She reached around his neck and gave him a long kiss.

Chapter 34 – Hotcakes Help Too

"What chance do I have with the barnacles?"

Lin sat with her arms crossed at one end of the couch, facing a sleepy Gabriel slouched against the other end with Nomad close by.

"I have no idea, Lin. Those spaces in between the Islands were never my thing, so I never spent much time there. Well, not 'time.' You know what I mean."

"But you know what it's all about, don't you?"

"I know some."

"And you still think if I could somehow drag Gloriana back here, something else might tag along? Gabby, you think those things have their claws in her right now?"

"Yes, she's probably got some hooks in her."

"There must be some way to, I don't know, cut them loose or chase them away."

"Maybe there is. But I doubt even she could tell you. Lin, those things are meant to destroy everything that passes from Island to Island."

"Okay, I don't understand something. In the magic, there's no time. If you or Renato are mostly in the magic, you live almost forever."

"That's true."

"If I stay in the magic, the barnacles will never get at me either?"

"That's right. It takes great strength to survive there, though. Few can do that."

"The magic comes in waves, and if I slow the waves down enough, I find the spaces in between them. That's between the Islands of Time?"

"'Slowing' might not be the right word, but I know what you mean. Yes, and it takes great strength to do that too."

"There's infinity *in* each wave of magic, and there's also infinity *between* each of the waves?"

"Yes."

Lin shook her head slowly while staring at the ceiling and listening to the heavy snow beating against the glass.

"You've been through a lot the last couple of weeks, Lin. I think that's why."

She turned down only her eyes to look at Gabriel, who wore a smile.

"Why what?"

"Why you're not asking the obvious questions."

She gave up on the ceiling and faced Gabriel.

"What are you talking about now?"

"You've been between the Islands several times now. Some of your trips were quick, and you were back as if no time had passed. But one time, Jack had to sit with you for four hours. And your very first journey lasted three days for those of us that were still alive."

"Yeah, I was dead a long time, but what are you getting at?"

"The first question is this: since there's infinity between each two Islands, even if you stayed in that space for a long time, why would you not come back to the very next Island? How does anyone ever know you were gone?"

"Well, now that you mention—"

"How could you die between two Islands and return from between another two that are much later in time?"

"Yeah, how does—"

"How can I be around so long, Lin? Why wouldn't my eternity last only until I return to the same Island of Time?"

"Gabby, I—"

"How can you find Gloriana no matter which two Islands you die between?"

Lin stared with her mouth moving slowly but saying nothing.

"There's infinity in each wave of magic, but they are all part of the same infinite magic. There's infinity between each two Islands of Time, too, but altogether, they are just one infinite emptiness. That's the answer to all your questions, Lin."

"But that doesn't make sense. When I use my mayhem, I'm in the magic, and I know I could stay there forever—I have all the time in the world. Wait, I didn't say that right. I mean that I have forever, if I want, before I let time start again. No, I mean before I come back to the world. I mean . . . I know I never really left, but—"

"Your mind, Lin. It has limits. You have no hope of understanding this with your mind."

"You're right—I don't understand it. But you do, don't you?"

"No."

"But how could—"

"Our minds are not made to understand it."

"Do I need to?"

Lin smiled and Gabriel nodded.

"A bit of understanding will help you."

"How? With what?"

"Navigating. I could wait a century to see you again, but no one else you know could."

"God, Gabby, that really is possible?"

"Hopefully not if I can explain it to you. I'll fail, of course, because it can't be explained to our minds, but it's worth an attempt."

"Tell me, Gabby. I'll try to understand it."

"If you were in the ocean and floating at the very top of a wave, you'd be connected to the ocean, wouldn't you?"

"Yes, of course."

"And that ocean might as well be infinite. At least it would seem that way to you."

"Yeah, it would."

"And the sky above you?"

Lin had a brief thought of the real sky above them all, one packed tightly with puffy snowflakes.

"That's kind of infinite too."

"Now, if that wave tossed you to the next one, for an instant, you'd be apart from the infinite water, and you'd belong to the infinite sky."

"Until the next wave catches me?"

"Yes. But you'd be alive only when you're on a wave. Most people can't do it, but your intent is strong enough that you can dive into that wave. You haven't gone very deep yet. Every time you've used your mayhem, you've come right back up to the top of the wave. But if—"

"If I dove down deeper, I could come up to a different wave? Is that it?"

"Yes, but here is where our minds fail us. The wave is part of the infinite ocean, but the wave is also infinite on its own. When you've used your mayhem, you were swimming around in the top of an infinite wave. But when you and I joined with those wonderful creatures in a real ocean somewhere, we dove deep into the wave. We dove into the infinite ocean."

"And when I was a bird with Jack? Then, too?"

"Yes. And do you remember how it felt to come back each time?"

"Yeah, I sure do. Like I was dying."

"And why was that?"

Lin stared and stayed silent while remembering the experiences, recalling the anguish she'd felt both times.

"I think it's because of how it started each time. Gabby, I felt like I was somehow being born."

"That's exactly right, Lin. And for both of those travels, you no longer existed here. Time continued without you."

"That's why we had to hide in that alley? We really did vanish?"

"Yes."

Lin smiled and said, "Our clothes too? How could—"

"For a short journey, you will take everything with you. Remember—everything is made of the magic, and your intent gathers it all up. If you were to go for many more Islands, right now, you wouldn't have the strength to bring back your fashionable wardrobe. You'd come back without your clothes, Lin."

Lin only stared and shook her head as Gabriel waited. She didn't speak, so Gabriel continued.

"When you begin a long march, you're strong, and you can carry some luggage if you wish. But on the return trip? You're tired, and you will have left your belongings somewhere along the way."

Lin shook her head again and said, "Okay, I don't think I'll ever need to worry about that. But that's how it feels to go deeper into the magic? Like being born? Why is that?"

"It just does, Lin, and all we can do is accept it. The deeper one goes, the more profound the feeling of birth."

"And the harder it is to come back?"

"Yes."

"When you're gone fighting evil in the magic, that's what it's like for you?"

"Yes, it's difficult to come back. It's hard to even want to."

"I was a bird for maybe two seconds, and I cried my eyes out when I got back. And that wasn't because I could hear God's Words, it was because I was in the magic?"

"No, it was because you heard God's Words. The deeper one goes into the magic, though, the more it feels the same way. There are no Words, though."

Lin stared in silence for a few seconds.

"To journey into the magic is like hearing God's Words?"

"Haven't you been drawn to the magic since you first found your mayhem?"

Lin closed her eyes and felt herself shaking inside. She knew that it was true. Every time she'd witnessed the magic, she'd felt like going deep into it, even though it was madness.

"How could you be strong enough to return from the magic?"

"I only come back when I'm asked. And if I am asked, I know it's important. I find the strength."

Lin felt tears pooling up and hoping to spill out.

"Gabby, you didn't want to come back to help me, but you did anyway?"

"As much as it feels like dying for me to return, my desire to answer that request is stronger. I will always find strength enough to do what is asked of me."

"Coming back, you felt like I did after being a bird for just a moment, but worse?"

"Yes, worse."

She couldn't help letting tears flow out and down her cheeks.

"Do you remember when I first arrived, Lin? How you cried as I held you?"

Lin could barely speak through her quiet sobs.

"Yes, I remember."

Gabriel's eyes closed.

"I wanted to cry too."

Lin wiped at her eyes and forced them to remain open. She wondered how she could have such unbelievable strength to use the magic, yet tears could be impossible to stop.

"But you didn't cry."

"I returned for you, Lin. Comforting you was all that mattered."

Fresh tears flowed from Lin's green eyes.

"How could you do that, Gabby? Aren't you still sad here?"

"You are a sustaining joy of my life. That helps more than you can know."

Lin stared through her wet eyes, feeling again like that crying fifteen-year-old girl in Gabriel's arms.

With opened eyes, Gabriel smiled and said, "Hotcakes help too, Lin."

Through her tears, Lin managed a soft laugh and Gabriel joined her.

* * *

After her tears had dried, Lin gave her eyes one more wipe with the back of her hand.

"Okay, Gabby, but I need to hear more about this navigation business. You're saying that if someone can go deep enough into the magic, the waves will continue past them?"

"Exactly right, Lin. The waves bring time to the living. Many waves pass while I'm in the magic fighting evil. If you add up all my time spent alive—the time when I'm on the Islands—I have only one lifetime. It was the same for Renato."

"He told me that. He told me he had only one life. And it's the same if I'm tossed up into the infinite sky—that's the spaces in between, right?"

"Yes. Gloriana also has only one lifetime."

Lin slumped back into the couch cushions with a relieved grin.

"Now, it's clear what I have to do. When I'm going to that space in between, I need to intend a return to the exact moment that I leave. That would do it, right?"

"Yes, but there are no guarantees. It's all about your intent and how strong your hold on it is."

"My hold is unbreakable, you know that. I won't ever be gone a century."

"Not unless it's by choice."

"I would never choose that."

"There was a time when I chose to remain in the magic rather than do something worse."

"What? You had to escape from something?"

"The forgotten numbers, Lin, the ones that were purged from all knowledge and memory. I was hunted for knowing of them by many men who were sent to kill me. I chose to wait and let time pass rather than destroy them all."

"If they also knew about the numbers, why would—"

"They didn't know about the numbers or why they hunted me. The last other living person to know of them sent a small army after me. But after she explained to them that there was a serious reason why I had to be killed, they understood right away that she had to die too. So, they murdered her and set out after me."

"Why would they—"

"Those were different times, Lin. Everyone knew the danger of powers without limits. They accepted their task without reservations."

"So, you left?"

"Yes."

"But then, everyone you knew, all your friends, everyone who—"

"They all lived their lives to their ends without me, Lin."

Lin felt more tears looking to escape. She wiped at her eyes and forced them to stay open.

"Gabby, I pray I never have a reason to even think of doing that. Hey, wait a second . . . can't you dive deep into the magic and find the waves from long ago?"

"If there's a way to do that, I have no knowledge of it."

"Is that what Lancaster Wolfe offered to teach you?"

"It's what he said, but things like him thrive on deceit. Still, it was easier to refuse his offer believing that it was impossible anyway."

"I felt like Gloriana took me back in time when I relived those events from her past."

"Perhaps her intent conjured up a world just to show you that."

"I don't know what to think about that. When she took me from the couch back at the cabin, I didn't just see what happened back then—I felt it."

"She was powerful beyond belief, Lin. It seems she still is."

Lin showed just a trace of a smile and looked down at her lap. Gabriel rubbed Nomad's ears and waited for more questions.

"I'm starting to get why I see infinity when I use my mayhem. But I'm not really *seeing* anything, am I?"

"No, not with your eyes."

"These lives that we live . . . we're right there on the edge of infinity, right on the fringes of it all the time, aren't we? Whether we know it or not?"

"Yes. Rather humbling, wouldn't you say?"

Lin turned to look at the icy white window and let out a deep breath.

"Yeah. And exhausting, Gabby. I'm done for the night. Tell Jack I'll see him around."

Chapter 35 – Strange Sweet Hunger

Leaning against her closed bedroom door, Lin studied the raging snowstorm slamming against her window. With a soft groan, she walked over and snapped the curtains closed. A look around her room showed her nothing of the problems outside its walls. It was a refuge, a safe place that she'd soon share with her Cowboy. In the morning, she knew she'd have to travel again to see Gloriana, and the possibility of being lost between the Islands for a century brought out another groan.

A steaming shower helped, followed by a leisurely towel drying, and she slipped on a thick white robe. Before doing anything else, she found the thermostat and aimed it toward a warmer room, one where clothing wouldn't be missed.

But what clothing? she wondered. She took a look in her closet and saw plain pajamas and t-shirts on one side and her sexy wardrobe on the other. She knew that Jack liked her innocent and wearing plain pajamas. But he also liked her dressed up. He liked her being a tease and playing that game—her new favorite game.

Thoughts of more play with Jack led to memories of strangers in dream worlds liking her best in her sexiest clothes, the ones that showed every inch of her legs and so much more. Everyone wanted her to tease them and tempt them. But most of all, they loved how she ended up without the clothes and doing what she was told.

She picked up the baggy pajama pants, rubbed the fuzzy material between her fingers for a few seconds with a frown, and threw it aside.

Then, she gathered the outfit all of them wanted most, including her: the shortest skirt, the highest heels, and a tight blouse that would cling to every little detail. She stretched it all on and sat at her vanity, where she began long, steady strokes with her hairbrush. Excited green eyes looked back at her from her mirror as she squirmed in her seat.

With a strange sweet hunger burning inside, she sat in the room's plush chair and crossed her legs. She looked down at her bare leg bouncing over her knee with the ankle strap twinkling in the dim light. She emptied her wine glass, poured another, and set it and the bottle on the table to one side. A thought of Jack and what they'd be doing soon led to her extending both legs out, and her left hand found the bottom of her skirt.

Without her seeking them, memories of her other lives pinned her down and pushed Jack into the shadows. She easily traded him for a replay of what a tease she'd been in those imaginary worlds. How cheap she'd been. And especially, how Ben had treated her.

She let out a slow breath and opened herself to the steamy recollections.

One memory flooded her and demanded her attention, and she welcomed it with a soft moan. The sweet abandon she'd felt when she'd stood in front of Ben wearing only her panties and heels, rotating herself gently and watching him stare. She remembered the thrill of glancing at the door to his room, locked and chained, and preventing any escape.

The danger had been intoxicating, and she'd only wanted more. So, she'd provoked him enough to slap her before she obeyed and got down on her knees for him. And when he'd called her a tramp, just a cheap tramp, a girl that dressed to tease and strutted all around for everyone to see, she'd realized that she really was a tramp. No, more than that—she'd *wanted* to be nothing but a tramp.

A sharp wave of pleasure touched her at the memory of being nearly naked and helpless and on her knees for a dangerous man. Then, she added her own fun detail to the memories, making it all that much more gratifying. She imagined taking another slap that compelled her to grab the thin elastic around her waist and begin to roll it down over her hips. She felt the tiny garment pulled tight between her thighs, leaving nothing hidden from him. She couldn't resist embellishing even more—she added getting another strike from a second stranger before removing it completely and standing in the middle of the large group wearing only her heels.

That would be better, she thought, while sunk deep into her chair in her quiet bedroom. It's always best to leave all her clothes on the floor. That's how strangers wanted her. That's how all the strangers would always want her—completely naked and helpless.

And after they'd forced her to her knees, there'd be no chance to even try to escape—they'd never let her free anyway. So, she'd have to reach out the very short distance and open the nearest belt and zipper. Before going any further, she'd know what she needed first, and one of them would give it to her. With the fresh stinging on her cheek, she'd have no choice but to do what she wanted to do anyway, so she'd—

Lin snapped her eyes open, felt her heart pounding, and found that her own hand had helped with the memories. She crossed her arms and sat up straight.

Oh, thank God, she thought. Those were only fake worlds—something Gloriana had concocted.

She fought to reclaim the image of Jack's solid, muscular body, his strong hands all over her and taking whatever he wanted. The reality that would soon be hers raced through her imagination, and her heart continued a steady, forceful beat.

* * *

The house grew quiet outside of Lin's warm bedroom. Minutes later, the door swung in slowly without a sound. Jack walked in wearing only his torn jeans and boots, his lean muscles highlighted by the dim lamp on the nightstand. He locked the door and walked to stand in front of her as she sat with her legs crossed and her skirt working its way up. She could see how wide his eyes opened as he looked down on her.

"My God, you look damn hot."

From her seat, she looked up into his smiling brown eyes, and past his cravings, she saw the undeniable love he had for her. She looked at his lips, then down along his hard chest, his trim waistline . . . all the way down to his tight jeans. So near to her.

She hadn't planned it, but she didn't fight it either. She relaxed and welcomed the memories finding an opening and taking her. No harm in that, she told herself, and she felt large pieces of herself moving around and finding new patterns. She knew that they were seeking the arrangement they'd found before in that fake world. And she felt like hurrying them into their places, jamming them in tight to again make her the woman she'd become in her dreams. The woman she wanted to be this night.

It's just for tonight, she thought.

"Oh, I can heat you up, mister. Do you want to play with me?"

"You want to play again, huh?"

Even in the faint light, she noticed how eager he'd become.

"Oh yeah. I'm dressed to be played with."

Jack smiled and shook his head slowly.

And a memory of Ben standing before her, ready for her, became a bit more real.

With a tangled mix of love and desire for Jack, and invading memories of being a tease for those other men, Lin finished her glass, stood, and pushed against his chest to move him back a few steps.

"I bet you want me out of this shirt. Would you like that, stranger?"

Jack started to laugh but stopped himself at seeing that Lin wasn't smiling.

"Yeah, damn right. Lose the shirt," he told her with a grin.

Lin unbuttoned it, slid it slowly back over her shoulders, and let it drop onto her chair. She remembered how she'd held her hair back for Davey when she'd lost her blouse, and she thought maybe Jack would like that too.

"Mm . . . that's better," she said with her hands up under her hair as she rotated slowly, swaying them for a staring Jack. She felt strangers staring too. She lowered her hands and held them behind her, just like Davey's gang had done.

"You like that, big boy?"

"Oh, God yeah. I—"

"How about this skirt, big fella?"

"Oh yeah. Yeah, take that off too."

"You just might want what's under there, mister. I doubt I could stop you."

Jack continued to grin and shake his head. He looked down to her waist, and his smile became a determined stare.

Lin slid her fingertips inside the top band and began stretching it down over her hips. He watched without blinking as the elastic of her panties came into view first. Then, he could see the thin, lacy material as she slid her skirt down her thighs. She shimmied it all the way, and it fell to her ankles, where she stepped out of it and pushed it to the side.

"There, I'm almost naked now, mister. I'll keep going if I have to. If you make me."

Jack looked up.

"Why would I have to—"

"Just one tiny little thing left, mister. Look how thin and tight it is."

She pulled it up, stretching the sheer material over her.

"Yeah, that's—"

"I'll take that off for you, if you insist."

"Yeah. But why would I have to—"

"I'll do whatever you say. I bet you want me completely naked, don't you?"

Jack shrugged, shook his head, and grinned.

"Yeah, damn right. Get that off too."

Lin hooked her thumbs into the strap at each side and began to slowly roll the string over her hips.

"Damn, you're such a—"

He stopped himself and stared at the elastic wrapped over her thumbs.

"I'm a what, mister? What am I?"

"I was going to call you a tease. You really are," he said as he shook his head.

"Oh, I'm something more than just a tease," she said as more pieces inside found new places.

Other men already know what I am, she thought.

"Just like you wanted." She peeled down the small patch of white cloth. With nothing covered, Lin felt most of the moving pieces find their places.

"There we go. Didn't have a choice, did I? Now, it's there for everyone to see."

"Everyone?"

She let it drop to her ankles and stepped one heel out.

"Mm-hmm. For everyone to enjoy too," she said without a smile as she leaned her hips forward and framed herself with her palms pressed against her skin.

He looked up into her eyes with a big smile.

"Really? That's more than just a tease."

"Yep. There's another name for a girl like me."

"For everyone to enjoy?"

She smiled and nodded.

"Oh yeah, mister. Everyone gets a turn."

Only part of Jack's smile remained.

"You mean, you'd let anyone . . . anyone could—"

"Can't say no, big boy. A whole gang could have that any way they want."

Jack stared but couldn't speak. She slid her hands up to her breasts and held them.

"These too, mister. They're so smooth and soft. I can't stop anyone from touching them and playing with them."

"But—"

"Mm . . . that's just the kind of girl I am."

Lin ran her hands down and rubbed the insides of her thighs.

He stared into her eyes. She looked back with a calm expression.

"What do you call a girl like me, mister?"

Jack shook his head a couple of times, but he found his voice and grinned.

"Oh, you're a hooker. You are one damn sexy hooker."

"Yeah, I could be a hooker. I sure like stripping, but I'm not about to get on my knees, stranger."

"Well, I guess nobody said—"

"You want me to, don't you?"

"Yeah. God yeah," Jack said with a laugh, and he kept smiling like a convert.

Lin took a few steps and stood right in front of him. He took a long look all the way up from her heels to her eyes, grinning at everything in between.

"You'll have to make me."

"What? I mean—"

"It's easy, mister." Lin swept her hair back and turned her cheek up. "You could force me to get on my knees."

"No, I can't . . . I mean—"

"You know what I'll have to do there, don't you, stranger?"

Jack began to shake.

"Well, yeah, but—"

"You want that, don't you?"

His fists were clenched at his sides, and she smiled at him.

"God, do I, but—"

"Imagine how that will feel. You want to make me do that, don't you?"

She turned her head to give him a good angle, and she noticed he'd unclenched his right hand. But Lin didn't get what she wanted from him, and she fought to keep her mayhem from taking him and forcing him.

"It's easy. You know you want to."

Jack reached up quickly, but he only placed both hands on her shoulders and pushed her down. The moment her knees touched, she felt most of the pieces inside wedge in tight. Only a couple still moved around.

"Get on your knees, you hooker."

Lin knelt in front of the man and swept her hair back. She looked him in the eye and gave him a barely noticeable smile.

"Oh, I think maybe I should leave, mister." She started to rise.

She liked how quickly the man grabbed her shoulders and pushed her back down, and she felt the coarse area rug rough against her knees. He didn't let her go.

"Is that enough to get what you want from me?"

His hand was a blur as it found Lin's upturned left cheek, but he only touched her gently. He left it there as they gazed into each other's eyes. Lin nodded once. He pulled it back an inch and tapped her cheek as he looked down on her and shook his head with a grin.

From the thrill of even that modest slap while she was naked and on her knees, Lin felt her eyes flash green for just an instant. When the man looked scared and tried to take a step back, she grabbed his belt and held him in place.

"Okay, stranger, I have no choice, do I?"

She opened his belt and worked his zipper down.

He stopped looking so scared.

"Oh, I think maybe I'm more than just a hooker."

She reached in.

He didn't look scared at all.

"Don't be a gentleman. You should call me what I am."

Lin smiled, looked up into the man's eyes, and waited. But he didn't answer.

"This is what I was made to do. What you're forcing me to do. You know what I am."

The man was shaking and could barely speak.

"I love getting on my knees. I give everyone a turn. Call me a tramp, mister."

Lin held on and looked without smiling. He found his voice.

"You're a tramp. Damn, you are such a tramp."

The final pieces inside found their places and locked solid.

Lin sighed and said, "Oh, you are so right," as she looked at what she'd found and was holding so close.

"Is that what you want, tramp?"

The man had quit smiling.

"Maybe I should just leave. I don't think—"

Without waiting for a nod, he gave her left cheek another tap, more like a gentle push, enough to turn her head and cause a quick flash of bright green. She didn't let go, and he made no attempt to escape. She saw mostly hunger in his eyes.

"What should I do now?"

Lin continued to stare as her smile left her.

"You know what to do."

"I'll do what you tell me. You sure have me naked and helpless."

She shook her hair out of the way and held him with both hands.

"Just do what a tramp does," the man said through clenched teeth as he pulled all of his hair back with both hands and gripped it tight.

"You mean what I love doing on my knees, one after the other? No matter how many are waiting in line? Because I'm such a—"

The stranger's hand was quick but light, turning her head to her right, but not hard enough to sting. Lin's eyes flashed again for a second, and she had a fleeting thought of destroying him. Instead, she lowered her eyes to look straight ahead.

"Tramp. Yeah, like you love doing to—"

"Everyone."

"Yeah, everyone. God, do it already, you hot tramp."

She turned enough that her right cheek could take the next one.

She looked back into his eyes, smiled, and nodded while saying, "Maybe it's not your turn, mister."

He shook his head and placed his hands on her cheeks. Lin looked into his eyes and nodded, prompting him to tap both cheeks. She waited, so he drew back and tapped harder with both hands, good enough to cause a slight smacking sound on each side.

Able to feel a slight sting in each cheek, and with her heart pounding a sweet tempo, Lin looked down from his eyes to what the stranger demanded of her.

"That's it. God, you're such a tramp."

"Mm-hmm . . ."

* * *

"Oh . . . my . . . God, Lin," said the stranger after Lin had finally allowed him to stop. He stumbled over to the chair and slouched deep into it. His eyes were thin slits, and his breaths were quick, but he still managed to unlace his boots and pry them off.

"Yeah, that was a sweet time," said Lin. "So far."

"Oh God, I don't know. Your powers . . . how many times was that?"

"A lot."

She rubbed her bare belly with her right hand, but her left was too busy.

"You really played that part well. God, it didn't seem like you were acting."

Lin gazed at the man blankly. It took a few seconds for her to remember her real life, but it finally came into focus, and she remembered his name.

"Well, I'm an actor, Jack. You know that."

"A damn good one too."

"Once I got going, it kind of took over, and it just felt like me. Like I wasn't acting. I probably couldn't have stopped."

"I'm sure if you wanted to—"

"Oh, I didn't want to stop."

He stared at her for a few seconds.

"And you didn't want me to stop."

He shook his head and smiled.

"Admit it, Jack. You like that game."

"Yeah. Yeah, I sure do. I was worried there for a while until I figured out what you were pretending to be. Wow, hell of an act."

"Oh, Jack, that wasn't—"

She saw the look in his eyes.

"I mean . . ."

"What?"

"It wasn't all that bad," she said. "You enjoyed it, didn't you?"

"God, yeah. And don't worry, I know you're not really a tramp. But damn, if you ever decided to be one, you'd be the hottest tramp ever."

Lin bit her lip and felt the burning memories crowding around her and demanding her attention. She followed them long enough to hear other men calling her a tramp too.

Jack will have to accept that I might really be a tramp, she told herself, and she knew that she'd give him a lot more opportunities.

Now sounded good.

She strutted over to the chair, still completely naked except for her heels. She knelt in front of him and rubbed the hard muscles of his thighs.

"You look so damn good."

Lin smiled and leaned in close to kiss him, and she felt her breasts hanging, aching for his touch.

He reached out and held them in his rough hands, and Lin said, "You do too, Jack. But . . ."

Jack didn't stop caressing her, but he waited and listened.

She stared at him for a few seconds with her lips moving but saying nothing. She let out a deep breath.

"I really am a . . . a . . ."

"A what?"

She saw the love in his eyes.

"A good actor," she said with a forced smile.

And before he could question her, she pressed her lips into his and summoned her mayhem. She aimed it like she'd just done so many times. He moaned against her wet lips as his enthusiasm greeted her in an instant.

Lin stood and reached out for him. He couldn't resist, so he stood, and without letting go, she pulled his jeans down, and he kicked them aside. She led him to her bed, and there, she yanked down the covers. Still holding on, she crawled onto the bed and rolled onto her back.

"I'm a bad girl, Jack. A really bad girl. Looks to me like you're ready to do something about that."

She looked into his eyes while the memories began burying her real life.

"Yeah, you're bad. You're such a bad girl," he said and smiled through his fatigue.

"Mm . . . you know how to treat a tramp like me," she told him.

He climbed onto the bed, and she didn't let go of him until the very last second. And several seconds later, as she held onto the headboard, she struggled to remember him and her life. That other life.

More seconds passed, and she let the other life go. She wanted no other life except to tease and satisfy the stranger above her. And whoever was next.

Lin's powers brought her a long line of eager strangers. She urged all of them to do anything they wanted to her, and to make her do whatever they wanted too. They did every possible thing to her, and when they got forceful, she obeyed every order, even though they never got nearly rough enough.

Before she'd been completely satisfied, she feared she might kill the stranger holding her hips if she didn't let him rest. So, when he finished, she let him collapse onto the hot sheets.

Lin lay beside him and finally felt her own fatigue as her life returned. And she saw that Jack appeared more dead than alive.

With his eyes drooping shut he said, "God, I love you, Lin."

She kissed him and said, "I love you too, Jack."

His eyes closed, and his head slumped into the pillow.

"But what am I going to do, Jack?"

She shook him but got no response.

"Jack?"

Jack was gone, so she rolled onto her side, facing away, and pulled his arm over her waist. He snored into her hair.

"I love being your girlfriend. But Jack, I think I really am a tramp."

His snoring continued.

"And I love that too."

Chapter 36 – Just Amusing Memories

Lin lifted Jack's arm off of her and sat up enough to switch on the nightstand lamp. She looked back at him and watched for half a minute. She couldn't be sure, so she leaned in close and felt his breath soft against her cheek.

Before rising, she remembered the night before and how she'd used her powers on him, just a part of him, over and over. With every renewal, she'd raised his passion just as high. His eyes had shown the wildness that had animated him and a reflected green glow. Every time.

And now, he was spent like a dead man again, except for his slow, deep breathing.

She also remembered how she'd felt. How the memories had taken over. How she'd forgotten Jack and cared only about what was demanded of her. And how she'd loved complying.

She shook those thoughts away and promised herself she'd think about it later.

Time to check the weather instead, she told herself.

A tiptoe walk across the cold wood floor brought her to the window. She parted the curtains and gasped—the snow was almost as high as the window, and it continued to fall. Streetlights still struggled in the predawn air thick with snowflakes. They could only muster a weak glow near her house, and they gave up completely several houses away.

At least we have power, she comforted herself.

She pulled the curtains closed and went to her closet, where she dressed in jeans, a sweatshirt, and hiking boots. She walked back to the bed and kissed Jack's cheek, snugged his blankets up to his chin, and switched off the lamp.

It was time.

*   *   *

"Gabby. Gabby, wake up."

Gabriel peeked out above a thick blanket that also covered part of Nomad. The big dog did no peeking and continued to snore lightly.

"Okay, Lin, I'm awake . . . I think. What's going on?"

"Snow. Lots of it. This isn't normal for November. This has to still be coming from Taylor."

"Have you checked on her?"

"No, not yet. I'll go take a look."

Lin tread quietly down the hall and nudged Taylor's door in. A few careful steps took her to the bedside, and she could see that Taylor was fast asleep. She resisted her urge to wake her up or even to kiss her. And in spite of the growing disaster outdoors, she couldn't help but smile at seeing her daughter home again and sleeping in her own bed. She closed the door and went back to Gabriel.

"She's sleeping, and she looks quite content. Not agitated at all. Is she still causing all this?"

"Maybe she doesn't have an active role anymore. She got it started, and now it has a life of its own."

"That's how it works? It won't stop until Taylor stops it?"

"I don't know, Lin. That knowledge has been lost in history. Except—"

"For Gloriana," said Lin. "She probably knows all about it. And Gabby, I don't think she's going to tell me. Not unless I bring her back."

"I did recommend against that earlier. But now, it might be the only way."

"How can I know if I'm strong enough? What could happen to me?"

"You're strong enough. I believe all that's needed from you is to hold open the door, so to speak. You provide that path, and when you return, so will she."

Lin was stooped down beside the couch talking with Gabriel. The room housed mostly shadows, and icy pellets continually struck the living room window, making pleasant tapping sounds and belying the danger piling up. Nomad's big paws protruded from under the blanket and twitched without a sound.

"Okay, so maybe that's not so hard to do. But what can I do about any barnacles she might have stuck to her?"

"I can't even guess about that. You can ask her, though."

"You know, that's not a bad idea. It's early, and Taylor's probably not going to be up for a while."

"Neither will Jack," Gabriel said with a smile.

"Oh, Gabby, you didn't—"

"No, I didn't hear anything. Just a lucky guess. You have a good life ahead of you, Lin. I know you don't want to use your powers to hurt anyone again. Jack's here, still by your side after everything. And you have Taylor back in your life. And this guy,"—Gabriel grabbed one of Nomad's paws and shook it—"will always be around to help too."

"But you won't. Is that what you're saying?"

Gabriel paused and looked into Lin's eyes but didn't let go of Nomad.

"I can't sleep on your couch forever. Should I get a job somewhere? An apartment?"

"You could."

"Yes. But I'm made for war, Lin. You know I'm a destroyer. That battle rages on, and—"

"And it's been doing just fine without you. I saw you as you really are, Gabby, when you fought Wolfe and his demons. I saw the destroyer—the you that never smiles. The you that can't even remember how."

"Yes, that's who I've become, Lin."

"But I've also seen you laughing, playing with Nomad, and eating stack after stack of blueberry hotcakes."

"That's all part of me as well, but—"

"And you want to be a rock star. Yes, you're a destroyer, but you're also this,"—Lin pointed at Gabriel—"fun-loving, helpful, protective, the most loving being that I've known my entire life. Can't you fight evil here too? And at the same time, can't you enjoy life like you deserve to?"

Gabriel's eyes closed, and Lin wondered if tears were being held back. Did Gabriel ever cry?

"You're very persuasive, Lin. And you're right—I'm doing good here too."

"So, you'll stay a little while longer?"

Gabriel's eyes opened, and a smile appeared.

"Do you know how to make hotcakes?"

Lin smiled and fought her own tears.

"Yes, I sure do. Piles of them, Gabby. I'll pile them as deep as the snow that's still—"

Lin turned to look at the blizzard steadily burying them and everyone in her neighborhood. She wondered how large of an area was now deep in snow. How many people were in danger?

"I have to go. I'll try to keep it quick."

"Will you be able to do that?"

"My hold on my intent is unbreakable. That's my only hope."

"And you'll ask Gloriana about Taylor?"

"And about the Islands. I've seen how the magic hits us in waves, creating us anew with each blast of it. And those spaces in between, where Gloriana's been trapped for centuries."

"Yes, it's quite amazing how we exist. How the world exists."

"And I need to ask her about how she created worlds and put me in them. Those crazy, mixed-up worlds where I wasn't really myself, just some bizarre version of me."

"That seemed to upset you at first but not so much after a while."

"You're right. Now, the memories are just . . ."

"Just what, Lin?"

"Just amusing memories, that's all. It was kind of fun to be a different version of myself for a while, even though it was all really crazy."

"Are you sure it's all just amusing now?"

"Yeah, sure. What else could it be? But how was all that possible, Gabby?"

"You should ask Gloriana about those worlds too."

"I still haven't told you all about those, have I?"

"Some. But I'm sure there's more."

"I think what matters is what I learned from them. In the first one, God, I was a tease. Really trashy. For anyone to see. I'm done with that."

Lin had a quick thought about the provocative clothes she'd just worn for Jack, if only briefly.

"You look very good dressed how you are, Lin. You don't need the other outfits anymore."

"Yeah, I don't need that style. And I don't want it."

Lin looked down quickly.

"What else?"

"The second one was like the first. I was trashy again, but I was also drinking an insane amount. I'm done with that too."

But she remembered craving the wine before the fun with Jack. She'd enjoyed being a tease and drinking more alcohol.

"You won't miss it. What else?"

"The third one was the worst. I was excited by violence, giving it *and* receiving it. It was a thrill either way."

Lin recalled how badly she'd wanted Jack to strike her, to force her to perform for him. She'd loved being a tramp, drinking wine, and craving every slap he gave her.

"And I enjoyed causing so much pain. It was Ben at first, not that that makes it okay. But I enjoyed destroying him piece by piece. I had no mercy, Gabby."

"And then, Ben became Taylor?"

"Yeah, and I don't ever want to hurt anyone again. I suppose I will if I have no choice. But I'll always have a lot of choices. That's free will."

"Yes, that's all true. So, even though she tried to trick you each time, you survived, and you learned."

"I guess if you put it that way, yeah."

"Anything else, Lin? You look like there's more on your mind."

"Yeah, Gabby. I was a tease in the first one and a drunk in the second. And in the third, I craved violence too. But I was more than just a tease. I was . . . something else in all three of them. That was consistent."

"What do you think that means, Lin?"

"Probably nothing. I'll ask Gloriana about it."

"I'm eager to hear her answers too. Make it quick, Lin?"

"Okay. That's what I'm intending anyway."

Lin spun around and sat with her back against the couch. She turned to her right and saw Gabriel watching her with the blanket pulled up close. She looked to her left and saw Nomad mostly covered up and snoring again. A last look straight forward revealed the wide white window that appeared painted.

With crossed arms and a deep intention of going for only a second, Lin closed her eyes. She intended her mayhem, and even with eyes closed, she saw the world as a flat calm surface. She felt the magic flowing into her, creating her. She intended the magic to slow down, and it became distinct waves washing through her, one after the other. Timeless waves of infinite magic, giving her life.

She slowed it further and came to rest between two waves. A pinpoint of black appeared, like a hole in the world. And beyond it . . . nothing. The nothingness grew and pushed the world away until the darkness covered her. Her breaths stopped, and she couldn't think anything about that. Couldn't feel anything about it. She waited for what would come next, and it did.

Her heart stopped.

Lin held her intent in the silence of her death. There were no plans and no objectives. The idea of returning to her world was no longer even a memory. Centuries could have blurred past before a white dot captured her attention. She couldn't look away as it raced toward her, scraping away the night as it covered her with a new world.

A strong, steady heartbeat welcomed her to the new world. She could think and feel again, and she savored the warm ocean air that expanded her lungs.

* * *

Lin left her eyes shut and enjoyed the slight scent of an ocean as she continued to breathe deeply. There were no sounds, so she opened her eyes.

She looked down at the familiar stone floor, its large pieces fitted together with an impossible precision. Just over the short wall in front of her, she looked down to see an ocean so far away that no waves could be detected—she thought it could have been a giant window painted blue. No sun rose from her left, and no moon, whether caring or indifferent, looked down upon her. She realized that this world, the one that she knew had never lived, was dying.

Without looking to her right, she said, "Hello, Gloriana."

"Lin Finity."

Long moments of silence passed.

"Your world here is dying."

"It is only for us to speak. I feel a love for my tower, where I spend countless happy, triumphant days with those I love. Looking down on all that I love. It cannot continue."

"Because your strength is leaving you."

"Yes. I keep remnants of this world as the living count many seasons. Soon, it is only the dark."

"Unless I help you."

Lin heard a deep sigh.

"Yes."

While continuing to stare toward the horizon, Lin said, "I need your help too."

"With the Glyphin. Your daughter."

"Yes, her. She's destroying part of our world. She started something, and it's running on its own now. She can't stop it."

"What she has started can be stopped. Tell the Glyphin to . . ." Gloriana paused.

"What? Tell her to what?"

Gloriana took a deep breath and continued.

"I give you this answer."

Lin waited.

"She must remember the word. She must see it by itself and not do anything with it. She must hold it as a simple word. Then, she must be strong enough to see only letters. What is done is undone when the word stops being a word."

"That's it? That's all it takes?"

"It is not easy for a Glyphin to see only a word or only its letters. Can you?"

"No, I doubt I ever could. But that's what she needs to learn?"

"Yes. It is difficult for all but easier for a Glyphin. Still difficult, though."

"But she'll be able to do that?"

"She must try. You have more questions."

"Yeah, one more. You tried to trick me three times, but it didn't work. How did you do that?"

Lin turned to look at Gloriana. The ocean wind carried her wild hair back over her shoulders, and her caramel eyes looked into Lin's with a deep weariness. Her cinnamon gown fluttered and outlined the body of a warrior.

"I cannot trick you into helping me. You must choose that on your own. Your intent must choose it."

"I barely got through without being tricked. How did you create those worlds like that? How is that even possible?"

"I only nudged you." Her eyes glowed more brightly. "Are those worlds familiar to you?"

"Yeah, the worlds were mostly parts of my memories, but mixed up."

"You find enjoyment in those worlds?"

Lin stared but didn't answer quickly.

"Well, they were . . . I mean—"

"And you." Gloriana smiled. "Are you familiar, too, in those worlds?"

Lin paused and said, "I was kind of like me, but not like . . . I'd probably never—"

"Each world is not far from the path you are on. Three times you lived different strings of Islands."

Lin stared silently into Gloriana's caramel eyes before looking back out over an ocean with nothing above its horizon.

"What are you saying? That somehow, some part of me is really like that?"

"What do your feelings tell you, Lin Finity?"

Lin sensed her intent beginning to send her home, back to her own life.

"But how . . . those worlds . . ."

Lin noticed a point of blackness near the horizon.

". . . they seemed real. How?"

"They are as real as they need to be."

"What does that mean?"

"Know that in each world you travel, *you* are real."

"But you're not saying . . . you don't—"

"They are not meant to trick you."

"You *did* try, but each time, I learned that it was all a trick. And none of your tricks worked."

Lin's eyes locked on the dark spot, and it began its race toward her. She knew that if she were alive, tears would be streaking down her cheeks.

"You are wrong, Lin Finity. What you call 'tricks' all find success."

Lin could no longer hear anything from Gloriana, the ancient queen standing beside her on a tower that didn't exist. The blackness covered her, she died, and she waited in silence in the eternity that reigns between every two Islands of Time.

* * *

Eternity ended when a speeding world covered her, and her heart began again. Life returned. Her life. Her string of Islands. Lin took a deep breath and stared into the white window in front of her.

"Lin," said Gabby, "you should go soon. Before Taylor wakes up."

Lin turned to see Gabriel looking back at her over the edge of the warm blanket. She looked to her left and saw Nomad twitching with the blanket above him bouncing.

She looked again at the white window.

"Intent is everything, Gabby."

Chapter 37 – Timeless Caramel Eyes

"Taylor. Wake up, Honey."

"Why, Mom? Let me sleep."

"Honey, the storm. It's getting worse, but I think we can fix it."

Taylor sat up, rubbed her eyes, and looked at the blizzard pelting her bedroom window.

"It's been going like that all night? Sorry, I didn't mean it."

"I know, Hon. Come on and get up. I'm making hotcakes."

Lin left and walked to the kitchen, but no one else stirred. Gabriel and Nomad remained under their blanket, and as far as any casual observer could tell, Jack was still dead.

The smell of blueberry wafted into the living room, drawing in Gabriel and Nomad. Lin gave the bedroom door a single knock and walked in to see Jack opening his eyes. She knelt beside the bed and leaned in close, giving him a big smile.

"Lin, oh my God. What a night. I feel like I just finished a marathon."

"You kind of did, Jack," she said before leaning in closer to kiss him.

"Sorry about that, Jack. I think I got carried away."

"Don't be. You make the rules, and I'll play the game. You were so, so hot. A little scary at times, but so damn hot."

"Oh, Jack . . ."

She leaned in for a hug and gave him a long wet kiss. She pulled away and said, "I really am a bad girl, Jack," and she stood and looked down on him.

"Come on, breakfast is about ready."

"How's the weather?"

"Worse, but maybe Taylor can fix it. We have to at least try."

She left him and found Gabriel at the table and Nomad pawing at his empty bowl.

"Jack'll feed you, my sweet boy. Try to hang on."

As soon as Jack entered the room, Lin said, "Jack, fire up the backhoe—Nomad's hungry."

"Funny. You beat me to it."

He pulled the bag out of the pantry, filled the big silver bowl, and Nomad's eager crunching competed with the wind howling over the roof.

Taylor shuffled in, her slippers scuffing across the cold floor as she rubbed her eyes, and she stood in front of the dining room window and looked out over their backyard. The wind had kept a thin strip along the house clear, and the snow rose up steeply from there. Lin's six-foot-high fence poked above it in only a couple of places.

"Oh my God, Mom. Are we going to be okay?"

"Yeah, I think so. How about if we try something?"

"Heck yeah. Anything."

"What you need to do is focus on the word you used when you brought this storm. If you could just—"

"Wait, Mom. Why didn't you tell me this yesterday?"

"I, uh . . . I mean—"

"You died again, didn't you? While I was asleep?"

The wind picked up and howled under the eaves, and a weighty blast of snow hit the window.

"Honey—"

"No, Mom. You have to stop dying. I just got you back into my life. What if you didn't come back? I couldn't even go looking for you. You'd just be dead on the kitchen table."

"Taylor—"

"Or maybe on the couch."

"Honey—"

"Or wherever you decided to die."

Another boom shook the house, and everyone looked at each other with big eyes.

"We can have that discussion later, after we fix this, okay?"

"Fine. How?"

"What word did you use? What word started all this?"

"If I think of that word, it's only going to get worse."

"We have to try, Hon. What was it?"

"Dead. The word was 'dead.'"

The wind increased.

Lin turned to Gabriel and said, "It's never easy, is it, Gabby?"

"The magic can be a minefield, Lin."

"Taylor, think of the word. But *just* that word. See it as only a word. Don't play with it, okay?"

"I'm looking right at it, Mom, and it's pissing me off."

"Try to see it as only the letters. Not even a word, okay?"

Snow continued to pummel the windowpane, and another boom rocked the house.

"Can you try harder, Hon? It's just a word that doesn't mean anything. It's not even really a word, okay? Just look at the letters. It's only four letters, and they don't mean anything."

Taylor took a seat at the table, and Nomad walked up to her. He laid his huge head on her lap, and she looked down and smiled.

The wind's pitch lowered a notch.

She rested her hand on his head and began to play with his ears. He looked into her eyes before she closed them.

"Okay, Mom, it's just a couple of letters. No big deal."

The wind continued, and thick snow fell heavy around the house.

"But it spells something, Mom. Something that really pisses me off."

"Try, Hon. I know you can do it."

Taylor sat quietly, rubbing Nomad's ears, and the weather didn't change. She opened her eyes and focused on Lin.

"Mom, tell me you're never doing that again."

Lin turned to look at Gabriel, who only shrugged. She looked at Jack, and he shook his head slowly.

"Taylor," said Jack, "your mom doesn't ever want to leave you. She doesn't want to die anymore."

"You're a good guy, Jack. And that's a good try. Hey, that rhymes."

"Do you still want to be an author?" said Gabriel.

"It's better than killing a whole city, Gabriel. Not the kind of story I want to tell."

"The wind has slowed down some," said Lin. "Maybe you can get the snow to stop too?"

"Okay, Mom. I'm going to try real hard, and then we're going to talk, okay?"

"Sure, Honey. That roof can only hold so much snow."

Taylor's hand rested on Nomad, and even his eyes held still. She closed her eyes again, and a calm expression replaced the frown. Everyone waited in silence.

The winds slowed and could no longer be heard. The snow quit hitting the window and fell softly, still adding to the deep drifts already on the ground. Then, the snow lessened and stopped altogether.

Taylor opened her eyes and began scratching behind Nomad's ears. He let out a low groan and jumped up to place his heavy paws on her lap. She laughed as he kissed her and nuzzled his big snout around her neck and throat.

"That was for you, you big fluffy beast."

She tried to reach around his mane for a hug, but she couldn't get her arms that far. She squeezed him as well as she could and looked to Lin.

"Mom, I feel like I'm holding the sky up. I don't know how long I can do it. How do I make it stay normal? What do I do with that word?"

"Oh, Honey, I don't know. I told you everything I know."

Taylor turned to look at Gabriel.

"Gabriel, you must have some kind of good advice, right?"

"No, Taylor, I know very little about Glyphins. There's only one who knows about that kind of power."

"The dead queen?"

"Yes."

"And the only way my mom can get her help is to die again?"

"Yes. I'm sorry."

Taylor looked down into Nomad's big eyes and flicked his ears up and down with both hands.

"I don't want to kill you, Nomad."

She looked around at three sets of eyes staring at her.

"Or the rest of you either. Really."

"Taylor, Honey, the dead queen wants me to help her get back here."

"What? How can that happen?"

Lin pointed out the window at the deep snow.

"Oh, yeah. Magic, right?"

Lin nodded.

"I think I should bring her back. You have to be okay with that, Taylor. I'm getting better at it, and you probably won't even know I'm gone."

Taylor frowned and stared at her.

"Alright, Mom. But she's not sharing my room, okay?"

Taylor gave Lin a weak smile, and Lin felt tears pushing their way out.

Not yet, she told herself. There's work to be done.

"Of course, Hon. She won't even stay in Pennsylvania. I'll explain later. Are you sure you're going to be okay?"

"How the heck can I be sure? I'll try. Can you go now, before I change my mind?"

Lin nodded.

She found her intent and lost her life.

* * *

Lin saw that she was surrounded by the glow of a world. She felt the stone floor beneath her feet and an ocean breeze lifting her hair. She took a deep breath and looked to her right.

Caramel eyes gazed at her from behind long dark hair blown about by the ocean breezes. Neither said a word, and Lin turned to look out at the ocean, which ended not far from the tower. Beyond its ragged edge was only gray emptiness.

"You're running out of time," said Lin.

"Time."

"Right. Anyway, even your ocean is fizzling out."

"Yes."

"What will you do if you get back to the Islands of Time?"

"Live a normal life. It takes the last of my strength to return. I give up powers to live the life of a normal human woman."

"How do you know that?"

"It is part of the deal. It is the only way this can work."

The edge of the ocean drew nearer, and the breezes dwindled.

"You'll lose all your powers? You'll be—"

"Weak on the Islands. But a normal life bears a unique type of magic too, Lin Finity."

Lin turned to look back into her caramel eyes.

"How so?"

"To know your end is coming is to appreciate every moment of life."

"Yeah, or go crazy wondering when it'll end."

"Yes, there is that too."

Lin looked back at the ocean.

"What dangers will I face if I help you?"

"It will weaken you."

"It won't kill me?"

"No."

"How do you know that?"

"Using our powers never kills us. But it does borrow from our strength."

"What do I need to do?"

"Do just what you do to travel here. Use your intent to return to the Islands. Hold on to your intent until you are caught by the next tide."

"What's that about a 'tide?'"

"The magic picks you up in its own time. Well . . . not 'time.' It puts you on an Island, and time carries you."

"I don't know if I'll ever understand all of this."

"You cannot. My words are nonsense even to me."

She turned back to face Gloriana and laughed lightly.

"Okay, pack a bag."

"You are funny, Lin Finity. I am ready. I already miss my islands."

"There are other islands. Okay, I need to look into your eyes, is that right?

"That is all. We travel together. Thank you."

"Well, we're not there yet."

Lin gazed into Gloriana's timeless caramel eyes and found her intent. The gleaming pools of caramel became surrounded by night, and Lin continued to gaze into them. The eyes never changed, but the darkness expanded in every direction before racing toward her and covering them both. She held on to her intent in utter silence, in an emptiness without beginning or end. And she knew that Gloriana's intent remained near.

A white point appeared before her, quickly expanded, and sped toward her until it covered her in her own world. Lin noticed her heart begin a steady beat, and she could feel and think again. She took a deep breath that smelled like home.

* * *

"Really, Mom, before I change my mind."

Lin looked at Taylor's puzzled expression, then she glanced at Jack. He only stared back at her, so she looked at Gabriel.

"Did it work, Gabby?"

Gabriel pointed to the doorway leading to Lin's living room. A beautiful woman with dark skin and wild dark hair coiled down far past her shoulders stood gazing at them with big caramel eyes. Her cinnamon gown left her arms uncovered, and she shivered as she stepped from one bare foot to the other on the cold wood floor.

Gloriana stared into Lin's eyes as her feet ceased their unproductive shuffling. She showed the beginning of a smile before her eyes rolled up high, and she collapsed to the floor.

Chapter 38 – A Hidden Part

"Mom, you did it!"

Gabriel and Nomad rushed over to each side of Gloriana, where Nomad began nosing her hand. When that didn't get a reaction, he began rooting around her neck.

"And she's gorgeous, Mom!"

"Taylor . . . Jack . . . I . . ."

Lin began to fall out of her chair, and Jack caught her enough to ease her to the floor. He sat with her in an embrace as he looked to Gabriel.

"Lin will be fine, Jack. What she just did is an astounding act of power over the magic. She must be very tired."

"Her too, Gabriel? She looks more tired than my mom."

"I believe she only fell asleep. Yes, she must be very tired as well."

Nomad gave up and trotted back to Lin's side. He poked all around with his wet nose, but he got no response from her either.

"This is impossible, Gabriel. Snow's one thing, and rain, but this . . . how can—"

"Jack, it's okay. Can you get Lin to her bed? She'll be fine, but I don't know how long she'll need to rest."

"Sure, Gabriel." Jack stood and lifted Lin into his arms.

"Good thing you've been tossing tons of dog chow, Jack."

"That's funny, Taylor. Can you help me get your mom to bed?"

Taylor rose from the table and walked with Jack, who carried Lin and laid her on her bed. Taylor drew a warm blanket up to her chin, and Jack leaned down and kissed her cheek. She didn't move. They closed the door and returned to the kitchen to see Gabriel carrying Gloriana, whose gown and long hair draped toward the floor.

"Right this way with the dead queen, Gabriel," said Taylor, and within seconds, Gloriana was fast asleep in Lin's guest room.

They returned to the kitchen table, and Gabriel laughed before speaking.

"We forgot all about the hotcakes. But they should still be good."

"Try the microwave, Gabriel," said Taylor. "It's kind of a new thing. Here, I'll show you."

With a tall stack of hot blueberry hotcakes, Gabriel sat and waited for Jack and Taylor to get a plate.

Jack said, "Hey, don't bother waiting. Get 'em while they're hot."

"They are called *hot* cakes, Gabriel," said Taylor. "That's kind of funny, you know. Even when they're cold, they're still hotcakes. How could food be like that? It's kind of crazy."

Gabriel stopped to look at Taylor.

"Like a dead queen in the guest room. That's crazy too, Gabriel."

A heavy wind rolled along the length of the house.

"How could things like this happen, Jack? Oh, how would you know—you don't have magic powers. But you do have a dead queen. In the guest room. It's really crazy, Jack."

A fresh wall of snow hit the window, and they both stared at Taylor.

"It's going to be okay, it really is," said Jack. "Your mom's only sleeping, remember?"

"Sure, Jack. But I don't know anyone that has a dead queen . . . wait, I kind of don't know anyone. Period. And one of the few people I know is a dead queen. She . . . Jack . . . I . . ."

Jack leaned over from his seat and embraced Taylor, who began sobbing quietly with her head on his shoulder. The sky ripped open and fluffed out heavy snowflakes. Jack gave Gabriel a puzzled look, and Gabriel only shrugged.

Then, Jack saw Gabriel look above his head and stare for a moment. He turned to look, but he saw only the decorative mirror on the wall near the sink.

"Gabriel, why don't we finish up these hotcakes, and then, maybe Taylor and I can get some work done? Does that sound okay, Taylor?"

"I'm hungry too, Jack. But don't worry—I'm not 'hangry.' Not yet."

"I'll heat you up some breakfast, okay? We'll deal with this after we eat."

"Okay, Jack. Mom's a good cook."

"These sure are delicious. I wish your mom would have made more before she—"

"Died and came back with a dead queen? Yeah, I know."

* * *

They ate without speaking as the winds hammered Lin's house and snow swirled thick over her backyard. When all the plates had been cleared, and they all should have been full, Gabriel decided to make a fresh batch.

"I don't doubt you'll do a good job," said Jack. "While you're cooking and eating, Taylor, let's you and I go shovel the drive."

"I don't think I'd be much help, Jack."

"Let's give it a shot. I'm sure Nomad will lend a paw."

"You're a funny guy, Jack."

They bundled up as well as they could, with Taylor borrowing Lin's winter jacket, and they took Nomad out in the blizzard.

* * *

Gabriel suspended the breakfast project and walked in to see Gloriana. She didn't move, but caramel could be seen through thin slits.

"Lin has helped you. Will you stop taking her to other worlds now?"

"I never took her there. I only pointed her in one of her own directions."

"So that you could trick her into helping you?"

"No. I never sought to trick her into helping me return."

"She saw your eyes each time. She said you tried to trick her into using her intent to save you."

"I intended my eyes there for a reason. It was for her own good."

"I don't understand. What was the reason?"

"It forced her to flee from each of those lives. She found her intent and came back to this life."

"That's pretty clever. If you weren't trying to trick her, what was that all about?"

"It is a deal I made to escape from between the Islands. I could regain my life if I would help Lin Finity become a better person. She is more good now, is she not?"

"Yes, she is. She learned something each time. That was all arranged? She said some of it was very upsetting. She was a much different person in those dreams."

"They were not dreams, but you know that. I only nudged her. Perhaps a hidden part of her came to the surface. That could not be anticipated. Is she troubled?"

"Yes, but she's very strong. I think she'll be fine. I must watch her closely, though."

"I owe her very much. My deal is complete, and here I am. I gave up powers. It is not enjoyable, Gabriel."

"No. But it's better than where you were."

"Yes."

Gloriana's eyes closed, and Gabriel turned and left her to check on Lin. She still lay sleeping beneath the thick blanket, so Gabriel returned to the kitchen for more hotcakes.

* * *

"Nomad's perfectly fine out here, isn't he, Jack?"

"Yeah, he sure is. With all that fur, this must be what he's made for."

"I think he's made for more than that. Can dogs play with magic?"

Jack froze and stared at her.

"I, uh . . . I don't know. Probably not. And we better get this driveway cleared. We might have to run out for food soon."

"But it's snowing so hard, Jack. What's the point?"

"Yeah, well, if somehow the snow would stop, then—"

"Oh, I see what you're up to. You're pretty smart, Jack. You're not *telling* me to stop. You're *showing* me why I should make it stop."

"Who, me? I just want to be able to drive if the roads get plowed."

"Sure, Jack. Uh-huh. I'll try harder."

"Good, I know you can do it."

"Mom's really going to be okay?"

"Yes, she really will."

"And that dead queen, she—"

"She's just a friend that's visiting. That's all she is now, Taylor. If you think of her that way, it's not so bad."

Taylor stared at Jack from inside a ring of fake fur around the hood of Lin's jacket. Her cheeks had gotten rosy, and a smile began to show.

"You're a good guy, Jack. I'm glad you like my mom."

"I do. I really do. Are you going to be okay?"

"I think so, Jack. But maybe we don't have to stand around in the snow for no good reason?"

"Good, it's horrible out here. Not so much for Nomad, though."

"He's jumping in the snow! Look at him go, Jack!"

*　*　*

By the time they'd brushed each other off and walked into the house, the winds had already died down. They got their coats and boots off and walked over to the dining room window to see only a trace of snow falling. The smell of fresh blueberry hotcakes filled the house.

"You seem to be done with the snow," said Gabriel, who again looked above Jack.

"It's a struggle. For now, at least, I'm okay."

Jack turned to look, saw nothing, and turned back to Gabriel.

"You're freaking me out. What's going on?"

"Nothing. I hope."

"I don't like the sound of that."

Jack looked down to see Nomad staring at the mirror too.

"Great. Nomad sees something too. What is it, Gabriel?"

"Jack, we should just—"

"Is it a barnacle, Gabby?" said Lin.

"Mom! You're awake already!"

Taylor ran over and hugged Lin, who rocked her and smoothed down her hair. Taylor didn't let go, but she looked into her mother's eyes.

"What do you mean by 'barnacle,' Mom?"

Lin looked at Gabriel, who only shrugged and poked around at the hotcakes.

"Gabby. What do you see?"

"Something, Lin. I don't know what."

"From back there, you mean?"

"I believe so. And I don't really see it. It's more like a feeling."

"And I bet it isn't a good one," said Jack. "I have no idea what you two are talking about."

"Me neither, Mom."

Lin sat, took a breath, and looked at the questioning faces.

"Taylor, it's nothing to get upset about. But where Gloriana came from, or where she was anyway, isn't a good place. There are . . . things . . . there. One of them is trying to get through here."

"Things, huh?"

"Okay, I won't try and kid you, Hon. They're bad things. They're the things that kill everyone and everything. Eventually, they get to us. They're why everything dies."

"Real cheerful stuff, Mom."

"Sorry, Hon."

"You mean 'really' dies. Not pretend, like you do."

"Yes, that's right. Gabby, are we in any danger?"

"I don't think anyone can answer that. But I believe it might succeed in getting through. It knows the way now. It watched you two leave."

"So, what do we do?"

"Wait."

"Wait for what? Who do we—"

Lin saw a black point directly in her line of sight. Her eyes locked on, and it compelled her to stare. The point grew until the blackness swallowed her. She ended up alone in the nothingness—dead and holding her intent.

*   *   *

"No, Mom! Not again!"

Jack grabbed Lin as she began to topple from her seat. He held her by her shoulders, but her head sagged straight forward.

"Jack, Gabriel . . . bring her back. Right now!"

A bright flash was followed by a loud boom right above the house. The lights flickered but remained lit.

"Lin," said Gabriel. "Hold your intent, Lin. Come back to us."

Fresh wind gusts pounded the house, and the windows in the dining room rattled.

A loud yelp from Nomad caused Taylor to scream, and Jack stood up, still holding Lin upright in her chair.

Nomad hung his head and wailed so low he could barely be heard. He dropped to his belly and rolled onto his side, where he lay with his mouth open and taking rapid breaths.

"It's Nomad! Look! Help him, Jack!"

*   *   *

Lin felt years passing as she waited in silence. Then, a light rushed toward her, wrapping her in her own familiar world. She felt her heart begin a comfortable beat, took a deep breath, and opened her eyes.

The first thing she heard was the thunder. Then, Taylor.

"Stop it, Mom. Just stop it, okay?"

"I'm fine now, Hon. I just got a little dizzy and—"

"I know a dead mom when I see one. I can't take this anymore."

Jack released Lin and stood behind her. Taylor sat beside Nomad and petted his thick fur.

"Mom, what's wrong with Nomad?"

Lin shook off her confusion and joined Taylor, and she held Nomad's head up. His eyes were glazed over and out of focus.

"Oh, Nomad, what's wrong, Baby?"

"Did that thing get him, Mom? While you were dead again? Is that what's going on?"

The snow began a steady fall, and winds drove it into the glass.

"Lin, I know you don't want to use your powers, but it might be necessary this time. Look at Nomad's spirit. See what you can find."

Lin stopped time in an instant. Her mayhem began to rise as she looked out at infinity in every direction, and the world became a calm, flat surface. She took a moment to gaze out at the multitude of thick snowflakes waiting in the air. Below, bottomless mountains of magic swirled and broke apart, joined together, and painted mad designs that few would ever see and none had any hope of understanding.

Her intent focused on Nomad's spirit, and the sight sickened and saddened her. His pure green spirit had something dark and menacing jabbed into it, something like a dagger. She looked closer and saw that it had a jaw, with sharp teeth locked onto Nomad's spirit.

So, that's what that thing does, she thought. She looked for Nomad's narrow space, hoping that she could invade him and help him to fight what was killing him. But his spirit was joined perfectly to his physical form—there was no room for her to sneak in and take control.

Lin scanned in every direction, seeking whatever had left that grisly piece of death. But there was nothing to be seen—only infinity and endless chaotic magic. And Nomad, with a set of pointed teeth chewing on his spirit.

She allowed her mayhem to end, and time resumed. Infinity could no longer be seen, and the world had returned to its familiar appearance.

Everyone remained where she'd left them before her mayhem rose up—no time had passed. She looked down at Nomad and saw him still lying on his side and his head still in her hand. And a large growth had appeared over his ribs, pushing his fur up in random, unwelcome patterns. Lin reached out to touch it, and he yipped, but he didn't move.

"The thing is gone. I never saw it. But Nomad, he's not okay. Whatever that thing did, it's still there."

"Can you fix him, Mom? I love Nomad! Mom, you have to fix him!"

Jack only stared with his mouth hanging open. Lin saw beyond him that the heavy snowfall had returned.

"He's sick now, Gabby. I can't even take control of him. What can I do?"

Gabriel paused to look at Nomad on his side on the floor before looking into Lin's eyes.

"Call Lee."

*　*　*

"I didn't think you'd ever want to talk to me again."

"I didn't know either, Lee. That surprised me—you being that way."

"Lin, that was impossible for me to resist. I never felt anything like it. All I could think about was doing it again."

"And now?"

"Before I left St. Simons, I stood on the pier and stared at the ocean. I think it was for a couple of hours. There's a massive peace in the sea, Lin. I have it under some control now. It was one thing for me to keep quiet about my powers. All I ever did was fix myself and keep myself in good shape. That all started to change when I healed Taylor and Ben."

"Is Ben going to be okay, Lee?"

"He's healthier than he's ever been. I know what I'm doing when it comes to that."

"But he's terrified of you now, is that it?"

"Who wouldn't be? I beat the crap out of him, and then, if he felt even one-tenth of the ecstasy I felt, can you imagine how that would mess someone up?"

"I tried to check on him," said Lin. "I've called a couple of times, and I sent some texts too. He hasn't answered any of it."

"I don't blame him. I really smashed him up."

"Have you gotten control of yourself? We need your help."

"I think I'll be okay. I needed some time to get some perspective, and I think I have it under control now. What kind of help? What's the problem?"

"It's Nomad. I can explain better when you get here, but he's sick. It looks like he has a big tumor or something. I work at a vet's office, and the times I've seen anything this bad, the vet couldn't help. You're our only hope, Lee."

"Where are you?"

"I'm at home in Pennsylvania."

"I'll get on the first flight. Text me the address."

*　*　*

"Mom, is Lee going to help? Can she?"

"She's coming, Honey. You saw Lee fix her own bullet wound, remember that? Some minor problem with Nomad is nothing to her. She'll fix him right up."

"You don't have to act brave for me, Mom. What can I do?"

"This snow, Honey! It's got to stop, or Lee will never make it to us. Can you try real hard? Please?"

"I'll try, but you know this can't be easy, Mom. You were dead again, we have a dead queen in—"

"Gloriana, Hon. Just Gloriana, okay?"

"Okay, we have a house guest, Nomad's sick . . . it's just a lot."

347

"Maybe it'll help if you go lie down somewhere quiet. What do you think?"

"Who knows, Mom? Sure, let's give that a try. Jack, don't grab your shovel, okay? Let me see if I can fix this."

Jack got a big smile.

"I believe you can, Taylor. Nomad will be fine."

After hugging Lin, Taylor touched Jack's shoulder on the way to her room.

"She's got to do it. Jack, you think she can, don't you?"

"Hell yeah, Lin. She's very strong, just like her mom. She'll figure it out."

"Gabby, what do you think?"

"I think we should wake up Gloriana. Maybe she can offer some advice. And yes, I do have faith in Taylor."

* * *

It took Jack shaking her and Lin yelling to wake Gloriana, and after she sat up on the bed, Lin held out a thick sweater for her. She shivered as she put it on, but a small smile lit up her face.

"Lin Finity, I am alive. I knew you had strength enough for us both."

"Welcome to Pennsylvania. I'd love nothing more than to chat with you about absolutely everything. But right now, we have a big problem. Oh, this is my boyfriend, Jack, and this is Gabriel."

Gloriana nodded at Jack and turned to face Gabriel.

"Yes, I know of Gabriel. Gabriel is well-known in many places. And times."

"And we can talk all about that later. Nomad's sick. Something came from between the Islands. I got pulled in there again, and while I was there, it reached through somehow."

"Who is Nomad?"

"My dog."

"You keep animals in your palace?"

"Well, it's not exactly a palace, and Nomad . . . he's family. And he's sick now from whatever that thing does."

"I hoped it would be left in its place. It has tormented me for many centuries. It is one of the worst."

"Well, it came here while I was stuck again back there. How can we stop it?"

"You cannot. You must keep that door closed. It exists outside of time, even as it can appear in the Islands now. It also exists outside of our knowing. It does not live, so it does not die."

"That's not very encouraging. I have to get back to Nomad. Join us?"

"I am weak. I will need to sit."

"We have a chair for you. Are you hungry?"

"Lin Finity, your imagination cannot tell you how much. Ah, the simple joy of food. Please, offer me food."

* * *

Gloriana took a seat at Lin's kitchen table next to Jack while Gabriel was busy whipping up more hotcakes. Lin sat on the floor beside Nomad and rubbed his ears gently.

"It stopped snowing, Lin," said Jack. "Whatever Taylor's doing, it's working. I'd like to go in there and thank her, but I better not. Just let her keep at it."

"And the sun is coming out," said Gabriel.

"I have never seen such a sight. It is like a thick layer of sea foam. Is it warm like the ocean?"

"Oh, you're in for a lot of surprises, that's for sure. No, it's icy cold. And we need it gone. The sooner the better."

"If I could use my powers still, I would take it away. But I cannot."

"There's too much of it anyway," said Lin. "My daughter, the Glyphin, seems to be making some progress."

"She caused all of that?"

"Yep."

"She is very powerful. I hope she can be just as careful."

Gabriel set a stack of hotcakes in front of Gloriana, and she made no effort to eat. She only looked from face to face.

"You're going to have to feed yourself," said Lin. "Life is going to be a bit different for you now."

Gloriana picked up a fork, and with Jack demonstrating the proper technique, she began to eat.

"It is good. This is very good."

She attacked the plate with enthusiasm.

*   *   *

Under a clearing sky, patches of sunlight broke through and began melting Taylor's handiwork. Snowplows cleared the roads, and Jack headed out for some shoveling. After finishing off a second plate of hotcakes, Gloriana's eyes started sagging shut, and Lin helped her back to the guest room.

Lin took a quick look and saw Taylor sleeping in her own bed in her own room. She closed the door without a sound and took her place sitting on the kitchen floor next to Nomad. With one hand on his mane, she rubbed his ears and the top of his head while trying to understand her fascination with the compelling lives she'd lived in Gloriana's fake worlds.

Chapter 39 – What You Imagine

"I'm confused about a lot of things, Gabby."

"What things?"

"When I told Gloriana that she tried to trick me three times, she said she didn't try to trick me, and that the tricks worked. But they didn't work. I figured out what was going on each time. When I saw her caramel eyes, then I knew it was a trick."

"She is right, Lin. She did not try to trick you. And the tricks did work. But I wouldn't call them tricks."

"Yeah, like that's not confusing. What on Earth are you talking about?"

"A couple of weeks ago, your mayhem started to erupt after you'd buried it inside you for over thirty years. And soon after, you had to make a choice about Ben. You thought you'd kill him or hurt him very badly if he came after you again."

Lin felt she visited Ben's hotel room, but she quickly focused again on Gabriel.

"But I didn't hurt him. I saw that he'd been damaged by my mayhem and so many other things. I knew that healing him was the right thing to do."

"Yes, and after you made that choice, I knew it was time for you to remember who I really am."

"I remember how that felt. It was like all my memories were rebuilt with the real you, not the other you, the one that wasn't real, the one . . . I don't even know how to describe it."

"And do you remember one of the first things I told you?"

"Yes, that I was important. And not long after that, you explained to me why I was important. You said you'd ask me to come with you to fight the war against evil in the magic."

"And you said you didn't think you were ready for that."

"I'm not. I don't believe I'm strong enough. Or good enough. You're impossibly good. I'm nowhere near being that good."

"You are more good now than you were just a few days ago."

"No, I'm just trying to help Taylor and Gloriana. I'm trying to hold all of this together. Is that what you mean?"

"She told you the tricks worked."

"But they *didn't* work. I saw her caramel eyes, and I knew each time that she was trying to fool me into helping her get back here."

"That wasn't the trick."

Lin stared in silence.

"You're losing me. Okay, what was the trick, then?"

"The first world, the first trick, was for you to reclaim the modesty that you had to give up to remember everything you had buried. The second was to avoid things that cloud your judgment—you're too powerful to be stumbling around intoxicated."

"And the third was to hate violence in any form. God, Gabby, you knew this? You knew what was going on?"

"No. Not until Gloriana told me."

"So, now I'm a better person, huh?"

"Yes. Once things are straightened out, you are ready to join the battle."

"Oh no, Gabby. No, no, no, I can't. I don't feel anywhere near good enough. Or strong enough. I'm not ready for you to even ask me."

"You are ready, Lin. I have to ask you, but it's always your choice."

"Even if I wanted to go fight evil in the magic, what about my life? I have a life here. I can't just walk away from that!"

"I understand, Lin. You're not obligated."

"Why did Gloriana do all that? What's in it for her?"

"She helped you become better so she could have a life here on the Islands of Time."

"That's how it works? How does—"

"For her, yes. You could say she made a deal."

"A deal with who? Oh, you can't be serious. You mean—"

"Yes. I told you that you were important. *I* can't interfere, but there's one who can and does. As often as necessary."

"God, I really must be important."

"Well said, Lin."

She stared quietly before the next question fought its way out.

"If it wasn't a trick, then why the eyes? The caramel eyes?"

"She said it was to cause you to leave those lives. When you saw the eyes, you knew to focus on your intent, and you returned."

"Wouldn't I have returned anyway?"

"Maybe not, Lin. Any one of those lives might have kept you."

"But they were messed up like crazy dreams. Even though Gloriana told me that they were as real as they had to be, whatever that means."

"Those worlds were only real enough to offer you lessons about yourself."

"So, how would those fake worlds keep me?"

"I said that the lives might have kept you, not the worlds."

"I don't understand what you're—"

"Who you were, Lin—that's what might have kept you."

"You mean who I was there?"

"Yes. You probably couldn't have stayed in those worlds much longer than you did."

"But I would have stayed that way? Even when I got back?"

"That's the power of imagination, Lin."

"That's what I suspected. I imagined the whole thing. Somehow, she tapped into my imagination."

Lin rubbed the top of Nomad's head and played with his ear while Gabriel watched her for a minute.

"You've never asked me about free will, Lin."

She stopped and stared as silent seconds crawled past.

"You already explained it. It's that narrow gap humans have between their bodies and their spirits. That's what gives us the ability to shape the slow magic of the world."

"But you've never asked, 'how?'"

Lin sat with her mouth open, staring into Gabriel's big brown eyes. Her hand rested on Nomad's head.

"I never . . . I mean—"

"Okay, you're not going to ask," Gabriel said with a smile. "So, I'll just tell you: imagination."

Lin continued to stare.

"But that gap, that allows us to focus our intent, even though it's too weak in most people. But that's it, right? We can focus our intent, and—"

"Focus it on what, Lin?"

Lin didn't blink, and her green eyes kept staring.

"Well, on what we're trying to do. What we're trying to change. Is that it?"

"And how do you even conceive of what that might be?"

Lin paused, and a smile took over.

"Imagination?"

"Yes. It's a simple thing. You use your intent to enact what you first imagine."

"And you said no other creatures have free will. So, they also don't have—"

"Imagination. They are content with the path they've been given. They can't choose a new one. They can't even imagine a new one."

"It all fits, Gabby. Every time I do anything with the magic, I see what I'm trying to do first. And my intent is so strong I can make it happen."

"Yes, Lin. It really is quite amazing, don't you think?"

"Even the first time I used my mayhem on my Uncle Ray. I must have spent years somehow imagining having the kind of power I'd need to stop him. I imagined it, and it became real?"

"Only with a strong intent. What you imagine can become more real than any other possibility if the intent is strong enough."

"What other possibilities? What are you talking about?"

"It requires a lot of strength for anyone to change the path they're on. The Lin you know is mostly locked into who she is. Without any effort—without using your intent at all—you follow that path."

"Until I imagine a different path, you mean?"

"Only if you focus your intent on it. And only if your intent is strong enough, which yours is. Then, what first became real in your imagination becomes the real life you live."

* * *

Lin dropped Nomad's ear, and he didn't move, but she looked back up at Gabriel.

"Gabby, wait a minute. Something isn't right about those worlds. The first world was about my lack of modesty, right? The second was about alcohol. And the third was about liking violence. Do I have that right?"

"Yes, I believe that was the hope."

"But I was way more than a tease in all of them. In each dream, about the first thing I did was get back into my sexy clothes, and God, the things I was doing. You're saying that wasn't the plan?"

"I don't believe it was, Lin. Not according to Gloriana. The first was only about modesty, the second about alcohol, and the third about violence."

"Why, then?"

"Lin, those worlds where you were someone different, doing things you would never do in this life—in some way, those lives are real too, just not as real as this one. Not yet, anyway. You might also be that woman. In a somewhat real way, you did all those things."

Lin looked away and felt herself shaking. She noticed more parts inside shifting around.

"And the feelings you felt while you were doing all that? Those might be your feelings too. That path, that life, doesn't seem to be too far from this one."

"When I liked something, when I couldn't get enough of it, I really did? That's really me too?"

"Apparently so, Lin. Three times Gloriana used some of her intent to put you in a situation, a world where you could learn something. But your intent filled in the blanks, so to speak."

She couldn't let herself believe it. Gabriel must be wrong, she thought.

"In the first dream, did you dress more provocatively than usual?"

"Oh yeah, I sure did. I was walking around almost naked."

"You said in the second dream, you drank very much. Did you have more alcohol than usual?"

"Yeah, a lot more. I chugged from a whiskey bottle until I couldn't see straight."

"So, those parts of those worlds happened as Gloriana intended. But you said you were also very immodest?"

"Oh, more than just immodest. So, that wasn't part of the plan . . ."

"And in the third world, you craved violence, giving or receiving. But you were immodest too?"

"Yeah, I was brutal at the end. And it excited me to get slapped around too. And really, 'immodest' isn't the word for how I was acting. Somehow, that was me?"

"I believe so, Lin. I don't know how else to explain it."

Lin didn't speak, so Gabriel continued.

"When I'm in the magic fighting evil, I told you I exist continuously at the point of choosing good or evil. That's free will—we must choose. It's the same with our possible lives. A new life can start in your imagination at any time. Your intent focuses on it, and it can become your new reality. Not for just anybody, but for you because *you* are that strong."

"I really did all those things? That's me too?"

"Yes, that was you doing all those things. In those worlds, though—not this one."

"Gabby, don't ever tell Jack I told you this, but twice now, I've acted like that woman I was in those worlds. At least it started out like acting, but I fell right into it. I felt like I was back in those worlds, and I liked it. For a while, I couldn't even remember this life or who Jack was. That's what you mean—I'm always pretty close to that, right?"

"It seems so. That must be a strong possible direction for you. The plan was to exaggerate three sides to yourself like you've mentioned. The hope was that you'd decide to rid yourself of those traits, and you have. You've changed your wardrobe, you've stopped drinking as much, and you abhor violence."

"But I was also really cheap in all three worlds. And I loved it."

"I believe that came from you, Lin. You were put in those situations, but the lives you lived there were built also by your intent."

Lin stared in silence for several moments before continuing.

"When I was pretending to be the other Lin, I did some drinking, and I sure was trashy. And I didn't plan it, but I wanted Jack to slap me to add to my excitement. No, wait, that's not right. I'm not sure I even knew that was Jack."

"Did you care who it was, Lin?"

"No, but I was just playing. It was just a fun game."

Gabriel only nodded.

"I sure did like it, though."

Lin felt large pieces moving inside, almost fitting together in new ways.

"Jack liked it too. He likes me playing like that for him."

Gabriel waited.

"I'm not going to do it, but I have to admit that I like knowing I could instantly become the tramp I was in those worlds. It *is* a part of me, and it's okay for me to remember it. Just thinking about all of that is pretty exciting. I feel like I'm almost back there."

"You should be careful with that, though."

"What do you mean?"

"What you feel is not a return to those worlds. It's a return to who you were there."

"Well, what's the harm? I mean, I'm just—"

"You've voluntarily played being the other you, the one from those worlds. That's how it begins. You like how it feels, and if your intent pushes you, you will be the other you."

"I don't think I'd ever—"

"You'd be very happy to be back in that ocean, wouldn't you?"

"God, Gabby, you're right—it *is* something like that. I didn't want to come back. Same thing when I took Jack with me, and we became baby birds. Jack didn't remember anything, though."

"No, it takes a lot of power to even hold the memory."

"And it sure was sad to come back from that."

"Yes, Lin. With the amount of power you have, there are countless possible lives for you. You've earned the strength to make them real. Now, you must find the strength to hold the one you want most."

"I know you're right. I wanted so bad to stay in that ocean and even more so to stay in that nest. But right now, the other Lin—the cheap, easy Lin—I want that life too."

"They're all possible for you."

"And it would be the same way, like when I came back from being a baby bird? If I became that other Lin, I wouldn't want to leave that for some other life?"

"Did you enjoy being the other Lin?"

"Oh, I sure did. I couldn't get enough of it."

"Then yes, your tendency would be to hang on to that life."

"Okay, no more acting, then. I'll just use my imagination from now on."

Gabriel smiled. "I'm not sure you've been listening. Lin, your imagination will take you there just as easily as your acting."

"Okay, okay. Unless I'm going to go all the way, I'll have to stop thinking about it too. It won't be easy. I do feel it pulling me in."

"There's a price for freedom, Lin. You have infinite possibilities."

"It's not like this for everyone else, is it?"

"No. People can imagine whatever they want. Their intent is far too weak to make big changes to their lives. They can and do make small changes, though, if they can gather up enough strength for their intent."

"And what about dreams? Are those real too?"

"Not even close. They are imagination with absolutely no intent behind them. But a memory of a dream can get fixed in the imagination, and if the intent is strong enough, it can become more real. People do change their own course, just not as easily as you can."

Lin smiled at Gabriel and said, "Just knowing that I can is enough. It's my choice who I am. What I am."

"Yes. Exactly right, Lin."

"I learned from those worlds, and now I'm more good."

The smile left her.

"And that's why you're asking me to go fight evil. To leave my life, go into the magic, and fight evil every moment."

"Yes, Lin. It's vital for the world that the war be fought."

"If I wasn't so good, you wouldn't even be asking, would you?"

"No."

Lin felt her blouse stretched open as strong hands held her against a cold brick wall.

"But if I want to go back to being a tease, I can."

"Yes. You already have the wardrobe," Gabriel said with a smile.

Lin felt a short skirt tight around her hips and her bare legs ending in her favorite heels.

"If I want to be more than a tease, if I want to be cheap, I can do that too."

"Yes, of course."

Lin felt her legs spread wide, her heels in the gravel, and her wrists held behind her.

"I could forget about saving the world?"

"You could. Free will."

She was stripped down and on her knees on the hotel rug, cheek stinging and called a tramp.

"Last night, I loved it when Jack called me a tramp. It just felt so right."

"Hearing that might have made it more real for you, Lin. Was that a good idea?"

Lin didn't answer. She let go of Nomad, rubbed her thighs, and stared at the wall with a faint smile.

"I can change my life anytime. I can be whatever I want."

Gabriel sat quietly, nodding.

Lin stopped smiling and said, "It would be a relief to be nothing but a tramp."

Gabriel stared for several seconds before letting out a short laugh. Lin continued to stare.

"You could, Lin. With no regrets. This life, and me, will become but a memory of a dream. You already knew that was possible, didn't you? Is that what you want?"

Lin fell into memories she now knew were real. She relived feelings she now knew were hers. Memories of drinking and strutting around for everyone in her spiky heels and a short skirt, her legs long and bare, teasing them and tempting them . . .

"Is that what you want, Lin?"

. . . feeling hands tearing open her blouse and tossing it aside, wiggling her hips to help them pull her skirt off, greedy hands peeling her panties down along her thighs, leaving her standing naked among strangers and wearing only her heels . . .

"Lin?

. . . being forced to her knees and shaking back her mane before a strong hand grips all of it tight, more hands holding her wrists behind her, unable to stop them from touching her everywhere, hoping she looks sexy for them on her knees in the dim hotel room, knowing she's in danger if she doesn't obey, but having no choice . . .

"Lin?"

. . . and doing what she knows she's made to do, forced to her knees and doing as she's told, as they're enjoying her in every way, and she feels her heart jump every time she's called a tramp, nothing but a—

"Lin!"

"Oh! Oh, Gabby, I was just thinking."

"With a big smile. Are you okay, Lin?"

"I'm fine. Really, I think I'll be okay," she said and continued to smile. "Can those other possible lives drag me into them? Did I open some kind of door?"

"In a way, yes, you did. Those lives are more possible for you now than they were before. I knew that was a risk even when I made a comment about your style not long ago because of how much power you have. But it was a necessary risk. Now, you must be vigilant."

"Or what?"

"You can lapse into one of those worlds pretty easily now that you've lived them like you have. Your intent can push you into being that person if you're not careful. Same thing for a life in the ocean or a nest. You wouldn't be just acting. Were you acting like a bird, or were you becoming a bird?"

"I was more bird than Lin. And it took only a couple of seconds."

"You felt that with Jack, too, didn't you? It didn't feel like just an act, did it?"

"No, not at all. It was me. Why is that even possible? Why do I feel so close to that now?"

"Because now, you see it as real. You've lived it in this world, and . . ."

"And what?"

"Now you know you are also that woman, and . . ."

"And what, Gabby?"

"It's obvious you want it."

After several moments, Lin squirmed and said, "Well, there's no real harm in . . . I mean, if I were to—"

"Let yourself be a tramp, Lin? No, that's not like letting yourself become a killer."

"But I did kill one person. And I crippled up Ben really bad. I really did all that?"

"No, Lin, those worlds weren't real like this world is. But before you think you can do that just for fun, remember that *you* were the most real part of those worlds. And what you do, even in a world that isn't completely real, affects you. Those acts can change you."

"So, even if I could, I shouldn't go back to one of those worlds just for fun?"

"No, there's a real risk of changing you."

"If I were stronger, I bet I could play around in a world like that."

"Possibly. Is that appealing to you?"

"Hmm. Maybe. It sure would be a fun time."

"While you were living those lives, did you even think of Jack?"

"Well, his name came up, but—"

"But it didn't even slow you down, did it?"

"No, I didn't care about Jack. I see your point."

"You might never make it back from that. You might not be able to find this life again. If you spent enough time in another creature's life, would you ever come back?"

Lin thought about her brief life in the ocean and the time spent in a nest. And she thought about Jack and their life together. And she also thought about all the things she would love to be forced to—

No, she corrected herself—things that she *did* love being forced to do. Because that was all real too. In some way, she was also *that* woman. She felt it.

Two different human lives and countless others. Countless possible directions. All real. All so close. All pulling at her. So hard to fight any of them. Her choice whether to—

"Lin?"

"I'm not okay."

"It's safe to briefly remember living a different life. As long as you can resist it, you'll be okay."

"I'm not sure I can resist it."

"You're strong enough to keep this life, Lin."

"But why is this happening? Sure, I like dressing kind of cheap, and yeah, I do like strutting around. But it's just for fun. I've never had feelings like that before Gloriana put me in those worlds."

"You're sure?"

"Pretty sure. Maybe those worlds did this to me. Is that possible?"

"Not according to Gloriana, but perhaps she's not being completely honest. Or maybe even she doesn't know the possible influence of worlds like those."

"I don't think it matters now. It's not enough anymore just to look like a tramp. I want to *be* that tramp."

"You will have to fight it, Lin."

"Huh. A lot of the time, I don't want anything else. Gabby, I believe I'm going to be that woman. Hell, I already am."

"You don't have to be. You must fight, Lin."

"I should try, I know I should. But now, I know what I really am."

"It's up to you what you are. You can choose."

"And I'll have to make that choice. I know I love Jack, and I want this life too."

She continued to stare at the wall as quiet minutes crept past.

"Are you going to be alright, Lin?"

She shook her hair back, smiled, and looked at Gabriel.

"Yeah, I'm sure I'll be fine. Just fine. You don't need to sit around in here. Why don't you watch some TV? I'll keep an eye on this big guy."

Gabriel paused to watch her closely.

"Don't leave without saying goodbye, okay, Lin?"

Silence.

"Lin?"

"I'm not going anywhere. Thanks for helping me try to understand all of this."

"It's a lot, I know. But you're very strong. Just be sure to consider the life you already have."

"I will. Thanks, Gabby."

"I hope Lee arrives soon. I'm sure she'll be able to help Nomad."

"I hope you're right."

"And you know what? Let's forget I ever asked you about fighting evil. Just focus on your life."

"Oh, thanks. And I'll do some focusing, that's for sure."

Gabriel left, and Lin heard the TV switch on. Nomad raised his head at the sound, but he let it clunk back down.

Lin loosened her grip on the moving parts inside, letting them draw nearer to where they wanted to be. She felt her intent, the raw power of it, ready to push them and press them together to make a new arrangement. A new Lin. In a new life.

But she didn't pack them in tight. So close to jumping into that life, she let her imagination take her to a world where fighting evil was never mentioned. No one needed her for that. But everyone sure did want her for other things. They'd watched her strutting around, showing everything off, convincing them all how easily they could have her, and it was time for her to let them take what they wanted. Something she was happy to do. Just let them undress her. Just do as she's told. Just be what she really is . . .

*   *   *

The door to the garage rattled open, and Lin got pulled back to her life on the floor beside Nomad. Jack had finished his shoveling and tracked snow onto the kitchen floor.

"We're going to have to train you a little better, Jack," she said with a weak smile.

Nomad raised his head but never turned it toward Jack. He laid it back down without a sound.

"I'll learn. How long before Lee gets here?"

"I have no idea. I'll keep Nomad company, and you can hang out with Gabby if you want."

"You're really sweet, Lin. That big boy will be fine. I watched a hole in Lee's chest patch itself right up. She can fix whatever that thing did to him."

"I hope so, Jack." She laid her arm over Nomad's mane and kissed the top of his head. He didn't move.

"Do you want me to sit up with him so you can go to bed?"

Whose bed? thought Lin. Yours, Jack? Or maybe a stranger's in some hotel where—

"Oh, Jack, thanks, but I'm staying right here. You go off and get some sleep, okay?"

"Alright, but if you need anything or you want me to take over, just ask."

"I will. I know Nomad wouldn't leave if it was me on the floor."

He stooped down and gave her a kiss.

"No, he sure wouldn't. I'll just be in the living room."

"Okay. I have lots I want to think about, that's for sure."

"I bet you do."

"Goodnight, Jack."

Lin gave him a smile. And she gave one to herself, too, as she took a vacation from the challenges of her real life and savored the decadent, sweet taste of another, almost real life. Knowing she need only push herself with her strong intent.

The clothes were still in her closet.

Just a little nudge . . .

Chapter 40 – Promise Of Eternity

Lin awoke to the sound of impatient rapping on the front door. Her arm still rested on the fur of Nomad's thick mane, and he didn't move when she got up. But Jack had gotten to the door first, and when she walked into the living room, Lee was already taking off her leather jacket.

Despite the urgency, Lin still took a moment to gaze at Jack in his tight jeans and remember what her powers had done to him two nights before. How she'd turned him into a crowd, a gang of eager strangers, and maybe some of them would get rougher next time too. Well, she thought, he did make a reasonable effort last time. With more practice—

"I got here as fast as I could. Where is he?"

"Thanks for coming, Lee. He's right here in the kitchen."

Jack took her jacket, and Lin gestured for Lee to follow her. She took a few hurried steps and stood looking down at Nomad on his side on the cold floor.

"I've never done this before. I mean, with a dog. But I think it should work."

Lee sat on her knees near Nomad's head, and she took each of his heavy front paws in her hands. Within seconds, her eyes rolled up high, and she began to tip. Jack rushed over and laid her on her side facing the big dog. Nomad remained still, his paws in Lee's hands.

* * *

Lee returned to her home, a patch of thick green grass in a peaceful valley. A brilliant blue sky stretched over her, and her old friend, the sun that never moved, rained its healing rays upon her.

She looked down on her stones, all forty of them arranged in a nearly perfect infinity symbol. She wasn't surprised—she felt strong and healthy, and only two of the stones needed minor adjustments.

Lee looked back up at her sun, and she couldn't help but smile, remembering what pleasure it could bring. But not this time. She remembered that she was there with a serious mission: to help Nomad.

But how? She'd seen Taylor as a trapped bird, and freeing the bird had cured the girl. Ben, at least the first time, was a giant oak tree with branches pinned to the ground. The tree had cried softly, and it sounded like only the wind until Lee freed the branches. The wind sound stopped, and Ben's injuries had been healed. And after that, the other times with Ben . . . no, she couldn't think about that now. She had to find Nomad.

She spun herself around slowly, looking first at the lush grass all around her. Everything appeared normal. Then, at the edge of the grass, she saw the taller weeds rising up. Above the weeds, she saw only blue sky in every direction except for one. She felt she was looking south, but since her sun never moved, she could never know. The sky high above was a brilliant blue, but near the horizon, there was a region of white. Not a true white—more like a light gray.

Across the grass, Lee hiked until she reached the taller weeds. She expected to feel a weakness or a pain like she had before. Instead, the farther away from her stones she walked, the lighter she felt. Each step propelled her forward, and she glided until she came down, touched the Earth, and pushed off again.

The wall was within sight, and she hoped she wouldn't drift away before she reached it. As she came to rest closer to its base, she looked up and saw that it wasn't flat across the top, and it wasn't a single wall. There appeared to be two walls connected down the middle, and each of them rose to a high, rounded peak. Above each wall, Lee could see the blue sky of her home.

She glided another step and barely made contact with the ground. She felt that even a gentle push would send her flying, never to feel the Earth again. Lee looked up at the walls and saw that they had an odd texture, as if some pattern had been molded into their surface. She reached out to touch it, and it felt solid.

Her eyes scanned left, then right, then up . . . and she saw it: something dark protruding from one of the walls high above the ground. She knew that she had to risk another leap, whether she'd ever come back down or not. She pushed against the ground very gently and began to rise along the walls.

With her eyes looking up, Lee floated along the hard wall surface until she reached the curious item. When she'd gotten close enough, she reached out and grasped it. It stopped her from floating away, but it saddened her at the same time.

It was a large black dagger plunged to its hilt into the wall. Lee held it with both hands and listened with her legs floating out away from the wall, but there was no sound. She looked at the ground far below her and felt a moment of panic. But she knew what had to be done, no matter what the risk.

She held the knife in her right hand and pushed against the wall with her left. The blade had been lodged in tightly, and she strained to make any progress. With her best efforts, the knife had moved out only a small amount. But even with that modest progress, Lee felt a difference in the wall—it had become a bit softer.

With a renewed grip, Lee pulled with all her strength. The thickest part of the sharp metal had already been pulled away, and she found that it began to slide more easily. She pulled slowly, mindful of the risk of her tumbling out of control high above the ground. She felt the wall getting even softer. And she saw it becoming whiter too.

After the sharp tip of the blade pulled free, she cast it toward the ground, but it vanished shortly after leaving her hand.

She watched as the wall's pattern came alive. What had been a curious texture, repeated in every direction, became an array of soft, individual pieces, each long and laying over the ones below it. Lee paused a moment to stare at the complexity of one of them. A gracefully curving central piece held hundreds of parallel strands branching out, shorter on one side than the other, and holding onto each other to make a shimmering surface. The entire wall glowed a soothing white.

But Lee had nothing to hold, and the force she'd exerted against the wall caused her to float away from it. She knew that she was lost, and she knew that it was okay. She could only hope that she'd somehow helped Nomad.

Still afraid of looking at the Earth so far from her, Lee looked up. The tops of the walls began to turn in unison toward her, revealing a brilliant white light that rivaled the intensity of her sun. She tried to continue her gaze, hoping to understand it, but the light had become blinding. She snapped her hands up to cover her eyes. The sudden motion sent her spinning out of control, and still, she had no regrets.

Then, she felt the soft walls fold around her, cradling her from every direction and stopping her spinning. She looked up between parted fingers and again saw the blaze and felt its warmth.

The walls wrapped her tight like a blanket, and Lee couldn't help but cry. Not from fear, but from a feeling she'd never known before. A feeling of acceptance. Of love. And a promise of eternity.

Then, the walls pulled away, and Lee felt the grass of her home beneath her. She lay there with her hands still covering her eyes, thankful to feel the ground pressing against her like it always had before. She looked south and saw only blue sky.

Causing more tears to spill down her cheeks, Lee looked down and saw in the grass near her feet one perfect white feather.

* * *

Lin watched from a short distance away and prayed Lee could help Nomad. Lee remained lying in front of the big dog just as Jack had left her. She still held his meaty paws in her hands.

"Mom, look!"

They all stared at Nomad's side where the swollen mass began to shrink. His fur moved with the changing shape until his side had returned to normal.

It seemed only seconds more had passed before Lin saw tears dripping from Lee's closed eyes and pooling on the floor below. She opened her eyes, and the tears continued to flow. Thirty seconds passed as Lee stared only at Nomad. No one made a sound.

Then, Nomad opened his big eyes. He remained still and moved only his eyes. He looked into Lee's left eye, then her right, then back to her left. Lee's tears increased, and she tried to hide her sobbing, but she couldn't look away from him.

He shifted forward and licked Lee's cheeks before pulling his paws free and rising up on his thick legs to stand over her. She tried to keep looking, but she covered her eyes, and her quiet sobbing shook her.

Lin felt her own tears, and she could hear Taylor crying too.

"Nomad? Are you okay?" Taylor said while wiping her cheeks.

Nomad turned to look at her, stepped closer, and jumped up to put a paw on each of her shoulders. Taylor cried as Nomad licked her face before turning his head to look at Lin.

Lin dropped down and sat back on her heels with her arms open and tears trickling down her cheeks. He walked over with his bushy tail swishing, where he kissed her and tried to help with her tears, too, until she'd started to smile.

"Oh my God. My Nomad!" Lin continued to hug him around his thick mane. "Lee, you're a miracle worker. You healed him. You—"

Lin stopped when she saw that Lee wasn't listening.

Lee had uncovered her eyes, and she stared at Gabriel with tears still streaming down her cheeks.

"Nomad," she said between sobs. "Is he . . . he's really—"

But she fell silent at the sight of Gabriel's steady gaze and slowly shaking head.

Chapter 41 – Sick Of Magic

Tears became gentle laughter when Nomad turned away from Lin and toward his bowl. His heavy steps brought him to it, and he nosed it around across the floor before looking into Jack's eyes.

"Where's the dump truck, Lin?" he said while blinking hard and wiping at his eyes. "Nomad has his appetite back."

Lin smiled and dabbed her fingertips at the last of her tears.

"Oh, Jack, he's really okay, isn't he?"

"He's hungry like always, so I'd say yes, he is."

Jack found the dog food and shook the bag over his bowl. Every face smiled as crunching rang through the house.

Lin brushed her hair back and turned to Gabriel.

"We can't let that happen again. Whatever that thing is, it's going to try to come back. If it drags me back there, the door will be open, and it'll get in again. And maybe next time, it'll figure out how to stay."

"I believe you're right about all of that, Lin."

Lin looked at Lee.

"Lee, that was another miracle. I can never thank you enough for saving him, but we can't ask you to heal everyone that that thing might attack."

"I would, but that was exhausting. And you don't understand, Lin. Nomad, he must be . . . I mean, I think he's really—"

She looked at Gabriel, who only looked back with a more serious expression.

"I mean, he's really wonderful. I'm thrilled I was able to help him. But you're right—I can't go around healing everyone. What 'thing' are you talking about? Something did that to him?"

Gabriel spoke. "It's something that doesn't belong roaming the Earth. It came from a place that doesn't exist, not like the world around us. Lin, we need to discuss this more with Gloriana."

"Who's Gloriana?" said Lee.

"I am," said a voice from the doorway.

Gloriana had investigated Lin's closet and found clothes more suitable to Pennsylvania in late November. Lin's faded jeans fit well enough, and a blue hooded sweatshirt covered a white long-sleeved t-shirt. Even Lin's old sneakers seemed to be working well enough.

"I am a friend from long ago."

"Gloriana, this is Lee. Lee, Gloriana. Okay, I'm glad you're up because we need to talk."

"And while we converse, perhaps Gabriel can prepare more of those cakes?"

"Looks like you found my closet," said Lin.

"Yes. I chose this and not your finer clothes. Why do you not wear those, Lin Finity?"

Lin held her breath and stared, and she felt a knot gather inside while she imagined the feeling of a skirt tight around her hips and barely hiding any of her legs, with a silky top stretched tight with nothing under it, while hands of strangers—

"Maybe another time."

Taylor's door opened, and she joined them while still rubbing her eyes.

"How's that, Jack?"

"Nice work, Taylor. I knew you could do it."

She gave Jack a big smile.

"Speaking of food," said Jack, "I'm going to head out to the grocery store and stock up while the roads are clear. Before this one,"—Jack leaned his head toward Taylor with a big grin—"decides to show off some more."

Taylor giggled and said, "I want to go too. Okay, Jack?"

"Yeah, I'll need your help anyway to carry the dog food," Jack said with a big smile as he looked at Lin.

"Oh, Jack, that's a good idea. Maybe Nomad would like to go too?"

"Yeah, let's take him, Jack!"

They put on lightweight jackets and boots to help with walking through the slush, and Taylor grabbed Lin's sunglasses off of the counter. Nomad barked once and led them out through the garage.

* * *

Gabriel set a stack of fresh blueberry hotcakes in front of Gloriana and sat beside her. Lin sat across the table from them, and sunlight brightened the room.

"None for you, Gabby?"

"You've run out of eggs."

"There are waffles in the freezer. Why don't you try those?"

With the toaster loaded up, Gabriel leaned against the counter while Lin sat with Gloriana and Lee, who leaned forward with her face buried in her crossed arms.

"Gloriana," said Lin, "we—you know, I'm not trying to be difficult, but your name is kind of long. Do you have a nickname or some other way that people address you?"

"It is also acceptable to address me as 'My Queen.'"

Lee looked up, stared a second, and put her head back down.

"Okay, well, that's not going to do. This is a different time and a different place."

"You are right, Lin Finity. I will—"

"Oh, and just 'Lin' is fine."

"Lin. Yes, Lin, I'd like the name 'Sunny.' My islands were always sunny. I will always miss that world. A new name for a new life."

"Sunny is good. Okay, we need to talk first about Taylor. I get it—she's a Glyphin now. What can you tell us? She needs to be able to control that power. You can see how frustrated she is."

"It is so simple to speak of," said Sunny. "But she will need practice. Part of what must be done is what I have already said. She must know the word that was used to bring the change."

"'The change?' That's what you call it?"

"It is a change a Glyphin brings. When a Glyphin combines the known with the unknown, a change comes."

"A normal word combined with a meaningless word . . . that's what you mean?"

"Yes, Lin. But remember that they are only words, even the unknown ones. The words themselves have no power. The Glyphin *is* the power that brings the change. The words are only a path."

"And how can Taylor stop a change before it ever happens?"

"She must learn to not dwell on any word. She can read it and understand it, and then, she must move beyond it."

"And if she slips up and brings a change—how can she fix it?"

"She must undo what she has brought. She must take apart the word that was used. The more she can bring it to nothing, the faster she can heal what she has caused."

"I don't know how to teach her any of that. Gabby, do you?"

"No, Lin. As we talked about, it's a very ancient knowledge."

"I will work with her, Lin," said Sunny. "She will learn quickly if I talk with her."

The toaster popped up, and Gabriel brought a plate with four hot waffles to the table.

"What about that 'thing?'" said Lee, turning her face up to look at Lin. "What exactly are you talking about?"

"It is a hunter," said Gabriel between bites. "It's one of the many things that hunt us—a part of us that's more like our spirit—until we cannot continue. It leads us to our deaths."

"But that wasn't Nomad's spirit. That was his body that took the beating."

"What that thing does to that part of us manifests in the destruction of our bodies too."

"Sunny, what do you know of that thing? How can we stop it?" said Lin.

"It cannot be stopped. It has tormented me forever—all the time I have been between the Islands of Time."

"Lin," said Lee, "'Islands of Time?' I'm never going to catch up with what's going on. I'll get some waffles myself and stay out of your way. You just tell me how I can help."

With that, Lee put four more waffles in the toaster, dug through the freezer, and took out a bucket of chocolate ice cream. She leaned back against the counter, closed her eyes, and took a deep breath.

"Its essence is destruction. It is accustomed to uncaring darkness and remaining unknown. Perhaps the opposite can be used against it?" said Sunny.

"Someone pure of heart and dedicated? And very focused?"

"A person like that might have a chance," said Sunny. "But it is not likely."

"I know who to call. He's already offered to help. Maybe there's some way?"

* * *

"Lin, hearing your voice is unexpected. Are you well?"

"Yes, Tayo, I'm doing fine. There are problems, though."

"You're not in Georgia, I surmise? You've journeyed back to your home?"

"Yes," Lin said into her phone with curious eyes and ears all around her at her kitchen table. "How are your injuries?"

"The bone structure is healing, albeit slowly, but I can't yet support any significant portion of my weight over the injured leg. Soon, I hope."

"I really didn't want to hurt you, Tayo, but—"

"Lin, you could have easily terminated my existence. You showed mercy where it would have been understandable to deny it in any form. I am in your debt."

"And I'm calling in that debt. Where are you?"

"I'm at my home in Baltimore. I relocated here for its proximity to The Shield's operations center. This recovery time is giving me the opportunity to study up on a number of things that have piqued my interest. I'm reading scientific journals, books on ancient civilizations . . . even the Bible. The world is a more mysterious place than I had ever believed."

"Put the books aside for a while and meet me in Allentown. Can you do that?"

"I can be there in about three hours. Where shall we meet?"

"How about the place where we first crossed paths?"

"I will never forget any of what transpired that day. I'll see you in three hours."

"Thanks, Tayo. See you soon."

Lin ended the call and turned to Lee.

"Lee, how about a road trip in a couple of hours?"

"Count me in, Lin," she said while chewing and leaning against the counter with her eyes closed.

Lin looked over at Sunny, who smiled between taking bites of her waffles.

"Sunny, do you have any plans for what you want to do with your life?"

While still chewing, she said, "It will take time to accept this. I lived my life with such power and accomplishment. I must learn to carry less expectations."

"There's nothing wrong with living a normal life. You'll be surprised at how much happiness you can find. You don't need to create your own islands."

"I will adjust. May I stay here in your palace—your home—until I find a life?"

"Yes, of course. You still look exhausted. I know I am. You're welcome to keep that guest room until we get you on your way. You'll probably need to rest some more."

"I shall. But . . . more waffles first."

Gabriel gave Lin a big grin, and she only shook her head and smiled.

* * *

Jack returned with Taylor and Nomad, and after they'd carried the groceries in, he refilled Nomad's bowl. With loud crunching coming from the kitchen, they all sat around in the living room.

"Well, we're quite a bunch, huh?" said Lin. "Where do we go from here?"

Taylor spoke first. "Are you going to keep dying? I'm barely holding myself together."

"Honey, I'm trying. Just remember that I'm not really dead, okay? It's just a weird magic thing. We'll figure it out."

"I'm kind of sick of magic, Mom. It's not fun like so many people think."

"I know, Hon. Nothing's easy."

"I'm going to my room. It's still a struggle."

She put on her headphones and left for her bedroom. Jack waited until Taylor had closed her bedroom door.

"She doesn't want to upset you, Lin, but she needs help, and she knows it. While we were driving, she was looking out the window, and I saw her jerk a couple of times, like she was fighting with something. And each time, there were gusts of wind that shoved my truck around. I had to keep talking to her to keep her distracted."

"You're a big help, Jack. We'll figure it out."

Lin looked over at Sunny, but she was staring out the window and not listening to anyone.

This reality must be hitting her by now, thought Lin.

And she knew it was hitting her hard too. Being asked to go fight evil in the magic. She knew that she could imagine a new life instead. One where she didn't have life and death responsibilities. Where the only goal was enjoyment. Where being sexy and willing was all that—

"I don't feel like I need to get home right away," said Lee. "Alessa likes spending time with her grandma, so if I can just hang with you a while?"

"Sure, Lee. As long as you want."

Lin looked from Lee back to Jack and said, "Jack, about Taylor. She—"

"I miss my islands, Lin Finity," Sunny said softly.

And I miss showing off my legs, thought Lin.

"It's just 'Lin,' okay? And I'm sorry, but those islands of yours are gone. Jack, Taylor should—"

Nomad jumped onto Lin's lap and began licking her face. She wrapped her arms around his mane and pulled him in close.

"Jack, she—"

"Lin," Gabriel said, "I'm glad you're well on your way, and so many problems are behind you. We—"

Lin tilted her head away from Nomad's kisses and said, "No. Don't even think about it. There's too much left to do."

"I'm trying to tell you that I want to stay a while longer. You're right—the war will carry on without me. I'll go back, but not right away."

"Oh, Gabby, that's wonderful. Plan on taking the couch. As long as you want, okay?"

"Thank you, Lin. And since I plan to stay, I must find a direction for my life."

"You will. I know you will."

Sunny said, "I must find a direction too. What is my purpose now, Lin?"

"You should just be glad you're not still in between somewhere. You'll find a good life."

So many questions and so much confusion, Lin thought. Nothing confusing about seducing—

"I have plenty of work waiting for me," said Jack. "I still have house building to get back to."

"I know, Jack. And you've been such a big help with everything."

She smiled, thinking about kneeling and undoing his tight jeans, whether she had a chance to strip first or not, but knowing it's better if she's naked because he likes her naked. And she wouldn't care who else was there—only pulling at that denim. And maybe he'd have to slap her a couple of times, maybe without being told this time, then she'd—

A black dot appeared on the wall across the room. Lin stared and felt thin trickles of tears on her cheeks.

"Your intent, Lin," she heard from Gabriel. "Remember your—"

The darkness swallowed her, and she died. But only for a moment. The speeding light draped her world back over her, and she took a deep breath as her life returned.

"That was quick, Lin," said Gabriel. "How did—"

A scream from Taylor's room caused them all to stand, and Lin ran to her bedroom and opened the door.

Taylor lay on her bed staring at Lin as her body shook from her strained, shallow breaths. Her arms and legs were straight and stiff and tears flooded her eyes.

Lin's intent focused on the magic within her, and time stopped in an instant. She saw infinity in every direction, but she ignored it and quickly went to Taylor's magic.

And there, she found a dark dagger with razor teeth gnawing on her daughter's spirit.

Chapter 42 – Service To Humanity

Lin knew that she couldn't remove the death from Taylor's spirit, so she let her mayhem recede, and time resumed.

Lee had joined her, and they both looked down at the ill girl.

"I'll try, Lin."

"God, please hurry, Lee."

Lee approached Taylor's bed and sat next to her. She took Taylor's hands in her own, and Taylor looked up at her as rapid breathing vibrated the bed. Lee closed her eyes, and within seconds, Taylor's eyes rolled up and closed.

* * *

Lee found her home—a patch of dense green grass beneath a brilliant blue sky. Right away, she noticed that her sun didn't shine as brightly as it should. She looked up to see a menacing cloud just big enough to block her sun and keep its brilliance from reaching the ground.

She looked down and saw some of her stones pivoting and sliding away on their own. The infinity symbol was still obvious, but there were gaps, and the smooth curves were becoming ragged. Without any apparent reason, they continued to scatter in the shade from the dark cloud.

Lee felt her energy begin a sharp decline, and she knew that she had to set her stones before she could look for Taylor. But was that cloud causing her stones to move? How could she move the cloud and let her sun shine? She watched her stones continue to shift about.

She hurried to put them all in their proper places and welcomed the rapid increase in her strength. While staring at her stones and hoping they'd stay in place, she saw two saplings sprout up through the grass and shoot toward the sky. Thin branches linked them together at a consistent spacing, forming a ladder. She saw that it reached all the way to the invading cloud.

Lee knew that Taylor would have to wait. She began to climb, but she felt her health again begin to fade. Standing on the fourth rung, she looked down to see a few of her stones again moving away from their places on their own. She jumped to the ground and placed them where they belonged, and her health returned.

She looked up and saw that the cloud had grown and blocked more of the sky. She rushed back onto the ladder and felt her weakness return. From the third rung, she saw her stones begin to scatter again. Tears ran down her cheeks as she jumped down and put them back in order.

When she looked back at the sky, she saw that the cloud had swelled, and her home was darker than she'd ever seen it. Sobbing uncontrollably, Lee began to climb the ladder. Weakness pulled her down like an iron blanket, and she stumbled back to the ground. On her hands and knees, she fought to move her arms and form infinity from her stones.

When she'd set them properly, and she held as many as she could to keep them from rolling, Lee collapsed across the symbol and wept. She knew that she could do nothing but return to the world.

* * *

Lee opened her eyes and slumped into the blankets next to Taylor. Her eyes immediately closed, and she began shallow, choppy breaths. Taylor continued to stare into Lin's eyes.

"Mom . . ."

Winds attacked the house from every direction, and heavy rains came down. The last traces of snow began to wash away as small streams and rivers cleared Lin's yard.

"Gabby, what can I do? Lee couldn't help her, and now they're both dying. Gabby?"

"Put me back there, Lin Finity."

"What? How could—"

"It knows me all too well. I believe it will follow me back."

Lin looked toward Gabriel, who quickly nodded.

"She remembers how to fight it, Lin. She will survive. You must do it right away."

Lin looked again at the fear in Taylor's eyes, then she looked into Sunny's caramel eyes and watched an empty darkness surround them. Lin found her intent, and while staring into those caramel eyes, she got her unbreakable hold on it.

The night around Sunny's eyes grew, and Lin could not look at anything else. The darkness hurried to cover her, and her lungs locked up. She could no longer feel or think anything. She had only her heartbeat as she waited in the black emptiness.

Then, her heart stopped.

*　*　*

The tiniest pinpoint of light appeared in front of Lin. She focused on it and watched as it sped toward her until it covered her with a world that didn't exist. Her heart raced before slowing down, and she felt her feelings and thoughts return. She took a deep breath and opened her eyes.

There was only gray. No ocean and no sky. Beneath her feet, she saw a small square of stone floor, and to her right, a cinnamon gown hanging limp with no breeze to carry it.

Lin shook her head slowly and looked into Gloriana's sad caramel eyes.

"Lin Finity."

"I'm sorry, Gloriana. It was the only way to save Taylor and Lee. They haven't lived their lives yet. I had to—"

"It is fine. I am practiced at surviving here."

"But you don't have your powers anymore, do you?"

"Here, I still have my intent. To live on the Islands of Time again, I must let powers go."

"That was the deal, huh?"

"Gabriel explains to you. Yes, that is my only path."

"You'll survive, then?"

"I survive."

"But there's hardly any of this world left. Where will you go?"

"I remain in the emptiness."

Gloriana turned to look out at where an ocean could once be seen. "All alone? How could—"

"No. Not alone."

"That thing. That's coming after you again, isn't it?"

"That is our plan. That saves two good lives."

"I'll come back for you. I'll figure out a way. Just hang on, okay? Can you?"

"I can."

Lin found her intent. A dark spot showed itself in the gray where an ocean used to be. It rushed toward her, and she died, until a white cover had been pulled over her, and life returned.

*　*　*

Still standing beside the bed, Lin found that she hadn't even had time to fall over. She'd returned Gloriana to a place and time that didn't exist. And she saw Lee breathing normally and lost in sleep next to Taylor, who still pleaded silently with her eyes.

Lin shook Lee awake, and she sat up.

"Lin. Oh my God, that was impossible."

"I think that thing is gone. Are you okay? Can you try again?"

"Yeah, I do feel better. Tired, though. Lin, I never got a chance to even find Taylor that time."

She looked down at Taylor shaking next to her.

"I'm going to give it another try. It'll work this time."

Lee reached over and held the hand closest to her.

* * *

Lee dragged herself back to her home. She looked at the sky and saw no cloud blocking her sun. With growing confidence, she looked all around. Something near the weeds caught her eye, but when she looked directly at it, she could see nothing. She began walking in that direction anyway.

Just behind the first few tall weeds, she saw a white dove burrowed in among the stalks. She shivered gently and gazed into Lee's eyes.

Lee knew that the bird's ailment was mostly fear, so she cautiously reached down and gave her a moment to study the hand in front of her. After several seconds, she crawled up and wrapped her claws around a finger, and Lee lifted her up. She held the scared bird there, and without a word, convinced her, just by holding her gaze and feeling the wonder of her home, that there was nothing to fear. Before long, the dove began to coo and bob her head.

She extended her arm straight out, and the bird jumped off with strong flapping of its wings. She circled Lee's home only once and flew toward the horizon.

Lee watched the bird's flight and delighted in its restored freedom. Feeling only flawless health, she looked at her sky, a clear expanse of pure blue, and she saw her sun shining down on her from directly above.

A quick walk brought her to her stones, and she saw with relief that none were moving on their own. A small adjustment to several of them produced her precise infinity symbol, and Lee knew it was time to leave her home.

* * *

Lin watched as Lee's eyes rolled up and closed. Within a few seconds, Taylor's breaths calmed, and she opened her eyes. She looked directly into Lin's eyes, and Lin rejoiced at her daughter's restored health.

Until Taylor spoke.

"Damn it! What the hell was that? I was better off sick, lying in a damn hospital bed!"

Thunder boomed above the house.

"Lying around lying, all by myself—that's what I was doing!"

More thunder shook the walls and furnishings.

"Wishing I could just fly the hell away!"

Buckets of rain slammed into the window.

"This is crazy, Mom. It's all crazy!"

Lin climbed onto the bed and hugged her sobbing daughter, who fell asleep in her arms.

The rainfall increased.

"Gabby, what the hell?"

"I doubt there's rain in Hell, Lin."

"I know you're trying to lighten the mood, but it's not going to work. If you have any advice for any of this, I'd love to hear it."

"You could just leave things as they are. Taylor is healed. Lee will recover."

"But what about Sunny? Well, I guess she's Gloriana again. What about her?"

"You can't save the entire world, Lin."

"I know, but there must be a way."

Jack had walked in when Taylor began screaming, and he put a hand on Lin's shoulder. Lin still held Taylor in her arms, but she wondered if Jack's rough hands would someday strip her and force her to her knees, where she'd have to do to him, and all the friends he could find, whatever they wanted from her. He had to have friends. Oh, he must have lots of—

"It's really pouring out there, Lin. Worse than before. And the winds are picking up too."

"See, Gabby? It's not like everything is fine. Taylor's still a Glyphin that can't control herself. Something has to be done."

"There is one hope. Go and meet with Tayo."

"Why? I never should have bothered him. This thing is too powerful, and he doesn't have any powers."

"No, but he still might be the one to fight that thing. There's something special about him, Lin. You know that."

"Yeah, I believe there is. But how could he? No one is that strong."

"It seems his fate is leading him to just such a confrontation. He needs to be of service to humanity. That we know."

"Maybe you know it. Or maybe he's just some guy that worked with The Shield, and since I didn't destroy him, he feels like he owes me."

"And he wants to pay that debt. Perhaps you should ask him?"

Lin looked down at Taylor asleep in her arms. Then, she looked at Lee, still unconscious next to them. Jack stood waiting for whatever would come next. Even Nomad had joined them and watched patiently.

"I'm going to Allentown."

More thunder rattled all the windows.

"Before I have to swim there."

Chapter 43 – Hold That Thought

"Jack, can you stay and keep an eye on Taylor? She might sleep until Lee and I get back from Allentown."

"Yeah, whatever you need."

Oh, Jack, I'm not sure you know yet what I really need, she thought.

"Gabby might be able to help, too, if that thing comes back."

"Alright."

"I'll try to help in whatever ways I'm able, Lin," said Gabriel.

"Nomad will help you too, Jack. He'll find a way to help."

"Alright, we'll handle it. Do you want to take my truck? You might run into some high water out there."

"No, you might need it if you have to try to outrun the Glyphin storm. My Temt8tion will have to do. It's a short ride, Jack. We'll make it."

She shook Lee awake.

"Oh, okay, Lin. How's Taylor?"

"She's fine, Lee. At least physically. She's very upset about the whole situation, and she can't control what she's causing out there."

Lee looked at the window to see the driving rain slamming against it.

"God. Well, I can't help with that."

"No, but if you come with me to meet Tayo, I know something you can help with."

"Sure, let's go."

Gabriel and Nomad had settled again in front of the flickering TV. Lee had gone ahead into the garage, and Lin and Jack were alone in the kitchen. He came up from behind her as she gathered her things on the counter and slipped his arms around her waist.

He whispered in her ear, "Be safe, Cowgirl."

She spun around and wrapped her arms around his neck.

"Oh, my Cowboy. I don't know what I'd do without you."

She gave him a long, deep kiss and realized that no stranger could compare with Jack. No matter how many of them were undressing her, holding her down, touching her, making her—

She groaned, broke free, and picked up her keys, and Jack grabbed her arm as she turned to leave.

"There's something I've been meaning to ask you, and there never seems to be a good enough time."

Jack found the engagement ring in his pants pocket.

"Hold that thought, Cowboy." She gave him a big smile, a smile so big that he happily let go of the ring.

"Alright. Maybe when you get back, then?"

If I'm still who I am right now, Cowboy. And I hope I don't end up killing you by trying to make you into a gang, because I don't want to kill you, so maybe I should just find a real gang that'll treat me like what I am, like all I want to be, and you'd still be alive somewhere, and I'd be stripped naked and helpless, drunk, slapped around, and finally—

"There's just a lot on my mind right now, you know, Jack?"

She smiled, blew him a kiss, and headed out to her car.

* * *

"Oh, Lee, the last time I was here."

"I was here too, Lin. I stood right there on the sidewalk and watched you drive away."

"I saw you in the rearview mirror. That was quite a night."

"Good thing you had this fast car."

"I can still remember that fever when I had to leave my life behind. All I wanted to do was drive."

Lin shut down the powerful motor and held the steering wheel. She looked at the restaurant entrance and wondered if Tayo was inside.

"I can't believe it's happening this far."

"What?"

"The rain. And who knows how much farther."

Lee stared out at the downpour and said nothing.

"Let's go, Lee. He might already be in there."

They got out of the car and splashed through the lot. A few steps inside, Lin looked up to see Tayo at a table on the balcony. She took a moment to look around the restaurant, and across the room, seated at the bar, she saw Anna on Lin's favorite bar stool and Daria next to her. Anna's short skirt showed a lot of her legs, and her low-cut sweater showcased assets that she'd kept to herself when working for The Shield. Daria grabbed Anna's arm, the one not holding Ozzy, which shook her cocktail and spilled some on the bar.

Just wonderful, she thought, as she and Lee climbed the stairs, and Lin thought about how nicely a skirt would ride up while climbing those stairs. If she were wearing one. And if it was short. Oh, it would be much shorter than Anna's, and showing so much of her bare legs would make clear to everyone just what kind of woman she was as she lifted each heel to the next step, giving them all a good—

"There he is, Lin."

Lin saw that Tayo wore his usual long-sleeved shirt, all black and white stripes. His jeans looked crisp and new except for the part that had been cut away for his cast. He didn't stand, but he did manage a courteous smile.

"Hi, Tayo. Don't get up. Is there an elevator in this place?"

"Hi, Lin. Yes, it's located back around that corner."

"You remember Lee."

"Yes. Hi, Lee. Anna and her daughter chose to remain outside of some safe radius from you. What assistance may I offer?"

Lin glanced over the rail.

"Huh. They're not safe." She turned back to Tayo. "Why did you join The Shield?"

He hesitated, but he pushed his thick black glasses up and answered. "I'm reluctant to speak truthfully because few would understand."

"If anyone would, it's us," said Lee.

He looked at both women and nodded.

"Very well. I must help mankind in whatever way I can. I've been given generous gifts. My reason. My health. My passion for doing what is right. It must all be put to good use. I tried to learn the Words of God for that very reason."

"I understand," said Lin. "And there's something monumental that you could help with. It's very dangerous, though, and I'm not sure you could help at all. Most likely, you'd be destroyed before you got a chance."

"Well, now I am truly intrigued," he said with a smile. He leaned his head back, and his long locks fell away from his forehead for a moment.

"What task do you propose?"

Lin looked at Lee before she looked back at Tayo and continued.

"You will have to take my word on what I'm about to say until you see for yourself."

"Yes. I understand."

"Diseases are like spirits. They attack whoever they can from a part of creation where no life exists. We pass through there countless times in every moment. They hunt us. They find us, and their teeth bite into us. Some of us they kill quickly. Others take longer."

Tayo's eyes grew wide, but he didn't react, so Lin continued.

"One very bad, dangerous hunter thing knows the way into the world now. We have to find a way to kill it. Except we don't know if it can be killed because it's not even alive. We're asking you to try."

Tayo looked between the two, and he started to laugh. He quickly caught himself and frowned.

"You seem serious."

"Deadly serious."

He rubbed his chin and brushed his hair to the back.

"I must pursue something that hunts in a place without life. And when I find it—if I can find it—even though it's not alive, I must find a way to kill it? Is that all?"

"Yeah, we're asking a lot."

He looked down at the table with one hand around his coffee mug. Several minutes passed as his eyes occasionally darted from one side to the other. He looked up and held Lin's gaze.

"Tell me what I must do."

*　*　*

A server came to the table and refilled Tayo's coffee. Lin and Lee declined ordering anything, and after the young girl had left for tables on the main floor, they continued.

"I don't know what to tell you yet. Mostly, I wanted to see you and ask you if you'd help. I really have no idea how this will all play out."

But if you tore this shirt off of me, she thought, you'd be happy at what would be out, and oh, I'd sure have to play. The things I would do. The things you'd enjoy forcing me to—

"You could have asked me in our telephone conversation, you know," he said with a cheerful smile. "I had to ask Anna to give me a lift. Driving is impossible with this." He swung his cast out from under the table.

"Yeah, I can imagine. Are you and Anna friends now?"

"We've been associates for many years. I think we're both grateful for our familiarity and the experiences we have in common. You must know, there's no way we can share our stories with anyone about any of this."

"You're right, of course. I take it for granted I have someone who understands all of it."

"Gabriel? Who exactly is Gabriel?"

"Oh, a very good friend. I can't explain any more than that. But there's another reason we needed to meet in person. How would you like your broken bones fixed?"

391

Tayo's eyes grew wide, and he looked from Lin to Lee and back again.

"That is possible?"

"Not for me, but Lee here, she has that talent. If you doubt it, just look at her. And she eats cotton candy and cheesecake all day."

He glanced quickly at Lee's toned physique and then back at Lin.

"I've started calling her 'Lee Ternity' because she doesn't age anymore. Isn't that right, Lee?"

"Yeah, but Lin, I don't know about the whole 'eternity' thing."

"What do you mean?"

"When I tried to help Taylor, I watched as my stones kept rolling away from where they should be. It was just a couple of them, and I was able to get them back in line. But I wonder . . . what if they all started moving? I'd never be able to put them back."

"Let's hope that never happens, okay? Maybe Gabby would know something about that. But in the meantime, can you patch this guy up?"

Before I find my own way to help him, she thought. I'd need to get naked first—that's always best. I'm sure he'd be real happy to have me naked for him. He'd like me helpless too. All that smooth, soft skin there for the taking. Then, anything he could imagine, I'd have to—

"Compared to what I just tried to do healing Taylor, I'd say yeah, nothing to it. Right here, Lin?"

"Yeah, if you can. Then, we have to get back before the roads wash out."

"Okay, Tayo, give me your hand."

Tayo laid his arm on the table, and she covered his hand with her own. Within seconds, he fell forward across the table, and Lee slumped back into her seat.

* * *

Lee went home. She stood looking over her stones, all arranged perfectly in the symbol for infinity. She saw the thick green grass in front of her and taller weeds and plants beyond. The sky was a familiar clear blue, and her sun shined down from directly above her. She smiled at her old friend, and she was sure that it smiled back.

Remembering that she had a purpose for her visit, besides the usual maintenance she always did to keep herself in peak health, she took a look around. She immediately saw a wooden bench by itself at the edge of her meadow. She began walking toward it, and with every step, she felt a growing hunger.

It took little time to tread across the lush grass, and she reached out to touch the wood. It felt warm from her sun, and she observed that three boards made up the bench surface. All were straight and smooth, but the middle one had mud smeared all around near its midpoint. She wondered how the mud could have gotten there, and the sight of it stoked the hunger burning inside. She knew that it was odd and unlike the other times she'd healed, and she also concluded that fixing the problem would be easy.

She stooped down next to the bench and began wiping at the mud, trying to sweep it off to each side. Most of the large pieces moved easily, and soon, there was only a thin film left covering the board. She knew that it needed to be cleaned completely to restore it, so she began wiping at it with the palms of both hands. And she felt her hunger becoming ravenous.

She knew that she was running out of time. Her hunger was a beast that would soon consume her, devour her from the inside. Her palms had become coated with mud and had lost their effectiveness. Without thinking, she swung a leg over the bench, and from there, she rubbed at the mud and wiped it on her jeans over and over. She knew that she was getting dirtier every moment, but it was the only way.

And she felt her sun hot above her burning her with pleasure. Wave after wave of heat and ecstasy, feeding that monstrous hunger inside. As a gigantic tide of ecstasy began to crash . . .

. . . Lee remembered that she wasn't there for pleasure—she was there only to heal. And even though the bench had been cleaned completely, she couldn't stop rubbing at it.

She knew that she had to get back to her stones and back to the world, but she also knew that there wasn't enough time. She had to get back to the world without delay.

Lee opened her eyes and rejoined the world.

* * *

"I like being healed!" yelled Tayo from flat on his back with Lee straddling him and grinding up and down. Her hands were on his chest, and her mouth hung open as she continued to rub him all over.

"Okay, okay, Lee," Lin said as she grabbed Lee's arm and tried to pull her up.

"Oh, I'm so sorry!" Lee said as she quickly stood up with her black snakeskin boots pressed against the outsides of his legs. He looked up with a big smile along her muscular thighs wrapped in tight faded denim.

"I don't know what got into me—I'm very sorry!"

Tayo laughed and made no effort to free himself.

"It is quite alright! I only wish I had more extensive injuries!"

He continued to grin as Lee swept one boot over him and got back in her seat.

"Lin, that wasn't supposed to happen. I was just—"

"It's okay, Lee. You didn't hurt anyone, that's for sure."

Lin smiled while shaking her head.

Tayo continued to lie on the floor in the restaurant's balcony, grinning and staring through his fogged-up glasses. He rolled over and pushed himself up, then he stood and put his full weight on the leg in a cast. He smiled and pounded it against the floor.

"This is astounding. My leg feels entirely healed. I only need to get rid of this cast!"

"And the pants. You'll have to change those pants, too, since the cast is coming off," said Lin.

"I'm sure I need to change my pants now anyway," Tayo said with a bigger smile.

* * *

Lin turned to view the stairs and saw Anna, her dog, and Daria looking over the rail. They all stared without blinking, and Daria was smiling. Lin took a look at Anna's short skirt and frowned. She reached down and felt the thick denim covering her own legs.

She sure is ready for some fun, Lin thought.

Daria started to reach for her pocket, and when Lin shook her head, she lost her smile and returned her hand to the rail.

"Well, Tayo," said Lin, "this has been interesting. Lee fixed you up?"

"Oh my, yes. Thank you, Lee. I have never felt better."

Lee smiled and said, "Anytime, Tayo. It was my pleasure."

"Then it was an equitable arrangement. Lin, what's next?"

"We're going back to my house to take care of some stuff, but I'll be in touch. I don't know if you have a chance with this, but what you'll be trying to do will benefit mankind more than trying to read the Words of God."

"I am at your service," he said with a quick bow. "Lee, perhaps we'll meet again?"

"Yeah, we probably will."

"Goodbye, Tayo. We'll talk soon. Be ready for anything now."

Lin and Lee turned and began walking toward the stairs, and Anna and Daria scurried down to get out of their path. Lin noticed that Anna wasn't as quick as her daughter, and she knew that it was because she'd need more practice walking in heels that high, even though they weren't as high as her own. The ones she should be wearing. The ones that she'd keep on after everything else was scattered around the dim room . . .

* * *

The two women splashed through the pounding rain and jumped into the Temt8tion. Lin started the powerful engine and put the wipers on high, but they couldn't keep up.

"Lee, what the hell was that? Right after you closed your eyes, you dragged him to the floor and mounted him like a carnival ride."

"Sorry, Lin. Maybe this thing isn't completely under control yet. But I fixed him, right? He looks like he's ready to go now."

"Yeah, he's ready now. Maybe he's ready for more of your 'fixing.' Let's get back home. We still have to deal with this nightmare that Taylor's causing."

Chapter 44 – Every Living Thing

After several detours to bypass flooded roads and washed out bridges, Lin steered her car around Jack's truck and into the garage. Strong gusts had pushed them all over the road, and after the garage door closed, she held the steering wheel and let out a loud sigh.

"We made it, Lin. Nice driving."

"Thanks. And we still have so much to do."

Not the kinds of things I want to be doing, she thought. After I lose my shirt. After my skirt is pulled down, and I feel lots of hands up and down my legs. When I'm—

She shook her head, and they got out of the car, and out of habit, she slammed her door much harder than necessary.

"There has to be time for some fun, don't you think, Lee?" she said without a smile.

Lee shrugged and watched as Lin approached the door. She didn't reach for the knob, but she leaned in close and listened. It took only seconds before a loud "Woof!" resounded from inside.

"Well, that was sure easy," said Lin. Like me, she thought and pried the door open a few inches.

Nomad's giant snout poked through, and he wedged his wide furry mane into the doorway, shoving the door all the way open. He stood and reached for Lin's shoulders, and she moved in close so that he could hold on.

"Oh, my sweet fluffy boy."

They hugged quietly in the doorway while Lee waited, and after a minute, Lin said, "Okay, boy, we need to get inside."

Nomad dropped with a loud thump and led the way into the kitchen.

* * *

The sound of the TV resonated from around the corner, and Lin saw Gabriel sitting at the kitchen table lost in thought.

"I'm glad you made it, Lin. Did everything work out okay?"

"Yeah, Lee healed Tayo,"—she turned to look at Lee—"probably more than he needed." She looked back at Gabriel. "He's ready. But ready for what, Gabby? Any ideas?"

Nomad brushed past Lin, and he and Lee disappeared into the living room. Within seconds, Lin heard Nomad crunching on something, and she tried to laugh inside, remembering how she'd always weighed everything he ate. No more. There were too many other concerns.

"Yes. I do have an idea, but I don't know if it's even possible."

"Well, I got nothing. I'm all ears."

And legs. And other luscious things that everyone would enjoy after they get me naked and helpless and—

"Gloriana is very powerful while she's in between the Islands of Time. She'll lose that power in order to live here again. But while she's there, she—"

"She can't kill that thing. She said so."

"Yes, but she could do something else. You remember that she transformed Renato into a scroll."

"Yeah, a dangerous one too. It was both Renato and a scroll at the same time. How does that help?"

"Can she somehow force that thing into some kind of object? You were powerful enough to change Renato back to just a man. You are also very powerful, and with your help, could the two of you do it?"

"But Gabby, that thing, that hunter . . . it isn't even alive."

"No, but it still interacts with the intent of things. It has some connection to the magic. We can't understand what it is, but we do know that much."

"True, but I also know that Renato had to find a way to offer his unconditional submission . . ."

She paused and gazed above Gabriel's head.

Mm . . . 'unconditional submission,' Lin thought. Oh, that sounds good. That's what they'd all get from me when I'm—

She shook her head and continued.

". . . to the transformation. He told me so. That thing won't give it. We can't even ask it to."

"You're correct, Lin. It wouldn't be a predictable operation, and it might have some bizarre result. This has never been tried before, but we can't say for sure that it's impossible."

"I know that Gloriana's more powerful probably than anyone ever has been. If anybody could do it, she'd be the one."

"You're very powerful too, Lin. Both of you together? What might that do?"

I'll tell you what I'd like to do, she thought. I'd rather be . . . no, she told herself. Stop those thoughts. That's not my life!

My life could be back in that nest, she thought. Back where everything made sense, where I had no doubts, where—

"I'm tired, Gabby. I'm not over everything I've been through the last couple of weeks. I feel like trying any of that would kill me."

"You really are beyond that, Lin. Using your powers will never kill you. You will get very tired, though."

"Okay, I need to understand very clearly what I'm trying to do."

"Yes."

"Gloriana and I will try to transform that thing into something. Something in this world?"

"Yes, that's the goal."

"And when we do, we'll see if Tayo, a dedicated man with a pure heart, can somehow find a way to destroy it before it destroys him?"

"It's the only way, Lin. It knows how to get here now. It will keep coming through, especially if it tires of Gloriana."

"Or if it kills her."

"Yes."

"I need to die again?"

"I'm afraid so."

"Okay, then I'll go sit in my car. I'd rather Taylor doesn't see. It's already raining so hard."

"And try to make it quick."

Lin stopped and looked into Gabriel's eyes.

"Sure, Gabby. Maybe I should cook some dinner while I'm out there too?"

"Now you're just being silly, Lin. That can wait until you're done."

Lin could only shake her head and stare at her unexplainable friend.

"Are you still okay with everything, Lin?"

"No. I don't know if I can fight this. She . . . those worlds . . ."

"Perhaps you can—"

"There's no time to understand it. Or fight it. I have to go."

She turned, walked out into the garage, and took a seat in her Temt8tion. She clicked on the stereo and tuned in Gabriel's classic rock. The deep base seemed to be shaking around the big pieces moving around inside her, vibrating them all into an arrangement that Lin knew she wanted and was barely holding back.

Then, she thought about driving. Leaving for somewhere warmer, far away from all the problems that had no solutions. Taking off all of the boring clothes. Maybe soaking for a while in a hot bath. Brushing her hair back and slipping on a pair of heels. And opening the door to a dim bedroom and the waiting strangers, how many she wouldn't even know. A slow walk into the middle of them. Hands all over her, touching her everywhere. Then, strong hands holding each arm and leading her to the bed. Held down on her back with more hands holding her ankles, pulling at them, just helpless and not caring about saving the world as they all—

Lin screamed inside and found her intent. It took only staring out through the windshield to see a tiny black dot on the wall in front of the car.

She knew exactly what would happen. She watched the spot begin to grow as its edges sped toward her, dragging emptiness along with it. When it had covered her, and she could see no more of her own world, she couldn't breathe. She couldn't think, and she couldn't feel.

Then, her heart locked up solid.

* * *

After an eternity, Lin saw a familiar white point racing toward her until it covered her with a world from long ago. When all darkness had gone, Lin's heart began again. Feelings and thoughts returned, and she took a deep breath of still air.

"There isn't much left," Lin said as she looked down at the single stone supporting her and Gloriana.

"No. I am not spending any more strength to make a world. I need it all to fight."

"We have a plan."

"I wish to know your plan."

"You transformed Renato into a scroll. Let's try to do the same with that thing, that killer."

"Renato gives complete control to me for his transformation. He agrees completely. He becomes what I want him to be."

"Yeah, and this will be different, that's for sure. Together maybe we can transform that thing into . . . I don't know what. But if we do, it'll be trapped."

"It cannot hold. It surely frees itself."

"There's a man who's agreed to help. His name is Tayo. He's a good man. He's dedicated like no one I've ever known. He'll devote his life to finding a way to destroy it."

"You are good and dedicated, too, are you not?"

"You know, since you brought it up, I feel like I'm about to fall into one of those other worlds. The ones you said were real too."

"You cannot fall. Perhaps you wish to jump, Lin Finity. Those lives are also very real for you. Do you like those lives? Perhaps you would like to jump."

"I don't know, that was—"

"If there is happiness there, it might be your best life. You say you are different there."

"Yeah, I was really cheap, and all I wanted was to have a good time. It felt good to not have any other cares than that."

"Your powers bring you hardship?"

"My powers are amazing, but sometimes, it's all too much."

"And you have enjoyment without those powers?"

"I don't ever want to be without my powers. But it sure was fun to forget about them for a while. Being helpless was kind of exciting."

"If you leave your powers, would that not be even more excitement for you?"

"Yeah, it would. I wouldn't be just pretending . . ."

Even on the meager remains of a tower, in a time and place that didn't exist, standing next to an ancient queen no longer alive but too strong to die, Lin imagined the thrill of being naked and helpless without her powers. The danger would be real. She'd have no choice but to comply. With no possible escape. She imagined what it would be like to be naked and surrounded and *truly* helpless and—

"Then, perhaps you can jump and release your powers."

Lin shook her head and looked down at the stone beneath them.

"Hmm . . . I don't know about that. How would I do that anyway?"

"It is easy. You intend to be a woman without powers."

"That's it?"

"Yes. Become what you wish, then cast away your powers. Then, you are powerless, which brings you happiness."

"What if I change my mind later?"

"If you could reclaim your powers, you would not be entirely helpless. And I believe you are happiest when you know you are truly powerless. It makes feelings stronger for you. Is that true?"

Lin felt a sharp excitement at the prospect of being so powerless with no going back.

"Oh yeah, *truly* helpless would be the most thrilling."

"Wanton and completely helpless is what you desire most?"

"It would be a relief."

Lin looked again into the emptiness all around them and felt the hold those lives still had on her. And she knew that Gloriana was right.

She could become a tramp and then give up her powers. She wanted that. She knew that it wouldn't take anything at all. A little bit of intent, and—

"You deserve happiness, Lin Finity."

It would be so easy, she thought. Just be a tramp, a cheap Lin with no powers and no way to get them back.

"I saw your finer garments. Are you happier wearing those?"

Lin imagined herself dressed in her shortest skirt and highest heels, hands reaching for—

"You are happy dressed that way and sharing all you have?"

Lin felt her sexy clothes peeled off of her and thrown aside until she stood naked among them, no choice but to share every—

"It could be done at any moment, could it not?"

Just a little push. Just a nudge, and she'd be—

"I can help if you have need."

Sexy and powerless with no way back—

"I can help you, Lin Finity."

"Would you? I mean . . . maybe I—"

"Yes, decide, and you begin your new life."

Lin saw across a chasm, impossible to ever again bridge, the faces of Jack and Taylor and Gabriel and Nomad. Their eyes stared as the gorge grew wider, pulling them away from her until they sank back into a grayness that smothered even her memories of them, of the lives they shared, of the love she felt for—

She shook her head and said, "Maybe later. We have a mission."

"Yes, I wish to return. Then, we help you to be happy. Tayo? You said his name is Tayo."

"Yes, Tayo Tersoo."

"I must remember his name when we have our attempt. I must try to give a direction to the change."

"'The change?' You're using Glyphin magic?"

"No. I have only my intent in this place. It must be enough."

"Well, whatever it takes. I'll help in any way I can. Where is it? That thing?"

"It is here. Its teeth will soon be on my throat."

Lin shuddered at the enormity of what they were about to attempt. And the endless misery Gloriana would endure to hold onto whatever life she could.

"I don't know what to do. In the real world, we'd use the magic, right? But there's no magic here, is there?"

"We have only our intent. Focus your intent on what we are trying to do. And do not lose your hold."

"My hold is unbreakable. I hope it helps."

"It does help. We begin now."

Lin knew only to focus on her intent as if she were trying to return to her life. But just as she'd held lightly the goal of finding a destination for her and Jack, she stayed aware of the entity they were attempting to trap. She felt her intent join Gloriana's, and they twisted and blended and circled around something, a thing that didn't flee or resist in any way.

But it did what it does, and the teeth and claws that Lin had felt when she was thrown outside of Gloriana's intended world began to bite. Began to shred.

She heard her own silent scream echoing through her along with desperate shrieking from the woman who she knew must still be beside her on the remnants of a tower. She grasped her intent more tightly, fighting as much to save herself as to capture the hunter, the thing that brought death.

Knowing only her unbreakable hold on her intent and the shared scream ripping through them, as she felt countless biting teeth and tearing claws, she squeezed the thing tighter and tighter.

Lin sensed Gloriana directing their intent, giving it a direction, leading it toward a black dot that had appeared out in the emptiness before them. Their intent rushed out to meet the darkness, dragging along whatever it had snared in its grip.

All at once, the blackness raced away from them, and Lin's intent abruptly returned to her. She took a deep breath as she leaned forward to brace herself against the low stone wall. From there, she saw the blue sky and bluer ocean stretching to the restored horizon. She stood next to Gloriana, and a warm breeze of sea air lifted their hair back over their shoulders as they looked out over the detailed world Gloriana had intended. She saw that Gloriana had even intended colorful flags that fluttered and snapped above many of the lower towers. She stared in disbelief at seeing ships in the canal, people walking the paths, children playing, some even looking up and waving at Gloriana. Lin waved back.

"This is much nicer. Wow, it's beautiful. I take it whatever we did worked?"

"I am free of that thing. Where it is, I do not know. But I can expend some strength and make this world one last time."

"And I can bring you home. We have to hope that thing is trapped, wherever it is."

"It is no longer here. It surely kills somewhere else, Lin Finity."

"Still, we must try. Tayo must try."

"I do not want to give up any powers, Lin."

"Neither do I."

Gloriana turned and gave Lin a smile. She said, "Perhaps when we are done."

"Sure, maybe. And you will have other powers. Your beauty alone is quite a power."

Gloriana sighed and nodded.

"Thank you. You are right. I am ready."

Gloriana looked out over her ocean for the last time then turned to face Lin. Lin turned and looked into Gloriana's caramel eyes. She found her intent and got a solid hold on it. She gazed into the sad caramel glowing softly and intended a return to the world of the living. To a life on the Islands of Time.

The eyes became embedded in the approaching night, and Lin couldn't look away. The darkness expanded, blocking Gloriana's face, then the stone tower behind her, then all of that world built only by Gloriana's intent. When everything around them had been covered, Lin's lungs seized, and her thoughts and feelings left her. She was left with only the beating of her heart, and she knew that it would stop.

It did.

* * *

A white dot appeared, and Lin couldn't ignore it. It hurried toward her, dragging a natural world in its wake. She felt her heart start up, followed by the return of her thoughts and feelings. She inhaled the coconut of her car's air freshener and heard the classic rock still playing.

She looked to her right and saw Gloriana in the passenger seat. Her eyes were closed, and she breathed slowly and deliberately. She opened her eyes and turned to look at Lin.

"Welcome home, Sunny."

"I am happy to be here, Lin. Thank you for saving me."

"And together, we might have helped save the world from something. If it's here. And if Tayo can figure out how to stop it. That's a lot of 'ifs.'"

"I choose to be optimistic. And I am not choosing to be hungry. But still, I am."

"I'm just tired."

"As am I. This thing we are in—it can take you away?"

Lin's fatigue prevented any resistance. Her thoughts raced to a dim hotel room where she'd be stripped and forced to her knees. Surrounded by strangers, she'd think of using her powers to save herself. As strong hands jerked her arms behind her, as a solid grip on her long hair held her in place, she'd feel herself on the edge of a cliff, ready to take a step and fall, and with a strange heat squirming all through her, she'd intend being a woman without powers. Every last trace would leave her in an instant. Any chance of stopping them would be gone, and she'd be trapped, with no powers or hope of escape, just a strong beating heart as she knelt there naked and helpless and forced to—

"It could," she said with a deep sigh, "but let's go inside."

She gave Lin a quick smile, and they got out of the car. Lin didn't bother with the Nomad game at the door since she'd been gone only a few seconds. They walked in to see Gabriel still seated at the kitchen table.

"That was quick, Lin. And welcome back, Sunny."

"I am happy to be back. And tired. More hungry than tired."

Sunny kept a hand in contact with the table and counter as she found waffles for the toaster.

"Well, let's see how things go, Gabby. We did something, but we don't know what."

"I don't hear anyone screaming. It's better now than before."

"That's for sure. We can't have that thing crashing into the world anytime it wants and trying to kill people."

Jack came into the room and pointed out the dining room window.

"Lin, it's getting worse out there. Taylor's been trying to stop it. I know she has. But she can't. What are we going to do?"

"Oh, Jack, I have no idea. And I'm so tired." She sat at the table and leaned forward onto her folded arms.

Tired of dressing like this, too, she thought. My legs were made to be shown off, to tease and tempt. I was made to be shared, passed around like a treat for every—

Stop! she told herself.

"Don't tell her, but I just went back again."

"I figured," Jack said as he glanced over at Sunny, who leaned against the counter near the toaster with her eyes closed.

Taylor walked into the room, and her mouth hung open when she saw Sunny.

"She's back, which can only mean one thing."

Lin sat up. A loud boom rang out over the house.

"Mom." Taylor shook her head slowly. "Not again, Mom."

More rain slammed into the glass.

"Honey, I only—"

"I can't take this, Mom. I've been trying, but I'm losing my mind. I'm exhausted from fighting it."

More thunder shook the walls.

"But Hon, I don't need to go back there again. We fixed it, Sunny and I, and—"

"'Sunny,' now? She's some dead queen, Mom. I finally get healthy, after lying around lying, Gabriel. I get my life back, and now, there's some dead queen in the guest room *living,* and you keep *dying.*"

The winds picked up and rolled heavily over the roof.

"Lying, drying, trying, and now *dying,* Gabriel!"

"Taylor," said Gabriel, "your mom is going to be—"

"Just stop! I've heard it all before. You know what? I don't even care anymore. Let it rain. Let it snow. Whatever the hell it wants. Let it bury this whole goddamn town!"

Lin looked to Gabriel, then Jack and Lee. No one had any advice.

"I need a break from this, Mom. I'm stuck in the middle of a nightmare, and there's no way out."

I'd love to find my way out of this, too, Lin thought. First, I'd jump right into a tramp's life. Then, I'd get rid of my powers and leave all these problems behind. Easy, just like Sunny said. The things I'd do. The things I'm made to do. That bedroom full of strangers, where I'd be held down on the soft blankets. I'd want to say something, but there'd be so many of them, all keeping me so, so busy. That's where I need to be: stripped down and helpless, heart pounding, doing whatever they—

"Maybe if I just had time to think about it, Mom, but I don't."

Taylor leaned her forehead into the wall and began sobbing. The thunder reverberated without pause. Sirens howled from every direction.

Lin fought with all her strength to push aside her hungers and desires. She struggled to focus on the world ending around them as her own daughter's out-of-control Glyphin powers brought down upon them, and likely the rest of the state, everything the heavens could offer.

And during that brief thought of Heaven, an idea flashed through her like one of the countless lightning bolts carving up the sky, an idea that was so compelling that it seemed to be sent from God.

She knew that it was outlandish and probably dangerous, but she also knew that there were no options left. Taylor had reached her limit and was about to destroy a larger area than any of them could know.

Lin knew that she was weakening too. That fork in her road was exhausting. No, it wasn't a simple fork. There was Jack and a good life in one direction, with responsibilities, problems, and the expectation to fight evil in the magic.

In another direction waited a life of strutting around half-naked to tease, tempt, and satisfy, enjoying all the sex, booze, and violence she could find—however much she could attract. She knew that she could stir up as many thrills as she needed. And without her powers, which she could intend away anytime, it would all be so much sweeter.

And maybe the most tempting direction of all: the simple life she'd lived in that nest. Or a life in the ocean. Or maybe as—

Stop! she screamed to herself. She couldn't let herself escape to any other possible life. Her daughter needed her more than she needed whatever simple or wanton life she could intend.

Gabriel would be fine and could leave anytime. The war was waiting.

She'd made plans for Sunny. Sunny would have to figure it out.

Nomad would get plenty to eat. Jack was strong enough to keep shoveling all that food.

And what of Jack? She knew the question he'd been wanting to ask, and she knew her answer. She knew that she loved him.

But she knew that he was only one man. She'd kill him if she kept trying to make him more than that. And he'd never accept what she really was. He thought it was a game. She'd have to show him just what a tramp she really was. His friends would be happy to help. She'd need her bedroom full of them, and when he walked in and saw her naked and—

Stop! echoed through her.

And Lee? Lee would have to find her own way and deal with her new temptations as well as she could. Perhaps Tayo would seek her help if he needed it.

Crushed under the weight of all that she'd seen and all that she'd done over the last three weeks, and the challenge of what Gabriel had asked of her, and especially knowing her true nature, the one she couldn't fight and didn't want to fight, Lin's intent focused on her decision. She felt the beginning of an intense wave of intent deep inside her.

It was the only way to save Taylor and stop the destruction she'd begun. And she might save herself, too, she thought. Or would it push her across some kind of line? She'd have to take that chance. She knew that she was close to nudging herself into another life, any one of the infinite possible lives that were all just as real as the one before her eyes.

With her unbreakable hold on her intent, Lin called for the right conditions. She knew that she couldn't plan it. She couldn't predict it. She'd be as surprised as everyone else.

It was as though she'd lit a fuse, and it could no longer be stopped. She'd given her intent a direction, and all of her power poured into it, aiming for a solution that Lin couldn't begin to imagine.

There was a good way to do this, she knew. It had to be right for Taylor, even if no one watching would believe their eyes.

Well, she thought, Gabriel would understand. Maybe Jack would too.

But she knew that she couldn't tell any of them goodbye. It might be a one-way trip anyway, but saying goodbye would probably guarantee it. She felt her old life peeling away, leaving her with nothing but her intent. There was nothing more to be said.

She took Taylor's hand and pulled to get her walking with her to the garage. When they walked out and stood on the wet concrete next to her Temt8tion, Jack, Gabriel, and Lee followed, while Sunny sat sleeping against a kitchen cabinet, a waffle in one hand. No one spoke. She guessed that they must have seen the look on her face and knew to let her be. To wait and see what would happen.

Lin looked into the stillness inside her and focused on the unbreakable hold she had on her intent. She trusted it. What would happen next couldn't be planned. Couldn't be arranged. But her intent would bring it, that much she knew.

She clicked the garage door, and it rose up, giving them all a good view of the torrents falling into rivers running down the driveways and into a flooded street. The trees shook and lighting lit a sky shattered by incessant pounding.

And all across the driveway, over the sidewalk, and into the road and in the yards across the street, crows stood wing to wing. Some hopped, and some bobbed and rotated their heads, but they all stayed in their places. Silently waiting. Packed so tight that the soggy ground couldn't be seen.

With Taylor's hand in hers, Lin began walking into the flock congregating in the deepening water. None made a sound.

"Mom, what's with all the birds?"

"Shh . . . it's okay, Hon."

"I'm sorry about the storms, Mom. I can't stop . . . I just—"

"It's going to be okay, my dear girl."

Lin felt the rain soaking her, and though it was cold, she felt no discomfort. She flicked her hair back and dragged her free hand across her wet eyes, eyes that she knew had begun glowing a fierce green. Every bird froze, stared into her flaming eyes, and began chattering as she walked among them.

She gave one more thought to all the possible lives, the lives that waited only for her nudge.

But she loved Jack, she knew. Only Jack.

And this was the only way.

Taylor had stopped crying, and she squeezed Lin's hand and stared at the field of birds with her mouth open. They walked quietly together as a sudden agitation swept through the flock, and they all began rocking from leg to leg, but still, none flew. They moved aside to let them pass, and the crowd closed after them.

"Why aren't they flying away, Mom?"

"We will, Honey."

"Mom?"

Jack, Gabriel, and Lee watched Lin and Taylor walking through the rain, across the flooded street, and deep into the carpet of birds. Jack held the ring in his pocket, and with a heavy sigh, he let it drop.

When they'd made it across the road and into the center of the flock, they turned to face the garage. Lin and Taylor looked to each side and all around them and saw every crow staring at them as they chirped and began fluffing their wings.

Lin turned to look at the confused faces gazing at them from the garage. Jack raised his hand.

Then, she felt her intent ignite like an unstoppable sun within her. She felt her intent radiate out in every direction and touch every crow that had come for them. The hot tears from her blazing green eyes mixed with the cold rain as she heard Jack's words through the downpour.

"Lin! Remember that I—"

The flock came to life with a roar and the purpose of a single spirit. Every wing began flapping at once, and a cawing cloud of black billowed up from the ground and through the falling rain, and every living thing escaped into the sky.

* * *

The rain stopped instantly, but swift rivers continued to flow everywhere. The thunder ceased, but sirens still wailed, and a gentle breeze allowed all of the leaves to begin shaking themselves dry. A break in the clouds permitted the first slivers of warmth to reach the ground.

"Uh . . . what just happened?" said Lee.

Gabriel looked only at Jack.

"She will return, Jack. Taylor too."

Jack shook his head, and tears seeped out of eyes still staring at the empty yard across Kingsbury. After many long moments, he answered with a shaking voice.

"No, Gabriel. She transformed us once. I didn't remember it, but she did. I've never seen her so sad to be here. To be human again. I held her and thought she'd never stop crying."

"She's strong, Jack. She'll come back to you. And Nomad. You must be strong now too."

Jack turned to look into Gabriel's eyes, and for the first time, he saw the profound love and peace that Lin had always found there. He felt a reluctance to look away.

"Alright, Gabriel, I won't give up hope."

"Good, Jack."

Jack placed a hand on Nomad's head and flopped his big ear around.

"Besides, someone has to feed Nomad," he said with a weak smile.

"Because you love Nomad too."

"Yeah, of course."

"He's here for you, Jack."

"Yeah, now that Lin's gone, he—"

"No, Jack. Nomad was always here for *you*."

Jack stared blankly into Gabriel's kind eyes. Gabriel held his gaze and nodded.

Jack took a breath, looked away, and found he could speak again.

"Where will you go?"

"Lin gave me something earlier that will help us. Sunny and I will leave when she wakes up."

"Where?"

"Back to St. Simons. It will help her to be on an island again."

"If Lin comes back, I can—"

"*When* Lin comes back. I will know, Jack."

"You're not staying at least for Thanksgiving?"

"No. It's best that Sunny settles into her life sooner rather than later."

Jack looked at the drying driveway and wiped at his eyes, and his voice continued to shake.

"Lee? What will you do, go back to Jacksonville?"

Lee continued to stare at the empty lawn across the street. All expression had left her face, and her voice was flat.

"Yeah. At least to check on Alessa. I think I might be needed soon."

Jack felt Nomad nosing his hand, and when he began scratching the big dog's head, Nomad looked up into his eyes. He didn't make a sound.

He stooped down so that their faces were inches apart. Nomad turned to look where Lin and Taylor had last stood. He turned back to Jack and looked into his left eye, then his right, then back, moving only his big eyes.

Jack reached out to hold Nomad's head in his hands, and he let out a deep breath. His voice had regained its calm and strength.

"Thank you, Nomad. I believe you."

Chapter 45 – Naked, Shivering, Squawking

"And why is the price for this one so high? What's so special about it?"

"Anything formed from the magic is precious. It carries more value than common items."

"Oh, of course—this is Sunny's Magic Island. Look, it's just too expensive. Lower the price some, and you'll have a sale."

"Very well. We can diminish its cost by one part in five."

"If you mean twenty percent off, well, now we got something here. Good, I'll take it."

Sunny rang up the dolphin sculpture and swiped the woman's credit card. She wrapped it carefully in paper, placed it in a plastic bag, and handed her the receipt.

"And I don't believe in magic anyway," the customer said with a grin.

Sunny blinked several times and held her gaze.

"Your belief matters not."

The woman didn't turn to leave. She only stared and shook her head slowly.

"It must be the lighting in here, but I'd swear I just saw your eyes glow."

"Is that likely without magic? Your conclusion must be that lighting devices can deceive you."

Sunny's caramel eyes stared back without blinking. Or glowing.

The woman stood frozen a few seconds longer, then backed toward the exit. She bumped into the door, jangling the small bells, and joined the foot traffic on Mallery Street.

Gabriel returned from the stock room with a donut in one hand and a coffee in the other.

"It is about time to close, Gabriel. Tonight is an occasion to people of this century?"

"Yes, they mark the passage of years with celebrations."

"I am starting to get used to strangers wanting odd things and giving us money. This is an unusual life, but not a bad one."

"Lin was wise to buy this place when we were all down here last month. She gave us a lot of cash that she got from The Shield, but it's best if we all earn our way."

"Yes, she is . . . *was* very kind."

"She *is* very kind, Sunny. And *when* she returns, she might need her money back."

Sunny nodded and looked away without a smile. She stared at the shop's door.

"And she did something else for me that I hope someday to thank her for."

"Yes. She returned you to an island. St. Simons Island. Lin knew that she was going to rescue you, and she worked it all out."

"I am very hopeful to speak with her again. I feel we have unfinished business."

"What kind of business?"

Sunny hesitated then said, "Only to thank her. I wish to thank her."

"Me too," said Renato, who no longer looked like the camper that he had joined when Gabriel had merged their spirits. Gabriel had found him, and Renato had known that he wanted only to see his queen again. And he was grateful that Gabriel had found a way to restore his appearance, though he felt some sadness for the camper who was mostly forgotten and living in the background.

"I am happy to have you in my life, Renato. We have many stories we can tell, do we not?"

"We can talk about our islands and our lives there. I thought I would always have to keep that to myself. I never dreamed I would ever see you again."

"I am surprised and happy to see you again too."
Renato looked at the floor with a smile.
"And Renato?"
"Yes?"
"I am happy that you can look in my eyes as you wish now."
Renato got a big smile and looked into her caramel eyes.
"Okay," he said. "On one condition."
"What is that?"
"When no one's around, when no one can hear me, may I still call you 'My Queen?'"

* * *

"This is Lee."
"Lee, this is Tayo Tersoo. Do you have a moment to converse?"
Lee had gone home to Jacksonville, and she stood on her deck eating a box of baklava and staring at the stars. Tayo stood without a shirt in his spartan third-floor apartment in Baltimore. The radiator under the window rattled, but the room remained hot. The muted TV, lost in piles of books, showed scenes of the New Year's Eve celebration in Times Square.
"Sure. What's going on?"
"Nothing good. I need you."
"Look, I never should have done that with you. I only meant to heal your injuries. It was fun, but—"
"Yes, that was exceedingly enjoyable. But I'm not telephoning about that. It's something else."
"What?"
"I've called Lin many times, but she has not responded. You're my only hope."
"Lin is gone, Tayo. She's just . . . gone. What's wrong?"
"She said the entity I must try to kill would appear somewhere in the world. And besides devising a way to destroy it, I had to locate it first."

"Yeah, that's right. Lin said she had no idea what it would be. Or where."

There was only silence.

"Tayo, did you find it?"

Tayo held a small mirror near his face and looked at his back in the larger mirror above his dresser. What had been smooth, perfect black skin was now completely covered with raised welts forming unrecognizable symbols. Each one was small, and rows and columns of them bunched together and covered all of his back from his shoulders to his waist and from side to side.

"It has found me."

* * *

The door slammed behind Jack as Nomad ventured out into Lin's frigid backyard. The big dog had finished every crunchy morsel in his bowl, and a nudge from his wet snout on Jack's hand had made his intentions plain. Despite it being a brisk and windy day, icicles reaching down beneath the gutters dripped from a sun that offered a subtle heat from its place in the cloudless blue sky.

"Happy New Year, Nomad. It's cold, boy—let's keep moving. Look, I shoveled you a path. Go ahead, big boy."

Nomad barked once at the sky and ran along the fence until he'd taken care of business, then he circled the yard and came back around. He jumped up to put his snowy paws on Jack's shoulders and licked his face once before nuzzling under his beard. Jack felt the wet kiss freezing on his cheek, but he smiled and patted the dog's sides, causing Nomad to lean back. The big dog lifted one of his paws off of Jack's shoulder, and while gazing calmly into his eyes, reached for his cheek.

"Alright. Good dog. We should go—"

He felt the cold pads packed tight with thick fur, small chunks of ice, and just a hint of his claws. With a gentle push, Nomad turned Jack's head to face the roof of the house behind Lin's, across snow-covered yards and beyond the high fence.

At the very peak, beside a brick chimney tossing white balls of smoke into the passing air, two crows stood together on the icy shingles. Both were silent, and Jack thought that they could have been sculptures placed there as a reminder. They stared directly at Jack and Nomad.

Jack felt Nomad's paw retreat back to bear down on his shoulder, and his watery eyes and Nomad's large clear eyes stared. He removed a glove and found the ring that he always carried in his pants pocket.

The smaller of the two birds began looking to the sky and fluttered its wings. The larger bird continued to stare. When the smaller one flapped and jumped into the sky, a sky without storms, the larger one gazed at Jack and Nomad only a moment longer, then it followed.

With Nomad's thick paws heavy on his shoulders, they watched the two birds glide over the treetops and out of sight. Jack let the ring drop down into his pocket.

He put on his cold glove, dragged it across his eyes, and said, "Alright, big boy. It's just you and me. Let's get back inside where it's—"

Jack heard a fluttering overhead and felt a cloud of snow falling from the roof above him. He looked up and saw a large crow leaning over the edge and looking down on him. It blinked once and stared. Jack glanced down and saw Nomad motionless by his side, his neck craned, and his big eyes staring at the bird. Jack looked back up.

Another cascade of snow got kicked down on them with the sound of wings, and when they could look again, they saw another, smaller crow had joined the first one. Both stared down on them without blinking.

"Nomad," Jack whispered as his heart thumped in his chest, "don't even breathe, okay, big boy?"

A raucous roar arose beyond the trees, and Jack and Nomad turned to see thousands of crows flapping over a tall stand of pines and winging straight toward them. They descended on Lin's backyard and swooped close, so close that they felt the wind from their flight. Countless birds, all racing past them, and near enough to graze them with wings and claws.

And then, they began to land on them.

Jack covered his head and leaned over, and he looked to see that Nomad had a dozen on his back, all twitching their big wings and screaming. Jack felt just as many on his shoulders and hood, their claws stabbing into his thick coat.

He shook his coat open and spread it over Nomad's head, and they both cowered as the clamor of wings and angry chattering surrounded them. They felt countless cawing birds landing on them, holding on for a second, then swatting their wings and launching back into the cold air, chasing swirls of snow in every direction.

They were both pushed into the frozen ground as the riotous birds covered them with grabbing claws and whooshing wings and deafening screams that blocked out the world. Just when Jack was sure the murder would kill them both, the claws began to pull back. A straggler pounced on Jack and jumped off with a bitter yell, and the screeching and snapping of wings dwindled as they all fled back over the trees.

Jack felt a hand on his shoulder and heard a familiar voice speaking rapidly.

"FIXED it FIXED it FIXED it! TAYLOR too TAYLOR too!"

Jack looked up with his heart pounding like thunder and saw Lin's unblinking green eyes focused on his. She didn't smile.

"My God, Lin, you're back! Fixed what? What about Tay—"

"TOO cold TOO cold! TOO cold TOO cold TOO cold!"

And he heard more urgent shouting behind him.

"INside INside INside INside! INside!"

Jack jumped to his feet and Nomad to his paws.

A laughing and crying man, a barking and howling dog, and two naked, shivering, squawking females rushed into the warm house to begin a new year.

Enjoy The Story?

Thank you for reading! Please consider leaving a review and/or a rating at your favorite bookseller or with your favorite book club. Help your fellow readers meet Lin Finity!

For more about Edward Allen Karr and his books, visit:

www.LakesideLetters.com

And follow him at:

Facebook: EdwardAllenKarr

Instagram: Edward_Allen_Karr

Next in time in the Fringes Of Infinity world:

Lin Finity And The Flights To Forever (Book Four)

Tempted by nearly-real worlds of her own creation,
Lin risks being lost there forever.
What is it about her flights
That captivates her more—
Gaining new powers? Or chasing her fantasy?

Lin Finity made a desperate decision to take her daughter and end their lives as women. They've returned after six weeks, but they're not quite themselves. Lin learns that becoming herself again will take more than chocolate. Jack's steadfast love helps and so does the timeless wisdom of her remarkable friend, Gabriel.

A seductive nemesis, Gloriana, is again part of Lin's life, teaching her and Taylor long-forbidden Glyphin skills even as she schemes to seduce Jack. With her typical style and humor, Lin juggles her return to human life, her desire to destroy Gloriana, and helping a past friend survive bizarre horrors. She finds solace in using the strength of her intent to take her on flights to nearly-real worlds of her own creation—worlds where she hones her powers and pursues a perilous fantasy.

"Where are those worlds, Gabby?" ~Lin
"You might as well ask where this world is. There's no answer to that, Lin. This world and whatever worlds you inhabit on your flights exist in the vast forever our minds can't comprehend." ~Gabriel

ABOUT THE AUTHOR

Edward Allen Karr was born, raised, and continues to reside in Ohio, USA. His adult life has followed a meandering path, ranging from working an automotive assembly line to designing space flight hardware. And through all of it, he's seen that life is a captivating and ultimately unexplainable endeavor. His writing seeks to add a splash of wonder to a world already awash in it.

*　*　*

Lin Finity returns for more magic, adventure, and romance in:

Lin Finity And The Flights To Forever
Fringes Of Infinity Book Four

www.LakesideLetters.com

www.ingramcontent.com/pod-product-compliance
Lightning Source LLC
Chambersburg PA
CBHW031609180726
48284CB00005B/1461